Note on the author

Fiona Cassidy (better known as Fionnuala McGoldrick) is from Galbally but now lives in Donaghmore, Co Tyrone. She lives with her partner Philip and their five children (hers, his and theirs). She is an Outreach and Promotions Officer for a rural charity and is a self-confessed jewellery addict who also has an incurable shoe fetish which means that she needs a bigger house, preferably boasting a walk-in shoe cupboard! *Anyone for Seconds?* is her debut novel.

Acknowledgements

Where do I start? So many people have been involved in my journey to publication!

I suppose the best place to start is at the beginning and to extend my deepest love and gratitude to my mammy and daddy, Peter and Eileen, who have been the best parents any child could wish for! They gave me one of the most precious gifts any parent can give a child and that is a love of books. From as far back as I can remember, reading always thrilled me and drives in the car and days out were always wasted as I was never interested in doing anything else other than curling up with a book!

Secondly, thanks to my partner Philip, a wonderful man and a fantastic father. The last nine years have been precious – and I look forward to many more happy years ahead! Thank you also to our children Colm, Úna, Catríona, Ciarán and Áine who inspire me each and every day and have helped me to keep the dream alive. Thanks for putting up with someone who spends all their free time glued to a laptop and for all your interest, excitement and pride! I love you all very much and am proud to call you "my family".

Thanks also to my circle of close friends for always being there for me when times have been tough (and there have been plenty of those). Noeleen, Katrina, Rachael, Joanna, Carrie-Ann and Denise, I love you all! I took all the best bits of your love, wisdom, friendship and wit and put them together to make the perfect friend – Ruby – and I hope that when you read the book that you will see yourselves coming to life!

I would also like to take this opportunity to thank my extended family, namely the wonderful McGoldrick clan (which I am proud to be part of now and always) and the McAllisters (Glengormley and Sydney, Australia), as well as neighbours and friends in Galbally and Donaghmore for all the local support I've received. I'd also like to mention my work colleagues, both formerly in Victim Support and Dungannon Court and now in Rural Support and Loughry College who have always been interested and supportive of my ambitions.

A special mention must go to Jim Hamill (photographer extraordinaire) and his lovely wife Rossy who live in my street and are constantly cheering me on!!

To Ruth Daly, a big thank-you for all your guidance and friendship and for being my proof-reader, PA (when I was on holiday at a crucial time with no internet access), negotiator and meetings facilitator . . . is there anything this woman can't do? And thanks also to hubby Finbarr (known as De Godfadder in our house).

Anyone for Seconds?

To Rachael McCrory who also read the book before anyone else, thank you so much for your enthusiasm, constructive advice and friendship ... everyone should have a "crisis buddy" like you!!!

Thanks to Pat, Natasha and Paula from the Donard Hotel in Newcastle, Co Down for an unforgettable holiday the week after I got my publishing deal and for the lend of the laptop (Maeve) and facilitating that all-important phone call (Liz).

A special word must also go to Denise and Kieran Fitzsimons and their gorgeous little daughter, Aoife, who are an inspiration and epitomise the sheer determination of some couples to have a baby! (You'll understand why I mention this when you read the book!)

I also want to extend thanks to the "Write-On" gang especially Jacqui (fancy a spin to Aughnacloy anyone ... ahem) Megan, Oonagh, Claire, Angie, Jo and Shirley. I have been part of the Write-On community now for three years and these girls are unwavering in their support and have travelled the road with me! I'd also like to thank Fionnuala Kearney, Clodagh Murphy and Trina Rea for their encouragement. Appreciation must go to Claire Allan for kindly reading the book and giving me a quote for the front cover as well as supporting and promoting me where possible (tweet tweet!). I also can't forget Sharon Owens who I hope to meet in person one day soon and neighbour and fellow-writer Emma

Heatherington. I couldn't think of a nicer group of girls to be flying the northern flag with! Special mention must also go to John Bradbury (a brilliant mentor), Mona Kelly and Patricia McSorely for their encouragement and enthusiasm. Thank you for the memories, craic and your listening ears. I will never forget those Creative Writing classes at An Creagan where it all began!

Finally, thanks to the people who are giving me this wonderful opportunity and believing in me. Immense gratitude to Paula Campbell and the lovely people at Poolbeg and to Gaye Shortland for her attention to detail and brilliant editing expertise. A heartfelt word of thanks also to my agent Emma Walsh for her guidance, advice, friendship and all the brainstorming sessions we've had over the phone, as well as that fabulous night in a Dublin tapas bar!

To you, the reader, thank you for buying the book! I hope you enjoy reading it as much as I've enjoyed writing it!

For Philip, my true love and best friend . . .
and all our children who make us complete.

Chapter 1

It was the cold and frosty month of January but instead of being miserable because I suffered from SAD and depressed because as usual I was broke, I was rather pleased with myself. The source of my pleasure was the fact that I had just recently met the man of my dreams. His name was Owen Byrne and he was a lecturer at the college where I'd been temping as Public Relations Officer for the past two weeks. He was tall with brown hair and he'd got that distinguished sexy look that only a man who wears glasses can carry.

He said that someone advised him to get contact lenses and I told him no way, that I thought his glasses suited him. I think he was rather surprised by my conviction, especially when I made him take his glasses off, studied him, walked around him as a vulture would circle an object of prey and then said "Definitely not" in a purring voice.

I've always been rather obvious when it comes to my feelings. My mother used to chastise me as a teenager when I'd come home from the discos and tell her that I'd met "Him".

"Frankie McCormick, will you stop wearing your heart on your sleeve?" she would say sternly, hands on hips, wearing her floral dressing gown and trying to inconspicuously (not one of her stronger attributes) smell my breath lest the demon drink had passed my lips. "Men don't like that sort of desperation. It makes them want to run away and hide."

Personally I didn't think my mother was qualified to talk about what men like or don't like. She'd had the same one for forty years, therefore had been out of the running for quite a long time. Things had changed substantially since my mother was dancing the two-hand reel and Daddy was walking her to the end of her lane.

Getting back to Owen though. He hadn't been hiding from me. In fact, the other girls in the office had been telling me that he'd been asking subtle questions about me.

"Was Frankie with you when you went for a drink last week?" he reportedly asked Ruby, my stalwart companion and best friend.

"No, she had to go home. No baby-sitter, you see."

"She has children?"

I was told that this was said with more than a little intonation of surprise.

Ruby proceeded to tell him about my "experience" which she peppered with expletives. She was not my ex-husband's biggest fan. Sometimes I thought she disliked him more than I did.

Ruby is best described as being an eccentric fun-loving dynamo with a heart of pure gold. With spiky bright-red hair and a temper to match she's easy to spot. We'd been friends for about twelve years. It was she who put in the good word for me which enabled me to get my job.

Ruby said that Owen then clammed up and wouldn't divulge any details apart from saying he was a single father. She made a big deal of letting him know that I was on the market as well.

I had made the mistake of telling Ruby that I thought that Owen was rather attractive. Okay, who am I kidding – I think my exact words were that he was "a total screw" and that "given half the chance I'd love to put all six foot two of him in my pocket and take him home to be my willing slave".

Ruby is one of those people however who is as subtle as a bag of flying boulders and, stopping short of telling Owen that I would straddle him bareback without a saddle, she let him know in no uncertain terms that I liked him.

3

"She had no baby-sitter last Friday night but I'd baby-sit for her if I thought that she would have a good night out with a man who would treat her well," she said coyly.

"Do you know any men like that?" Owen reportedly asked with a mischievous twinkle in his eye.

"From personal and disastrous experience, no, but Frankie is one of these tiresome girlies who insist on seeing the good in people and likes to give them the benefit of the doubt until they prove otherwise. She loves the Clark Kent look. Men with glasses make her all hot and bothered."

When she told me what she'd said I smacked her around the head with the paper plate that held my soggy salad sandwich. (It was Monday – the one and only day I am ever on a diet.)

"Rubbeeeee!" I admonished, cringing at the thought of what he must be thinking of me

"Frankie, men are stupid creatures who need things pointed out and spelt for them. They don't do well with this female habit of trying to drop hints."

"Well, no one could ever accuse you of trying to do that," I muttered.

"Straight to the point; that's me."

I couldn't stay cross with her for long though, especially when Superman himself, minus his cape and manky-looking Y-fronts, came to ask if he could take me out. He took my number and promised to phone me that weekend.

It was Friday and I left the office waving goodbye to him with my heart pounding.

I'd already convinced myself that it wasn't going to happen. (It's a method of self-preservation when you've been hurt, you see.) You tell yourself that you're not worthy, that he's only doing it to be nice and that he'll come up with a suitable excuse as to why he couldn't phone. Ruby told me that he had a daughter so I'd already painted the scenario that one of her legs would fall off or something equally dramatic would happen to completely eradicate me from his mind.

"Bye, Frankie," he called in a friendly voice. "I'll chat to you tomorrow night."

"Sure," I said in a cheerful tone, still wondering what his excuse would be on Monday.

It was Saturday morning and I was up with the lark. The children were downstairs watching what they call "the funnies" on television and I could hear them giggling in high-pitched voices as somebody got a bucket of gunge dumped on their head from a great height.

I was changing the beds and as usual finding nine-year-old Ben's toy cars everywhere. No matter how often I told him not to leave them lying around I always inevitably ended up standing on one of them (in my bare feet of course, so that it hurt more). His room was an explosion of red in honour of his beloved Liverpool. I hate football but got an intense kick out of the fact that he supported an opposing team to his father and could never be swayed no matter what Tony (die-hard Arsenal supporter) said to him.

I picked up his dirty football kit and put it in my linen basket. He played for the Swiftstown under-tens and wore his blue and white colours with pride.

Carly's room was much tidier. It was pink and decorated with brightly coloured wall stickers and hanging mobiles. Her DVDs of *Cinderella* and *Beauty and the Beast* and other fantasy princesses were neatly stacked at the side of her little white TV and her *High School Musical* poster had pride of place above her bed. She loved singing and I could hear her warbling in her six-year-old voice as I descended the stairs, grubby duvet covers in hand.

"Muummeee!" she shouted as she put her arms around my neck and swung. She was tall and gangly for her age with a head full of blonde curls and was as light as a feather.

Everyone always jokes that there must have been a mix-up at the hospital where Carly was concerned as we are nothing alike. I am five feet tall and not a centimetre more and have a bit of a spare-tyre thing going on around my middle. My blonde hair is not really blonde but everyone told me that it suited me the first time I got it highlighted so I keep getting it done. I have large eyes and am blessed with long eyelashes and buying the latest mascara is my favourite hobby as I like enhancing the good features I have. I am also told that I have a lovely smile but equally that I can deliver the foulest looks on the planet when the mood takes me.

"What are we doing today, Mum?" came the all-too-familiar question.

Saturday was our treat day when we went to the Popcorn Club at the cinema or to the swimming pool.

Saturday used to be the day when their father would spoil them until he decided to move to America with his new Californian wife who had the cheek to have legs up to her armpits and look like a coat-hanger.

Tony (aka The Arsehole) came home one day about four years before this and announced that he no longer loved me but hoped that I would understand that he had found a soul mate. Stella was the American stick insect's name. Tony met her through business and it was the start of a beautiful relationship. It was just a pity that the prick didn't remember that he was in one with me at the time.

My children no longer saw their father and he didn't seem to care. He and his new wife were expecting a baby, I had heard, and were all loved up. Tony's sadistic old hag of a grandmother took great pleasure in imparting this particular piece of information just as I was unloading my trolley in Tesco's the previous week. My first thought when I had digested the news was that I hoped that the baby had an unusually large head. Perhaps if the bimbo went through a tough labour she wouldn't be so keen to get pregnant by other people's husbands and her sprog wouldn't be nicking Ben and Carly's father either.

Saturday evening came and we were all pooped. My children loved saying or rather singing that word, should I say. We all loved the film *Father of the Bride*, you see, so the kids liked to indulge in a verse of "Every Party has a Pooper" and stick in "Mum" where George Banks' name should be.

The day had been hectic. We went to the circus at Ruby's request. Ruby was a child at heart and not having children of her own she often used mine as an excuse to do things that she should have grown out of years ago. She loved the circus so accompanying Ben, Carly and me was a good reason to go. The children had always called her Auntie Ruby and she was like one of the family. A very noisy, boisterous addition in fact.

"First one to bed gets a bottle of chocolate milk!" I shouted and heard the children scrambling to beat each other into their rooms. Of course they knew I had one sitting in the fridge for each of them but they didn't seem to care about that as I announced the competition.

An hour later and I had finally settled in front of the Saturday-night film with a glass of White Zinfandel. I was trying my best not to keep looking at the phone but I couldn't help it. It was sitting in the corner of the room mocking me by remaining silent.

I repeated the mantra over and over again in my head. *He's not going to phone. He's not going to phone. He's a man. He's not to be trusted and he's not going to phone.*

Midway through my inner speech the phone rang and I sloshed wine all over my jeans.

"Hello?"

"Hello, can I speak to Lois?"

"I'm sorry, you must have the wrong number," I said with bitter disappointment in my voice.

"That's a pity," the caller said. "Because it's Clark Kent here."

Chapter 2

We'd been an item for four weeks. (Longest relationship since the marriage fell down round my ears.) Everyone had an opinion about our romance. Ruby, I was willing to listen to – everyone else I wanted to physically hurt as soon as they opened their big mouths. My mother, Celia, was one of those on the "hurt" list and, as she was highly opinionated, she aggrieved me more than most.

I'd heard it all from her. The last visit was particularly irritating which is why I was now avoiding my parents' home like I would a biblical plague of Egypt.

"You've got two children, Frankie."

"Really, Mother. Thank you for pointing that out. I wasn't aware of that."

"Don't be so sarcastic, Frankie. It doesn't suit you," she said in a prim voice which made me want to go out to the nearest field and roar in annoyance. "I'm simply looking out for my grandchildren, that's all. He could be anybody."

"He's not anybody – his name is Owen, Mammy – and I'm not about to frogmarch him into the house and demand that the children call him 'Daddy' any time soon."

"I should hope not, Frankie. You need to know what you're dealing with before you go moving him in."

At this point I choked on my tea and succeeded in spitting it out on the table.

"Moving him in!" I gasped. "Where the feck did that come from?"

"Don't swear," my mother said disapprovingly. "Moving in is what you young ones do even though the Pope says you should be married first so I'm just trying to pre-empt what might happen."

At the ripe old age of thirty-two I was chuffed at being referred to as a young thing but peeved never-theless. I need to explain that my mother is a proud Irish Catholic Mammy but that she is not averse to giving off about the Vatican and some of the weird goings-on that seem to take place there. She is very much with them on the whole not living-in-sin thing, however, and I really wasn't in the mood for a lecture.

"Well, stop pre-feckin'-empting," I said. I prayed for Daddy to come and save me but instead of doing that he decided to go and walk the dog.

Banjo got walked a lot during my visits as Daddy often felt the need to get offside. Translated this meant that the women in his life drove him bananas and he would rather walk the roads around Swiftstown than have to listen to us.

Having said that, however, there weren't as many of us as there used to be. My sister, Ella, moved to Scotland, after hooking up with a kilt-wearing Scotsman from Edinburgh. She knew all about Owen but had declined to comment as of yet, although I knew that our mother had been feeding her all sorts of stories.

I thought that working with my "luvva" would have been uncomfortable or the source of a bit of unease but this was not the case at all. Owen was brilliant. Outside work he was wonderful company and great fun to be with and when he was in the college, suited and being called Mr Byrne (which I found very attractive and masterful), he was discreetly attentive lest he gave the office gossips too much scope to do what they did best.

Mandy the receptionist was positively aglow with the fact that she actually had something to talk about that she didn't have to fabricate. She was the sort of girl who loved a story and also loved adding on a clump of untruths to make it more appealing to anyone who would give her the time of day. It was a wonder that anyone did any more since the entire place had been victimised by her tongue and her rogue imagination.

"So what's the story, Frankie?" she purred one morning when I went into reception to send a fax.

"Nothing much unless you have it, Mandy."

Reverse psychology is a wonderful thing. Once you become a mother you are instantly provided with a large dollop of the stuff and you discover that it works on most people as well as your own offspring. Not on Mandy though, more was the pity.

"I don't have any," she answered sweetly. "How are things with you and Owen?" (Nothing like taking the bull by the horns then.)

"Well, actually," I said with what I knew was a thoughtful look on my face which nearly sent Mandy into a frenzy, "they're how would I put it ..."

"Really good?" she interjected excitedly. When I shook my head, still looking thoughtful, she made another suggestion. "Really bad. Is he crap in the sack?"

"Actually, Mandy, they're grand. That's the word I was looking for and when I want the rest of the country to know any more I'll make sure that I tell you first so you can get out your loudhailer and make a party political broadcast on my behalf."

She gave me a filthy look and didn't speak to me for the rest of the week. Not that I minded ... Getting interrogated on your way into the office in the morning can be a bit intimidating.

Ruby told her to "piss away off" on one such

occasion and succeeded in scaring the shite out of her to the point that whenever she went into the office Mandy always pretended to be on the phone.

Owen and I discovered that we had a lot in common. Not only had we both had disastrous relationships where we had been badly treated by the other party but we were also devoted parents.

Owen had a fourteen-year-old daughter called Angelica. She sounded like a good kid who'd been through a rough time. Owen told me about the breakdown of his marriage but I had a feeling that I'd only heard part of the story.

His wife disappeared one day leaving a note in her wake saying that she wasn't cut out for motherhood (it only took the silly cow nine months of pregnancy and seven years to figure it out) and that she was going somewhere hot and sunny to "find herself". I hated people who said things like that. I'd have loved to tell them that they'd be better off going to look for someone else instead. I mean if they didn't know who they were by now it was just a little bit sad. In my opinion that type of behaviour was just pretentious bullshit and an excuse for acting like a twat.

I could only sit back and thank God that my children were both too young to realise what was going on when Tony and I split up.

Obviously none of the children had been made

part of the Owen equation yet. I made it very clear to him, and he was in full agreement with me, that we shouldn't involve them for a long time. He hadn't mentioned our relationship to his daughter yet and mine didn't know anything either so it was all going according to plan.

I loved going out with Owen and by "going out" I mean just that. We had proper dates where we made arrangements and I got all dressed up and he collected me and we went out and had a great time together. We talked a lot when we were in each other's company. Owen and I shared a similar sense of humour and when we laughed it could get quite loud and raucous.

Ruby of course was gloating at her success and kept making jibes about wanting a mention when Owen made the speech at our wedding. (Like I said, it had only been four weeks. The hat shops didn't need to panic yet.)

"I can just hear him," Ruby would say. "'We wouldn't be together only for our chief groomsperson'" – Ruby was a complete tomboy who hated flouncy dresses – "'who started a bit of harmless flirting about Clark Kent and Lois Lane and sure look at us now – aren't we just great with our Von Trapp family?'"

She also kept asking me how I was going to cope with handling someone else's child. "It won't be the easiest job, you know," she warned, wagging a finger. "Look at the evidence that kids have to go on.

Cinderella's stepmother was a stinker and so was Snow White's and sure even the Children of Lir were turned into swans by theirs."

"Ruby, I haven't made a lifelong commitment to be anyone's stepmother, you know," I reasoned. "For all we know I could be back to speed dating in a matter of weeks but for now I'm just happy to go with the flow. And can I just point out that I'm not living in a fairy tale? Although sometimes I think I am." I hugged myself dreamily as Ruby made gagging noises and rolled her eyes.

"Yeah, okay, Sleeping Beauty, you've been asleep for a hundred years and you've just been woken up by your prince. You'd need to have been sleeping or drugged or something to have married what you did."

"Ruby, I may not have made the right decision about my choice of husband but my children were meant to be here for a reason and I wouldn't swap them for the world."

"Okay," she conceded begrudgingly. "But I still think that you must have been mad."

As I said, Ruby hated Tony. I think my height brought out the maternal instinct in her. She liked Owen though so I was glad that I had her vote of approval on something.

"So I'm not insane or sniffing glue or anything then?" I said.

"Definitely not. The Owen one was a good

decision, but then it was always going to be good. I made it for you so you had no choice."

I thought it was a good move too. It was "Golden Oldies" night at the cinema and Owen and I were going to watch *Dirty Dancing*. What other man would have even entertained the idea? Had I struck gold or what?

Chapter 3

Time was passing nicely and our relationship was continuing to progress at a steady pace. Owen and I saw each other every day at work, talked most evenings and went out at least once a week. I suppose we could have spent more time together but I wanted to limit it so that Ben and Carly wouldn't feel that they were playing second fiddle to their mother's love life. It was with surprise therefore that I received an unusual phone call from Owen one Saturday morning.

"Hello, you," came the dulcet tone as I held my mobile phone to my ear and tried to control an over-excitable Carly who had just pirouetted her way into my room and performed a double-pike somersault into my bed.

"Well, hi there, handsome, how are you?" I said back in an exaggerated American drawl.

"I'm just fine, little lady," he quipped.

"Less of the little," I said sternly. "Just because you're a lanky big eejit with legs up to your neck does not give you the right to look down on the rest of us."

"Eh-hem, Frankie," he said, trying not to laugh, "I think you'll find it does."

"Shut up," I said. He had started to call such statements "Frankie-isms".

"I think you'd better shut up," he said "unless you want to add to my ever-expanding list."

"Mmmm," I hummed into the phone.

Carly thought I was playing with her and immediately started to mimic me.

"Mmm mmm," she sang. "Mum, who are you singing to?" Quick as a flash she grabbed my phone and started to hop around the room with it.

"Shit!" I said before grabbing it and glaring crossly at her.

"Bless her," Owen said. "She sounds like a sweet little thing. She even talks like you. What age did you say she was again?"

"Ha ha."

"Are you doing anything today?"

"Spending time with the wee ones."

"We're going to the park to do the pedal boats with Mum!" Carly sang.

"Do you think that perhaps Auntie Ruby could be roped in to help with that task?" Owen asked tentatively.

I was a bit shocked at this request. In the four months that we had been together Owen had never wanted to infringe on my Saturdays as he knew that they were my special time with the children.

He noted my silence and responded quickly. "Frankie, I don't want to intrude but I was hoping that I could borrow you for a while today. It's for a very good reason. I wouldn't ask otherwise."

"What is it?" I asked as Ben appeared, sleepily rubbing his eyes, and came to me for a hug. His spiky blonde hair was standing on end and his pyjama bottoms were too long for him (an adverse side effect from inheriting the short-arse gene from his mother).

"I'd like you to meet my mother," Owen said gently, instantly grabbing my attention. "She's only visiting for the weekend, you see, and I've told her about you and she'd like to see you."

Owen's mother lived in Dublin. She couldn't cope with life in the north of Ireland without Owen's father, Jack, who reportedly was a living breathing legend, so she left and set up home in an apartment in Malahide. As a result she expected others to visit her (sounded a bit like having an audience with the Queen) but on this occasion I knew that she was making the trip because it was Angelica's fifteenth birthday. Angelica was apparently the apple of her grandmother's eye, hence the special visitation.

"Frankie, are you still there?" he asked.

"Yes, Owen, sorry," I spluttered. "I'm sure that would be okay. I'll phone Ruby now and get it organised. But I thought that we had agreed that we would have no contact with the children until we had been together at least six months?"

"That still stands," he explained. "My sister has promised to take Angelica out for a special birthday tea so that will give us an hour or two on our own with my mother."

I had to admit that I was relieved by this revelation. I'd need to psyche myself up for about a month before preparing to meet my boyfriend's child. I wondered what she'd think of me when I eventually did. I hoped she'd like me.

I had expressed my concerns to Owen on numerous occasions but he'd always said the same thing. "What's not to like?"

I quickly dialled Ruby's number and was greeted by a grumpy voice which obviously belonged to a hungover owner.

"Oh shit, Ruby, I'm sorry," I said quickly as I saw that it was still only ten o'clock.

"This better be good," she said slowly. "I feel as though my eyes are glued together. I'm going to talk to you with them shut and then I just might be able to avoid being sick. I was drinking Aftershocks last night and I think that my liver has finally packed in."

I had a feeling that she wasn't going to like what I

was about to say but I took a deep breath and prepared to ask her anyway.

"Ruby, I wonder if you could do me a big favour?"

A few hours later and Ruby was standing at my door wearing a tracksuit with remnants of last night's make-up still evident around her eyes.

"Auntie Ruby, Auntie Ruby!" the children shouted in excitement as they spied her. I didn't tell them that she was coming as I knew that they'd appreciate the surprise. Ruby, however, didn't.

"Is there a volume-control button on those two?" she asked, cradling her head.

"I'm afraid not," I replied, "but I've talked them into going to the cinema instead of going out on the boats today."

"Oh my God, couldn't you just see me barfing out the side of a boat with two children in tow?" said Ruby while dissolving two fizzy pain-relievers in water. "They'd be calling Esther Rantzen and *Childline* before you could say 'alcoholic'."

"Okay, I'm going to get ready now," I said.

"So what are you wearing for the first meeting with the future mother-in-law then?"

"What's a mother-in-law?" asked Carly, looking puzzled.

I shot Ruby a warning glance. She had a tendency to forget that children have enquiring minds and my daughter could hear the grass growing. She's like that little cartoon character, Mindy, who always asks "Why?" and then ends every conversation with "Okay, I love you, bye-byeee!".

"A pain in the arse mostly," Ruby muttered under her breath in answer to Carly's question.

"Nothing, darling," I answered. "Go and get ready quickly and talk to Ben because you have to decide what you want to see."

Ruby looked apologetic as I motioned at her to sit down while I went upstairs to change.

I finally decided on a pair of grey trousers and a pale-pink knitted top with some funky beads. I fluffed out my hair, applied a little make-up and finished off the outfit with my favourite pointy boots which came complete with a four-inch heel. I didn't want this woman to think that her son was going out with one of the seven dwarfs.

I had arranged to meet Owen at one o'clock at his house. He lived in a renovated cottage on the outskirts of Swiftstown. I loved his home. It was full of character with high ceilings, an open fire in the living room, wooden rafters in the kitchen, five spacious bedrooms and a bathroom decorated entirely in black and white marble-ware. His backyard opened out onto a lake and there was a beautiful garden with terrific scenery all around. It was pure bliss. Owen had managed to sneak me in one evening when Angelica was at a friend's house and I'd been daydreaming about the place since. (Lady of the Manor – I mean, Cottage, really suited me, I thought, as a title.)

Today I was nervous as his house came into view. I always had fears as to what Angelica would think of me but I could come up against more opposition from his mother. Would she think I was good enough for her son?

As I knocked on his door I could already see her rear view through the window. Her hair was silver and coiffed perfectly. She was wearing pearl earrings and a tweed suit.

Owen smiled his gorgeous smile as he opened the door and stooped to kiss me. We always joked that I would need a stepladder to reach him. However, with my heart rocketing to the soles of my shoes I wasn't much in the mood for jokes.

"Mother, I'd like you to meet Frankie," Owen said as he presented me with a wave of his arm.

"Frances," she said as she took my hand and looked closely at me.

Uh oh. I felt like I was six years old again and had just broken the garage window with my tennis ball. My mother only ever gave me my full title when I had done something wrong. Already I sensed that this was not a good omen and the woman had only uttered one word.

"Mrs Byrne, it really is lovely to meet you."

She frowned and began to chastise me. "Call me Esme," she commanded. "I dislike being called 'Mrs'. It brings back too many painful memories for me. I miss my Jack so much. Life has never been the same since he died."

She looked like she might cry and I was inwardly telling myself to stop being a moron when Owen brightly suggested that we have tea.

That might be a good idea. Perhaps if I had something to chew on then I wouldn't be inclined to stick my great foot in it.

"So you work with my son?"

I realised that it was simply a rhetorical question which required no input from me when she went on to boast about his success in the teaching profession.

I remained silent and nodded politely.

"And you've just started working in the college yourself?"

"Yes, my speciality is Public Relations."

"Really?" she said, looking entirely unimpressed (obviously teaching had much more credibility attached to it).

A rather awkward silence ensued where I picked imaginary pieces of fluff from my clothing, studied my nails and pondered my future in the field of public relations, taking into account the fact that I was in a room with only one other person and couldn't manage to drum up a hint of small talk never mind conversation. Esme was studying me from the corner of her eye and sniffed and turned away when we finally made visual contact.

This was not going well. Where the hell was Owen? Was he going to China to source the feckin' tea himself?

"How do you like living in Dublin, Esme?" I finally asked before the atmosphere in the room smothered me.

"I was never meant to be living there on my own," she said, avoiding my gaze. "My late husband and I had always talked about retiring there so it just makes his absence all the more hard to bear although living here would have been worse."

Oh good. She was now on the verge of tears again and I was contemplating sellotaping my mouth shut.

"I'm sure it's nice to come and see your family though, Esme."

"My family is very important to me," she said, turning and looking at me properly for the first time. "I hear you have children."

"Yes, Ben and Car—"

"My granddaughter has been through a very traumatic time. She lost her mother when she was young and is very insecure as a result. Therefore I hope you understand that Owen's first duty will always be to her. He can't suddenly drop everything to be a stand-in father for someone else's children. I hear your husband left you."

I was more than a little stunned by this statement and could feel my blood starting to boil.

Owen obviously saw the warning signs as he entered the room and attempted unsuccessfully to intervene.

"What my mother means is —"

"Your mother has made it perfectly clear what she means, Owen," I responded angrily, "and now I would like to make myself clear. Esme, I would never in a million years expect anyone to neglect their own children to be a father to mine and I'm not actually looking for a 'stand-in father' as you so nicely put it. I can manage quite well on my own. I've had no choice but to learn. My husband chose to go to another country and start a new life without his children so I know what it's like to be abandoned and can empathise with Angelica. I am certainly not selfishly expecting Owen to drop everything and dance attendance on either myself or Ben and Carly."

"I'm glad to hear it," Esme answered. "Angelica is a sensitive little soul who needs to be loved and understood. She is very confused and fragile at the moment. The teenage years are hard regardless of circumstances but the poor lamb has had it harder than most."

"I can appreciate that it has been hard on everyone, Esme. I am looking forward to meeting Angelica and getting to know her." It took all my willpower to encourage my jaw to unclench itself so that I could smile.

"Here's your opportunity," Esme announced, her mood lightening and her expression softening instantly when she heard a car door slamming outside, suggesting that we were about to be joined by more company.

"Auntie Maura took me to that poxy restaurant with the crap menu. Nothing but meat, meat, meat and I don't eat it any more!"

Esme smiled adoringly at the fire-snorting monster that had just come into the room (fragile my arse and did Esme know what a lamb was?). The girl was followed by a woman in her mid-thirties who looked quite like Owen.

"Well, that didn't go according to plan," the woman said in a tight voice. "Apparently we are now a vegetarian and don't like eating the flesh of dead animals. Mind you, we don't like vegetables either so it was a very worthwhile lunch." Then she smiled at me and proffered her hand. "Hi, I'm Maura."

I shook her hand and we shared a knowing look. I instantly knew that I was going to like this woman.

"Angelica, come and meet Frances," Esme said as she gestured towards me.

Angelica was tall with shoulder-length brown hair which had red and blonde streaks in it. She was thin, had blue eyes and was dressed entirely in black. She looked very pretty as she smiled at her grandmother but her smile left her face as she turned towards me.

"Hi, Angelica," I said, trying to smile. "I hope you have a lovely birthday."

"Thanks," she said, curling her lip at me in a bizarre fashion and immediately turning her back to me. Then she suddenly swung around, recognition dawning on her face. "You're Frankie, aren't you?" she said. "I hear my dad talking to you on the phone."

"That's right," I said, looking pleadingly at Owen who had suddenly decided to examine his shoes. "We're good friends," I added seeing as the cat had been very busy whipping everyone else's tongues out.

"I'm fifteen tomorrow and I'm not stupid," she said with her face dangerously close to mine, "and I know that you must be more than just friends."

As I looked into her eyes I saw an unsettling look of contempt there which I didn't like and I knew I was facing a challenging time. A very challenging time indeed.

Chapter 4

"Is he on something?" I asked Ruby when I returned home. "How the hell can he sit and calmly tell me that he thinks that fiasco went well? It was a God-awful nightmare from beginning to end. I managed to insult his mother within the first ten seconds of meeting her and she insisted on addressing me as Frances and making me feel like I'm six. As for that daughter of his, I can see nothing but trouble ahead on that score. I'm trying to be understanding and look at things from her perspective but there is just no excuse for being that rude. Even her own aunt seems to have reservations about her."

I stopped for breath and noted that Ruby was looking quizzically at me.

"I did tell you that it wouldn't be easy," she said. "Step-families are notoriously difficult to cope with and you're just unlucky that the girl is at a bit of an icky age as well. What did Owen do?"

"After she sneered at me and ran out? Well, after standing and ignoring me and acting like a stuck pig, he eventually went after her," I explained. "And I think he may have had a word but whatever he said didn't work very well. Angelica was upstairs peering out through the curtains as I left and giving me the evil eye."

"Did Owen say anything when you were leaving?"

"He's phoning me later," I said, my heart skipping a beat as I uttered the words.

What if his mother and daughter had both ganged up on him and told him that they'd disown him if he didn't dump me? Esme might have been willing to give me a chance but one word from Angelica would sway her. She seemed to dote on her granddaughter and be entirely blind to her rather disturbing behaviour.

Angelica was to be pitied, though, I told myself (very sternly). With her circumstances she needed love and understanding. I tried to believe it but a niggly little voice kept telling me that it looked suspiciously like a smokescreen for teenage angst and behaving like a stroppy brat.

Owen phoned me that evening and sounded very sheepish.

"Are you okay?" he asked solemnly. "I'm sorry to

have put you through that. You weren't meant to meet Angelica under such circumstances."

"She doesn't like me," I blurted out. "In fact I think she hates me."

"She doesn't hate you, Frankie. She's just confused and messed up. She's only starting to realise now that her mother left of her own free will and has never bothered to return. How would you feel if your mammy suddenly decided after seven years of having you that she didn't want to be a mother anymore? It's almost like saying that she wished you were never born. Birthdays are hard for her as well. Can you imagine what it must be like to go through the anniversary of your birth and wonder if your mother remembers either it or you?"

I thought about this, and had to agree that when it was put like that, it was understandable the pain and confusion that such thoughts and feelings would cause.

"You're very quiet," he said. "If you want to put it all down to a bad experience and call it a day I'll understand. You have enough problems without me adding to them."

"I think that's my decision, don't you?" I said, annoyed that he would give up what we had so easily, unless of course he saw this as the perfect excuse to end it all (bloody men are all cowards). "Is that what you want?" I went on in a huffy tone. "If you want us to finish you don't have to try and trick me into doing your dirty work for you. You have a mouth of your own so just say the word."

I think he may have been stuck for an answer as I wrapped the phone flex round and round my finger.

"Is that what you want?" he asked.

"Stop putting it back on me, Owen!" I snarled through gritted teeth. "I am perfectly happy and willing to make a go of it but I only want to do it if you are also committed to making it work. I've encountered scarier things in my life than your daughter and I'm sure that I'll cope."

"Frankie," he said slowly.

"Yes, Owen."

"God but you're sexy when you're cross."

A few days can make all the difference in these situations and soon I'd convinced myself that it was a one-off bad experience which I'd learn from. Owen was trying to be upbeat about it too even though it was painfully obvious that he was very preoccupied.

"Are you all right?" I asked as we ate slices of pizza after watching a film.

"That's the third time you've asked me that this evening," he answered, sounding peeved with me.

"Well, perhaps if you'd stop lying and tell me what's really on your mind then I wouldn't keep asking."

"Look, it's nothing to do with you so stop worrying.

You're the one thing that keeps me going and makes me look forward instead of back."

"Ooh, that's deep," I said, wondering what in God's name he was going to say next.

"It's not meant to be deep," he said. "It's just an observation. Look, Frankie, I've been thinking …" He paused as if he seemed unsure about what to say next.

(Just for the record – when a man says he's been thinking it's never going to be a good outcome.) I was bracing myself for a conversation that was going to start with the words "I think we should slow down".

"Owen, what is it?" I prompted impatiently.

"I think we should introduce the children to one another," he said. "My mother's been shouting her mouth off and Angelica feels quite threatened by the fact that you have children and I think if she met them and got to know them that it might go a long way to convince her that I'm not about to abandon her. Being part of a proper family unit might be good for her as well."

I *sooo* was not expecting him to say that. I thought about his proposition for all of three seconds before coming to the conclusion that it was the worst idea he had ever had. My poor wee Carly was too young to be mauled to death by a bad-tempered teenager. If Angelica was capable of reducing me to a gibbering wreck I could only imagine the damage that she could inflict on a sensitive six-year-old. I could visualise all of Carly's tight little curls uncoiling themselves and lying lank against her usually vibrant little head as she received yet another insult or put-down from Angelica. As for being part of a family unit, I had a sneaking suspicion that Angelica would probably rather eat her own arm than ever view me as a potential mother figure.

"You look very worried," Owen said.

(No kidding.)

"I've got good cause to be," I said. "Owen, I think we need to think very carefully about this."

Luckily that seemed to stall him in his tracks.

"I think it would be better if we left it until the summer months to make introductions. We'll have more time and there won't be the added pressure of school for any of them then," I said.

However, I also felt secretly annoyed that his daughter had seen me when my children hadn't clapped eyes on him yet but were curious as to where I went on the evenings I socialised. I had always been really careful to make sure that Ben and Carly were in bed and asleep if Owen came round and the nights that he picked me up he never came in.

"On the other hand," I said uncertainly, "it isn't fair that now Angelica knows but my kids are still in the dark."

"Here's a solution," Owen said quickly. "Why don't I come over early on Saturday evening and spend some time with Ben and Carly? Angelica is staying at a friend's house and need never know."

I must have looked quite alarmed as he then assured me that Ben and Carly weren't on the menu for tea.

I was still unsure but reluctantly agreed. I suppose technically he was only being obliging and doing as I asked. I just hadn't expected or wanted it to happen so soon. (Me and my big gob.)

Chapter 5

"I don't know what you're so worried about," Ruby commented the following day over our morning tea break. "You're happy, aren't you?"

"Of course I'm happy. That's the problem. I'm afraid of putting 'the scud'" (bad omen of the Northern Irish variety) "on it by not having the patience to wait a while longer before letting it get so serious."

"You're only introducing him to your children who will probably find him a novelty for all of ten seconds before sticking their heads back in their computer games again."

"I know you think I'm overreacting but I don't want to go introducing them to a man" (acceptable reference) – "Mummy's special friend" (I hate that) – "Uncle Owen" (no chance) – "only for something to happen. I'd look like such an irresponsible parent to allow my children to get close to someone only for them to disappear like their father."

"*Hellllooooo*, lighten up please and stop being the Princess of Doom and stop worrying about what bloody Peggy will say! I know you too well and I know that that's what's really bothering you."

I was loath to admit it as I liked to pretend that I didn't care what anybody thought but I did care — especially when they were just looking for an excuse to expose me as an unfit mother.

I suppose at this point in my story I need to take a walk back in time and give you a history lesson. This may explain why Peggy Colton, Ben and Carly's great-grandmother aka "Nebby Peg" ("nebby" conveying in local parlance the fact that she is the sharpest, most vicious-tongued woman in the world . . . and I'm being diplomatic) and I are less than friendly.

The common belief is that grannies everywhere are sweet, good-natured individuals who remember birthdays, eat sugared almonds and are generally cuddly and loving towards their grandchildren (and their grandchildren's choice of girlfriends). Peggy must have been in a different queue when the aforementioned traits were being handed out. She seemed, instead, to have received the nation's quota of vindictiveness and sarcasm.

I first met Peggy when Tony (the philandering two-timing fecker) brought me to his mother's house for Sunday lunch when we had been together for a few weeks. Tony's mother, Liz, was a lovely woman who I had instantly warmed to. She welcomed me into the bosom of their family and fussed over me like I was the most important person there. I always loved the chats I had with her. She was the sort of person who gave you a warm fuzzy feeling when you were telling her a bit of news because she was so interested and concerned for your welfare. Tony's father, Lawrence, was a bit of a mystery. He was quiet and conservative and I never really got to know him. Peggy was his mother and she always made me feel uncomfortable and I wasn't the only one. I always had a strong suspicion (to be confirmed later) that she never thought that Liz was good enough for her son. She was constantly making snide comments which usually held a barbed criticism. She always smiled sanctimoniously when she was delivering these statements and it really irritated me and made me want to grab her by the two ears and shake her. How Liz put up with her I never knew but one thing I did know was that she didn't like me and the fact that Liz and I got on so well was fanning the flames.

Tony and I had been together for about a year when tragedy struck and his parents were both killed in a horrific car accident which left the family and community at large shocked and stunned. As Tony was an only child like his father before him and his mother had no relatives to speak of, Peggy stepped in and became his nearest and dearest. Anyone else (anyone remotely normal, that is) would probably have been concentrating on picking up the pieces of their grandson's life which had just been shot to bits – but not Peggy. Instead Peggy had only one agenda and that was to get rid of me. I was speechless when she turned to me in the graveyard, after burying her son and his wife, and told me that she wasn't going to stand by and watch me ruin her grandson's life the way her son's life had been destroyed by Liz.

I had to hand it to her that she did her best to turn Tony against me. There seemed to be no lengths that she wouldn't stoop to. I was accused of only being with him because of what he stood to inherit and she tried to make him believe that I was seeing other men. Luckily for me (or in hindsight maybe not) Tony was unwilling to leave my side and two years later we married. Peggy wasn't there and we had a wonderful day. When the children came along I could see that she was seething with rage as she knew that her control was slipping. I was giddy with the feeling of having the upper hand in those days. It gave me such a thrill to know that she was so annoyed with the situation (immature and silly, I know; but she was supposed to be the mature one growing old gracefully – but doing the direct opposite).

My upper hand toppled magnificently, however,

when Tony announced that he was leaving me. Peggy was beside herself with glee and took every opportunity to let me know that it was all my fault that my marriage hadn't worked out. Apparently her grandson wouldn't have been seeking solace in the arms of another woman if I had been enough for him (yeah, right – it wasn't my problem that his fly came undone at the sound of an American female accent).

Nebby Peg and I rarely saw each other any more. I think (if truth be told) she was as miffed as I was when her precious grandson took off on a jumbo jet and left his children behind. On the few occasions that I have met her, however, she never fails to twist the knife by talking to the children as if I'm not there.

"Hello, Ben, aren't you handsome just like your father?" she said one day. "You do remember your daddy, don't you? He'd probably be here now if your mother had been a better wife."

It was a good job that Ruby was with me or else the old crone would have been taking out a restraining order against me with my foot still lodged in her rear end.

I had only met her once since and that had been when she had cheerfully told me that Tony and his wife were expecting a baby (whoop dee feckin' doo).

I hoped that it would be a long time before our paths crossed again but, knowing my luck, it would be sooner rather than later and I certainly didn't want to give her any ammunition.

Chapter 6

The children and I were walking out of the cinema on Saturday afternoon and I was feeling more buoyant and optimistic about the arranged meeting that evening. Ruby had finally persuaded me to stop giving myself an ulcer over it and I had also confided in my sister who had agreed. I had spoken to Ella the evening before and we had spent nearly an hour on the phone catching up with each other. Maybe it's female intuition, perhaps it's a sister thing or it might simply be that I'm gifted but I sensed that Ella was worried about something. Her conversation had been flowing freely when she was advising me about what to do with my tangled love life but when I asked her how *she* was she seemed unwilling to talk.

I was contemplating phoning Ella again to make sure she was okay when I heard a harsh and aggressive voice talking loudly behind me.

"That's her. That's my new stepmother apparently."

I turned and saw Angelica staring at me with two other girls in tow. They were all brazenly looking me up and down and nudging each other and making me feel like a prize heifer at a farmers', mart.

"Hello, Angelica," I croaked. (Why today? Of all the days in the year why the hell did I have to meet Little Miss Attitude today?)

"What's a stepmother, Mum?" Carly enquired.

"Somebody with bad roots who needs to go on a diet obviously," Angelica sneered making her friends smirk as they walked away laughing.

"Who was that?" Ben asked as we looked at the girls' retreating backs.

"Erm . . . just somebody I know," I said lamely.

"I don't think she liked you very much, Mum. I think she was laughing at you." (Thanks for pointing out the obvious, son.)

"But why would she do that?" Carly said in a quivering voice. "Everybody likes Mum."

"Look, there's no need for either of you to concern yourselves with what people think," I reassured them. "As long as you like me then I don't really care what anyone else thinks." (*Liar liar, pants on fire!*)

Owen arrived punctually that evening bearing a beautiful aromatic bunch of lilies for me. He kissed me on the cheek and spoke easily to the children as if he had known them all his life. He made a friend in Ben almost immediately as practically the first words he uttered were "Fancy a game of footie?" whilst producing a football emblazoned with the Liverpool logo. I enviously looked on and wondered whether he was simply brilliant with children or whether my children were blessed with good genes and nice manners and didn't delight in insulting potential step-parents. It had taken Herculean strength for me not to cry, have a hissy fit or go and smack Angelica when she had been so nasty to me. I had gone home, stripped, examined myself in front of the mirror and sadly come to the conclusion that I did indeed need to go on a diet. I had also booked an appointment with the hairdresser for the following week. Technically, I suppose she had done me a favour but there are two ways of saying something and on second thoughts I think I would have preferred it if she had zipped her mouth closed. I wasn't going to say anything to Owen about it as I reckoned it would spoil the evening and as much as I thought she was a brat I didn't want him to know that.

Carly shyly stood and watched whilst Owen kicked the football around the backyard with Ben and was delighted when he produced a bubble-making machine for her.

"How did you know I love bubbles?" she asked, treating him to a lopsided smile with her two front teeth missing.

He tapped his forefinger on the side of his nose and told her it was a secret but that he also knew she loved *High School Musical* and maybe we could all go and see the musical that the local youth club were producing. (Jammy fecker! Why hadn't I thought of something like that?) I was gobsmacked and my enviousness had now turned to full-blown green-eyed jealousy at how easy he was making it all look.

I had told the children that we would have a barbecue if the weather stayed fine and as the sun (surprisingly, given the fact that it was an Irish sun) was keeping its end of the bargain I began to unload sausages, burgers and steaks from the fridge. Owen immediately took everything from me, donned an apron and lit the barbecue whilst waving a fish slice around his head in a manic fashion. I have to ask a question at this stage as I know that it is the source of much discussion with women everywhere. Why do men, who have no interest in cooking, and would look at you like you were sprouting horns if you suggested that they wear an apron inside the house, suddenly think they're Gordon Ramsay (complete with his temper and assortment of colourful swear words if you try to help) when they're positioned in front of a barbecue? I wasn't complaining, mind you, it was nice to sit outside on the wooden decking and enjoy the evening sunshine without having to do anything and Ben and Carly thought he was the best thing since sliced bread.

By ten o'clock the children were in bed and I had pronounced the evening a success. Owen and I were enjoying a glass of wine and he was telling me how proud I should be of my cherubs as he thought that they were wonderful. He paused and looked at me and I realised that this was the point where I was meant to return the compliment concerning the not-so-angelic Angelica.

I decided to smile and nod and play dumb as I was afraid that I might go to hell for telling such a downright lie. Besides, I was having trouble speaking as I was concentrating all my efforts on holding my stomach in and running my fingers through my hair to hide its natural colour.

Owen left a few hours later and when I went to check on the children Ben was sound asleep but Carly was awake and asking for a drink.

"Is Owen our new daddy?" she asked innocently.

I was shocked that she had even been thinking like that.

"Owen is Mummy's special friend," – I couldn't believe I'd said that – "and we're going to take our time to get to know him." Then I ventured, "Do you like him?" I had promised myself earlier that I wasn't going to put any pressure on them by asking such questions.

"He's really nice," she answered with a smile. "If he is going to be my new daddy can you let me know soon, Mum?"

"I'll do my best," I said trying to hide a smile. "Why do you want to know?"

"It's just that everybody else talks about their daddies and I'd like to talk about mine too."

I nearly cried as I looked at her beseeching little face and at that moment made a promise that if it was the last thing I did I would try to find a suitable applicant who could fill the most important job in the world of being my precious baby's daddy. Whether the post would be filled by Owen would remain to be seen.

Chapter 7

The following day I had a frank discussion with the children and asked them, in a roundabout way, if they'd mind not telling too many people about Owen. When I say "roundabout" what I mean is that after several disastrous attempts at trying to make them understand that there was nothing wrong with Owen, and that he wasn't a criminal as Ben suggested, I would just rather that they didn't talk too much about him being Mummy's special friend (yuck ... yuck ... yuck).

"Is he your boyfriend?" Ben asked with a giggle. "Owen and Mum up a tree K-I-S-S-I-N-G!"

"Yes, yes, yes, thank you," I said in response to this impromptu rendition of the classic school yard chant. "That's enough now. I want you both to get dressed because I've decided that as it's such a nice day we're going to go to the amusement park in town."

"Yeeeeeah!" they both yelled as they ran enthusiastically to get changed.

We had a lovely afternoon going between the swing boats and the Dodgem cars (even though I was nearly bankrupt due to the constant demand for money) and I was just beginning to cite this as possibly the most enjoyable weekend I'd had in a long time (excluding the comments about the size of my waist and the state of my bonce, of course) when my phone rang and I registered that it was Ruby checking up on me to see how last night had gone.

I answered the phone and started to walk away from the picnic bench where we had decided to end the day by enjoying our pasta salad and sandwiches. I continued to walk round and round whilst regaling Ruby with the story of what had happened the previous evening.

"Sounds like she needs a good clip round the ear – you're not fat," she said loyally when I bemoaned how I had been abused outside the cinema.

I was just starting to tell her about Owen and his culinary expertise at dishing out barbecued steaks when I saw the children talking to someone. Someone old and cross-looking who was standing doing the perfect impression of a fishmonger's wife.

"Ruby, hang on a second," I said as I removed the phone from my ear and hurried over to investigate more thoroughly. "Shite and bollocks, I have got to go," I said in a frantic whisper as I realised that my poor innocent children were being subjected to the evil ramblings of none other than Great-granny Peggy (and there was nothing great about her).

"Peggy," I said in a monotone bored voice by way of greeting.

"Oh, so you're here then. I was just about to call the police and tell them that I had found two innocent children who'd been abandoned by their mother."

"No, I think you'll find that it's the father who does all the abandoning in these situations," I retorted.

"With so many paedophiles and strange people lurking around I'm surprised that you left them like that," she said with her scary smile.

"Oh, I know, Neb– Peggy. You turn your back for two seconds and you never know what sort of crazed lunatic with age-spots might be talking to your children. Must dash. Lots to see and do when you're being both mother and father to your children."

Peggy looked at me with a soured expression but then beamed at Ben and Carly.

"Now remember what I told you, children."

Oh God. What lies had the old bat been filling their heads with?

"She said it was a secret," Carly complained when I threatened to banish Zac Efron (of *High School Musical* acclaim) from her room if she didn't tell me.

"Carly," I said in a warning tone.

"She told us that all men were bad and that Uncle

Owen was probably just one of loads of new uncles that we were going to have."

"The cheeky oul bit– . . . hold on a minute . . . how did she even know about Uncle –" (was I on drugs?) "Owen," I spluttered furiously.

Carly looked worried and Ben refused to look at me.

"I thought I told you two that you weren't to tell anybody about Owen."

"You said not to tell tooooooooo many people," Carly whined. "So I thought that that meant that we could tell a few people."

I counted to ten and breathed like a rhinoceros. Obviously the heavens were conspiring against me. It was my own fault for having the cheek to think I was having a good time for a change. However, like every black cloud there had to be a silver lining somewhere and mine came in the form of knowing that I had well and truly pissed off my arch-nemesis.

Great-granny Peggy had not been amused to find that Mummy had a special friend. Indeed she'd gone so far as to tell the children that Mummy was lucky that she had any friends at all, given how she had made poor Daddy run away to the other side of the world.

"What's a compliment, Mum?" Carly had asked.

"Why do you ask, love?"

"Granny Peggy said that you sent Daddy a compliment, Mum."

I found it very hard to believe that anyone would think such a thing. Most people knew that the only thing that I would like to send Daddy was a bullet with his name specially engraved on the tip. I knew where I'd like to shoot him with it too.

"I sent Daddy a compliment, did I?"

"No, you sent him *to* a compliment," she said, looking at me strangely. "Somewhere far far away from here and Granny is sad because she misses him."

"I think you mean a continent," I said, suddenly understanding. I wished Granny would go and join Daddy in the continent far far away. Interfering, nasty old bat. Apparently it was okay for Tony to act like he was suffering from amnesia and conveniently forget his vows (whilst we were still married I hasten to add) but it was a crime for me to do likewise (after he had started playing happy families with a stick insect and got her knocked up).

Life was full of inconsistencies and definitely unfair but I felt strangely at peace as I made my way home with the children. I suppose, I had surmised, that as Nebby Peg knew what was happening I no longer had to worry about her finding out. All I had to worry about now was my other stumbling block which came in the form of a stroppy fifteen-year-old who didn't relish having me around.

Chapter 8

It was the month of June and a very busy time in the college. Exams were in progress, the marketing people and I were working on a campaign to secure enough student places for next year and Owen had been chosen at the start of the year to organise the upcoming highly prestigious Graduation Day and I'd been asked to help out with the publicity of the event.

Preparations had been ongoing for several months and it had become a standing joke at work now. Everyone kept making references to Owen receiving his prize at the end of the night and I had started to stick my middle finger up a lot. I didn't do this in front of the management though as rumour had it that they were actually quite pleased with my work and that my "temporary" position might become "permanent" if I managed to impress with my creativity on this job.

My predecessor had been on long-term sick leave but apparently had now decided not to return. Wise choice, I thought, even if I was slightly biased.

Owen and I were sitting making a list of final preparations that needed to be looked at when he got an urgent phone call from Angelica's school to ask if he could pick her up as she was sick.

"But what about all this?" I asked, gesturing at the invitation lists, catering quotes and general plans that we had to make decisions about in less than three weeks.

This was the first day all week that we had managed to get a free minute to work on it and I had to admit that I was more than a little annoyed to discover that it was all going to be ruined by flamin' bloody Angelica. I could nearly lay money on the fact that she wasn't sick at all. She probably had an exam that she wanted to get out of or a teacher that had hired a hit man to take her out on a contract or something.

"Can Brenda not pick her up or is that a stupid question?"

Brenda was Owen's ex-sister-in-law who Angelica worshipped and she was a barge of the highest order. I'd never actually met her but Owen had had her on speaker phone a few times and that was enough to convince me that she was a nasty piece of work. She had a voice that was best accompanied by headache tablets due to its brutal nature and I reckoned that she'd make a great Sergeant Major in any army.

"Stupid question," Owen said in response.

Brenda worked as the money-hungry Chief Executive of a retail outlet which sold designer bags and accessories and was always tied up in meetings or training sessions.

I felt contrite as I looked at Owen. His shoulders were slumped, his head was down and he looked deflated.

"I'm sorry. I know you're only doing your best," I said. "What's wrong with Angelica?"

"They just said that she was upset and feeling light-headed. It happens a lot. She's very confused and Brenda doesn't help with her mad ramblings. She told Angelica that I was unfaithful to her mother when we were together and that I was bad to her. It's all lies but Angelica doesn't know what to believe and it plays on her mind."

"I could never do that to Ben and Carly," I said in a firm tone. "Their father has deserted them but I'd never tell them anything like that even though in their case it would be partly the truth. There are some things that children never need to know."

I looked at the table in front of me which held all the information that I had been so excited about earlier. It no longer seemed that important in the grand scale of things.

Owen left to collect his daughter and I sat and sorted through some more papers until Ruby came and physically dragged me to the canteen for a much-needed caffeine fix.

"Christ, Frankie," was her response when I told her the latest excerpt of the saga that was my life. (If they were ever stuck for a storyline on any of the soaps I could soon give them some good ideas, all true of course.) "Why did that stupid woman ever bother having a child? And what's her sister got to do with the whole thing? If I was Owen I'd be telling Brenda to sling her hook and stop interfering. Surely she has no rights over Angelica?"

"She has no legal rights," I explained, "but she has always had contact with Angelica and Owen doesn't want anyone else suddenly disappearing without a trace. He reckons that as she doesn't have her mother he shouldn't try and keep her away from her mother's family, even though they try and blame him for what happened."

My phone vibrated and rang at that point and I answered it quickly and cheerfully when I saw that Owen was the caller.

"Hi, hon. How's the patient?" I asked.

There was silence on the phone. I took it away from my ear and stared at it, wondering if the signal had suddenly disappeared.

"Hello, Owen, are you there?"

"I'm here. I'm at the hospital with Angelica," he said in a strange strangled voice.

"Hospital," I spluttered, suddenly alert and holding the phone with a firmer grip.

"She's been brought in for observation. Apparently she hasn't been eating and fainted in school. The school nurse took a urine sample and said that her blood sugar was terribly low. They're hooking her up to a drip as we speak and hoping to get a child psychologist to come and see her. What am I going to do, Frankie? They think that she's got an eating disorder which has been created by stress and I think that it's all my fault."

Shit. I was overcome by feelings of helplessness and guilt. I was helpless because I couldn't apply some antiseptic cream and a bandage and make it better and riddled with guilt because obviously I had been ignorant of the full facts. I had been making rash assumptions on something that I didn't understand and didn't want to understand.

"I'll be there now," I answered him. "Do you need anything brought over?"

"Just you," he said with his voice breaking.

The phone went dead and I looked at Ruby and my eyes filled with tears. "I am a first-class heartless bitch and I should be horsewhipped," I said.

"Yeah. You're a real selfish cow that thinks of nobody but herself," Ruby drawled back.

Some time later I found myself at the hospital and ready to spit nails. At last I had got to meet the delectable Brenda and I didn't think I had ever met a scarier woman in all my life. She was positively toxic. Hatred exuded from her every pore and she seemed entirely blind to the fact that her niece was ill. Angelica had apparently begged Owen to phone Brenda and reluctantly he had agreed, knowing that she would exploit the situation to her own advantage.

I was shocked at Angelica's appearance. She was pale and vulnerable-looking and didn't react even when she saw me. Although I had disliked her brash attitude it was preferable to the crushed little girl I saw in front of me and I longed to see a spark, any spark of life in her.

"Who the hell are you and what are you doing here?" Brenda asked me, when she took time out from shooting dagger looks at Owen.

"This is Frankie, Brenda," Owen said in what sounded like a soothing tone.

"Really? Well, I hope that you're pleased with yourself. Whilst you've been gallivanting about the country getting laid, you've been making your daughter sick. I hope the little fling was worth it."

With that she stomped out demanding to see a doctor, causing the nursing staff to look at each other in amazement. She hadn't even spoken to Angelica or so much as given her a cuddle, instead preferring to devote her energies into a game of one-upmanship where Owen was an unwilling participant.

My heart went out to Angelica. I thought of my mother and how nice it was to be cuddled and consoled in sickness or anytime for that matter. It was now obvious to me that this child desperately needed a female role model in her life (who wasn't a psycho) who would love her and not use her as a pawn.

"I'll leave you two alone," I said, looking at Owen and willing him to be strong. "I brought you a few things, love," I said gently, giving Angelica (who was unresponsive) a bag containing some magazines, grapes and a bottle of fizzy flavoured water.

I was sitting in the waiting room when I narrowly missed being severely brain-damaged by a bottle being flung at my ear.

"My niece doesn't need anything from you!" Brenda snapped at me, showering my face with saliva in the process (say it, don't spray it, love).

She was like a she-devil and I was glad when one of the nursing staff appeared and told her to keep the noise down at which point she breathed deeply, puffed out her chest and flounced off back in the direction of the ward.

If she got what she needed from your family perhaps others wouldn't feel the need to compensate, I thought, looking after her incredulously, then walking out, shaking my head.

I had given up smoking years before but at that moment could have smoked like a trooper as I stood outside the doors of the hospital and watched longingly as a woman took long draws on a cigarette.

"Frankie?"

I swung around. "Maura," I said, smiling when I recognised Owen's sister.

"What's happened now?" she asked. "I got a garbled message from Owen about Angelica being here and came as soon as I could."

"She looks terrible," I ventured. "They seem to think that she has some kind of eating disorder."

Maura rolled her eyes and breathed deeply. "Right."

"You don't sound convinced," I said.

"Believe me, it's just the latest in a long line of dramas that Angelica is at the centre of. The poor kid has had a terrible time but she doesn't make life easy for herself or for Owen either."

"He's really worried about her," I said. "Her Aunt Brenda is there too. She certainly is a force to be reckoned with."

"I should have known that she'd show up like the proverbial bad penny," Maura said in disgust. "All she ever does is cause trouble but Angelica hangs on her every word and tells everyone that she's her favourite aunt even though some of the rest of us do more than simply try to apportion blame and make excuses for the fact that Jane was too selfish to be a mother."

"Jane?" I asked.

"Angelica's mother."

"What happened?" I asked gently. "Owen never speaks about it and I don't like to pressurise him."

"Jane always struck me as someone who had itchy feet. Always wanted to travel and see new places and meet new people," Maura explained. "Owen never shared her enthusiasm though and she always resented that. She was absolutely horrified to discover that she was pregnant and was going to get rid of the child only Owen threatened to leave her. She must have loved him back then because she stopped talking about abortions and adoptions and continued with the pregnancy. Owen was so happy when Angelica was born but Jane used to accuse him of loving their baby more than he loved her. She must have eventually convinced herself of it as she walked out one day and never came back."

I shook my head in disbelief. "She sounds like a very self-centred person."

"Oh, she was that all right," Maura said. "She left Owen to pick up the pieces with a seven-year-old who was devastated that her mother had just abandoned her. Jane's family were desperate to cover up the fact that their daughter and sister was obviously at fault and started rumours about Owen being some sort of wife-beating philanderer."

"So I gathered," I said.

"My mother doesn't help the situation either,"

Maura said ruefully. "Angelica is no angel but Granny Byrne suffers from a very bad case of 'first and only grandchild syndrome'. Angelica could go and murder somebody and her granny would come up with an explanation as to why she was driven to it. Why do you think Owen and I persuaded her that she would be better off living in Dublin?"

"It sounds like you've your work cut out for you."

"We have but not half as much as you do," Maura said, raising her eyebrows at me. "Believe me, you better think long and hard about what you're taking on," she added before making her way through the main doors of the hospital.

Chapter 9

Days later, as I served the dinner of potatoes, carrots, sausages and gravy to my children I was delighted to see that they were sniffing the air enthusiastically and lifting their cutlery in anticipation of the meal. I imagined that Owen would give his eye teeth to have the pleasure of seeing Angelica eat something and truly enjoy it.

Angelica had been using food, or rather the lack of it to seek attention. She didn't have a full-blown clinical eating disorder but it was certainly a cry for help as most of these complaints are. She was using food to punish herself for what she apparently saw as something which was her fault. A meeting had been arranged with the hospital psychologist and Owen had asked me to accompany him and there we had both sat in disbelief at what we were hearing.

"Why would she punish herself?" Owen argued.

"Her mother leaving was certainly no fault of Angelica's nor mine for that matter. If truth be known I'd say that it's Jane who needs your help more than my daughter. Why would Angelica suddenly start acting like this? She's always been a terrific eater – well, she used to be before she started all this faddish behaviour, wanting to be vegetarian, only eating dry bread, not having breakfast."

The psychologist looked pointedly at Owen and Owen studied his hands. Without looking up he spoke again.

"I should have known, shouldn't I?" he said sadly. "All the signs were there but I chose to ignore them all."

I started to feel a hot flush creeping up my neck as the full implications of Owen's words sank in. He had been too busy with me to notice that in an attempt to get his attention his daughter had been making herself ill.

We didn't speak as we sat side by side in the car before Owen dropped me home.

"I'll see you later," he said in a forlorn voice. "I'd better go and spend some time with Angelica."

My thoughts were interrupted by a little hand tugging me by the sleeve and a little voice enquiring as to why I looked sad.

"Mum, why do you look like that?" Carly asked me. "Your bottom lip is like this."

She made a face and hung her lip.

"I don't look like that, do I?" I said laughing.

"You looked like you were dreaming but that it wasn't a nice dream. I cry when I have dreams like that and then you take me into your bed," she said, still looking very solemn and peering into my face.

I wrapped my arms around her and held her close and thanked God for her innocence.

"When is Owen coming over?" Ben asked with a broad smile. The football fanatics were bonding. Owen had promised to take Ben to a real Liverpool match so what started as a tentative friendship had now turned into a very serious case of hero worship.

"I don't know, son. He'll maybe come over at the weekend and spend some time with us then."

I said this as I knew his mother was coming up from Dublin so he wouldn't mind leaving Angelica. She was certainly in need of some reassurance and her daddy was the best one to give it to her although I was sure that Granny Byrne would also be laying it on thicker than usual, if that was possible.

There was a knock at my door, someone entered and three faces broke into beaming smiles as they registered that Owen was the surprise caller.

"Gosh, if I'd known that you were going to be so thrilled to see me I'd have rung first and then you could have formed a proper welcoming committee."

Carly pretended to blow into a bugle and play a fanfare and Ben started to bow in front of Owen. He stood and laughed and came and kissed me on the cheek and ruffled my hair.

"Hi, gorgeous," he said in a husky voice and immediately I felt myself tingle in response.

There hadn't been a lot of time for any intimacy lately so to say that I would probably have eaten him alive and without salt would be an understatement.

He saw the look I gave him and smiled his sexy smile which gnawed at my insides and made me go all aquiver.

"Kids, why don't you go upstairs and play?" I suggested to moans and groans of protest before they dragged their feet and left the room.

"I've a bit of news for you," Owen then said. "My mother is coming up on Thursday and taking Angelica to Dublin with her for the week so we'll have some time alone. Would Auntie Ruby be interested in a spot of baby-sitting this weekend? All weekend – because I think we've earned ourselves a few nights away in a hotel with a Jacuzzi spa, a four-poster bed and a door with a 'Do Not Disturb' sign on it. I have the perfect place in mind too. It's a hotel in Fermanagh complete with its own marina and cocktail bar."

I wondered had I started to drool yet or if there was a neon sign flashing on my forehead that said "Shag Me Stupid" as I looked back at him.

For the first time in a few weeks life was looking up and I couldn't wait to start living it.

Chapter 10

Carly was looking forlornly out the window and Ruby was whispering something to her as she waved to me and we pulled away.

"I feel as if I'm abandoning her forever," I said as I swivelled myself around in the passenger seat and kept waving.

"Jesus, talk about the long goodbye," Owen sighed and rolled his eyes. "Do you want to go back?"

I looked at him thinking he was joking but realised he wasn't by his hard-set jaw-line. A ripple of annoyance surged through me.

"Excuse me for being concerned about my daughter," I said through gritted teeth. "Or, sorry, do you have the monopoly on that?"

Ooops, maybe I shouldn't have said that. In fact I knew I shouldn't have. All thoughts of a shagfest had gone from my mind as we drove along in a stony silence.

Companionable silences I could handle. Friendly silences I could cope with but this business of having a bad atmosphere where two parties sit and have murderous thoughts about each other I hated. I took a quick sideways glance at Owen and decided that he must be really angry with me. He would probably drive to an isolated spot, boot me out and tell me to make my own way home. In fairness he could be forgiven for it if he did. Me and my big mouth. Not only did I stick my foot in it but I managed to squeeze in my leg and my arm as well.

I looked sideways again and caught Owen doing the same. We both looked away quickly and stared straight ahead. We sat like this for a few moments until I heard the sound of quiet laughter.

"Shut up, you," I said, trying to keep a straight face. I sucked in my cheeks and tried to think sad thoughts but I ended up gurgling with laughter too. "I'm sorry, Owen. That was a terrible thing to say."

"It's okay," he said. "I'm going to have to try and lengthen my fuse. It's been very short of late and I've started to become rather intolerant of others. Don't worry about Carly. She's in good hands and she knows that you'll be back."

We smiled at each other and I wriggled into the seat and sighed comfortably. Good! The shagfest was officially back on the agenda!

I was happy and serenely content as I combed through

my wet freshly washed hair and selected a body lotion to slather on my skin. I had just had the most glorious bath.

If Carlsberg did an advertisement for the best bath in the world that would have been it. The water temperature was perfect, the bubbles were fabulous, the champagne which I drank was deliciously sparkly, the music softly playing from the room was relaxing and best of all there were no interruptions in the form of small persons banging on the door demanding "Get out of the tub, Mum, because I need to pee!".

Yep. Life was good!

I had just phoned home and my children were tucked up in bed after having an exhausting day of madness which I think Auntie Ruby had enjoyed too. They went to the zoo, had lunch in McDonalds, got ice cream on the way home and then got DVDs to watch. Ruby was in the middle of watching *Match of the Day* when I rang. She laughed at me when I asked her if Carly had settled down.

"Settled down, Frankie? She doesn't want you to come back. I am the new mummy of the house now and it's largely due to the fact that when you take her to get ice cream you only allow her to pick one topping. Stingy tight-arse Mum!"

I laughed at her and told her to go back to drooling over Gary Lineker and shouting at the referee. "How's my boy then?"

"He's fine."

Ruby answered this question a tad too quickly and in too cheerful a tone and I immediately smelt a rat.

"Ruuubbbeee," I said in a warning tone which she knew not to treat lightly. "What's going on? Is he being bold?"

"Of course he's not being bold. Ben is the best boy in the world. Look, it's nothing for you to worry about. He's just been asking a lot of questions about his father."

"He's been *what*?" I shrieked.

"Oh bloody hell," Ruby whispered. "Me and my big mouth. Now don't let this spoil your time away. It's nothing I couldn't handle."

"Tell me," I commanded.

"It can wait until you come home, Frankie."

"*Now*." I had a very scary way of saying that word with just the right injection of menace in it. It worked a treat on the children and obviously had some effect on baby-sitting adults also as I could sense Ruby starting to waver.

"Why do you have to know so much?" she complained. "Feck off and go and have a good time and leave me in peace to watch the football highlights."

I started to breathe forcefully now and she knew that I would drive straight home and strangle her if she didn't spill the beans.

"He's been asking about the new baby and if

they'll ever see it and he wants to know if it's a boy if he will be Tony's son instead of him."

"Oh no," the words caught in my throat. "I didn't even think that he knew about the baby. I certainly didn't tell him and I'm very careful not to talk about such things in front of the children."

"We did bump into Nebby Peg earlier although I largely ignored her and tried to steer the children out of her way."

"What is it with that bloody woman?" I said. "Has she got spies camped in my garden reporting our every movement? Did she speak to them?"

"For about a second."

"Well, that would be just about long enough for that poisonous, cantankerous old witch to cause a row in heaven. I swear I am going to commit murder when I get home."

"Never mind about committing murder," Ruby chided. "Go and commit a few other deadly sins before you come home."

"I intend to," I said as I looked in my wardrobe and picked out a little black dress. (In my case it was a very little "little black dress". Those of us who do not have legs up to our armpits can't get away with anything which is of a normal length – Carly would probably be able to wear it next year.)

"Tell Ben I love him," I said as we signed off for the night.

"Do you think I haven't already done that?" Ruby asked.

I knew that she would have handled the situation very diplomatically and I also knew that a certain elderly lady (I use the term "lady" loosely) would be getting a visit from me when I got home. I hoped for her sake that I would come home refreshed, relaxed and utterly sated or she would be in for a very brutal verbal assault.

I dressed quickly, piled my hair up and clipped it, added some eyeliner, mascara and lippy, squirted some perfume, dotted cream blusher on my cheeks and did a twirl in front of the mirror. I liked what I saw. I seemed to have lost weight as my dress was looser than before. Being in love definitely suited me.

Oops! Did I just hear myself use the "L" word?

Owen was waiting in the bar for me when I came down and he whistled admiringly as I approached him.

"I'm sorry but what did you do with the rather less glamorous woman I came here with? She's about so tall, never shuts up and is like a little spitfire if you so much as look at her in the wrong way."

"What? The one with the greasy hair, unironed jeans and the bad attitude?" I teased.

"The very one," he said.

"I flushed her down the plughole a long time ago and replaced her with the new more sophisticated version."

Anyone for Seconds?

"I like the new version very much," Owen said as he ran his eyes over me appreciatively.

"Your seats are ready in the restaurant, sir, madam," the maître d' announced, leading the way with a smile and a flourish.

We sat in silence for a time examining our menus and watching as other diners took their seats, placed drinks orders and were served. I felt like Owen and I were the only lovers in the world and that the people milling around us had simply been put there for added effect.

"Would you like to see the wine list, sir?" a young waiter said.

Owen quickly scanned what was on offer and decided on a bottle of red Australian Merlot whilst looking at me for approval which I gave with a smile and a nod.

"Lovely," I said several minutes later when the waiter came back and poured a small amount in a glass to let us sample it.

"Are you ready to order?"

Our eyes locked and I was transported to another place where we would be alone with no one to intrude on our precious time together.

"Waiter, can we eat in our room?" I asked.

As the waiter gaped in surprise, I pulled Owen to his feet and led him to the lift which would take us back upstairs.

Chapter 11

I woke up to a shrill noise reverberating in our hotel room. Owen was muttering and I was completely disorientated and sat bolt upright in bed, expecting Carly to spring on top of me any second. When I realised that the noise was coming from the phone I shook my head and wiped the sleep from my eyes. It was only when I actually went to answer it that I looked at my watch and realised that it was only six thirty in the morning.

"Hello?" I said with a sense of urgency. I didn't think that the hotel staff would be ringing their guests on a whim unless there was a problem. A problem at home. Oh shite! The bloody house had probably burnt to the ground or the wee ones had got food poisoning from a wonky undercooked McDonald's burger. Oh Jesus, I was never leaving home again!

"This is your morning wake-up call, madam." An over-polite English voice said.

"What?" I shrieked. "I thought you were the police or the fire brigade or somebody!"

"Who?" the voice said in confusion.

"Who?" Owen said as his head suddenly jerked up.

"Did we order a wake-up call?" I asked.

"No, we feckin' did not," Owen said.

"I'm so sorry," the voice said in a hurry before making a hasty retreat off the phone.

"Sweet Jesus," I breathed, "I thought that something had happened at home."

"You don't say," Owen said, looking quizzically at me. "I must tell Auntie Ruby that you think that the fire brigade and the ambulance service as well as the police need to be on alert when she's baby-sitting."

"You can't blame me for being nervous. I'm not used to being away from the children. Besides, I have reason to be worried about Ben."

"I thought it was Carly who was pining yesterday."

"It was. But it appears that Ben has been thinking about his father and putting a voice to his fears by bombarding Ruby with questions about the new baby."

"You never said."

"I didn't get the chance. I was speaking to Ruby before I came down to dinner last night and then I came down –"

"And then we came back up." Owen said this with a smirk playing about his lips and I blushed at the memory.

I was still tingling from head to toe. After a brief but very satisfying encounter when we reached our room the night before, we did actually order dinner. Then, after I had consumed my Teriyaki steak with roasted vegetables and drunk two glasses of wine, I had a tiny peek at the dessert menu but then looked across at Owen, saw him watching me and made a quick decision about what I wanted for afters. Being in a relationship was definitely good for your figure as faced with a choice between Death by Chocolate and Owen I knew what would give me most satisfaction.

"What are you looking like that for?" Owen now asked me.

"Nothing. I'm just reminiscing about good times," I said.

"Well, speaking of good times and now that we're awake anyway what are we going to do until it's time for breakfast?"

I looked at Owen, took the phone off the hook and prepared to further improve my diet by skipping breakfast altogether.

As we had a marina in the grounds of the hotel Owen was keen to make good use of it so he eventually talked me into leaving dry land and hiring a boat for the day.

I had to admit that the weather was ideal for it. The

water was calm, the scenery lovely and the thought that we had another night left on our own was just pure bliss. I phoned Ruby before we left our room and had to sit on Owen to make him stop making noisy comments in the background about police stakeouts and having the Doctor on Call on high alert.

"You sound like you're having a good time," Ruby said when there was a lull in the conversation and she'd convinced me that my children were both in a stable frame of mind and in good health.

"I am having a good time," I said, looking at Owen and treating him to a broad grin.

"Is he there with you?" Ruby demanded. "I can hear it in your tone of voice. You're all loved up."

"Yep. Loved up and loved out," I declared. "I'm going to need a holiday to recover from my activities this weekend."

"Yes, thank you," Ruby said. "You can tell me about your sexual gymnastics some other time, preferably when I'm not head and ears into cooking scrambled eggs and sausages for a pair of starving children."

I smiled as I thought of them and my stomach gave a tiny lurch. I missed them so much and although I was having the time of my life I couldn't wait to get back home to the noise, the chaos and the love. I thought of Angelica. What on earth was her mother thinking of? I wondered if she ever gave her daughter a second thought.

"There you go again," Owen said as he looked searchingly at me. "You've got that brooding look on your face. What are you thinking about?"

"Have you heard from your mother or Angelica since we've been away?" I asked.

"Not a dicky-bird and that's the way I like it," he answered. "It'll do Angelica good to get away for the week and I know that I'm a lot less stressed knowing that she's being well looked after. She talks to my mother a lot. More than she would to me. After my mother visits I find that she often tells me things that Angelica has shared with her. Thoughts and feelings that she wouldn't want me to know about. I never say anything about what I know. It's just nice to have that little bit more insight into how she's feeling."

I started to feel apprehensive again. What if Angelica told her grandmother that she didn't like me and that I was the cause of all her eating problems? Owen loved his daughter and would do anything to help her so if such a thing were to be revealed he would have to do something about it, wouldn't he?

Owen leaned across and took my hand in his and looked deep into my eyes. "She does like you. Stop thinking otherwise. We've only been together five months but already I can read you like a book. Have some confidence in yourself. Kids are great at spotting adult weaknesses and using them and Angelica knows that you're scared of her."

"That's a slight exaggeration," I argued. "I think scared is too strong a word." (Yeah, right, you big pussy!)

After we spent another hour rowing the boat and admiring the peace and tranquillity we decided to go and get something to eat in a little bistro bar that we'd found. I wasn't going to surrender any food this time as I was absolutely starving and dying for a good gawp at the bar menu. I also thought that half a pint of ice-cold cider would go down a treat. I kept forgetting that I had left my "responsible head" at home and that if I wanted to have a little drink then I wouldn't be labelled as a shameless mother as my children were in fact in someone else's dutiful hands.

Owen excused himself and left me to look at the menu which was making my mouth water. I went to powder my nose before Owen got back. As I entered the corridor in the bistro where the rest rooms were situated I could hear a raised voice. One that sounded very familiar.

I followed it and discovered that Owen was standing outside the fire-exit door having a heated argument on his mobile phone.

"Angelica, don't you dare even think such a thing. You know I love you more than life itself. Frankie doesn't want to replace your mother and me going away with her is not me putting her needs before yours and I do not love her children more than I love you. Stop being so silly. I thought you'd enjoy spending time in Dublin with your grandmother while I had a break as well. The past few weeks have been tough on everyone."

I watched him pace about in agitation as he listened to what was being said by the other speaker.

"Stop interfering, Mother. I was so happy that Angelica was going to be with you this week. I thought that it would be good for her to be away from all the stresses and strains of home for a while but instead I find that all it has been is one big long bitching session about my love life. It hasn't been a bed of roses for me either in recent years and I'm glad that I've found Frankie. She makes me happy and I love being with her. It wouldn't matter who I'm with, you'd still have reservations about them. God forbid that I devote some of my energies to something other than the mess that Jane left behind her."

I felt so sorry for him as I watched the emotions become evident on his face. He ended the conversation and I dived into the bathroom, my appetite suddenly wilting. I wondered if he'd tell me about the verbal exchange and if it would make any difference to his formerly relaxed and happy mood.

I sat at the table and absentmindedly scanned my eyes over the menu that had filled me with such enthusiasm earlier. My stomach was now knotted and I wasn't sure if I'd be able to eat a thing. Owen still hadn't appeared and I wondered who he was arguing with now in the name of defending my honour.

I watched the exit door and lowered my head quickly as I saw him appear, noting that he was smiling broadly as if nothing had happened.

"Well, my love? Do you see anything you like?" he asked me.

I knew I was probably being paranoid and if Ruby was here she would most certainly slap me around the head and tell me to wise up but I was annoyed that he felt he couldn't tell me about the argument. As I was inadvertently involved surely I had a right to know?

"Frankie, Frankie, are you still with us?" Owen was waving at me and trying to get my attention as the waiter had joined us and was looking at me expectantly.

"Oh, erm, I'll just have a side salad," I said quickly. "And some water."

"Are you feeling all right, Frankie? Have you looked at the menu? This is a top-class restaurant and you've just ordered salad."

"Well, maybe that's all I can stomach right now." I stood up, nearly knocking down the startled waiter who was still hovering at our table waiting for Owen's order. "Perhaps if I wasn't being lied to I'd be better equipped to enjoy a decent meal but at the moment I don't feel like that."

Owen looked like I'd just slapped him.

"What are you talking about?"

At this point the waiter sidled away.

"I'm talking about the fact that you've just had a

row with your daughter and your mother about me but instead of being honest and telling me what's happened you sit there and tell me off for not ordering something more fancy from the feckin' menu! Helllooo!"

My heart was pumping ninety-nine to the dozen as I threw my napkin onto my seat, lifted my coat and stalked towards the door. I was so confused and annoyed. I had walked for about ten minutes when my mobile shrilled. No doubt it was him wanting to talk. Upon inspection, however, I saw that it wasn't him but my mother. I was definitely not in the mood for a discussion with her but felt that I had to answer the call in case it was about the children.

"Hello, darling. Are you having a good time?"

Translated, this meant that she wanted to know if I'd mucked it up yet or not. My mother was a natural at picking up the pieces after disastrous events. Well, she'd had plenty of experience with me.

"It's fine," I answered in a tight voice. I didn't trust myself to speak in case I burst into tears. Why did mothers always have the effect of reducing you to a child who just wants cuddles again, especially when they use that particularly endearing tone of voice?

"It's not fine, is it?" she said gently. "I called because I could sense that something was wrong with you."

My mother's sixth sense was legendary in the McCormick household. Ella and I could never hide anything from her and even the best Oscar-worthy performances of putting a brave face on events would never fool her.

"It really is all right, Mother," I said tetchily. "There's nothing wrong with me or with us. Owen's flamin' family seem to have it in for me though."

"Why? What's wrong with you?" Mammy asked in a defensive tone of voice.

This is another of my mother's traits which I must share with you. She is extremely protective of her family. Her daughters in particular. She is allowed to give out yards about us herself but dare anyone else so much as look at either of us in the wrong way and she would be on the warpath. Tony learnt the hard way not to mess with her. He attempted to tell her one day that the breakdown of our marriage was all my fault and that if I had been a better wife then he would not have felt the need to go looking for "it" elsewhere. Not to put too fine a point on it, let's just say that he sorely regretted his words, especially as Mammy happened to have a particularly heavy load in her handbag that day. Apparently our neighbours saw him being unceremoniously booted out of our house before being chased by his handbag-wielding ex-mother-in-law who was screaming at him at the top of her voice. She said that if he had been more of a man in the first place perhaps I would be more upset at losing him but, as it stood, it was his loss and the children and I would be a lot better off.

"Take no nonsense from Owen's lot, Frankie. You're worth one hundred of that silly ex-wife of his. Any woman who can willingly leave her child in that manner needs her head well examined and I'd soon tell them that too."

"That's what I'd be afraid of, Mother," I responded.

Mammy had been dying to meet Owen and had been dropping hints the size of atomic bombs wondering when the meeting would take place. She had also been making huffy comments about her and Daddy not being good enough, especially in light of the fact that Owen's mother had met me.

"I would like to meet this boy, Frankie. I'm not going to let my mouth run away with me but I'd like to see him in the flesh instead of viewing him as your virtual boyfriend because I've never laid eyes on him."

"I'll see what I can do," I said unenthusiastically. I was agreeing to it because realistically I was wondering if I would still have a boyfriend in the near future. If I didn't manage to scare him away myself with my own mad antics his family would undoubtedly influence him to leave me.

"Another reason why I was ringing was to tell you that Ella and Hamish are coming home for a couple of weeks."

"Oh!" I momentarily forgot my own troubles as I digested this news. I was surprised as Ella usually liked us to visit her which I always did obligingly as I loved the shopping in Edinburgh.

"Is there anything wrong?" I ventured. "Why is she coming for so long?"

"Well, between you and me, Frankie, I have a feeling that there may be problems."

I knew I was gifted. "What sort of problems?"

"I don't know, love. I'm not psychic."

"Makes a change," I muttered.

"You must be starting to feel better. You're answering me back and giving cheek again. Hello, darlings!" I heard her shout suddenly and in the background I could hear Ben and Carly. "Ruby, how are you? How's the love life these days?"

I laughed as I told Mammy I'd talk to her later and left her to interrogate Ruby who would no doubt kill me later for not jumping to her rescue.

A hand on the back of my arm stopped me in my tracks and I whirled round and looked at Owen who was staring sadly at me.

"I'm sorry, Frankie. I wasn't deliberately hiding anything from you. I just didn't want you to get upset. We've been having such a nice time here away from the stresses and strains of home that I didn't want to remind you."

"We're in this together, Owen. If someone upsets you or drags you into an argument (especially when I'm the feckin' topic of discussion) I'd like to know.

I'm so annoyed that your mother and daughter both think so little of me. They hardly know me."

Owen's expression suddenly darkened. "How long were you standing there? Do you always listen in on other people's private conversations or do you just reserve that particular habit for me?"

His face became angry and I now realised what my actions must look like from his point of view.

"I wasn't deliberately eavesdropping, Owen. I was going to the toilet and couldn't help overhearing you. If you will roar and shout like a banshee then I think that you have to expect people to hear. I heard my name being mentioned and have to say that I was very hurt by what was obviously being said although I was touched by how you defended me. I don't think that your mother or your daughter are ever going to warm to me or give me a chance. I might have got upset if you had told me but it's better than you hiding things from me and trying to cover things up. All the best relationships are built on trust and honesty and I had enough lies in my marriage to last me a lifetime."

I stopped my tirade, paused for breath and looked at him.

He pulled me close to him. "I've asked the restaurant to hold our table. I'll bet that you're hungry now after all the excitement."

I wasn't sure I had an appetite (dwelling on your

ex-husband and how his actions have left you with a supreme lack of trust tends to do that to a girl).

Owen enveloped me in a hug and after several hand-dangling moments where I was an unwilling participant I slowly let my arms encircle his waist. He smelt divine and I felt safe and secure while he held me.

My stomach made a loud noise and Owen looked at me with a slow smile playing about his lips. "So how about it then? Dinner for two minus the interruptions. Look, I'll even switch my phone off." He pressed the button and the screen started to fade.

I tried to bite my tongue and appear coy but my grumbling tummy gave the game away again.

"Chicken Chasseur with garlic fries, followed by Mint Chocolate Cheesecake." He raised his eyebrows suggestively at me. "Or could I tempt you to something else for afters, madam?"

"Well, considering that you've a lot of grovelling to do your menu better be as competitive as the one in the restaurant because I'm starving." (I was also incredibly turned on but I wasn't going to tell him that.)

Chapter 12

"Oh my God!"

No, this was not my response in the heat of a passionate encounter with Superman. This was my response when I saw the state of my house when I arrived home.

"Excuse me but have Libyan militants taken over my home and are they using my kitchen for bomb-disposal purposes?"

Ruby was swearing under her breath, Ben was backing out through the door and Carly was looking suspicious.

"I thought you said that it would be okay to mess up the house, Auntie Ruby?" she said. "You said that it hadn't been dirty in years and that it would do it good not to be scrubbed for a change."

At this point I must confess to being a tiny bit of a

clean-and-tidy freak. Ruby reckons I've got obsessive-compulsive disorder but I know that she simply doesn't understand because she's a mucky cow herself.

"Ahem. Yes, thank you, Carly," Ruby said, frowning. Her eyebrows were so far down her forehead that she was doing the best Les Dawson impression that I'd seen in years.

"We have to tidy this place up," I said in a stern voice. "Not just because you lot have lived like dirty pigs over the past few days but also because we're going to have guests."

Ruby stopped sulking for long enough to let her nosy streak present itself.

"Who?" she asked in surprise.

"Auntie Ella and Uncle Hammy are coming to stay," I answered bracing myself for the noise that this statement was sure to create.

Immediately the children started to dance around.

"*Yeeeeeeeeeeeeaaaahhhhhhh!*" they squealed as they jumped up and down in excitement.

"When are they coming?" Ben said, grinning broadly. He adored Hammy who was an avid Inverness Caledonian Thistle fan who would no doubt bring him to a pub with a big screen to watch the latest Scottish league matches.

"Auntie Ella will see how much I've grown and she'll bring me something nice because she says I'm her special girl," Carly said excitedly.

"Oh well, that's me blown out then," Ruby stated in a wounded tone. "Auntie Ella's coming so poor old Auntie Ruby gets forgotten about."

"You can share us with Auntie Ella, Auntie Ruby. There's enough of us for everybody," Carly said, holding Ruby's hand and looking solemnly at her.

Ruby and I couldn't help laughing at her serious expression as I began to pile dishes beside the sink and she started to unload the full-to-the-brim dishwasher.

"Well?" Ruby asked with an eyebrow raised.

"Well what?" I retorted, still removing plates and setting them on the kitchen counter. "Ruby, were you attempting to use every dish, cup, plate and teaspoon in the house?" I demanded, hand on hip. "Sweet Jesus I've never seen this thing so full."

"Well, that's because I kind of forgot to put it on until this morning," she answered, deliberately avoiding my gaze.

"So there has been no washing-up done in nearly three days," I squeaked. "I don't even want to know what state the bathroom or the bedrooms are in."

"We'll get right on it," Ruby said, running over and grabbing Ben and Carly. "They'll all be spotless by the time you come to inspect them."

"Are we allowed to tell Mum about the bath having too much water in it and the carpet getting wet?" Carly asked before Ruby clamped her hand firmly over her mouth and steered her towards the stairs.

"Hello, gorgeous."

"Hello, yourself," I said as I let Owen in. He looked freshly showered and shaved and was carrying a bottle of red wine and a DVD under his arm.

"Chill-out night," he said, waving his purchases at me.

"And, boy, do I need to chill out!" I said. "You should have seen the hovel that was trying to pass itself for my house earlier. Ruby does not know the first thing about housework or keeping things tidy. I forgot that she was so messy."

"Did she like her 'thank-you' hotel spa voucher?"

"Well, actually, I had to use it as an olive branch when she accused me of having a brush-shaft stuck up my ass and threatened to never baby-sit for me again. Do you think I'm uptight? It's not a crime to like having a tidy house, is it?"

A smile played about Owen's lips and I swatted him with the back of my hand.

"You wouldn't change anything though, would you?" he asked suddenly.

"Would I still have gone away with you, you mean? Of course I would. It was worth every dirty dish and plate and even worth getting my new bathroom carpet soaking wet for."

Owen looked questioningly at me. "Never mind. It's a long story. The house needed a good clean anyway. Ella's even worse than I am when it comes to everything having a place. I think having children has mellowed me a bit."

"Does she not have any? Children, I mean."

"She will one day," I said "but she's in no rush. She's a midwife and surrounded by babies all day so she gets her mammy-fix from her work."

"Speaking of work," Owen groaned, "we have a busy week coming up."

"I know."

I thought of the mayhem that would surround us in the coming few days. I had never been present at a college graduation but Owen assured me that the very words send staff and students alike into a frenzy. I was glad that Ella would be here by the time it happened. I was looking forward to seeing her but also a little apprehensive about her visit. I hoped that there was no negative reason for her wanting to come home for so long and at such short notice.

"I hope Angelica likes her present," I said, turning my attention to the other pressing matter that was in my head. We had bought all the children gifts while we were away but I had spent a long time choosing something that I thought Angelica would like. After going into several shops I had chosen a beautiful necklace with a jade stone in it. I thought that it looked very pretty and hoped that Angelica would understand the sentiments behind it. I didn't want to fight with her. I wanted to be her friend or I at least wanted her to know that I wasn't her enemy.

"I'm sure she will," Owen said. "I'm going to make sure and tell her that you chose it specially and that it was quite expensive."

"It doesn't matter about the expense," I said firmly. "I'd rather that she concentrated on the fact that it's a gesture. I'd like to get to know her better."

We were obviously more tired than we thought because I woke up at eleven thirty to find Owen asleep beside me and the TV showing a snow storm on the screen.

"Owen, Owen, wake up!" I shook him a few times but to no avail as he seemed to be dead to the world.

He looked so comfortable curled on the sofa that I decided to leave him there. After removing his shoes and throwing a blanket over him I made my way upstairs to bed. I wished that I hadn't fallen asleep. I hadn't rung Ella and I was dying to know all about her trip and the reasons behind it. I would ring her tomorrow, I decided, as I dressed for bed and checked on the children. Ben was lying across the bed breathing heavily and Carly was clutching her Angelina Ballerina ragdoll and sleeping peacefully.

It was good to be home. I snuggled into the

familiar lavender-scented pillows and fell blissfully to sleep.

Ben and Carly were delighted to find that they had a guest the following morning when they came down for breakfast before going to school.

"I didn't know that you were having a sleepover with Owen, Mum," Carly said as she smiled at Owen over her bowl of Coco Pops.

"It wasn't exactly a sleepover, darling," I said. "Owen fell asleep on the sofa and I made him comfortable and let him stay there because he was very tired."

"It doesn't look as if anyone slept there at all," Carly said, looking over at the neatly plumped sofa.

I inwardly chided myself. Perhaps my neatness does have some disadvantages. I should have left the blanket where it was. I didn't want the children getting the idea that Mum had overnight male guests to stay, even if it was Owen.

Owen seemed to sense my discomfiture as he immediately started to talk about how lucky we were having such a comfortable sofa to sleep on. Carly smiled and seemed convinced but Ben was rather quiet. I had yet to talk to him about his confused emotions concerning the impending birth of his half-brother or sister.

"I'll see you at work," Owen said as he drained his coffee cup and jingled his keys. "I feel like a dirty stop-out, wearing the same clothes this morning as I did last night."

I laughed and accompanied him to the door, kissed him on the cheek and told him I'd see him later.

When I got back to the kitchen the children were standing there looking at me.

"Why are you two standing there like that?" I asked.

"We have something to ask you, Mum," said Ben. "Is Owen going to be our new dad because our real dad doesn't want us anymore?"

I looked at the sincerity on my son's face and felt terrible. I should have sat him down and tried to explain the situation to him.

How was I going to approach this without confusing or upsetting him further?

I looked at my watch and knew that now was not the time for an in-depth discussion on fathers (absent or in the running to fill the position).

"I promise that we'll sit down this evening and talk about this. You can ask me anything you want and I'll try my best to answer it."

Their faces told me that they thought it was a long time to wait and an immediate answer now would have been better but it would have to suffice as we all had a long day ahead. A day that I hoped would be long enough to try and figure out what I was going to say.

Chapter 13

"Hello. I've been trying to get hold of you all day. What's wrong? Why are you coming home?"

"'Hello, Ella. How are you, sis? I'm looking forward to your visit.' That would have been preferable to the third degree, Frankie! Has it been that long since I've spoken to you that you've morphed into Mammy in the meantime?"

"Oh shut up! I'm just concerned, that's all," I said, kicking myself for being so obvious.

"Yeah. Mammy says that too and has been saying it consistently since I told her that I was coming. What's wrong with everyone? Why does there have to be a reason? Can I not just come home and see my family without there being a national feckin' enquiry?"

"Well, for a start, Sisssss, you never come home. You ring me and expect me to drop everything to fly over to Scotland when Take That are in concert or when Debenhams are having a sale. You always say that you can't be arsed getting on a plane and that the boat makes you sick and you're afraid to leave in case they need you to work at short notice."

The more I thought about it the more worried I was getting. This was totally out of character. (Oh my God, I *was* turning into my mother. Shit!)

"Look, Frankie, I appreciate your worries but honestly you have no cause for alarm. Maybe I'm coming home because I haven't been in a while; did you ever think of that?"

"Okay." I resigned myself to the fact that she wasn't going to tell me anything. I knew how irritating my mother could be when she started one of her tirades so I wasn't going to make Ella endure one.

On second thoughts, however, I was also an expert in sidestepping questions and trying to convince myself as well as everyone else that things were all right when in actual fact they were far from it, so therefore I recognised the signs when someone else was trying to do likewise.

I loved my sister dearly. There was only a year between us. Mammy always said that she wanted her family close together but I think things moved a little too quickly even for her in that department. What resulted in a handful for our parents, however, was a blessing for us. It took us a while to realise that sisters were supposed to love and look out for each other instead of threatening each other with violence if a Barbie doll happened not to be in its usual spot but once we had that figured out we were inseparable. We only ever had one major fall-out and that was when I was sixteen and Ella was seventeen and Ryan Bradley finished with her after he met me when she brought him home to meet Mammy and Daddy. We didn't speak for a week and then Mammy threatened to bang our heads together and not let us out the door for a month so we had no choice but to resolve our differences.

I would never forget the day that Ella announced she had met Hammy. She was so happy and we could all see why once we had seen him for ourselves. Hammy is a sweet gentle giant with a soft Scottish accent who worships the ground that my sister treads upon. It had been an awful shock when she told me that she was going to live in Scotland permanently but I couldn't blame her even though I missed her desperately. In the dark days when Tony and I first split up I would have done anything for a tight squeeze and a sisterly cuddle instead of endless tearful lonely chats on the phone.

"Frankie, are you listening to me?"

"Yes, I am."

"So you'll pick us up at the airport then?"

"Which one and what time?"

"I knew you weren't bloody listening to me," Ella said peevishly. "I'm only after telling you that we'll be arriving at the George Best Airport in Belfast at nine o'clock on Thursday morning."

"Yes, that'll be all right. Although I'll not be able to hang about because I have Graduation Day in the college the following day."

"I was just coming to that," Ella said with a hint of devilishness in her tone. "Are dirty weekends with the lecturers in everyone's job description?"

"No, they aren't, but I think they should be made compulsory. I can't wait for you to meet him, Ella. He is totally divine and makes me really happy. It's just a pity about the baggage he's carrying. I'll tell you all about it when I see you."

"I'll look forward to it," she said.

At that point our conversation was interrupted by the ringing of my doorbell.

"Better go. I'll see you on Thursday," I said briskly as I put the phone down and went to answer the door.

It was quite late and I couldn't think of anyone who could be calling.

As soon as I'd opened the door I regretted doing so. For standing looking at me was Nebby Peg, looking nebbier than ever.

"Where are my great-grandchildren?" Peggy barked without so much as a greeting.

I thought this was a bit of a liberty considering that

she was standing on my doorstep with her foot jammed in my door.

"Do you realise the time, Peggy? The children are in bed and I'm not disturbing them. If you'd like to arrange a time to call round and see them at a reasonable hour tomorrow you're welcome to come back then." (I must take the children for an overnight visit somewhere, I thought frantically.)

"I want to see them now. I have a duty to my grandson to make sure that his children are being looked after properly and from what I've been hearing you've been leaving them with that trollop with the wild hair whilst you run the roads with that fancy man of yours. I hear that he was here all last night. Turning into a right little tramp, aren't you?"

I was shocked. I was flabbergasted. My gob had never been so smacked and I was fit to be tied and boiling mad.

"I beg your pardon? Just who the hell do you think you're talking to and what right have you got coming to my doorstep calling me names and preaching to me about responsibilities? Your grandson hasn't given his responsibilities one moment's thought since he ran away to America with his mistress-cum-slapper-cum-wife. How dare you speak to me like that and how dare you tell my son that his father is having a baby with someone else?"

"Somebody had to tell him. You weren't going to.

All you're interested in doing is putting yourself about. Although I suppose you're to be pitied more than blamed. It must be hard to accept that your husband doesn't want you anymore. He always was far too good for you."

I started to laugh. Long loud hysterical laughter because if I didn't laugh I'd end up decking the mad old witch and get done for assaulting a pensioner.

"Is there not a home for the old and insane that you should be in?" I spat. "You can stand there and rant and rave all you like but you'll be doing it to a closed door and if you have not disappeared and gone back to your coven within the next two minutes I'll have the police remove you. Go away, you old bat, and don't ever come near me or my children again!"

"I think that that's a choice for the children to make, don't you?"

I saw that she was looking behind me, smiling, and I turned and registered with some dismay that Ben was standing at the bottom of the stairs.

"I came down to see what the noise was," he said sleepily.

"Oh, that was your mother shouting at me and telling me never to see you again. She's good at scaring people away. She did the same with your father and that's why you never see him anymore."

Ben looked stricken and his eyes darted between

his great-grandmother's and mine before I saw his face crumple and he ran back upstairs.

"Shit!" I said as I slammed the door. With any luck I had closed it on the wrinkly old bitch's foot. I took the stairs two at a time in the hope that I'd be able to catch Ben and explain the situation before he jumped to his own conclusions but, alas, life (my life in particular) was never that easy.

"Ben. Ben, please let me in!"

My son had locked himself in the bathroom and was thinking God knows what about me. My daughter had woken up to hear her brother sobbing and her mother begging to be given the chance to explain things. It was nearly eleven o'clock, they had school in the morning and to make matters worse I felt like an emotional wreck. My period was due any day and PMT had set in with a vengeance. Although with Peggy Colton around who needed bloody PMT?

I eventually coaxed Ben out from behind the locked door. His eyes were red-rimmed. He was shaking with the cold and he looked like a lost sheep badly in need of guidance.

I took him by the hand and led him downstairs.

"I'm so sorry about that, darling," I said. "I'm sorry that you had to hear that. Do you normally hear Mum speak like that?"

"I've never heard you talk like that to anyone before," Ben said, wiping his eyes and nibbling on the chocolate biscuit that I'd got him from the kitchen cupboard. (Bribery is a great thing in the absence of all other methods of persuasion.)

"Can we talk about this tomorrow when I've time to explain it to you properly?" I asked beseechingly, knowing full well what the answer was likely to be.

"No, Mum, you said that before," he said right away. "Tell me now."

At this point Carly appeared and I led the two of them into the living room and sat them down on the sofa. I sighed, closed the blinds, and then went back to the kitchen to put the kettle on and fished in the cupboard for the bottle of brandy that I knew was there. If I was going to do this I was going to do it with the accompaniment of a strong cup of tea.

Once I'd made my tea and added a generous dash of alcohol to it I rejoined the children who were looking at me expectantly. I sat down between them.

"Okay, what do you want to know?"

"I want to know if it's true," Ben asked. "Did you really tell Daddy to go away and never to come back?"

Carly looked shocked and immediately grabbed my arm and pulled me close. "Don't talk silly, Ben. Daddy left because he wanted to. Granny Celia and Mammy both told us that."

Perhaps my mother's meddling had its place sometimes.

"Daddy left because he didn't love *me* anymore," I

started to explain. "That doesn't mean that he doesn't love *you*. I'm sure if he was here now and saw how big and well-behaved and clever you are that he'd be really proud to say that he is and always will be your daddy."

"But if we're so good why doesn't he want us now?" Carly asked, her small eyes wide.

"He chose to go and live in America which is where Stella is from. America is far away and your daddy wants to be there because he loves Stella and that's where she wants to be."

"Did he want a baby so that he could have a well-behaved good child in America?" Ben asked.

I knew that he was really asking me if he was being replaced and it was a question that I didn't know the answer to. Damn Tony. Damn Peggy and her poisonous tongue and damn the whole situation.

"I'm sure that he would like a well-behaved and good baby but I'm equally as sure that he's glad that he's got you two over here. I'm sure that he's boasting about you to everyone he knows and that he'll come back and see you when he's ready."

"When will that be?" they both asked at once.

(Now where was my crystal ball?)

I put my arms around them and pulled them both close to me. "I don't know, darlings. Your daddy is the only one who knows the answer to that."

I turned and faced Ben and enclosed his smaller hands in mine.

"Please believe me when I tell you that I didn't ever want your daddy to leave and not come back. I never wanted that for you because I love you and I know that it's important that you see your dad. Sometimes people get married too young and make mistakes. They think they love each other when really they should never have been married in the first place because they're not right together. That's what happened to us. We made a bad decision but something good did come of it."

"What?"

"You two. My precious boy and girl were meant to be brought into the world so I'll always be grateful to your daddy for that."

"What has Daddy got to do with us being born?" Carly demanded. "I thought that the stork brought us here and left us down the chimney."

"So he did," I answered quickly. "Eh . . . erm . . . it's just that when we were putting in the order your daddy really wanted you both as well and without his signature we wouldn't have got you so fast," I faltered lamely.

Carly looked at me and then nodded her head as if she understood. Ben was disgusted. I knew that he was in possession of enough information about the birds and the bees to know that storks and order forms were not involved.

"Look, it's very late and we're all tired," I said,

jumping up from my seat. "Let's go to bed and get some sleep and then we'll talk some more in the morning."

"What about Granny Peggy?" Ben said in a worried voice.

"What about her?" I asked, trying my best to keep the contempt out of my tone.

"Have you scared her off?"

"I don't mind," Carly said. "She always smells funny."

I stifled a grin.

"I don't mind either," Ben said. "I don't like it when she says horrible things about you."

"She shouldn't have spoken to me the way she did tonight and she shouldn't tell lies either," I said. "I hope that you both know how much I love you and that I would do anything for you."

"We know," the children announced in unison before we had a big family hug and kissed each other goodnight.

"Night night, Mum," Carly whispered as I tucked her in.

Ben had already disappeared and I knew that he would probably sleep fitfully and restlessly just as I was predicting I would.

Chapter 14

I decided that I needed to let off some steam and by some (misguided) notion thought it would be a good idea to call in and see my parents for lunch the following day.

"She did what?" my mother was rooted to the ground and two pink spots were appearing on her cheeks. She was apoplectic with rage and I pitied Nebby Peg if she ever got hold of her (not).

"Old people are very cantankerous and annoying, aren't they?" Daddy interjected.

"If that's the best you can do under the circumstances, George, then I think that you better take that dog for a walk!" Mammy said, rounding on him. "How is Ben now, Frankie? How was he this morning when you left him off?"

"He was very quiet but then I did give them both

lots of food for thought last night. I think it's the first time that we've ever had a proper chat about the whole situation. Any time it's been mentioned before I've simply been answering questions that have arisen and then they've forgotten about it."

"We'll have to do something to take their minds off it. Next thing you know they'll be wanting to go to America to see him." (That's my mother – ever the optimist!)

Daddy raised his eyes to the Lord and shook his head. He clicked his tongue and the dog came running with the lead in his mouth. I think Banjo automatically got his lead when he saw me coming. Even a mere canine animal knew to disappear when my mother and I were in the same room.

"I'll not have to try too hard to distract them – Ella and Hammy will be a great novelty when they land on Thursday. I'll have a word in Hammy's ear and see if he can arrange to take Ben to watch a game."

"Good idea," Mammy said approvingly. "Have you managed to get to the bottom of why she's coming home yet?"

"She says she's just coming home to see us," I said but I knew by the incredulous looks that my mother was throwing around that she didn't believe a word of it.

"And what about Owen or the Invisible Man as I've started to call him?" said Mammy. "I'm sure that you'd like your sister to meet him. It's as well that you have somebody within the family that you're not ashamed to introduce to him." Mammy sniffed and adopted her hurt expression.

If Daddy hadn't already left I'd have offered to walk the dog myself.

I was saved by the bell from a further ticking off when the grandfather clock in the hall chimed two o'clock.

"Shit! I need to get back to work."

"Language!" my mother scolded as she continued to fuss around the kitchen.

I went back to work and found Owen in a state of pre-Graduation stress and running around like a headless chicken trying to get microphones set up, plasma boards in place and seating arrangements organised. Things never ran smoothly when you wanted them to. There was a problem with the caterers and the people erecting the marquee were one man down so the deadline that we had given ourselves was not going to be met. I sighed as Owen breathlessly imparted these facts in a hurried and tension-filled voice. As a precise and meticulous person I didn't usually like encountering problems but today I was glad of the distraction.

Owen noted my expression and gave me a quick and comforting squeeze. I had told him about the dramatic events of last night when I came in that morning and he was empathetic but not shocked. It took a lot to shock Owen. Ruby on the other hand was not empathetic or sympathetic. She was psychopathic. I didn't know what she was more offended about: the fact that her childcare capabilities had been called into question, being called a trollop or having her hair described as being wild.

"Cow! What an absolute tramp from hell! I thought that grannies were supposed to be sweet and cuddly and nice and give you money at Christmas and wear their hair in a bun?"

Ruby was so worked up that she didn't notice that Mandy had come into the office, looking curious and excited all at once. I could almost see her ears twitching.

"Frankie," Ruby said mournfully, "is my hair really that bad?"

I cleared my throat and stared straight ahead. Mandy looked pleased that she seemed to have caught Ruby having a self-confidence crisis.

Ruby followed my line of vision and spotted the intruder in our midst.

"What the feck are you doing standing there with a demented grin painted on your face? Feck off and answer the phone or type something, will you?"

Mandy looked like the proverbial deer that had just been caught in the headlights and seemed to be looking around for an escape route.

Ruby did not handle derogatory comments about her bouffant well and was determined to take her anger out on something. She started to bang things around her desk and slammed the filing-cabinet door so hard that the files within began to fall and topple like dominoes.

Mandy gave a small squeak and practically raced out the door. I'd never seen her move so fast.

"I swear to God if I ever see that decrepit old spinster Peggy I will smack her one. Her false teeth will be smiling out of her arse by the time I'm finished with her."

For the first time in twelve hours I burst out laughing. Ruby was hilarious when she was angry. The only one who didn't think so was Ruby herself which was why she was sitting scowling at me.

"Ruby, stop taking it all so seriously."

"She didn't just insult me though, did she? She had a go at you as well and she tried to blame you for what happened. What planet was she on when her prick of a grandson ran off with his fancy piece and abandoned his children?"

"Planet "My-Tony-is-a-saint-and-he-should-have-never-married-that-tart-because-he's-far-too-good-for-the-likes-of-her'," I said in my best squeaky old-woman voice. "I wouldn't mind so much but I was warned about him. My mother wasn't impressed the first time she met him."

I remember the day that I introduced him to my family like it was yesterday.

"You mark my words, Frankie, he's a shifty-looking so-and-so and I know for a fact that he's just going to break your heart," Mammy had announced after looking at him for five minutes.

The more I thought about it the more I started to think I should blame my mother for this whole sorry situation. If she had said that she liked him I probably would have dumped him immediately but as soon as she had voiced her disapproval I made it my mission in life to make sure that I kept him. (Mental note to self: always tell Carly that her boyfriends are wonderful lest she should make the same mistake as her mother and end up with a tosspot.)

"Frankie, I need you now," Owen called through the open door of the office.

"Not had it in a while?" Ruby said acerbically.

Owen poked his head around the door and asked me to chase up the PowerPoint presentations that were due to be shown to the graduation students and their parents.

"I'll get right on it," I said as I moved in the direction of the staff room.

I suddenly felt very tired. I wanted to be fresh and full of enthusiasm for both my sister's visit and Graduation Day but now somehow neither of those things seemed to be as important as they were.

Anyone for Seconds?

It was nearly five o'clock and time for me to collect the children from their after-school club. I felt a sinking dread as I wondered how Ben would greet me. Did he believe me when I said that this wasn't my fault or would he be convinced of something else, having had time to think about it all?

Chapter 15

When I arrived to pick up my son and daughter I was surprised to see Ben's teacher there.

"Mrs Grason, how are you?" I said in greeting.

"I'm not too bad," she said. "I'm here to see you as it happens."

(Shit.)

"Don't fret. I'd just like to talk to you about Ben. I thought I'd come and see you in person this evening as I don't think that we need involve the school. I'm very fond of him but a bit worried."

I breathed deeply. This day was getting worse.

I followed Mrs Grason into a private staff room in the community centre where the after-school club was based.

She sat opposite me and steepled her fingers together before tapping her fingertips against her lips.

Her greying hair framed her face and her blue eyes were kind. She seemed unsure of what to say so I decided to help her.

"Things have been a little complicated at home lately," I explained apologetically. "Ben is at an age now where he is starting to understand more about the situation concerning his father and he is having a hard time dealing with it."

"Ahh," Mrs Grason responded. "That would explain a lot."

I shut one eye and squinted at her with the other one.

"We had a little incident today in school," she said.

I didn't like that word. That word told me that he didn't just make a passing remark or answer somebody back. "Incident" meant that he must have done something.

"We were doing Religious Education today and studying families. I am very mindful of the fact that not all children live with both parents and as such I like to try and handle the subject as sensitively as possible. We started to have a discussion when suddenly Ben kicked the table and ran out of the room. He seemed very angry. I followed him and he started to babble. I couldn't make much sense of what he was saying – suffice it to say that he is very confused. He didn't want me to tell you because he thinks that you'll be hurt. I would normally view that type of behaviour as being disruptive but in this particular instance I know that it has been offset by confusion. I know a very good child psychologist who you could speak to."

"I know one too," I said in a tight voice, thinking back to my experience with Angelica. The man would think that Owen and I were a pair of loonies who were driving our children nuts if we went near him again but it was looking increasingly likely that his services would be required.

I assured Mrs Grason that I would speak to Ben and that there would be no repeat of today's display of temper. "Thank you for telling me about this," I said finally.

I looked through the glass door where the children were sitting and watched my son. He was drawing intently. He was probably doing a picture all in black which would tell any psychologist that he was emotionally disturbed and that his great-granny was a dead woman when I next got my hands on her. In fact, she could get in line after his father.

"Mum!" Carly squealed as she spotted me at the door.

She ran over and jumped on me. Ben looked up and tried to smile although it came out as more of grimace.

"Hello, son," I said as I sat down and joined him at the table where he was working.

"Hi, Mum. I drew you a picture."

"Did you, darling?"

(Please don't let it be a page full of black deep-grooved scribbles . . .)

"It's a picture of our family."

He held up the drawing which depicted four people. A woman, a man, a little boy and a little girl.

"This is you, this is me and this is Carly," he said, pointing at the woman and the children.

"And who is this?" I asked, pointing at the man in his drawing. My breath was catching in my throat as I waited for his answer.

"It's my daddy."

I had to turn away to stop the tears which were threatening to spill over from falling on him. Oh, how I wished life could be simpler!

"Mum?"

"Yes, son."

"That's the picture that I drew earlier. That's the picture that I would draw if my family was normal. I did another one just before you came which shows my family as it is."

Ben held up another drawing which had lots of people in it.

"And who are all these people?" I asked, my interest piqued.

"This is you and me and Carly. And this is Granny Celia and Granda George and this is Auntie Ruby and Auntie Ella and Uncle Hammy."

(I would not tell Ruby that she had been depicted with sticky-outy mad-looking hair which was purple in colour.)

There was one person left in the picture and he appeared to be wearing glasses.

"And this? Who's this?"

"That's my friend Owen. Mrs Grason told me that I'm very lucky. Other children might have a daddy but I have lots of other people who love me just as much as he does. She says that Owen might be more than my friend some day but for now that's what I'll call him."

(Mrs Grason, I salute you!)

I saw no depiction of Daddy, Stella, the new baby or evil Granny Peggy and whooped inside.

I decided to phone Owen to see if he wanted to come over for a glass of wine and a chat that evening. We hadn't been able to spend much time together since we came home from our weekend break.

Angelica answered the phone in a cheerful voice but her tone turned sour when she realised who she was speaking to.

"Hi, Angelica. How are you? How's the appetite?" I asked.

"If that was any of your business I'm sure I'd tell you," she answered snippily.

"Angelica, please. Stay on the line and talk to me

for a minute. I've been worried about you and thought that maybe we could do something nice and girlie together next week. Would you like to go shopping or out for a pizza one evening?"

Angelica seemed to find this suggestion incredibly funny as she started to cackle maniacally down the phone.

"If I want to go shopping I can do that with my friends or my aunts and if you took the time to get your facts straight you would know that I hate pizza. And, by the way, green is so not my colour so I pawned your crappy necklace at school today. I got a fiver for it and probably made a profit. My Aunt Brenda said that it was the cheapest piece of tat she'd ever seen and she would know." She paused. "Dad, it's some woman for you!" she shouted without another word leaving me bludgeoning the phone receiver against the banister in bad temper.

"Hello?"

"It's me," I said grimly. I was stung. I had never been so crushed or hurt as the result of someone's words. (Slight exaggeration considering my ex-husband told me he was leaving me for another woman but that was beside the point.)

"Oh, Angelica never said. I thought you were going to be some bloody awful sales person trying to sell me a mortgage or something. She mustn't have recognised you voice."

"Obviously not," I said crisply, trying my best to keep the irritation from my voice.

As it turned out Owen wasn't free but Angelica was staying with a friend the following night. Her friend must need her head testing – I wondered did the poor child's mother know the negative influence that her daughter was being subjected to.

I took a deep breath and held my temper and looked forward to tomorrow when I would have him all to myself minus the demonic, obstructive teenager.

Chapter 16

The next day was a whirl of stress, mayhem, tussles with workmen, arguments with computer technicians and cleaning.

My house was shining like a new pin in preparation for our special guests and the marquee at the college had been safely installed and was still standing (or at least I hoped it was). All the equipment had been set up, we had a dress rehearsal which was executed with military precision and the graduating students had been primed and warned that they were not allowed to get drunk.

I spoke to Ella on the phone and our excitement at being about to see each other was at fever-pitch level. It had been almost a year since I'd laid eyes on my sister and I couldn't wait to hug her. I could hear Hammy laughing softly in the background and Owen was sitting in my living room nursing a glass of wine with a bemused expression on his face.

When I finally got off the phone I tiptoed upstairs and looked in on the children.

Ben had fallen asleep still holding his *Harry Potter* book tightly and Carly was curled up with her hands under her head and her blonde curls splayed on the pillow. They both looked much happier than in previous days and I was so glad.

I returned downstairs. Owen patted the seat beside him gently. I knew that he was concerned about me.

I sat beside him and he began to knead and rub my shoulders with his fingers. I winced in pain.

"Relax, Frankie," he said. "You're like a coiled-up spring. Loosen up those muscles. You'll look like you've got a poker shoved up your ass when you go to the airport tomorrow if you keep that up and I don't think that that's how your sister wants to be greeted."

I did as he commanded and let my shoulders fall. I rolled my head from side to side, pretending to like the sensation and then got up. Usually I loved being touched in this manner but I had too much in my head and felt fidgety and restless.

"Can you stay the night?" I asked hopefully, knowing that Angelica was safely out of the way. Nebby Peg had also given me food for thought. There was nothing I loved more than to annoy her so I reasoned that there was nothing wrong in having Owen stay over occasionally. She already had me painted as a harlot so I might as well have some fun and live up to her image of me.

"I'd love to stay but that sofa of yours is a bit lumpy. I had an awful crick in my neck when I woke up the other morning."

"I wasn't planning on asking you to kip on the sofa," I said indignantly. "I only left you there the other night because you fell asleep and forty tons of explosives wouldn't have wakened you."

He arched an eyebrow at me and grinned. "So where exactly am I sleeping then?"

"Well, if you've no objections to sharing my bed then that's where you'll be laying your head."

"I see," he said. "And do all Mum's friends who might become something more in the future get this treatment or is it reserved for me?"

"I'm very choosy about what special friends I like to lie with, thank you," I said. "It just so happens that you are very, very special."

We'd had a long chat about Ben earlier and I showed Owen the picture. He seemed touched by the gesture and gave Ben an extra ruffle on the head before he went to bed. He didn't know how lucky he was – if Angelica was given the opportunity to draw her family I know that I wouldn't feature at all unless I was depicted wearing a pointy hat and riding a broomstick.

Owen told me that he'd had a chat with Angelica that evening and that we might be able to organise a bit of a get-together when Ella was home. Owen's theory behind that particular plan seemed to be that there was safety in numbers and hopefully his volatile daughter wouldn't kick off if there were more distractions.

If the plan had been to have fun and frolics upstairs then we were both to be sorely disappointed as within five seconds of our heads simultaneously hitting our pillows we were asleep.

I woke up the following morning and sighed with pure contentment as I nuzzled further into Owen's chest. It had been a long time since I'd had anybody in bed to cuddle who didn't call me Mum so it made a nice change – a very nice change. I looked at my watch and thought horny thoughts and wondered if we had time for a bit of activity before we had to go to work.

I turned to Owen and started to nibble his ear. "Morning, lover," I whispered as he opened his eyes, smiled and encircled me in his arms.

Because of our antics everything was running late. (Owen is extremely attentive and has lots of stamina . . . ahem!) When I am late I get stressed so by the time I reached the airport my brain was fried, I was red in the face and convinced that Ella would think I'd forgotten about her and get a taxi instead. My mother would be unbearable to listen to. "Imagine leaving your sister to make her own way from the airport! Well, that's just charming!" This statement would no doubt be accompanied by a lot of tutting. I always thought that my mother could give Skippy the Bush Kangaroo a run for his money in the tutting department. They could have a very lively conversation if left alone together.

I ran into the toilet in the arrivals lounge and brushed my hair, applied a little lip gloss and smoothed down my linen trousers which were crumpled from sitting in the car. Satisfied that I looked decent enough to greet Ella (hoping that she was still in the vicinity, that is) I returned to the public waiting area and stood watching as people started to mill through the gates.

It was with relief that I heard Ella's flight number being called and realised that it had been slightly delayed.

I watched with interest as the new arrivals who had just travelled from Edinburgh to Belfast emerged. I watched as an old couple greeted a young couple with a new baby. The elderly lady seemed emotional as she grasped the tiny bundle and hugged him closely. I smiled and nodded as they walked past me.

There was also a group of business people who were easy to identify with their briefcases and copies of the *Financial Times* tucked under their arms. A group of girls, one wearing an L-plate on her back were singing and laughing loudly and obviously on a hen night. I wondered if the bride-to-be knew what she was letting herself in for. I shuddered at the thought. I saw a woman in the distance walking through the doors talking to one of the stewardesses and decided that either she must be a model or have anorexia because surely nobody normal could be that thin.

Ella would laugh when I told her about my observations. She was always telling me that I'd missed my vocation and should have been a journalist. "At least then you'd get paid for being so pass-remarkable," she'd say for the hundredth time.

Everyone seemed to have filtered through and I frowned and looked at my watch. I was starting to doubt myself as I scrambled in my bag for the post-it note where I had hastily written down Ella's flight information when I was arranging to pick her up. My mobile was in my hand to call her and see if she was okay when I caught a glimpse of a pair of ultra-skinny legs and realised that they must belong to the anorexic model that I saw earlier. So it was with both shock and horror I looked up and registered that the skeletal frame belonged to my sister.

Her face was gaunt with sunken cheeks, her clothes were hanging off her and she looked pale and tired. Hammy was following behind her and making slicing motions with his hands and shaking his head vigorously. I realised that he was telling me not to say anything to her about her appearance and for his sake I decided not to.

"Ella," I said with more joy than I actually felt having had a good look at her and coming to the conclusion that either she was very sick or had turned into a size-zero fruitcake.

Oh my God, I just realised that my mother would have a fit when she saw her. She will be feeding her mashed potato intravenously to build her up and shovelling large amounts of apple tart and homemade custard down her throat whilst dragging her to the doctor and wanting to give her cod-liver oil, like she used to do when we were little.

"Hi, Frankie," she said, still having retained most of her Irish accent but with a definite note of a Scottish lilt.

"Hello, hen," Hammy said as he enveloped me in a bear hug that seemed to go on forever.

I was very concerned. They were both behaving very oddly and I was more perturbed than ever when I saw that my usually strong, brave sister had just sat down on one of the plastic chairs and was now crying with huge fat tears rolling down her cheeks.

I was in very unfamiliar territory. Ella had always been the strong one who had made it her life's work to pick me up and put me back together again when things had gone wrong. Now it appeared that she was falling apart and I was at a loss to know what to do for the best.

I stared wordlessly at Hammy who had sat down beside Ella and was whispering comforting words in her ear and stroking her hair. Ella allowed him to placate her for a few moments before getting up and going over to a window where she stood and looked out, seemingly needing to compose herself.

"Give her a hug and tell her that it's going to be okay," Hammy said in a low voice. "She needs to know that it's all going to work out."

"I'll do whatever you want, Hammy," I whispered. "But first of all I really would love it if somebody would tell me what is going on."

"It's just that the specialist was a bit more negative on her last appointment and she's very down about it."

Specialist. Another word I didn't like. Any illness that required intervention from a specialist must be serious and if the particular specialist in question was being negative then it must be very serious indeed.

I was moving towards Ella to put my arms around her when another thought struck me. Hammy seemed to think I knew what was going on when in actual fact I was more in the dark than Stevie Wonder.

I performed a 180-degree spin on my heel and steered Hammy over to a row of seats on the opposite side of the arrivals lounge.

"Hammy, what's wrong with her? She hasn't told me. This is really scaring me."

The tears came before I could help myself and I was more disconcerted than ever to see Ella coming over to join us. Two minutes later and Hammy was left cradling two emotional tearful wrecks who were covered in snot and sobbing noisily.

Ella reached out, grabbed hold of me and hugged me tightly as she said "There, there," and rubbed my back.

I couldn't believe it: even in her hour of need when I should be providing the support and understanding she was trying to comfort me and still wearing her Big Sister mantle.

"It's not something I wanted to talk about over the phone," she said in a choked voice by way of explanation.

I noticed that she seemed to be looking pleadingly at Hammy at this point.

I looked towards my brother-in-law and noticed that he was none too pleased. In fact he looked most pissed off which was no mean feat for someone with twinkly eyes and a mouth that was permanently upturned in a smile. He turned away and I could hear him muttering something about "an obsession taking over our lives" under his breath.

Ella whimpered, looked at him, then at me and flounced off in the direction of the ladies' room, slamming the door behind her.

I looked questioningly at Hammy and he sighed and rubbed the back of his head.

"I know that this must look bad, Frankie. I'm trying to be understanding, really I am. I want this as much as she does but it gets really hard sometimes. On days like this I wish that we'd never had any investigations done and then maybe she wouldn't be getting so stressed out all the time. Sometimes ignorance can be bliss."

I was quite taken aback by this statement. "Surely if she's sick, Hammy, it's better that she knows and that they've detected whatever it is early. Note that I'm still saying 'whatever it is' because nobody has feckin' told me anything yet."

He ignored the fact that I was still clueless and continued to speak. "She was quite reluctant to hear what the consultant had to say when we were called back. I think her nursing experience told her that it wasn't going to be good news and with her knowledge of how severe this can be and how hard it can be to treat she's been very depressed about it. You have no idea of the year we've just been through, Frankie."

"I know I don't," I said in my most patient voice. "Look, can you just spit it out. Is it operable? Is it curable?"

"I don't know Frankie. All I know is that it has made life very hard."

"Really hard, Frankie," I heard a voice saying behind me.

I turned to find Ella standing looking at me. She seemed to have pulled herself together a bit. She smelt nice and had brushed her hair.

"What the feck is going on?" I demanded, willing the last nerve I had left to stay with me until I got an answer once and for all.

"I've got unexplained infertility," Ella said, wringing her hands and looking at the floor.

"Is that all?" I said incredulously. "I thought it was something serious."

Chapter 17

Okay. With the benefit of hindsight and a stern ticking off from Hammy (who is very scary and unintelligible with his Scottish accent when he is cross) I realised that it wasn't the most tactful thing I could have said. It didn't convey the support, love and concern that I was feeling but I was so relieved that my sister didn't have a life-threatening illness that I couldn't help blurting it out.

The silence was deafening. We were in the car which was moving in the direction of home and Ella hadn't said two words to me since we left. She had to be escorted out of the ladies' toilet in the airport by Hammy who got shouted at by an elderly lady who thought he was a pervert so now he wasn't talking to me either. Owen had rung twice demanding to know where I was and the second time I spoke to him he told me that he was sacking me from my position if I didn't get my ass in gear and get to the college in record time.

I told him to go and feck himself sideways which was childish and uncalled for, I know, but two minutes before that I had my mother on the phone whinging about her cooked breakfast being ruined and threatening to feed Banjo the lot. Daddy had taken to the garden shed to seek solace by all accounts and I was seriously thinking of joining him when I got home. If I ever got home.

I knew that I was acting like a child but my family had reduced me to it. I had locked myself in the car and was refusing to speak to anyone after receiving nothing but abuse since I arrived at my parent's house.

"Frankie, Frankie," my mother mouthed through the window, "can you hear me?"

"No," I mouthed back whilst turning the radio up by several hundred decibels. I'd rather listen to The Feeling singing about being lonely than listen to another angry tirade.

"What have you done to her?" was the way I was greeted when Ella pushed past me and nearly knocked Mammy flying, mounting the stairs two at a time in her attempts to lock herself in the bathroom before anyone could stop her.

"Well, obviously it has to be something to do with

me?" I answered, feeling very put out that my mother had such a bad opinion of me.

"Well, you were the one who went to meet her. What's wrong with her?" she said, her voice becoming high-pitched. "Has she told you why she's home yet? Why is she home? Hammy?"

Hammy was a wise man. Sensing that the forces were starting to close in around him he disappeared out the back door and Mammy eventually found him sitting on an upturned plant pot deep in conversation with Daddy.

"Ella, Ella love! Please come out. What's wrong? Did Frankie do something to upset you?"

Mammy was hammering at the bathroom door. Ella was sullenly refusing to respond and it was at that point that I decided I'd be safer taking refuge in the car. It was just a pity that I hadn't had the foresight to throw my mobile out the window on the way down the motorway. It was one o'clock and I had promised Owen that I would be back at half past eleven at the very latest. Obviously I hadn't bargained on my sister being an emotional wreck and falling out with me therefore I was very late. Owen was extremely irate, if that was the correct word for someone who referred to you as being irresponsible, unreliable, bad at their job with no sense of priority and a pain in the arse.

"She won't listen to me, George," Mammy said as Daddy approached the stationary vehicle where I had rooted myself.

"Frankie, it's your father here," Dad said in his most important voice.

"Owwww!" he responded when Mammy nipped him in the arm and shouldered him out of the way.

"You are useless, George. After thirty-two years of referring to you as 'Daddy' I think she knows that. When I asked you to speak to her I meant you to say something sensible instead of stating the obvious."

Mammy was pink in the face and shaking like a leaf. I could hear her telling Daddy that Ella wouldn't talk to her. Hammy was being very non-committal apparently and she was not one bit happy. I heard my name being mentioned again but decided not to wait to hear anymore.

"Tell Hammy I want to talk to him," I said as I wound down the window.

"Frankie, what the hell is going on?" my mother demanded.

"The last time you looked were you big, burly, married to my sister and Scottish?" I asked.

Daddy propelled Mammy into the house before she could answer and started bawling at Hammy to "come and talk to that one who's sitting in the car and won't come out". The last thing I heard was "I always told you that boys would have been easier!" I didn't hear her reply – it seemed that for once she had the sense not to answer him back.

Hammy appeared at the front door looking uncomfortable and scratching his head.

"Tell Ella that I'll be over to see her later," I said. "And tell her that I didn't mean to be insensitive. I'm sorry for upsetting her but I was just so happy that she wasn't really sick. I know that she must be going through hell and I'll always be here for her, you know. Your room's ready and I'll pick you up as soon as you phone me to tell me that it's okay."

"No phone call required," Ella roared as she flew out of the house with my mother in hot pursuit still demanding to know what was going on. "Drive," she said, getting into the car, dragging Hammy in her wake.

Chapter 18

My heart was pounding as I eventually drove towards the college. I was expecting to be handed my P45 and have Owen bellow at me that I was single again. I had totted up twelve missed calls from him along with the bad-tempered voice message that he had left where he sounded raging mad. I was expecting him to be like a starved Rottweiller when I saw him.

I went in through the reception door and began to get nervous as I saw Mandy look at me, first with a look of pity and then with gloating satisfaction.

(Shite.)

Ruby met me before I went to find Owen and catapulted me into the staff kitchen.

"What, may I ask, have you done to our usually placid, even-tempered, esteemed colleague?" she asked. "He's bitten my head off three times today already and absolutely everyone is staying out of his way for fear of being devoured whole."

"Look, I've had a bitch of a day so far and it seems set to get worse and if Owen can't be supportive towards me in my hour of need then I don't think he's the right man for me," I said with a lot more conviction and forthrightness than I actually felt. "I'll tell you all about it later, Ruby, but for now I'd rather just let the inevitable happen and get it over and done with. The dole queue and the lonely hearts columns are beckoning to me even as we speak."

I knew that he would be in the marquee setting things up and without me he'd have had twice as much to do. I thought about the last few months and felt an instant lurch of nervousness and sadness. I really didn't want to go back to being on my own again.

As I approached the open flaps of the marquee I could hear voices, one of them unmistakably belonging to Owen.

"Look, she's had a terrible day. I spoke to her sister earlier and she told me that she was ill on the plane and that Frankie was unavoidably delayed at the airport and afterwards as well. She's put more effort into this Graduation Day than anyone ever has in the past and she doesn't deserve to have it all thrown back in her face over something that isn't her fault."

I heard Mr Reid, the principal's voice.

"If that's true then I'm sorry to hear it but this was

her chance to shine and show us what she can do and all she has proven is that in a crisis she's not here."

"She had a crisis of her own and sometimes family is more important that anything else," I heard Owen retort indignantly.

"We'll see," the principal answered. "I'm disappointed but I'll consider every angle before I give my final summation to the committee."

I heard Owen breathing heavily before he spoke again.

"Mr Reid. If Frankie isn't given her just desserts and made permanent then I'll be considering my position with the college very carefully. She deserves it."

"I understand that you and Ms Colton are conducting a relationship of sorts, Mr Byrne, but I'd ask you not to let that cloud your judgement in this matter. You've been a longstanding and valuable member of staff for many years and I'm sure you know that the interests of the college are of the utmost importance to me. The role of Public Relations Officer is a vital one. You know as well as I do that if we are not promoted properly in all the right places then we may lose our student numbers and if they aren't met we are in grave danger of closing down. We can't afford to leave this important task in the hands of someone who is incapable of being where they should when they should. "

"All the preparations that have gone into this day

have been largely down to Frankie. The contacts that we have are the ones that she made, the plans that were drawn up were of her making and the success and smooth running that we have experienced so far have been all down to her."

I was stunned. I was speechless (a rare occurrence) and so in awe of his loyalty and support that I was in shock. This was not what I had been expecting. Maybe he still loved me after all.

"Oh and by the way I'd rather that you didn't refer to my relationship with Frankie as 'a relationship of sorts'. That gives the impression that it's not serious or some type of fling and I can assure you that neither is true."

I peeped through the crack in the plastic and had a good look at Owen's face which was stern in the extreme; no wonder Ruby and the rest of the staff were hiding in fear of their lives.

Mr Reid stalked out as I dived out of the way and when I looked again Owen was taking his mobile from his pocket. I watched in a daze as he dialled a number and then jumped seven foot in the air as my mobile began to ring shrilly and he looked around in confusion.

Oh good. How was I going to explain this?

He took large strides towards where I was standing cowering and opened the marquee flap fully. I felt as though I was in the set of a *Carry On* film as I fell in the entrance and straight into his arms.

"Hello," I said cheerily as he gave me a long hard look.

"We'll talk about this later," he said abruptly as he let go of me. "Right now, we've work to do. A lot of work to do."

"I don't know anyone that has a better knack of talking her way out of things than you," Ruby said in a tone which was partly admiring and partly disbelieving. "And he hasn't said anything to you about not being there today?"

"We didn't have time to talk. I'm literally only in through the door and it's nine o'clock already. I haven't seen the kids at all, I've hardly spoken to Ella, who incidentally I'm not sure is talking to me anyway and I feel like I've been dragged through a hedge backwards I'm so tired and sore."

"I can't believe that he spoke to Mr Reid like that," Ruby said.

"I know," I gushed. "I'm so chuffed that he would stand by me so forcefully, especially when I was less than pleasant to him earlier."

"He must be really into you," Ruby said enviously.

"Well, we did have a rather good start to the day today."

"Ugh, don't," Ruby answered quickly. "I think I'm going to sign myself into the nearest convent. They'd accept me in ten seconds flat I'm living such a nunlike existence as it is. Are you sure that Owen has no eligible single friends?"

"Ruby, can you let me sort out my own relationship disasters before I start ruining your love life as well?" I laughed. "Besides I don't have time to talk. I need to have a bath and get into bed before I fall over. I only have one day left to redeem myself before they cite me as being unfit for the job."

"It sounds as if Owen has already sorted that one for you," Ruby said. "I'm sure Mr Reid will have listened to him and carefully considered what he said."

"Don't you ever breathe a word that I heard them talking," I said quickly. "I overheard a conversation he had with his daughter and his mother when we were on holiday and he went mad and accused me of snooping and eavesdropping – so please keep it to yourself."

"My lips are sealed," Ruby promised.

"Good," I said as I heard rustling sounds upstairs. "I need to go. I've got to talk to Ella and see how she is and whether or not she'll ever speak to me again."

"Good luck," Ruby said.

I had told her the full story and she was at a loss to explain how one person could have so much bad luck heaped on them from such a great height.

"Thanks," I said grimly before hanging up and ascending the stairs.

Chapter 19

"Ella, can we talk?" I asked tentatively as I poked my head around the guest-room door.

"I suppose so," she sighed, getting up from where she had been curled on the double bed wearing a comfy pair of striped pyjamas teamed with fluffy woollen bed socks. The pyjamas hid the fact that she was now so thin and I wasn't nearly as freaked out by her appearance as I had been when I first saw her at the airport. Her eyes were still the same. Ella's eyes were warm and kind and she had the sort of smile that lit up not only her face but the whole room. Hammy always said that the first time she smiled at him he knew that he was in love. I noticed that her chestnut-coloured hair seemed thinner than usual and that she had cut it.

We surveyed each other for a period of time before collapsing in each other's arms.

"I'm so sorry," I whispered into her hair which smelt of coconut and almonds.

"I'm sorry too," she responded. "I acted like a prize nut-job today. Hammy is getting sick and tired of me going off the deep end about it all the time and it's starting to affect our relationship. We've always been really happy but now we seem to be constantly strained all the time."

"Where is he now?"

"He's taken Ben out to the video shop to buy some kids' stuff – Carly is asleep – I already brought the children presents which I'm sure they would have been quite content with so it's just an excuse to get away from me and the situation as a whole which is made all the more frustrating because there is no apparent explanation for it." Ella paused and I saw her bottom lip tremble slightly. "We've both had tests and Hammy has a perfect sperm count and there doesn't seem to be anything wrong with me. Frankie, it's so unfair. I adore children, babies in particular. That's why I love my job so much. Is it too much to ask that I have a baby of my own to love and cherish instead of safely delivering them into the world for everybody else?"

She looked thoroughly miserable and I could see why she had difficulty talking about it. It wasn't an easy subject to talk about, made all the more acutely painful by the fact that her whole occupation was centred around pregnancy and the joy of babies.

Anyone for Seconds?

I thought of myself and how easily Ben and Carly were conceived. Ben wasn't planned and was a grave shock. I didn't have an easy labour, however, (twenty-three hours of pushing and telling Tony he was a bastard) and that ensured that there were no more babies until we planned to have Carly nearly three years later when I realised that Ben needed company. I started to fully appreciate how lucky I had been. I had a lovely pregnancy with Carly and my second labour was short and relatively pain-free. It was an experience that I will always treasure and I sincerely hoped with all my heart that my sister, who was so kind and patient and good to everyone else, would also get to experience it.

I stroked her hair as she leaned against my chest and sighed as I felt the sisterly closeness that we'd always shared return.

"I hope you didn't get in too much trouble today," Ella said, suddenly extricating herself from my arms to look at me. "Owen phoned and I kind of told a few fibs in the hope that he'd be more understanding. I was sick on the plane and had to be escorted off in a wheelchair if anyone asks, only for God's sake don't be letting Mammy get wind of it or she'll have a pink fit. I had to take your phone off the hook earlier because she wouldn't leave me alone. She seems to think that I'm suffering from some deadly illness and that Hammy and I are splitting up."

"The day that you and Hammy split up will be the day that the rest of the world officially loses hope of ever finding love," I said confidently. "You two fit like a glove. You are so right together and you'll get through this. Things like this make a relationship stronger."

"But look at what happened to you and Tony," Ella said, looking at me anxiously. "You loved him so much. I used to sit on the phone and listen to you sobbing about him after he left and I felt so helpless. There was nothing I could do to help you."

"I'm sorry," I said suddenly. "I forgot to specify that Hammy is a real man and not a ginormous hormone on legs."

Ella laughed and kissed me on the cheek.

"About the other little matter," I began slowly. I was going to have to choose my words very carefully and try not to stick my great foot in it again. "You can't really blame either Mammy or me for thinking that there's something wrong with you." I looked beseechingly at her. "You're so thin, Ella. Are you telling me the full truth? There's nothing else, is there? Because no matter what it is I'll always stand by you."

I could feel my eyes starting to well up. The thought of anything ever happening to Ella didn't bear thinking about. I missed her so much but at least she was on the end of the phone if I ever needed her.

"There's nothing wrong," Ella assured me. "It's my way of dealing with stress. I don't eat."

Anyone for Seconds?

If I coped with stress that way I would look like Geri Halliwell in her yoga days when she looked like a zip with a head on it. Unfortunately I seemed to cope with things by eating enough for at least three people.

"I know I should eat and I'm going to start right now," continued Ella.

"Why bother about deciding? Are you seriously deluding yourself into thinking that you'll have a choice when Mammy gets a proper hold of you? She was born with a teapot in her hand, you know!"

Suddenly I had an idea. I was going to help Ella in the only way I knew how.

"Extend your stay," I said. "Dump your return tickets and let me build you up again. I'll bet that losing all that weight has something to do with you not being able to conceive. Sure they're forever giving out about Posh Spice not being able to get pregnant for the fourth time because she's too thin."

"Oh, well, okay, doctor," she said.

"I'm serious," I stressed, in case she thought it was one of my hare-brained ideas. (Why does nobody ever take me seriously?) "Besides anything else, we haven't been together in a long time so it would be nice to rekindle our sisterhood and have some proper fun. Carly would love it," I added, using just a small tiny bit of emotional blackmail. "The poor child has no other aunts and you wouldn't like to deprive her of having the only one that she has, now would you?"

"Not fair!" Ella cried. "You know I do the best I can for her when I'm not here."

"I know, I know," I said "but it's not the same as having you here in the flesh where we can see you and hug you and feed you copious amounts of chocolate and spuds."

Our conversation was interrupted by the front door opening and two animated voices sounding in the hall.

I went out to tell them to be quiet as Carly was asleep but they had moved into the living room.

So I hung over the banisters and eavesdropped – it was becoming my favourite occupation – well, my second favourite.

"Wow and did you really see Jamie Carragher score the goal, Uncle Hammy?"

"I did, Ben. I was so near the sideline that I could practically touch him."

"Did you ever see Peter Crouch scoring a goal?"

"I did back a few years ago but that was nothing compared to when I watched Liverpool playing and saw them beat AC Milan in the Champions League Final where they came from a deficit of three nil at half time and went on to win in penalties. Steven Gerrard was rallying the troops that night. I'll never forget it."

"Are you really going to take me to watch Liverpool playing Aston Villa on Sunday, Uncle Hammy?"

"Indeed I am, son. We'll go early and get some chips beforehand and then we'll watch the match and leave the girls to their own devices."

"I love having you here, Uncle Hammy," Ben said.

I went back in to Ella and whispered, "See, that's another reason why you should stay. Ben loves Hammy so much."

"And Hammy loves children," Ella said sadly.

I stood up and put my right hand in the air.

"I do solemnly swear that before you leave, which better not be in two weeks' time, that I will have helped to build up your strength and that you will be returning to Scotland feeling happier and more positive. I also promise to enlist the help of St Gerard Majella who is the patron saint of childbirth and whose head I will have melted with prayers."

My phone beeped and I saw that I had received a message from Owen.

"What does it say?" Ella asked as she peered over my shoulder.

"He says that I'm a pain in the arse and that I've caused him no end of trouble today but that he still loves me anyway and that I have to give him a ..."

I stopped and blushed furiously as I read the rest of the message where Owen specified what exactly was required to make up for my tardiness.

"He wants a massage," I said hoarsely as Ella smirked at me.

"Sure he does," she said with a mischievous twinkle in her eye as Hammy entered the room.

"All right, my two hens?" he asked as he kissed Ella on the forehead and ruffled my hair.

"We're fine now," Ella said.

Chapter 20

I was up at the crack of dawn and in the bath humming to myself as I lay back in the cherry-scented bubbles.

I was planning my day. I needed to be in work at around eight o'clock, spruced, clean and looking suitably professional and with my hair straightened.

Owen and I had already got quite a lot accomplished the previous day. When we left the marquee the seats were all positioned neatly in rows, all the microphones were in working order and the plasma screen and video were wired and ready to roll. I was quite proud of myself actually: I had come up with the idea that I should tape the students getting robed and ready before they walked in pairs to the marquee where they were going to be presented with their certificates and awards. I thought that it would be a nice gesture to show the footage on the plasma screen while the proud parents waited for their little darlings to graduate. I had put it to Mr Reid the evening before and he had seemed impressed. He was trying his best to be nonchalant but I could see that he was quite taken with the suggestion. Owen had put in his tuppence-worth at that stage too and suggested that Mr Reid couldn't afford to lose someone who came up with such inspirational ideas.

I got out of the bath and dried myself and tried to think of any last-minute touches I could bring to the event that would help me to shine and sparkle and save me from the temping agency. Suddenly I snapped my fingers and grinned at myself as I brushed my teeth in the mirror. Owen was going to be so proud of me and Mr Reid was going to be begging me to stay and give me a raise.

In the immortal words of Hannibal Smith – "I love it when a plan comes together".

I was leaving my children in the capable hands of their Auntie Ella and Uncle Hammy for the day. The school holidays had kicked in the day before so my sister's timing was wonderful and she had kindly agreed to look after Ben and Carly until the beginning of July.

My stomach sank as I thought of the holidays. Part of me had been looking forward to the break but the other part was dreading it as I was going to have to keep my part of the bargain and allow Owen to introduce Angelica to Ben and Carly.

I had absolutely no idea how that would all pan out but I had a funny feeling that it wouldn't be without its problems, the biggest one probably being Angelica herself. (Her name was so unsuitable and obviously given to her when she was a small baby and incapable of answering back or being cheeky about her father's choice in girlfriends.)

Owen had been telling me that Angelica had been behaving pretty well of late. Probably because she'd had her father all to herself as well as being pampered by her granny. (Owen told me that his mother preferred to be referred to as "Nana" as it didn't make her sound so old but I wasn't playing ball on that one. If people would insult me behind my back then they needn't think that I was going to be merciful about any age-related concerns they might have.)

I arrived at work before Owen and slipped into the toilet where I touched up my make-up. I knew that I looked good. I had somehow managed to lose about half a stone in the last few weeks, my hair was straight and neat and the navy suit and turquoise wraparound top that I was wearing helped to bring out the colour in my eyes. I smiled to myself when I thought about what I had on underneath. I had taken out a pair of white lacy panties with a matching bra that morning but then I caught sight of the unworn light blue camisole with matching French knickers which I had bought the year before but had been unable to fit comfortably in. I slid them on and they had felt wonderful against my freshly moisturised skin. Owen might get his wish after all when he least expected it.

I couldn't believe that everything was going so well. Things were running so smoothly that I was suspicious. I was wondering when the sky was going to fall in or when Mr Reid was going to give me my cards and tell me to leg it to the job centre. Luckily they had all liked my new idea.

"The bath must be a very creative and inspirational place, Frankie," had been Owen's response when I told him how I had concocted my plan whilst tending to my ablutions that morning.

"It is," I assured him before going to get what I needed. At short notice I managed to contact all the graduating students. They were all under strict instructions to bring what was required without letting their parents know anything about it. I was gratified that most of them had followed my advice and brought images that marked all the other big occasions in their lives. I hugged myself with glee as I put them all in order and placed a projector in the appropriate place. Owen left me to my own devices but nicely tipped off Mr Reid that I had something up my sleeve that would thrill and excite every parent seated. I had also called members of the press and told them if they wanted to see a roomful of emotional tearful parents that they should be in the marquee at approximately two o'clock.

Owen had shown me how to operate the video camera a few weeks previously so I considered myself to be a bit of a pro. By the time I went to video the students getting robed in a haze of hairspray, aftershave and perfume I was relaxed and at ease using the equipment. Their faces were animated and there was an air of excitement as they made last-minute adjustments to their clothes and primped and preened in the student study room which had been converted for the purpose. At twelve thirty I saw Owen coming in to check on me and asked one of the other members of staff who was proficient in the art of video production to take over the task while I went and spoke to him for a few seconds.

"Hello, gorgeous," he said.

"Am I?" I asked, fluttering my eyelashes seductively at him.

"Extremely," he said, slipping his arm around my waist as he blew gently in my ear. "Do you come here often?"

"Only when I know you'll be here," I answered. "Am I forgiven for yesterday then?"

"How could I possibly stay angry with you? Your good nature always takes over in a crisis. How's your sister now?"

"She's feeling a lot better actually," I answered truthfully. "She's dying to meet you in the flesh."

"And she will. I'll be calling over tomorrow with Angelica. She's looking forward to meeting everyone."

I could feel myself stiffening slightly but quickly masked it to make it look like I was cuddling into him.

"There'll be plenty of time to be frisky later," Owen said whilst cupping my bottom with his hands.

"I'll take that as a promise," I said, as I kissed him and broke away.

I retrieved the video camera and continued to film. Once I felt that I'd got enough footage I quickly whipped out the tape and gave it to one of the technicians who planned to put it on a loop to play in the marquee.

I was busy for the next while putting together a presentation which I was very pleased with as the clock chimed one o'clock.

Now that everything was in order I took the opportunity to phone Ella and check on the children.

"Everyone's fine," she said.

"And how are you?"

"I'm feeling better," she answered after a short pause. "I've thought about what you said and I'll tell you what we've decided later."

"Okay," I answered, glad to hear that she seemed to be more upbeat.

It was half past one and the seats had begun to fill with expectant parents and family members all dressed to the nines. The video was playing in the background and Owen had teamed it with some appropriate music in the form of The Beatles "A Little Help from My Friends" and M People "Moving on Up". Very appropriate, I thought.

Mr Reid approached me and moved his mouth in an agitated fashion before he spoke. "Can you come with me, Ms Colton?" he asked in a pompous tone.

I was wondering if he would actually be cruel enough to tell me I was sacked just as the fruits of all my hard work were being aired to the public.

I was taken into a room where four other people who I didn't know were seated. There were three men and one woman. The men smiled but the lady in question looked me up and down and sniffed.

"I'd like to introduce you to some members of the Board of Directors. I've been telling them about your efforts since you've joined us and everything you need to know about where you stand is in this envelope."

With that he walked away from me, closely followed by his colleagues.

With shaky hands I ripped open the envelope and found inside a job description, a contract and a letter. The contract was for the post of Public Relations Officer which was a full-time position within the college. The job description outlined the list of duties which were to be undertaken by the appointed candidate and the letter was on headed paper and from Mr Reid.

Redmond College
Swiftstown
29 June 2008

Dear Ms Colton,
We are delighted to be able to offer you the full-time position of Public Relations Officer within the Redmond College campus.

Your full-time position, should you decide to accept our offer will begin in two weeks' time.

We are pleased with your performance to date but must include one stipulation. We are aware that you are having a relationship with a member of the teaching staff and ask that this be conducted discreetly and outside of college hours.

We look forward to your response.

Yours sincerely
Rodney Reid
(Principal)

I was sighing with satisfaction and contentment as I skipped into the marquee and looked for Owen in order to impart my glorious news. I found him looking pale and stony-faced while staring open-mouthed at the plasma screen which seemed to be showing a couple cavorting in a most undignified manner. Bloody students! They just didn't know how to conduct themselves!

Fuuuuuucccccccckkkk! On closer inspection I discovered that it was not students but a teacher and the newly appointed PR Officer who had just been warned in writing to keep her relationship with the said teacher discreet.

That was a short-lived promotion.

Chapter 21

Owen was foaming at the mouth and had gone in search of both the technician responsible for the video editing and the staff member who had obviously recorded us having a private moment together. He was threatening to take the video equipment and insert it somewhere unmentionable and irretrievable but he found either of them. He was severely pissed off by what had just been aired and aggravated further to find that his students all thought it was hilariously funny and were now calling him the college "Liaisons Officer".

I was avoiding all contact with Mr Reid and swore I was going to smack that silly cow Mandy if she sniggered at me behind her hand one more time. Ruby wasn't much better but after twelve years of friendship she had earned the right to laugh at my indiscretions.

Luckily the parents seemed to have a sense of humour. One father told me that he was available if I ever got sick of Owen. I was touched but decided not to impart that information to Owen who was doing a good impression of a bulldog sucking a nettle. "Oh cheer up," I said as he glowered at me. "At least the parents liked the presentation." I felt a pang of anxiety. I really wanted the opportunity to do it all over again next year.

My master plan which had been hatched mid-sud that morning had been to get old photographs of all the students from when they were babies up until the present day and show them on the big screen as they went up to collect their awards. There had been a large array of baby photographs, first school pictures featuring gap-toothed smiles and pictures of older children with bowl haircuts and quirky clothes. There had been lots of "*ooohs*" and "*aaahs*" as they had been viewed and I witnessed a few mammies wiping away stray tears as they watched the flashing images.

Thankfully the board seemed impressed as well as I got a few appreciative comments from them all, except for Mrs High and Mighty who looked positively outraged as she walked past me. I thought I heard her mutter the word "trollop" under her breath but could have been mistaken.

Mr Reid also looked less than amused and I was starting to sweat at the thought of having a job for all of five minutes before being told to get out for molesting the staff in front of an audience.

"A word please," Mr Reid said as he approached Owen and me. "Both of you," he added as I moved forward and Owen stayed still.

Shit, shit, shit. I could handle my own demise as PR guru within the college but didn't think my conscience could cope with carrying the strain of causing Owen to lose his job as well. How the hell was I supposed to know that the twat I handed the camera to was going to catch Owen whispering sweet nothings into my ear?

"This is not easy for me to do," Mr Reid began but before he had the opportunity to utter another syllable I interrupted and began to panic-speak unintelligibly.

"Please, Mr Reid, I know that you specified in your letter that we were to be discreet and we always are. My sister is ill at the moment and I was a little tearful and annoyed about it and Owen was simply comforting me. He is an excellent teacher and this is just a misunderstanding that is not his fault. I'll resign even though I really would have enjoyed the challenge and genuinely like working here. I'm so sorry."

Mr Reid was looking at me with a peculiar glint in his eye. "If I can get a word in edgeways I was just about to congratulate the two of you on a good day's work. I have had parents coming up to me all afternoon and telling me what a pleasure it has been to have put their young people through college with us. I was disappointed naturally that a stunningly ingenious idea was somewhat disrupted by a show of unprofessional behaviour but I am willing to overlook it this once. The press have agreed to do a large advertising campaign for us at a discounted price. Apparently someone suggested that the student football team display the name of the local newspaper group on the front of their football jerseys —"

"That was me," I answered excitedly before quickly closing my mouth again as Owen elbowed me and Mr Reid looked sternly at me.

"Sorry," I whispered before gesturing at him to continue.

"Do not mess with me again or I promise that both of you will be out of a job. I do not want our students influenced by such behaviour."

"It will not happen again," Owen said. "I am very sorry if we let you down but can assure you that our first priority whilst on the campus grounds is our jobs."

"Yes," Mr Reid said, sounding decidedly unconvinced. "Tell me, Owen, how do you show comfort by groping someone on the bottom?"

We hadn't been planning to stay too late at the festivities afterwards but as a direct result of being lectured and humiliated we both decided that there was nothing else for it but to go to the nearest pub and get roaring drunk and erase the embarrassment from our memories. That would possibly have been an easier task if everyone else hadn't decided to follow us and people didn't keep making smart unwanted comments.

"That wash a fabulush performance today, folks," Mandy slurred as we tried to have a private conversation together in a snug near the back of the bar.

We were in the middle of making arrangements about getting everyone together the following day. (It is surprising how much more endearing demon teenagers can be when one is under the influence of large quantities of gin.)

"Glad you liked it, Mandy," I said quick as a flash. "We wanted to remind everyone what it's like to be in a relationship. You haven't forgotten, have you?"

Mandy flounced off or did her best to flounce whilst attempting to retain her balance and not fall over.

"That was mean," Owen said, looking reproachfully at me.

"I'm only giving as good as I get," I countered. "If you don't give that one an answer she'll only make one up anyway so I might as well head her off at the pass. Feckin' nosy cow! It would suit her better if she went and got a life of her own instead of rooting into everyone else's."

"I don't think that private is the right word to use, dear," Owen said. "We were caught live on camera snogging today so accusing Mandy of prying into our personal lives is a bit unfair, don't you think?"

"Hmmm," I responded. (I was determined not to agree with him on this one and so was Ruby who was doing her maternal 'if you say one word about Frankie I will beat you about the head' act and had just sent Mandy scuttling to the ladies' at high speed.)

"Let's go home," I said eventually. I was tired and drunk and wanted hugs from my sister who was probably thinking that I was well and truly ripping the arse out of her good nature at this stage. Besides, I was dying to hear what she had to say about my idea of her staying on in Ireland. (I was full of good ideas. I would be a headhunted renowned PR genius in no time.)

"What's the craic?" I said as I fell over the potted plant at my front door and landed at Ella's feet as she came down the stairs.

"Good night?" she asked unnecessarily given the fact that I was grinning like an eejit and falling asleep on the floor. "Come on," she said as she manhandled me into the living room and attempted to remove my jacket. (I am a very awkward and stubborn drunk who could sleep on a clothesline and deeply resents being poked and prodded.)

I awoke the following morning feeling as if I had been

tap-danced upon by an elephant. My mouth was as dry as the Sahara desert and the kitchen might as well have been about forty miles away as getting there felt like an insurmountable task because my legs didn't seem to be working.

I was trying very hard to remember how I got to bed and into my pyjamas but my memory had completely evaded me. I could only surmise that Ella must have done it. I lay with one eye opened and one eye closed and tried to remember what she was talking about the night before but had no recollection. (This was why I didn't usually get pissed and why the last time I did I promised myself that it would never happen again.)

Had she told me that she was staying or did I dream that in my drunken stupor? If I asked her about it she was sure to bite my head off and hit me with her shoe for not listening to her and being a drunken scut.

I hoped that Nebby Peg didn't get wind of my antics or she would be round again shouting her mouth off and lecturing me about my responsibilities. The very thought of the woman made me cross and forced me to sit up quickly and jerk my neck. Sweet Jesus, I thought my head was going to fall off! (Note to self: next time I made a promise to stay away from copious amounts of gin I was to soundly take my own advice.)

"Hello, Mum! I missed you yesterday," Carly said as she bounded onto my bed and flung herself at me.

"I missed you too, darling," I croaked, trying not to sound like I was going to die anytime soon.

"We're going to have a lovely day, Mum," she said confidently. "I'm after talking to Owen and he says that he's got a big surprise for us today. He's coming round for breakfast and he's bringing his lovely daughter with him. He says that her name means Angel and that it's because she is one."

He must still be drunk.

"And, Mum?"

"Yes, pet."

"Granny Celia phoned as well and she says that she's coming for breakfast too. She says that it's probably the only way that she's ever going to get to meet the invisible man."

Chapter 22

Angelica was being as charming and sweet as the flowers of May and acting as if butter wouldn't melt in her mouth. I felt ill. Hammy and Ella thought that she was a very polite girl, Ben and Carly were delighted with her especially as she was (pretending to) take a very keen interest in them and their football and Disney Princesses and Owen kept looking at me and smiling. The only person who seemed to have any reservations was my mother. God bless her and her magical sixth sense for sniffing out trouble.

"She's too sweet to be wholesome," was her comment after being in Angelica's company for all of five minutes. "She'd make a good actress, I'll give her that. Most actresses, however, remember that their eyes give it away but obviously nobody has told her that. She's a manipulative-looking little madam and I don't envy you trying to work with her."

I felt obliged to stand up for Angelica even though she annoyed my happiness and made me want to squeal but I always disagreed with my mother so why break the habit of a lifetime?

"She's had it really tough, Mammy, so if she's defensive and hard to deal with it's because she's been badly hurt in the past. I don't know how I would have coped without my mother or how I would feel knowing that she had deliberately left me."

"Oh, I don't know about that," my mother answered in a huffy tone. "You'd have been short of a sparring partner that's for sure but you might have coped all right."

My head was starting to thump again and an argument with Mammy was not what the doctor ordered so I bit my tongue (so hard I nearly drew blood) and decided not to retaliate.

Carly bounded into the room with her curls flying and showed me a DVD of *Cinderella* which Angelica had agreed to watch with her.

"Angelica is lovely, Mum. She's like my big sister," she said as she ran away again clutching the box tightly.

Owen overheard her comment as he passed the room and smiled indulgently. I hated when he did that. He looked every inch the besotted father who was too overwhelmed by his little girl to notice that she had turned into a teenage version of a screen star diva who rants and raves until she gets her own way.

My mother was not oblivious to my fidgeting and gave me a knowing look. I hated that too. (Drink made me highly intolerant, I discovered.)

I went to walk out of the room but was accosted by Mammy before I had the chance to turn the doorknob.

"So have you found out anything yet?"

"Found out anything about what?" I asked in confusion. I wasn't in the mood for riddles or mind games.

"Your sister," Mammy said in the tone of voice that might be reserved for a particularly stupid child.

"Why don't you ask her?" I said in agitation.

"Because she won't give me a straight answer. How did I manage to raise daughters who treat me with such disregard? I didn't float up the river in a bubble, y'know. I'm intelligent enough to know that my Ella is thin and peaked and has a lot on her mind. She didn't just come home to see her family. It's a cry for help and I would only be too delighted to help if someone would confide in me and tell me what the hell is wrong."

"It's up to her to do that, Mammy. It's not my problem to discuss. I'm helping her all I can so just be content to know that she's being well looked after."

"Well looked after?" she shrieked. "If your appearance today is anything to go by then I pity her!"

"Everything okay?" Daddy asked, looking longingly at the door. He was obviously wishing that he had a dog to walk who could act as a decoy and get him away from all the madness.

"Does it look okay, George?" Mammy asked acerbically. "What sort of a family do we have who can't talk and discuss their problems?"

Daddy looked as if he would be a lot happier if nobody discussed anything and was absolutely delighted to see Owen, Ben and Hammy coming into the room talking about the football results.

"George, we'd like your opinion on something."

"Just name it," he said, practically running out and away from Mammy and her penetrating gaze.

"Angelica's not a bad girl," Ella said as she came in to see me. "I don't know what you were so worried about, Frankie."

"She has every right to be worried and suspicious," Mammy snapped. "That little imp will take Frankie for a ride."

"Oh stop it, Mother," Ella sighed. "You're not always right, you know."

"Call it a mother's intuition, Ella," Mammy said, leaning towards her and wagging her finger. "You don't know anything about that yet but you will one day if you ever decide to have children and stop dieting and letting your career take over your life!"

There was a deathly silence before Ella stalked out of the room. I could see that she was hurt to the bone but trying not to let it show.

"Your intuition is just feckin' marvellous, Mother,"
I said as I went after my sister in the hope that she was
not standing on the roof and threatening to jump.

This day could only get better. Surely.

Chapter 23

Ella was inconsolable when I eventually coaxed her out of the bathroom. (I was contemplating hacking the lock off the door with the nearest sharp object as I was getting sick of kneeling down and talking through keyholes.)

"If my own mother thinks that I'm a career-driven, diet-obsessed freak then that must be everyone's opinion of me. Bloody Hammy's mother keeps on making comments as well about when she's going to hear the pitter-patter of tiny feet and I want to jump on her every time she mentions it."

"Ella, would it not be better to just come clean and tell them all that you're having problems? At least that would stop all the questions and you'd not be driving yourself up the wall thinking that people are talking about you."

"And what?" she said bitterly. "Have them all pity me instead and say 'Ach, look, there's poor Ella. Can't have babies. It'll only be a matter of time before her husband leaves her.'"

As the tears streamed down her face I was at a loss to know what to do. I could go downstairs and attack my mother for being highly insensitive and seek out Hammy and tell him to forget about the football for five minutes in order to convince his wife that he loved her dearly and was not about to run away. But would it do any good?

"My bloody period came this morning," Ella said miserably. "I go through this every month. I hope and pray that something has happened and analyse every tweak or cramp that I have and pray fervently that it's not a sign that I'm going to bleed but I always do. I borrowed some tampons from your cabinet. You've got quite a stash in there."

"Have I?" I asked absent-mindedly.

"Organised as ever, Frankie," she said, wiping her nose with her sleeve.

We were both sitting on the landing when I heard a raised voice coming from Carly's room. I shot down the hall and stood against the wall. I longed to actually see what was going on but as the door was only slightly ajar I had to make do with simply listening.

"Don't say that about my daddy!" I could hear Carly saying, sounding like she was going to cry.

"He won't ever come back, you know," came Angelica's voice, "and I'm just telling you for your own good so that you won't be disappointed when it doesn't happen."

"But Mum says that he'll come back when he's ready and that he'd be really proud of me if he could see me now."

"Yeah, it's easy to be proud when you're on the other side of the world and not giving a shit about your children because you've left someone else to look after them."

"You said shit," Carly said accusingly.

"And what are you going to do?" Angelica asked in a menacing tone that made me want to do an Indian war dance in annoyance.

I went to storm in and rescue my baby but Ella appeared at my elbow, grabbed me and pulled me away from the door.

"If there's one thing I've learnt in life it's that if you stay quiet you'll hear more," she said quietly. "Besides, she'll only accuse you of eavesdropping and then Owen will be mad with you. She's obviously a very disturbed youngster to be coming out with talk like that."

"I am so sick of everybody doling out this crap about poor wee Angelica being a lost soul and needing understanding because she's confused. It's all just an excuse to act like a spoilt little bitch with a ginormous chip on her shoulder and I am fed up with it!"

I moved to go back to Carly's bedroom but Ella stood in front of me. "Think about what you're doing, Frankie. Tread very carefully. If you go in there and start fighting Carly's battles for her Angelica is only going to resent you."

"Harrumph!" I snorted before marching down the hall and into my daughter's bedroom, leaving Ella throwing her hands in the air and shaking her head.

"Everything all right, girls?" I asked, looking pointedly at Angelica and hoping that my look conveyed that I would personally strangle her if she upset Carly with any more of her unnecessary comments.

"We're fine, thanks," Angelica answered without looking at me whilst Carly studiously ignored me and looked intently at the ragdoll she was grasping tightly.

"That's good," I said in a clipped tone. "I'll be here if you need me, Carly," I added for good measure hoping that she'd squeal the place down and tell me to drag the attitude-ridden teenager out of her room but she didn't. Instead she just reassured me like she always did.

"I know you're here, Mum. You always are."

"That went very well, didn't it?" Owen said as we sat on the garden seat near the porch and got a moment's peace together before he had to leave.

I resisted the urge to check his temperature to ascertain whether or not he was delirious. I was getting tired of being the only one not wearing rose-tinted feckin' glasses.

"Great," I said in a non-committal tone.

"Is everything all right, Frankie?" he asked in concern as he whirled me round to look in my face.

"I'm just tired."

What I really wanted to say was that I wished this relationship didn't have so much damn baggage involved in it. Our bloody ex-spouses had a lot to answer for and if I ever got hold of his ex-wife I would string her up with my bare hands for leaving Angelica with such a monumentally bad outlook on life which I was hoping that she wouldn't transfer to my children. My mother's words about children learning from example were ringing in my ears and I was hoping and trusting in God that it would be mine that they'd follow and not the said grumpy teenager's.

Ruby pulled up outside the house at that point and momentarily distracted me from my morbid train of thought. Until she hopped out of the car, rushed over and waved one of the local newspapers in my face.

"I take it that you haven't seen this," she said as she pointed to a picture and an article entitled "*Sextra Curricular Activities at Local College*".

"Oh – my – God," I breathed as I looked at the picture and registered that it was an image of Owen and me clenched in an embrace.

Owen grabbed the paper as Ruby stormed off again in her car purposefully. He looked utterly shellshocked.

The photographer must have taken it from a video still and I was amazed at how clear the picture was. It bloody would be, I thought, close to tears. Bad publicity would lead to job losses. Job losses would lead to me being broke and unable to pay my mortgage and that would lead to a possible decampment back to Mammy's or setting up home in a cardboard box.

The cardboard-box idea seemed more appealing after Mammy spotted us from the window and, sensing drama, waylaid us in the hall as we went in. She grabbed the newspaper from me, peered at the photograph and started to breathe in heavy spasms.

"Mammy, are you all right?" Ella had come out of the living room to find Mammy hyperventilating in the hall. "Would you like to put your head between your knees?"

"Celia, stop that!" said Daddy before he too caught a glimpse of the headline and the photograph, turned forty shades of purple and in a strangled voice announced, "We are going home. *Now*, Celia!"

The children, who had been attracted downstairs by the commotion, were wondering what on earth was going on. I managed to wrestle the paper from Owen before Ben and Carly saw it but unfortunately Angelica's beady eyes were too quick for me.

"What a lovely portrait of the two of you!" she

said, her voice dripping with sarcasm. "I must keep it for Nana. She'll be so proud. Funny there were never any photographs like that of my dad before now."

"Angelica, that's enough," Owen said firmly.

"I don't think that you're in any position to tell me what to do, Daddy, and as for *you*," she said, fixing me with the filthiest look that I'd ever been on the receiving end of, "thanks for making me a laughing stock. My Auntie Brenda was right. You're just out to destroy Daddy because you hate all men because your husband left you! I'm not surprised – you're nothing but a cheap tart and I know that you don't like me. Well, the feeling's mutual," and with that she climbed into the passenger seat of the car, nearly unhinging the door in the process.

Owen said nothing which further fuelled my burgeoning temper.

"Are you just going to let her get away with that?" I demanded. "It seems to me that there is a severe lack of discipline in your house. I certainly wouldn't let my children speak to anyone like that, let alone somebody I'm meant to love. But I suppose when she has grown up thinking that she can get away with blue bloody murder because of her unfortunate circumstances then it's to be expected."

Owen was still silent but flushed with apparent anger. "Don't talk about things you know nothing about, Frankie."

"Excuse me but I'm a single parent too, y'know.

My life hasn't been a bed of roses either. You're not the only one to have suffered through a bad relationship. This whole mess is your fault. If you hadn't suggested bringing your daughter here when we were with the students yesterday I wouldn't have felt the need to cover up my apprehension and dismay by hiding my face and cuddling into you. Your daughter decided a long time ago that she doesn't like me, will never like me and will never give me a chance."

"Okay, so let me get this straight." Owen said, looking at me with steely eyes. "I say something you don't agree with, so instead of being open and honest about it you cover it up by putting your head in my chest which made us look like a couple of immature idiots with no self-control on video and now that the picture is gracing the front page of the newspaper it's my fault. But then I forgot that you were infallible and didn't make mistakes, Frankie, and that you also have a penchant for looking for someone else to blame when things go wrong."

"I didn't want to hurt you even though the idea of having Angelica here filled me with dread," I said desperately. "Can't you see that she's been conditioned to think that way? You heard her. Her head has been filled full of codswallop by that aunt of hers and she's willing to believe every single word of it. This goes much deeper than the front page of a newspaper and you know it, Owen."

I could see Angelica looking most pleased that her

father and I were having a hissy-fit fight on the doorstep and that everyone seemed to be angry with me. She looked like the cat who got the cream.

"You really are something else," he shouted. "You're being totally irrational and unreasonable, Frankie."

"Well, if that's how you feel then I think you'd better leave," I told him as he stalked in the direction of his car.

"No problem," he snapped before driving away in a cloud of dust.

"Out," I roared pointing at the door and hopping like a mad woman. I was going to kill my mother if she didn't stop talking.

"What did I ever do to deserve this type of disgrace being heaped on my head?" she wailed as Daddy made soothing noises and patted her on the hand. "I'll not be able to show my face in public for months. All the neighbours will be talking," she added darkly furrowing her eyebrows. "They'll be saying that my daughter is no better than a scarlet woman, putting herself on a plate like that and her the mother of two innocent children who will probably be bullied now because their mammy was photographed in a compromising position. Flamin' Peggy Colton will have a field day with this. You better watch that she doesn't send social services round here or that Tony doesn't get in touch with you demanding full custody."

Ella recognised the signs of my imminent spontaneous combustion through bad temper and firmly helped Mammy out into the hall. "Mammy, I know that you're only trying to help but could you please do us all a favour and close your mouth and go home."

After my mother had been unceremoniously booted out of my home I took a long look at the newspaper article and read the name of the vindictive shit of an excuse for a journalist who put it together. I was going to go to the newspaper office and knee him so hard in the groin that his balls were going to bounce off the roof of his mouth. How dare he treat me in this manner especially when I was hungover, tired and agitated and not in a mood to be trifled with? I was also extremely worried about the children. I had images of Ben going back to school after the summer holidays and being taunted by his friends about his frisky mother. Little girls could be much more vicious, however, and I was petrified about what poor little Carly might have to listen to. I voiced my concerns to Ella who thought I was blowing everything out of proportion.

"Frankie. I know that you're worried and justifiably so but it'll all blow over. Besides, it's the summer holidays. Everyone will have forgotten about it by the time the students come back to college and the wee ones go back to school. Anyone who knows you will know you wouldn't deliberately put yourself in that position and that it's been taken out of context. Actually, if you have a sense of humour and read it as an outsider might, then you can see the funny side of it. Stop being such a drama queen."

"I am not a bloody drama queen," I snapped defensively. "And can I just say that if you're being flippant in a bid to cheer me up you're doing a very bad job. I am being perfectly calm and rational about this and I am not completely devoid of a sense of humour but fail to see the funny side of being paraded in the press as the local bike when it was just a quick hug from my boyfriend or ex-boyfriend as the case may be now. It's not as if I was having an illicit affair or that I'm a student getting off with a teacher or anything."

"You see. There you go," Ella said in an annoying sing-song voice. "It could be worse."

I felt nauseous and light-headed as I sat and contemplated my life. I felt like hunting for my passport and emigrating to another country where no one knew of my scandalous past and I wouldn't get pointed at in the street for being the one who was caught on camera doing something that she shouldn't. (Obviously I would not be moving to America as I would only have to leave again in disgrace after murdering the children's father for being a complete and utter knobhead and the root of all evil.)

183

Just as I was sinking into the complete depths of despair and feeling truly sorry for myself, Ruby arrived back.

"Bastards!" she announced as she walked through the door.

"Hello to you too," Ella said.

I was feeling sorry for Ella. She came home for some peace and quiet and instead she had entered the Irish equivalent of the Bermuda Triangle where life got crazier by the second. The only consolation I had was that perhaps it was taking her mind off her own problems.

"Who's a bastard?" I asked Ruby as she stomped around the kitchen like a woman possessed.

"Mandy and her deranged brother who is now missing a testicle," she answered.

"Okay," my head was starting to thump again. "Start at the beginning, please."

"Well, as it turns out, Mandy's brother is a photographer for one of the local papers and was in attendance at the ceremony with other members of the press."

The penny dropped.

"So you're telling me that Mandy took him back into the marquee after we had all gone and rewound the tape to allow him to get a still photograph of Owen and me," I repeated incredulously. "The vindictive cow!"

"I think they thought it would be funny."

"Funny?" I fumed. "I'll show her funny when I wring her feckin' neck on Monday. Risking someone losing their job, putting a teacher's career in jeopardy and causing a perfectly happy couple to fall out and have a screaming match in front of a smug teenager is not amusing."

"I wouldn't worry," Ruby said. "It's all been taken care of. Mandy's darling brother won't be taking photographs like that in future."

"What did you do to him?" I asked in alarm. Ruby wasn't aware of her own strength.

"Let's just say that there is going to be a full and frank apology from the paper next week stating that it was a silly prank that went wrong and caused distress to many people. The advertising campaign is now going to be done for free. I had a word in the editor's ear and told him that unless he wanted to be sued for libel damages and using photographs out of context that he'd better do something to compensate. Hopefully that should put the smile back on Mr Reid's face for a while."

Ella looked at Ruby in admiration. "You're not one for hanging around, Rubes, are you?" she said laughingly.

"Definitely not," Ruby stated. "Why waste time fretting about things when you can scare the shite out of somebody and get them to rectify it for you?"

"Can you go and talk to Owen for me now and

tell him that I'm sorry for shouting at him and saying that it was all his fault when it wasn't?" I whined.

"No can do," Ruby said. "You'll have to do that yourself. Look on the bright side though. Think of all the making up that you can engage in once the apologies are all over and done with."

"He'll not want to touch me with a forty-foot barge pole after how I spoke to him today and Angelica has probably got him well and truly warped into her way of thinking by now."

"Don't worry about Angelica –" Ella began.

"If you say the words 'that poor child is confused'," I said, menacingly interrupting my sister's flow, "I swear to Jesus I will throttle you."

"Well, actually, smart arse, I wasn't going to say that. I was going to point out that it's all an attention thing. It's a very simple theory. Angelica wants attention and she will get it by any means possible even through bad behaviour because obviously adults react to that. If you learn to ignore her and she sees that she is no longer the centre of the universe and that life will continue as normal even if she is acting like a spoilt brat then she will tire of her games. She can't keep it up forever."

I opened my mouth and closed it again quickly as for once I couldn't argue with her.

"I did a bit of psychology in my nursing degree, sis, and find that it comes in handy in real life as well."

"Well, if you're so great at diagnosing problems then tell me why I'm feeling so rough. I've had hangovers before but this one is unbelievable. I feel like I'm going to die."

"You're stressed out," Ruby said. "You don't need a nursing degree to figure that one out. I'll baby-sit for you while you go and see Owen and sort all this out and I bet that you'll not feel half as bad when you come back."

"Why should I be the first one to make the move?" I asked stubbornly. (I was awkward when sober as well as when drunk.)

"Because you'd like to sleep tonight and because it's the right thing to do," Ella told me. "It wasn't Owen's fault and I'm sure that he feels as badly as you do about everything."

As it turned out I went to bed alone that night still feeling wretched. I'd called over to see Owen but the house was locked and no one was there. His phone was switched off and he hadn't contacted me at all. I had a terrible feeling of foreboding that I had definitely burnt my bridges this time.

Chapter 24

It was Monday morning and I felt sick as I drove through the gates of the college. I had butterflies doing somersaults around my stomach and my chest felt tight and restricted.

I hadn't seen or spoken to Owen since we had our argument. I left two messages on his phone and drove past his house about twenty times like a stalker but all to no avail. Obviously he didn't want to be with me and instead of being a man about it and telling me to my face he was spelling it out to me through his actions and expecting me to take the hint. Wimp!

I parked in the staff car park and noticed that Owen's car was missing. Mr Reid's car, however, was very noticeably there.

Well, this is just charming, I thought. Not only does bloody Owen get me in trouble but now he leaves me to deal with it all by myself. (Weird female psychology: had gone back to thinking that the whole situation was Owen's fault as it was easier not to like him if I persuaded myself that he had done something wrong.)

As I walked into reception I felt a fire in my blood that hadn't been there before and decided that I might as well be hung for a sheep as a lamb.

"Good morning, Mandy," I snapped. "Did you have a nice weekend?" Not waiting for an answer, I continued, sensing that Mandy was wishing that she had a panic button under her desk as I was starting to move towards her. "I didn't have a good weekend at all. In fact I had a positively rotten horrible weekend and it was all due to the actions of someone who thought that they were being funny and smart by exploiting a situation which had nothing to do with them."

"Look, Frankie, I'm really sorry about −" Mandy stammered nervously.

"Shut your stupid great big flapping mouth and listen to me!" I said, peering right down at her and feeling very superior and in control because I was standing and she was not. "You will never as long as you live talk about anybody within these offices ever again. You will make up no more lies about them nor exaggerate stories that you have heard to make them more interesting for your prospective listeners and you will most certainly never let my name pass your lips unless you want to talk about something which is public-relations related. Do I make myself very clear?"

"You do," Mandy answered, looking like she might jump out of the window with fright. "I'm sorry about what happened. My brother is new at his job and he needed to find something that no one else had so I was just trying to help him."

"Oh I see. Is that what you call it when you sensationalise a perfectly innocent situation that was accidentally caught on camera and make it public viewing?" (I shouldn't have worded it like that, should I?)

"He's very sorry. He's coming over this morning to apologise to you in person."

I was gratified that Mandy wasn't arguing with me and trying to justify her actions, as I expected that she might, so I felt marginally better when I finally got to my office where Ruby was waiting for me.

"Good girl yourself," she said, patting me on the back when I told her what I had just said. "I must be starting to rub off on you. How are you? You don't look well."

"Is that your polite way of telling me that I look like shit?"

"Okay. We've been friends for long enough for you not to thump me, I suppose, so yes in answer to your question. You do look completely crap, Frankie. You're pale and your skin seems to have broken out and your hair is a complete mess. If you were hoping to win back Owen's affections I'd suggest that you put on a bit of make-up, go and get some dry shampoo for your hair and plaster a smile on your face and do something about those dark lines underneath your eyes."

"Yes. Thank you, Ruby. There's nothing like kicking me once I'm down," I said before my voice broke and I ran and locked myself in the bathroom. (Locking oneself in the bathroom when the going gets tough runs in my family.)

Ruby was now doing my usual job and hunkering down at the door and whispering to me to please come out.

"Frankie, I'm sorry if I was a bit harsh but to tell you the truth you haven't looked well all week. Have you been feeling sick?"

"I suppose I have a bit," I answered sniffing. "It's probably due to all the stress I've been under between work and Ella's problems and going through things with the children. I'll be fine. I'll just have to pick myself up and go on."

"That's my girl," Ruby whispered in an encouraging tone.

When I came out I felt like a prize twat. If I had looked rough before, my appearance certainly hadn't improved with the addition of watery, puffy eyes and bright red cheeks.

"Owen has taken a week's leave," Ruby said gently before I started to cry again.

"I've really blown it, haven't I?" I said in a quivering voice. "It wouldn't be so bad if I knew what was going on. He's being so cruel leaving me in limbo like this. I'd never do that to him."

"Of course you would," Ruby said as she put one finger up to silence my protests. "You'd do exactly the same if you thought that it would teach him a lesson."

"What are you trying to say?" I asked, getting angry. "Are you insinuating that all of this is my fault because I didn't treat him right?"

"God, but you're touchy!" Ruby said in an exasperated tone.

"Obviously another one of my many faults then," I said as I stomped back to the car park and sat in my car.

After crying for a further ten minutes, thumping the steering wheel like a lunatic and grinding my teeth in the rear-view mirror I decided that I was not in the mood to be at work and took decisive action.

"Mr Reid, I'm not feeling well. Women's problems," I said ominously as I pointed to my nether regions and pulled a face.

"Right." He studied the ceiling intently taking great care not to let his eyes wander to where I had just pointed. (Men of a certain age always react like that – thank God.)

"Perhaps you should take the rest of the day off then," he said. "I'll need you here tomorrow though. I had the editor from *The Daily Reporter* on the phone and he wants to meet you to discuss the team logo for the new football shirts. He also assures me that the article which I am not supposed to mention to you was a mistake and that an apology is being issued this week. This apology could be what saves your jobs. I will have to review this situation with the Board and see what steps can be implemented to provide damage control. The college wants to distance itself from such behaviour. I trust that we will have no further mention of this unfortunate incident, Ms Colton."

"What incident would that be?" I asked, feigning mock innocence through my pain. "Oh and by the way, Mr Reid, could you call me Frankie from now on?"

"If you so wish," he said looking at me quizzically. "Of you go then, Frankie, and remember I want you back here looking bright-eyed and bushy-tailed tomorrow."

"I will be," I assured him before I left. I had been through worse than this in the past and I refused to lie down under this latest catastrophe.

I was officially off men for life.

Chapter 25

"Why are you not working, Mum?" Carly asked wide-eyed when she saw me.

"I decided that I would take the day off and spend it with you," I answered her, throwing my mobile out of my bag, determined that I would not spend another second looking at it and willing it to display Owen's name with a phone call or a text message.

"Goody, goody!" she shouted. "Ben, Mum's here and she's going to take us out for the day!"

I heard a door opening upstairs and could hear Ella mumbling.

"Frankie, what on earth is wrong with you?" she asked me as she came down the stairs.

"Nothing," I growled.

"Yeah, right," she said incredulously. "Look at you. You're a mess."

"So everybody keeps telling me." I grabbed my children and propelled them towards the car without another word.

I was doing my best to be upbeat and cheerful as I walked barefoot along the County Down beach. It was a glorious day. The sun was beating down and the children were in their element as they walked along eating candyfloss and watching the small figures that were dotted along the ocean trying to keep their balance on surfboards and paddle boats.

I looked longingly at all the couples I saw and wished with all my heart that Owen was with me making suggestive comments about doing things in the sand dunes and challenging me to a race on the Dodgems.

"Are you all right, Mum?" Ben asked, looking intently at my face.

"I'm fine, darling," I lied as I put my arms around him.

He didn't look convinced. I had to remind myself that he was nine going on ten and not as easy to fob off as six-year-old Carly who would believe anything as long as I smiled at her.

"Why has Owen not been around?" he asked, suddenly catching me off guard.

"He's been busy, love."

"He's never been that busy before that he hasn't

had time to call and see us." Ben looked at me through narrowed eyes. "You shouted at him the last time you saw him and he hasn't come back."

The accusation hung in the air between us. My son thought that this was all my fault and that old Nebby Peg had been right all along. All I had to do was open my mouth and suddenly people that he cared about started running away. Great! I could now add Ben to the list of people that I had managed to alienate myself from. I was going to book myself in and get my jaw wired at the earliest convenience.

I reached for my phone to touch base with Ruby as I always did in a crisis and then I remembered that I had no phone with me and that even if I did ring she probably wouldn't answer me anyway. I had walked away from her in a huff this morning and then left without so much as a by-your-leave even though she was constantly defending me and helping me in any way she could. If I'd had a wooden cross to hand I think I'd probably have gone and hung myself on it.

"I'm hungry, Mum," Carly said as she joined Ben and me.

"How can you be hungry when you've spent all day eating junk?" I asked.

"I'd like sausages and chips," she said matter of factly.

"I'd like a burger," Ben said, "with burger relish and cheese."

I could smell the chip shop before I saw it and my stomach gave a little lurch. As we entered the establishment and I looked at the vast array of greasy food in front of me I could feel my mouth fill with saliva and began to swallow very quickly before running outside and being sick over the shoes of a very startled elderly gentleman.

"Yuck!" Ben said as he peeped out at the mess from between his fingers which were covering his face.

"Mum!" screamed Carly as she saw me stagger unsteadily against a nearby wall.

"Do you want an ambulance, love?" a passing woman asked in concern. "Quickly, somebody call an ambulance. She looks like she's going to faint."

I managed to compose myself enough to tell her that I was okay.

"You need to watch yourself, pet. You shouldn't be exerting yourself more than you have to. It's probably the heat as well and maybe you should get your blood pressure checked."

I wanted to make a sarcastic comment and enquire where her stethoscope and white coat were but refrained from doing so in light of the fact that I'd realised what an evil tongue I could have.

"Thanks a lot," I said weakly before turning to the gentleman whose shoes I had pebble-dashed.

"I can't apologise enough," I said, hardly daring to meet his eye. I was cringing with embarrassment and thanking God and St Jude that I was in Newcastle where nobody knew me.

As the man smiled kindly at me without looking too disgusted and turned to walk away I heard a familiar voice.

"Just look what the cat dragged in."

"Granny Peggy!" Carly shouted as she saw her aging great-grandmother approach with a group of other pensioners.

(Great. Just bloody great.)

I had come to the conclusion that the planets must have united to give me the worst and most pessimistic horoscope reading for that particular day. I couldn't believe that the elderly gentleman whose foot attire I had used as a sick bag was on an Ulsterbus Tour trip with Peggy.

"This is my grandson's ex-wife," she announced loudly to her companions. "You know, the one that I was telling you about," she added in a stage whisper.

"And these must be your grandchildren," the lady with the purple rinse to her right said. "Poor little mites." She looked at Ben and Carly and then stared at her companions, shook her head and fixed me with a disparaging look.

God alone knows what stories Peggy had been concocting about me. From the way her friends were looking at me I was obviously an adulteress child-abuser who had a sideline in prostitution at the weekends.

"Mum was sick over someone's shoes," Carly announced, curling her nose up.

"Was she, pet?" Nebby Peg said, arching an eyebrow at me.

"She hasn't been well all weekend but I heard Auntie Ella saying that it's because she's a gin soak and that she'll have to behave herself when she's out in future."

I loved my daughter dearly but could have cheerfully belted her in the mouth with my flip-flop for being so loose with her tongue. I was also going to kill Ella.

Mrs Purple Rinse looked like she was sucking a lemon as she pursed her lips and surveyed me as one might look at a particularly slimy insect.

"You see," Nebby Peg said knowledgeably with a vicious glint in her eye, "I told you how bad she was and you all thought that I was exaggerating. My poor Tony had a lucky escape, y'know."

"Oh for God's sake," I began, all thoughts of minding my tongue going swiftly out the window. "It's the children and I who've had a lucky escape. Just look at them, Peggy. They are your precious grandson's flesh and blood and where is he? He's on the other side of the world and let me tell you something in front of all your high and mighty cronies. I would climb mountains and swim seas to see my children. I wouldn't let anything stand in the way of me and them but instead you and your grandson would rather devote all your energies into conducting a hate campaign against me. Well, if that's how you want to spend your twilight years then go ahead. I hope you talk yourself into an early grave and leave us in peace. And if the rest of you holier-than-thou folks lead such perfect lives that you are in a position to judge other people then it's not on a pensioner's day out you should be – it's in Rome receiving your sainthoods!"

Some of the crowd had the good grace to look embarrassed but Nebby Peg stood with her nose in the air and stared me out like I knew she would.

"We'll be late for the bus if we don't hurry up," she said casually. "See you later, children. Look out for one another now, won't you?"

My words, as usual, had fallen on deaf ears but I was past caring and starting to feel ill again.

"Mum was sick in the street," was the way that Carly greeted Ella when we arrived home.

(I was going to have to have a serious discussion with her about not telling all and sundry about her mother's misdemeanours. I had a disturbing image in my head of it being the first thing that she said to her new teacher when she went back to school.)

"What?" Ella was looking momentarily stricken. "Children, go to your rooms, please."

"Ella, I am in no mood for the third degree. I just

don't feel well and I'm stressed out, okay? It's no big deal so don't be making one out of it."

"Frankie, stop being such a martyr, please," Ella sighed. "Admit that you need some help. I think you need to see a doctor. There's more to this than meets the eye."

The phone rang and I ignored it. It wouldn't be for me anyway. I noticed that no one was mentioning that Owen had left any messages for me.

"I do not need to do any such thing," I said. "I'm always like this before I get my period."

Except I hadn't had my period, had I?

I had wondered what Ella had meant when she said that I had an impressive supply of tampons. I always bought them with my shopping every month but I hadn't even noticed that I had double the amount this time. My queasy stomach which I had been putting down to nerves and my bad temper which alarmingly everyone just thought was me being me were obviously down to hormones and the worst thing about it all was right in front of me.

As I stared at Ella and saw the worry lines that had formed around her eyes and looked at her frame which used to be buxom but was now tiny, I wondered how on earth I was going to tell her.

She had come home to me to get away from her problems and I had promised that I would help her. I had even persuaded her to extend her stay so that we could find a solution. So how on earth was I going to tell her that I was pregnant, that I wasn't sure I wanted to be pregnant and that the baby's prospective father would probably leave the country when I told him, if I told him?

Chapter 26

Any other morning the children would have been having a lie-in (if you considered nine o'clock a long nap), Ella and Hammy would be in their room and I would have been free to conduct my business in private. There was, however, a disorderly queue forming outside the bathroom door.

Ben and Carly were fighting like cat and dog and calling each other names.

"You're a big stupid tube!"

"Not nearly as stupid as you are. You're a silly girl and I'm going to pee first."

"I was here before you, Ben, so buzz off!"

"It takes you too long. At least I don't have to sit down to go to the toilet."

"Muummmeeee, tell him to leave me alone!"

As a result of the noise they were making Hammy

had appeared to see what the commotion was all about and Ella had gone to boil the kettle and make everybody tea. The pregnancy test (bought from the local twenty-four-hour garage at eleven thirty the previous night where I met half the country buying milk) was still sitting in its packaging and I knew that I needed to be in work early.

"Typical. Bloody feckin' typical," I muttered, unsure whether the uneasiness in my stomach was due to nerves, annoyance or morning sickness.

In a sudden fit of inspiration I decided that I would take it with me and do it in work. Lord knows I might actually get more peace and quiet.

When I came downstairs I saw Ella glancing nervously at me before beckoning at me to come out of the room.

"I'm fine," I snapped before she had the chance to open her mouth.

"Fine," she said in a tight voice. "I'm rapidly starting to dislike that word because it's all you ever say and it's a downright lie."

"Who's lying?" I asked.

"You. Constantly."

"I am not," I said as convincingly as one can when one is queasy and feeling decidedly dizzy.

Ella refused to answer me and instead folded her arms, pulled her dressing gown tighter around her and fixed me with a particularly incredulous look.

"Well?"

"Right, good luck," I said as I slipped passed her and opened the door. "I'm away to work. See you all later."

"Frankie, I'm talking to you."

"Pity I can't hear you then!" I sang as I got into my car.

I was worried and my stomach was filled with nervous anticipation but there was one advantage to this unfortunate situation. For the first morning in three days my immediate reaction to wakening up hadn't been to check my phone and register that yet again Owen had forgotten I existed.

When I eventually did the test I was absolutely starving and hopping from one leg to the other as I knew that the best time to do it was in the morning when the sample was at its strongest and nothing has been eaten or drunk. It was no longer morning, however, it was twelve o'feckin' clock and so far I'd had two major arguments, threatened a man with violence and nearly lost my job (again).

When I arrived at work Mr Reid was in a flap as he had been double-booked and wouldn't be there to meet the editor of the paper to discuss the logos on the student football jerseys. So I had to handle it all by myself.

As it turned out the editor in question was a lecherous git who kept wanting to look down my top and was prone to making suggestive comments about what I got up to with other members of staff.

"You can come and work for me any time, darlin'," he drawled with a wink. "I like a good snog at the Christmas do as much as the next man. Our nights out are for staff only so the wife need never know."

"What a lucky woman," I answered sarcastically. "She must lead a charmed existence with you around."

"Oh she does," he assured me with a grin. "And you haven't even seen my charm yet!"

"I'll try not to get too excited about that," I said, feeling bile rise in my throat and for once I was sure that it was nothing to do with my hormones as I looked at his nicotine-stained teeth and greasy hair.

"So where is he then?" he asked abruptly.

"Who?"

"The one you were getting down and dirty with in the video. Are you into that sort of thing? I can recommend a few websites that would cater very nicely for you. They might even give you a slot if you wanted to make the footage a bit more exciting by removing a few clothes. I'd keep the students in it though or maybe get a few of them to join in."

"Rubbbbbeeeee!" I screamed at the top of my voice, making the slimy little creep jump in the air and bang his knee off the table top.

Ruby, along with the rest of the staff on the floor, came running to answer the call as they all wanted to know who had cut my throat.

"What's wrong?" Ruby said breathlessly, looking from my face to his which was now looking terrified.

"Why would there be anything wrong?" he asked in a high-pitched voice.

"It might have something to do with the fact that since you came in here you've done nothing but be rude and obscene," I said. "I could have you for sexual harassment at this stage after what you've just suggested and in the ten minutes that you've spent waggling your extraordinarily long eyebrows at me you haven't once mentioned the bloody football shirts that you are supposedly here to discuss. I believe that you've already met Ruby? She loves testicles, you know, especially when they're fried and salted and served with a garnish."

The man visibly blanched, looked at Ruby whose teeth were bared and made noises about being late for another meeting.

"I'll be asking Mr Reid to phone your superiors to see if this is an acceptable way to conduct business. Oh yes – and what was the name of that website that you were suggesting that I contact? I'm sure that the police would be very interested to know that you'd advocate and encourage a group of minors to go frolicking about on it."

"Look, about the shirts," he said quickly. "I'll get them done for you at a good price in any colour that you want."

"I don't think so," I said with a terse smile. "You won't have time to worry about a set of football shirts. I'd say that you'll be too busy explaining to your wife why you talk about her in such a disrespectful way to other women when you're trying to get your grubby way."

"He did what?" shouted Ruby, starting to shake with uncontrollable rage as the man shielded his genital area from possible attack.

"Take your poxy T-shirts and shove them −" I began before Mr Reid walked in and demanded to know why there was no work being done, why everyone was standing about and why the editor of the local paper looked scared out of his wits. I also had to give an explanation as to how I was promoting the college by scaring the shite out of the local media and telling them to shove free merchandise somewhere it wouldn't fit.

"Frankie, are you constipated?" Ruby enquired as she came into the toilets, banging the door in her wake.

"Why would you think that?" I asked.

"It might have something to do with the fact that you've been in here for half an hour," she said, sounding cross.

Anyone for Seconds?

"I'm sorry I got you in trouble earlier," I said. "I didn't mean to drag you into it. Besides I thought Mr Reid wouldn't have been back for ages."

"Well, you don't think, do you?" she said crossly. "You haven't been thinking straight about anything lately and I'd like to know why. As your closest friend I think I deserve an explanation."

I watched the shocked expression on her face as I handed her the little white stick.

"What the hell −" she began before clapping her hand over her mouth. "Oh Frankie, what are you going to do?"

Chapter 27

Ruby was treating me with kid gloves and when I went to reach for a file that was positioned on the topmost shelf of the filing cabinet she screeched the place down and told me not to be stretching.

"Ruby," I said through my teeth, "please try and be discreet. I don't want anybody knowing about this."

Mandy had just come into the room and I felt my face become devoid of all colour. I didn't know what she had heard and whether or not she was going to spread stories and add bits on to make it exciting. I knew my fears were unfounded, however, when I saw that she had someone with her. Someone rather handsome and solemn looking, actually.

Ruby must have noticed as well as she was straightening her top, smoothing her trousers and wiping the corners of her mouth lest any remnants of the tomato soup she had for lunch be detected.

"Girls, this is my brother Luke," Mandy announced, motioning at her good-looking counterpart.

I glanced at Ruby and noticed that she was looking disgusted and deflated at the same time and had now sat down heavily on my chair.

"It's Frankie, isn't that right?" he asked, shaking my hand. "I missed you yesterday. I called to speak to you in person but then heard that you had already left for the day. I'm so sorry about that photograph. I didn't do it to upset anyone. I just thought that it was a bit of fun."

"We heard that you did it to further your career," Ruby interjected before I had the chance to speak. "And having met your editor, who by the way I wouldn't let your wife within a hundred yards of, I'm not surprised that he found it entertaining. He seems to get off on things like that, the sleazy little prick. He's lucky he left here with his balls intact."

Luke looked as if he wanted to laugh but then arranged his features into a serious expression again.

"Well, firstly, you'll be glad to know that I got fired today after our esteemed editor, who I also think is a prick, came back from his meeting with, and I quote 'the fiery wee blonde thing with the mad friend who would have raped me given half the chance.'"

"Raped?" Ruby said in an aggravated tone of voice. "Well, if that means that I'd have made mincemeat out of him then I guess that must be the right terminology."

"I take it that you must be the mad friend?" Luke said casually. "Although, can I stress that those are not my words?"

"Good job they're not," Ruby said, smiling in spite of herself. "I'm Ruby by the way. I can't have you going about calling me mad, even though it might be true."

"Pleased to meet you," he said, shaking her hand and holding it for a fraction longer than necessary. "Oh and just for your own information, Ruby, if I had a wife I wouldn't let her within a hundred miles of Spencer but as I'm currently single it's not a consideration for me."

I sucked in my cheeks and looked away but as my eyes met Mandy's I saw that she was wearing a similar expression.

"Ahem," I cleared my throat. "Getting back to why you're here, Luke, I hope that I'm still going to get the apology I was promised. That photograph caused me and my family a lot of distress. I believe that my mother has not opened the curtains in her living room since Saturday and that our family pet is the best-walked dog in Swiftstown as my father cannot bear to see my mother in such a distressed state." (The bit about the curtains was true as my mother had phoned me every day to tell me that she couldn't possibly face her neighbours in such circumstances and that I was to wear sunglasses if I was visiting. I exaggerated the dog-walking scene slightly. Daddy just wanted to get out of the house for his own preservation and had told me that he was thinking of becoming an entrepreneur and advertising his dog-walking abilities in the post office.)

"I am very sorry about that," Luke said, looking genuinely contrite. "I will do my best to ensure that you get your apology although given the fact that I got booted out this morning I can't guarantee it."

"Great," I said abruptly. "So I'm going to be left forever more with people thinking that I'm some sort of harlot and quoting websites to me that they think I should Google."

Mandy put her hand on Luke's arm and started to steer him back out through the door. I think she knew that I was capable of turning into a nut-job if I felt I wasn't being taken seriously.

Luke, however, had other ideas and shrugged her off and walked closer to me.

"I promise that I will do my best to rectify this for you, Frankie. I need to rectify it for myself too as I want to be taken seriously in my profession as well. I've already rung several of the other newspapers this morning and they laughed at me and said that they had already seen my work and that it wasn't what they were looking for."

I shrugged dismissively. I didn't see why I should feel sorry for someone who had in one fell swoop managed to ruin the happiest relationship that I'd had in a long time as well as driving my father closer to the nearest mental home because he'd given my mother more ammunition to complain about.

Not to mention that he was entirely responsible for leaving my poor baby fatherless, just like its brother and sister who were having such a hard time dealing with that particular state already. (I conveniently forgot that he had no part to play in the procreation process but I needed someone to blame because obviously none of this was my fault.)

All of a sudden the enormity of the situation hit me. In eleven years' time my unborn child would be coming to me and asking if his/her father left because I pushed him away and I'd have to explain all about how his/her mother was a floozy who allowed herself to be videoed and then photographed in the most undignified of positions at student gatherings.

"Oh Ruby, what have I done?" I wailed before bursting into noisy tears and throwing myself in her arms.

Mandy and Luke stood there observing Ruby cradling me whilst murmuring to me not to worry and promising that everything would be all right.

"Is your boyfriend around?" Luke asked. "I'd like to speak to him as well."

(Obviously the words "red rag" and "bull" didn't mean anything to this guy.)

"Well, when you find him tell him I said 'hi'," I sniffled. "Try and jog his memory and see if he remembers me and my children who were starting to look on him as a substitute daddy, seeing as their own father is about as much use as an ashtray on a motorbike to them."

"Okay," Luke said, obviously sensing that perhaps it was time to leave.

"See ya," Ruby said casually, even though I could feel her shiver slightly.

They left. I pulled back from Ruby and raised an eyebrow.

"This is no time to be thinking about how long it is since you last had sex," I said.

"Imagine Motor Mouth having a brother like that!" Ruby said, looking astonished.

"You better start being nice to her from now on," I said. "You don't want her running back and telling her brother that you're not as nice as he thinks you are."

"He doesn't anyway," she said, looking at her fingernails. "He was just being polite for your sake. I'll bet that she already told him that the title of Mad Bitch suited me well."

"She might well have done but it obviously didn't deter him from squeezing your hand and telling you that he hasn't got a wife and that he's single at the minute."

Ruby looked thoughtful. "This is mad," she

announced finally. "You've just found out you're pregnant and we're ignoring that issue altogether to talk about how attractive Mandy's bloody brother is when he is in actual fact the enemy and the creator of very big rows."

"I can't believe it, y'know. I knew I was pregnant before I did the test. A lot of things are starting to make sense to me now. I must have forgotten to take my pill when we were away for the weekend and what with Owen and me being alone and having no children there and him being a red-blooded male and me being a hot-blooded female and me being very distracted. I remember now being a bit uncertain one day – the pill was missing from the pack but I couldn't remember actually taking it. When I think about it now I can't believe I was so stupid. I know where babies come from and how they're made so why did I not take care?"

"Aside from all the negative stuff, Frankie," Ruby said, putting a consoling arm around me, "how do you feel about it all?"

"I think the timing could have been better and I think that it would be nice to have a man instead of being a bloody single mother yet again and I think that my mother is going to flip and that Daddy is going to be walking dogs around in circles for days after this news breaks and I just don't know how I'm going to tell Ella." I started to howl again.

"What about Owen?" Ruby asked gently. "He does have a right to know."

"Well, it's all very well having rights and needing to know things when you're around to receive the news," I said obstinately. "But when you purposefully run away then those rights disappear."

"He's only on holiday for a week."

"He could be on holiday a lot longer than that as far as I'm concerned."

"It's up to you," Ruby said. "You're the boss."

I knew that I was the boss of things in my own head but considering that my brain resembled a ball of goo and that my hormones were all over the place and that I was boyfriendless and my children were fatherless (again) I had never felt less in control of anything in all my life.

Chapter 28

Over the next few days nothing changed. I was stuck in limbo and no further forward. Ruby was the only one who knew my secret and I was driving myself to distraction with all the worries and concerns that were whirling around in my head.

Ella was not helping matters as she kept scrutinising me and following me to the bathroom. I had never used my shower radio before now. The kids got it for me for Christmas a few years ago and I always thought it was a useless contraption as I could never understand how you could hear anything over the sound of the water running. I had since discovered, however, that it was very good for drowning out the sounds of projectile vomiting and uncontrollable retching. (Can I just say at this point that it must have been a man who came up with the title "morning sickness"? Morning sickness my arse – all-feckin'-day sickness or morning-noon-and-night sickness would be more appropriate names for it.)

The children also knew that I was preoccupied and kept asking me questions.

Carly kept bringing me Lemsip as she thought it was going to make my "cold" all better and Ben wanted to know what I'd eaten that kept making me turn such a funny colour. I felt guilty for being selfish and wrapping myself up in my own world but I didn't seem capable of anything else.

I hadn't been to the doctor yet either. Going to the doctor and actually saying the words would only make it seem real and I still thought I was in the middle of a bad dream which I hoped I'd wake up from.

Owen still hadn't been in touch but I'd decided that it was his loss. The woman he loved ran away and left him to bring up their child alone and if he wanted to do the same to me then I'd let him. I would cope. I was used to coping. I always did.

It was Friday and I was glad that this hellish week had come to an end as I was exhausted both physically and emotionally. I knew that I'd lost weight as several people had commented on my gauntness. I was secretly hoping when Owen saw me on Monday that he would look at my pale skin and my sunken cheeks and feel so guilty that he would be sick.

I decided to prolong the time before I had to go

home and pretend to be normal by taking an impromptu trip into town and I was standing looking absent-mindedly into the window of a clothes shop when I heard someone talking to me.

"Frankie, is that you? How are you? Nice to see you again."

When I turned I wondered was this some sort of joke as I was looking at Maura Byrne who seemed to be pleased to see me and not at all put out that her brother and I had parted less than amicably.

"I'm grand," I faltered. "How are you?"

"All's quiet under the circumstances. I'm sure you must be missing Owen. He's hoping to be back from Dublin on Sunday evening. It was unfortunate that my mother was on her own when she had her fall. If there had been someone with her perhaps they could have got her to hospital sooner and she wouldn't be feeling so traumatised about being alone. I'm going down soon so you can have your man back again."

She was looking at me expectantly as if I should have been responding to this statement in some way, and I would have, only I hadn't the faintest clue about what I was supposed to say.

"Great," I said weakly. (Chicken-shit response because I didn't want to tell her that I'd been dumped.) I wondered if the fact that she didn't know was a good thing or a bad thing. Could it simply mean that Owen had been so preoccupied that he hadn't told her or could it be that he didn't want to say anything because he was planning to land on my doorstep with a massive bouquet of flowers, apologise profusely for being a dickhead and take me in his arms and tell me he loved me? (Or was Maura lying to get me to talk so that she could feed the gory details to her mother?)

Maura saw my discomfiture and looked at me with a frown.

"Is everything all right, Frankie?" she asked.

"Everything's fine," I said airily.

"Mmm." She was giving me a funny look.

"So how is your mother now?" I asked.

"She's doing better. She got an awful shock though. I've told her time and again not to be climbing and that she should wait for her housekeeper to help her but Mother is very independent and likes to consider herself as still being young."

I nodded politely. I could tell that she expected me to know exactly what happened in great detail.

"Yes, chairs can be so wobbly when you're stretching," I answered trying to look knowledgeable.

"Yes, they can," Maura answered. "But stepladders are obviously worse since that's what she fell off."

(Shit.)

"Yeah. I was just saying . . ." I trailed off.

"Fancy a coffee if you're free?" Maura asked. "I'm dying to sit down and take the weight off my feet for a while as I have a notion that I won't be doing much lazing around over the next few days. My mother can be quite demanding – perhaps you already know that? I'm sure Owen has been filling you in on what she's had him doing all week. He's been domesticated within an inch of his life whilst that lazy whippet Angelica cosied up to her grandmother and told her how hard her life is."

"I'm sure that she's told her all about the photograph," I said, suddenly filled with pique. (Okay, I thought. Please tell me that I did not just say that out loud. To. Owen's. Sister.)

"What photograph?" she asked pleasantly as if I was talking about a nice family snap shot and not the soft-porn image that I'd started to imagine it to be.

"Oh nothing, it doesn't matter," I laughed, sounding false even to myself.

As soon as we entered the coffee bar I knew that I'd made a mistake. I had always been a three-or-four-cups-a-day gal but since I'd discovered that I was with child I couldn't stomach it at all. Even the mere thought of a frothy cappuccino with cocoa powder swimming around the top made me feel nauseous. Suddenly it was no longer a thought on my part and I had to act quickly before another foot-splattering incident took place. Clapping my hand over my mouth I ran to the ladies' room as quickly as possible but not without engaging the attention of the whole shop and having Maura speed after me in an alarmed state.

"Frankie! Oh my God, Frankie! What's wrong?"

Anyone for Seconds?

Maura shouted through the door of the cubicle while I spat and gagged my way through my daily ritual of sickness.

"Nothing. It must be a bug or something," I said when I eventually reappeared.

I saw Maura take a step backwards. She looked like she wanted to run away and have a bath in bleach but instead she stepped forward again and came closer.

"I don't believe you," she said. "Owen has been acting weird all week. Even my mother has noticed that much, despite the fact she's not well and milking every last drop of attention from it. And you're pale and drawn and now you're sick and wringing your hands."

I looked down at where her gaze was positioned and saw that my fingers were tied in knots so great was my anxiety.

"I'm phoning Owen," she said as she put her hand in her bag and started to rummage about.

"No!" I screamed in a hysterical fashion causing a few people to run out of the toilets without washing their hands. "You can't. I don't want him to know anything about this."

"Know anything about what?" she asked, eyeing me suspiciously. "What's wrong with you? You're sick, aren't you? Owen has a right to know if you're ill."

It was at that precise moment that I snapped (or rather my patience did). I was so sick of everyone telling me what I should and shouldn't do.

"Owen has no rights over me or anything else for that matter," I said sharply. "We parted company on bad terms last week over a misunderstanding that got blown completely and totally out of proportion and which I might add was not my fault. Matters were not helped by your scheming little brat of a niece who took great delight in making nasty comments and I'm sure that having spent the week with her and your mother he will well and truly hate me now. Well, good luck to him."

Maura looked like a goldfish. She was opening and closing her mouth at a rate of knots.

"I think you're being a little irrational, Frankie," she said finally. "Owen has been through a lot and so has Angelica –"

"I am allowed to be as goddamned irrational as I like," I said, trying to stem the tears that were threatening to do a rendition of Niagara Falls down my cheeks. (Pesky hormones really get in the way when conducting arguments as you can no longer remain dignified but instead turn into a snivelling wreck.)

It was only when I got outside that I noticed I had vomit stains on my shirt, there was toilet roll sticking to the sole of my shoe and I realised that I had well and truly blown any chance of a reconciliation.

Chapter 29

It was Sunday and I knew that Owen was at home. Maura told me that he was coming home that evening. It had just turned nine o'clock so it was officially no longer "the evening"; it was night-time. I was staring at the clock in a manic fashion and for some reason kept lifting the phone and listening to the dialling tone to check that it was working. I appeared mad even to myself and couldn't imagine what my little six-year-old must have been thinking as she watched me and chewed at a strand of her hair.

She looked penetratingly at me. "Are you all right, Mum?"

"Me. Oh yes. I'm top of the world," I answered. (Who was I trying to kid?)

"You don't look like you're on top of the world," she said slowly. "You look like you're cross and you keep giving the clock funny looks and banging the phone."

"I'm just playing," I answered.

"Are you playing with me?" she asked.

"Yes," I said. "I'm playing 'house' and we have to pretend that we're waiting for a very important phone call."

Carly began to look animated. I hadn't played with her like that in a long time.

"Hello," she said into the phone receiver.

I was going to tell her not to tie up the line but reasoned that it hardly mattered as Owen was hardly going to be in a mad dash to get in touch. His sister had probably gone to Malahide early just to tell them all what a lucky escape he'd had and that I was a lunatic of the highest order.

"Mum says that she's waiting for a very important phone call," Carly said into the phone. "I don't know who it will be from but I like talking to you."

I smiled indulgently at my daughter, glad that I was taking the opportunity to spend a little quality time with her.

"Where have you been?" Carly asked. "I missed you. Are you going to come over and play with us? Ben hasn't missed you as much as I have because Uncle Hammy takes him out all the time."

I was starting to feel a bit unnerved. Who on earth did she think she was talking to?

"Who's that, darling?" I said conversationally, all in the spirit of the game.

"I'm talking to Owen," she said in an equally conversational tone. "He says he loves you and that he misses you."

"Yeah right," I answered sarcastically. "It's quite obvious we're in the Land of Make-believe now and not in the real world. I don't think that we'll be seeing Owen or nasty, horrible Angelica again, darling, so perhaps you should pretend that you're talking to Granny or Auntie Ella instead."

"But I'm not pretending, Mum," Carly said innocently. "Owen is here and he sounds very cross now. He said that he rushed all the way home from Dublin when he heard that you were sick but if all you can do is be horrible then he shouldn't have bothered."

Whaaaaaaaaaaaaaaaaaaat?

I was now on my feet and flailing my arms around like I was badly in need of a straitjacket. (Which wasn't too far from the truth. When did I suddenly turn into such a basket case?)

"Is he still there?" I croaked.

"Hello, hello," Carly said before slowly shaking her head and then hanging up.

"Bollocks and shit," I said before looking towards the door where my mother, father, Ella and Hammy were all surveying me with shocked expressions and looking pointedly at Carly. Ella grabbed her and covered her ears but it was a little late now – a bit like closing the gate after the horse had bolted.

"We came to see you," Mammy said a tad unnecessarily. "We were worried about you. Ella says that you haven't been feeling too well. All the stress and annoyance of your activities getting to you, are they?"

Daddy breathed out loudly before abruptly inviting Hammy to go for a walk with him.

"Do you have to do that?" Mammy asked sharply. "I thought that we agreed that we were going to sort out this problem together. Run along, Carly!" She gave Carly a packet of sweets and a pat on the head and propelled her out the door.

Everyone proceeded to seat themselves around me and I felt totally invaded now as well as angry.

"Problem?" I asked sweetly, trying to keep my temper in check. So that's what my family thought I was. I was nothing more than a mere problem that needed to be quashed.

"Well, obviously there's a problem," Mammy said. "There's been no apology and your name hasn't been cleared which means that we're all still in the frame."

"In the frame for what exactly?" I asked in a dangerously low voice.

"For unsavoury goings-on, that's what," she said, patting her hair and looking all around her lest anyone should overhear.

"I know, Mammy. It's a terrible situation for you,

isn't it?" I said in an even tone. "It must be awful to be living in a dungeon because you can't open your curtains in case your daughter might think that she's more important to you than what some old gutter-rag says. After all, your neighbours are all the cream of the crop with no guilty secrets and no skeletons in the closet, aren't they?" My voice was rising by the second. "Dotty O'Hare will just have to forget the fact that her husband left her for one of his pupils because she'll be so much more interested in what I've been doing and Mr and Mrs Donnelly will have to put their son's suspended prison sentence to the back of their minds because they'll be so outraged at my behaviour. Not to mention Susan Kennedy – maybe she'll forget that her husband has bone cancer because she'll be so busy standing guard at her window and waiting for you to show your sorry face in the street."

The room was quiet. I think I had stunned even myself with the amount of rage that I had inside.

Dad broke the silence.

"I knew that this was a bad idea, Celia. Let's go home now." His voice was strangely gentle which alerted me to the fact that my mother had tears streaming down her face.

Oh God. Maybe I went too far and said a teeny weenie bit too much. Daddy wasn't looking at me and I wished that Ella wasn't either because right now her angry stare was boring into my forehead.

"I'm sorry, Mammy," I said, taking a deep breath and feeling all the fight going out of me.

"No, I'm sorry," she said sadly. "I'm sorry that my daughters both have problems but that neither one of them feels that they can confide in me."

Ella sprang from her seat and with a defensive shrug went and stood beside Hammy who had got up and walked to the window when the conversation had got heated and was looking decidedly uncomfortable and shifting his weight from foot to foot.

Oh shit. The worms were wriggling out of cans in all directions.

I decided to take the pressure off Ella. "Look, Mammy. There's nothing wrong," I said. "I'm just feeling sorry for myself because I've made yet another disastrous blunder where my love life is concerned."

"What about you?" Mammy asked Ella. "Your love life isn't in a blunder, is it?"

The tension momentarily lifted as everyone cracked a smile.

"No. Our love life is fine, Mother," Ella said. "I just came home for a holiday and to see you all."

"She came home because she needs your help," boomed Hammy, making everyone jump. "As no one else seems capable of being straight and honest then I'll do the talking." He shrugged Ella off as she attempted to protest. "Ella and I are desperate for a family. We have been for some time but unfortunately Mother Nature doesn't seem inclined to work along with us on that one. We've been to see several doctors and finally we were put in touch with a consultant in the city who did some tests. The tests proved inconclusive as there doesn't seem to be anything wrong with either of us but, as we have discovered, it might have been easier to cope with if there had been a specific problem. It's very frustrating and upsetting for Ella, given the nature of her job, and I felt that some time at home with her family might do her some good. That was a mistake on my part, however, as instead of giving her any of your time you're all too busy getting worked up over stupid things. That photograph was forgotten about the day after it was taken, Celia. The remnants of that story have wrapped countless bags of chips by now. Frankie was stupid to get herself into that position but she has bigger things to worry about now. Are you going to tell them, Frankie, or am I?"

"Tell them what?" I said frantically.

"Tell us what?" Mammy said, looking like she was watching a tennis match as she jerked her head from side to side to look at us both.

Hammy looked at me and I knew that he was leaving me with no choice. Ella was crying quietly but stopped as she waited for me to speak.

Mammy was looking at me with her mouth open and I wanted to listen to Daddy's chest to make sure that he was still breathing as he was so still.

I closed my eyes and kept them closed as I didn't think that I wanted to see the shocked expression on my mother's face or the raw hurt in Ella's.

"I'm pregnant," I said.

Chapter 30

I was expecting chaos. I was expecting angst and cries of "What did I do to deserve this!" from my mother but what I wasn't expecting was for Owen to appear from behind the architrave of my living-room door looking most bewildered and demanding to know what I was talking about.

"What do you mean you're pregnant?" he asked.

"Excuse me a moment, Owen," my mother said with remarkable poise. "Get in line, please."

"Frances, what the hell do you mean you're pregnant?"

"I mean that I am carrying a child. I'm about seven weeks pregnant, I think, and I'm sorry that I've caused so much trouble. I didn't mean to hurt anybody and I definitely didn't mean to hurt you!" I rushed over to hug Ella who gave me a tight squeeze.

"I'm sorry," I repeated, looking at Hammy and

willing him to forgive me. "I know that I've been a selfish, unsupportive cow but I promise that I'll do all I can to help you both."

"And I'll do everything to help you," Ella said.

"Does it make you feel awful?" I asked tentatively, looking earnestly into her face.

"Does what make me feel awful?" she asked in confusion.

"Me being pregnant. Are you annoyed? I'll understand if you don't want to be around me now. It must seem like I'm rubbing your nose in it."

"If I felt that way about my patients I wonder how many babies would be brought into the world and how many mothers would want to have me hung drawn and quartered for abandoning them in their hour of need? I'm not going to shy away from you just because you have something I want to have some day. That would be very petty and foolish. I'd like to help you — that's providing that you're going to go ahead."

"What do you mean go ahead?" my mother shrieked like a banshee. "You're not surely suggesting that she —"

"Are you going to go ahead?" another voice interrupted.

I had forgotten that Owen was still in the room and I suppose that out of everyone present he had, more than anyone else, the right to know what was happening.

"Can we step outside for a minute?" I said.

He walked out of the room in front of me and I followed and closed the door behind us. I led him out into the cool night air and we sat on the garden seat near my porch.

"I'm sorry that you had to hear it like that," I began. "I might have told you sooner but you weren't here and you never contacted me." My voice sounded hostile and accusing and I saw Owen wince.

"My mother had a fall –"

"I know the full story. Maura told me everything and she obviously told you some things too."

"She said that you weren't well and that you were acting really peculiarly. She was surprised to hear that we had split up. I think that she thought it was the real thing."

"There was more than just her thought that," I murmured, looking straight ahead.

"Look, let's put the past where it belongs and start again," Owen said softly. "You've made mistakes but I don't want you going through this alone."

Mistakes? My head jerked up to look at him.

"Is that the only reason why you want to be with me?" I asked angrily. "Is this one of those sad situations where people think that they are forced to stay together for the sake of the children even though they are an unsuitable match? Do my mistakes not deter you from wanting to be with me because they obviously stopped you from ringing me all week? You knew that

I'd be worried sick so, if you set out to hurt me, then congratulations – you did a great job."

"I've made mistakes as well," Owen said in a reasonable voice which made me want to pummel him to the ground.

I didn't want him to speak to me as if I was a stroppy child. I wanted him to realise that I had every right to be angry and every right to question his logic.

"Damn right you have," I said obstinately.

"Okay, let's call a truce for long enough to talk about what's important," he said. "Have you been to see a doctor yet?"

"Not yet," I answered mutinously. "I did a home test and I haven't had a period so I think that's confirmation enough."

"How are you feeling?"

"Top of the bloody world and then some."

"Look, I'll admit that my timing was really lousy," Owen said. "I never would have left you to cope with all of this on your own if I'd known the circumstances."

"And if the circumstances weren't there? What would you have done, Owen? Would we be having this conversation or would you still be ignoring me and punishing me for my mistakes?"

He looked at the ground which was not the response that I wanted.

Anyone for Seconds?

"Why did you come here tonight?" I asked. "I don't think that it was to apologise. I think that you were coming to reprimand me for what I said about Angelica. Well, I meant every word of it and I don't take anything back. She's a spoilt manipulative little hussy who knows which buttons to press to wrap you round her little finger. She doesn't want anyone taking the attention away from her, least of all someone who is introducing two other children into the equation."

"Don't you mean three?" he said, looking at my stomach.

I wrapped my cardigan tightly around myself and looked away.

"I was coming to talk to you," he said. "We were going to have to work together tomorrow and I didn't want it to be awkward. I wanted to bury the hatchet and start over again. I do love you." He cupped my chin with his hand, forcing me to face him.

"I love you too," I said, beginning to cry. "But I'm so scared. I don't want to do anything rash and hasty and for the wrong reasons."

"Why don't we give it a chance and see where it takes us," Owen said. "After the experience I've had I don't want to be jumping into anything which could turn sour either."

I wiped my nose with my sleeve and sniffed.

"You still haven't answered my question," he continued.

"What was that?" I asked, my mind a sudden jumble of conversations, shocked expressions and angry words.

"Are you going to have the baby?"

"Of course I am," I snapped as I placed a hand protectively over my tummy. I might not have liked it at the start but I was starting to become fond of the tiny person who was developing inside me. (If I was honest I also liked the idea of having an excuse to have a pot belly and not to have to forcibly hold my stomach in.)

"I was just checking that it's what you wanted," Owen said softly, "because I know what I want."

"What's that?"

"I want you to smile and to stop crying and I think that they all do as well." Owen was pointing at the curtain which covered the glass panel of my front door and when I turned to look I could see my family all peering out at me looking concerned.

"I'm fine," I said to them as I walked back into the house. "We just needed to get a few things sorted."

"And did you? Get things sorted, I mean," Mammy said anxiously.

"I think so," Owen said as he put a comforting arm around me.

I would have liked to sink back and lean against him but something was stopping me. I still had misgivings and a little voice in my head was telling me to slow down.

Owen must have sensed my stiffness because he removed his hand from my back.

"Don't cry anymore," Ella said. "It's not good for the baby. The stress you've been under all week won't have helped and this is a crucial developmental stage where you need to be relaxed and take as much rest as possible."

"I'll see to it that she does," Owen said.

"Well, you haven't been doing a very good job of it so far," Mammy said before leading me to the sofa. "Put the kettle on, Ella," she commanded.

Soon I had a steaming cup of tea in my hand (with two sugars for the shock although why I needed the sugar was beyond me. I already knew. It was everybody else that had got the fright.)

"It's not what I would have wished for you," my mother said. "In an ideal world I hoped that you would be married before any more children came along but what's done is done and all we can do now is pray that everything goes well for you. As for you," she said, looking at Ella, "your mother is neither slow on the uptake nor stupid. I knew that something was wrong before you even talked about coming home. I could tell that you were strained on the phone. It's not the end of the world, pet. I think it's wonderful that they haven't found any blockages or problems. It'll just be a matter of time. Once you stop thinking about it and putting yourself under such pressure it'll happen naturally. Your father and I were married for two years before we had you and in those days people talked if you didn't come home from your honeymoon with news. Besides, Ella, if the worst comes to the worst and you can't have your own child, there are other things to consider. You could do worse than to adopt a child. You have so much love to give that I don't think it would matter."

"Well, we have to be honest and say that we've already been looking into that," Hammy said. "We've filled out forms and been through an interview. It won't be easy though. It's a very difficult process. The vetting is rigorous and there could be a long wait. We decided, after our last appointment with the consultant, that we'd review our options."

"We're going to keep trying," Ella said. "We can go for IVF as well but from my work I know how stressful and disappointing it can be. Besides, technically there is nothing wrong with either of us. I'm starting to think that maybe it's a sign. Thailand is a country which has suffered terribly since the tsunami and as a result there are quite a number of children there who have lost parents or whose parents aren't able to look after them due to poverty or circumstances."

"Those children are so attractive," Mammy commented, looking wistful. "I can just see you with a beautiful dark-haired, dark-skinned child. That would be lovely and you'd be doing something so worthwhile and giving a child who otherwise didn't stand a chance a home and love and happiness."

Hammy and Ella shared a look and I knew at that moment that they could get through anything as long as they had each other.

I finished my tea and walked Owen to the door. Ben and Carly were peering through the banisters and waving and smiling at him. I knew that they were fond of him and that he was good to them. I was just seriously confused.

"I'm sorry about everything," he said. "I do love you and I'll just have to keep telling you that until you believe me. I shouldn't have been so hard on you and I take on board your comments about Angelica. I know she can be difficult but –"

"I know. She's had a lot to deal with."

I wondered how she would cope with the idea of having a half brother or sister with me as its mother and suddenly any enthusiasm that I had mustered died a swift death. Teenzilla and a baby. What the hell had I done to myself?

Chapter 31

I woke on Monday after a fitful night's sleep and stretched before I eased myself out of bed. I had learnt not to stand up too quickly in the mornings for fear of making my already delicate stomach even more unbalanced.

The first thought that came into my head was that I should have been happy. I should have been ecstatic, in fact. Owen was back and what's more he had accepted the news about the baby and actually seemed to be happy about it. So why was I not?

I thought back over our conversation for about the hundredth time and for the hundredth time bristled when I heard Owen's voice echoing in my head when he told me about the "mistakes" I'd made. Since when had he received his feckin' sainthood, I thought angrily, standing up abruptly and promptly gagging.

Ella was already up and humming quietly and making breakfast when I came downstairs. The smell of toast made my insides churn.

She turned around when she heard me approach.

"Are you all right?" she asked in concern. "I heard you being sick. You forgot to turn the radio on this time."

I smiled sheepishly. How could I think that I could hide such a monumental fact from my only sister? My only sister who could probably recognise a pregnant woman at twenty paces.

"Never mind me," I answered. "Ella, listen to me." I forced her to look at me. "I'm really sorry about everything. I never meant for any of this to happen and I feel terrible. Are *you* all right? I'm so worried about you. Are you not feeling hurt and betrayed by me?"

"Betrayed?" she asked, looking confused. "How did you betray me? You haven't been having lustful thoughts about my husband, have you?"

"No," I laughed before wearing a more serious expression. My worry about Ella had kept me awake half the night. "But I wasn't very sensitive about your predicament when you first arrived and then I was really preoccupied and now I've gone and got myself pregnant and I'm sure you think I'm the worst sister in the world."

"I do wish that you'd stop sounding like a broken record, Frankie," she said, busying herself with pouring boiling water into the teapot. "I do admit that you're about as tactful as a flying brick and that you're a complete disaster when your love life is in the pits and that you're one of these sickening girls who seems to get pregnant by simply looking at a man. But having said that I wouldn't change you for the world."

I could feel myself welling up (again), although in fairness sisterly soppy conversations always got me going regardless of how rampant and mad my hormones were.

"What about Owen?" she asked.

"What about Owen?" I responded, shrugging.

She stopped what she was doing and turned to face me with a puzzled expression.

"What? You've been walking around here all week with a face on you like a wet weekend in Donegal and now that you've got what you want you're shrugging at me like you don't care?"

"I don't know what to do or how to feel. Owen appearing back last night should have been like a dream come true given the circumstances but things he said upset me and I'm wondering, if this hadn't happened, whether he'd be back at all. Besides, I think I'm starting to go off him."

"Go off him?" she repeated.

"Yeah. Do you think it's a symptom?"

"Not one that I learnt about in my nursing degree or have read about in any medical journals, Frankie," Ella said with a smile. "But then again you could just be reacting to the fact that he left you for so long. We women are funny creatures. We adapt situations to suit ourselves and we're also very good at wanting what we can't have and then when we get it becoming complacent about it."

"It's not that," I said firmly. "It's more about the fact that he spoke to me like I was one of his students in this condescending, patronising voice like he was chastising me or something."

Ella handed me a cup of tea and a plate of toast and marmalade. "You're going to be late if you don't get a move on," she said, eyeing the kitchen clock which was the shape and colour of a bright red rooster.

"I know. I'm going," I hastily took a few mouthfuls of tea and carried my toast with me to finish in the car.

When I arrived at work Ruby informed me that Mammy had already rung three times demanding to know where I was and how I was. She had also stipulated that I was to phone her the minute I came in.

"Oh no!" I wailed. "This is the start of it. She could fuss for Ireland at the best of times but she'll have turned it into an Olympic sport by the time this is all over."

"Sooo. Tell me," Ruby said, inching closer and perching herself on the edge of my desk. I had sent her a rushed text message the previous night letting her know that Owen had come to see me and told her that I'd fill her in on the rest when I came to work.

"He came to see me. He knows. He went home," I said making a face.

"Please don't tell me I've listened to you sobbing and complaining all week about being deserted and that now you're going to explain how the whole thing was rectified in three choppy sentences," she responded, looking crossly at me.

"I don't know if it's going anywhere or if it ever was going anywhere," I said.

"Don't say that!" Ruby cried, looking shocked. "You're the perfect couple and you will get through this. It's just complicated at the minute."

"My life was complicated enough before all this," I retorted.

Ruby looked towards the door and motioned at me to be quiet as she saw Owen approaching.

"Good morning, ladies," he said cheerfully. (Did he have to be so happy about life on a Monday morning?)

I smiled tightly at him and walked to my desk. "I'll see you for tea later," I said.

I could see that he was baffled by my obvious indifference but I didn't care and felt a thrill of satisfaction when I saw him walk towards the staff room with his head down.

"You're not being very sociable this morning," Ruby commented, raising her eyebrow at me.

"Perhaps I'm not in a sociable mood," I retorted before sitting down and lifting the phone to ring my mother. I no longer wanted to talk about that subject.

Chapter 32

Six weeks had passed and I couldn't believe the changes that had taken place and I wasn't just talking about the fact that I seemed to be allergic to Owen these days. The very look of him irritated me. The physiological changes that occurred in pregnancy were also very evident. My skin and hair seemed to have improved overnight with no help required from Nicky Clarke or a team of expert make-up artists. My clothes were also starting to feel rather tight and I was now the owner of a magnificent chest that would rival Jordan's any day of the week.

I couldn't believe how supportive and calm everyone was being just when I had tipped my entire family as being in the front running for a very messy meltdown.

My mother had opened her curtains again and didn't seem to be the least perturbed about her neighbours and what they might or might not think. Banjo had even started to look a bit on the chubby side as Daddy wasn't walking the paws off him in a manic fashion.

Ruby had also turned into a very bolshy Florence Nightingale who kept suggesting vitamin supplements I could take and Ella was trying to persuade me to go to yoga classes. I had made the mistake of telling them that I had headaches and wasn't sleeping very well at which point they both started to fuss.

Ella was also looking a lot better. Obviously the old saying was true "a problem shared; a problem halved". Since "fight night" when Mammy had been determined to sort out her daughters, Hammy had put the world to rights and Owen had discovered I was pregnant, Ella had seemed a lot more content. It was like a weight had been taken off her shoulders now that she didn't have to harbour her awful secret all on her own. She was still sad sometimes but not as upset and she seemed to have regained her appetite and had started to look more like her old self as she had put on a few pounds and was slowly getting her colour back. She and Hammy had been spending a lot of quality time together and I could see that it was making a difference to both of them. Hammy had also returned to his ever smiling, twinkly personality and was the resident clown as far as the children were concerned. Ella and I had grown closer then ever in the last few weeks and I knew that having her leave me again would be the same as losing a limb.

Of course Mammy was taking all the credit for the change in Ella .

"It takes you to come home to your mother to feel better, love, doesn't it?"

(Obviously I had done nothing to help then.)

"You're better than The Priory any day, Mammy. You should start advertising," Ella had joked.

"The where?" Mammy asked. "Is it a guest house?"

Ella and I had solemnly agreed and then killed ourselves laughing. "Yep. It's a guest house."

"A very expensive and exclusive guest house," I added, "for celebrities badly in need of a break from their drink and drug-fuelled lifestyles but a guest house all the same."

I wished I could deal with things more sensibly myself. I was studiously avoiding Owen and taking the coward's way out. It probably would have been easier to just tell him what was wrong but I didn't have the energy to get into it, so I didn't.

I knew he was hurt but to my mind it was karma doing a good job of evening up events. What goes around comes around and all that.

He kept repeatedly asking me if I was all right and kept getting the same short answer every time: "Fine." (Ella's favourite word.)

When I returned home from work later that day an official-looking envelope with the hospital logo stamped on it was waiting for me. My heart skipped a beat as I opened it in anticipation of its contents. I gave a little whoop of delight when I discovered that it was a letter detailing the date of my first scan which would take place in a week's time.

When I told Ella my good news she said: "Well, at least that gives you time to sort it out before you go to the hospital together."

"I beg your pardon. What are you talking about? Sort what out with who?"

"Well, Frankie, unless you're very talented and this baby was the result of an immaculate conception or a little tryst with the Angel Gabriel then you're going to have to tell Owen about the scan date. You can't leave him out. I think you're being unfair. I know he hurt you but do you not think you've punished him for long enough now? I think you should concentrate the rest of your efforts on the baby and forget about playing games."

"I am not playing games," I said stubbornly.

"Frankie, how many missed calls have you got on your mobile from Owen today? Please don't try telling me that you didn't hear the phone because I know you did. I saw you check it and throw it away when you saw it was him. You can be such a child."

"Am not."

"Are."

"Am not."

"Frankie, I am not doing this with you," Ella said

sternly. "I think that you should seriously think about what you're doing and what you want from the future. You've been lonely for a long time but now you have the chance of happiness in a proper family. Are you really prepared to risk losing that by being so pig-headed?"

(Me? Pig-headed? I didn't know what she was talking about.)

I slept restlessly that night and laid the blame squarely at my sister's feet. She could be such a killjoy sometimes. I was only trying to prove a point but as it happened I tended to agree with her (although I certainly wasn't going to tell her that). Maybe things had gone far enough. I would talk to Owen but I intended to be brutally honest with him.

Owen and I had a long talk about everything over morning coffee and for the first time I told him exactly how I'd been feeling and why he had annoyed me so much. He seemed shocked that I'd taken things so much to heart and promised to be more sensitive. He told me repeatedly that he loved me and that he couldn't wait for us to have our baby. His eyes positively began to dance in his head when I told him about the scan and I felt a wave of love and affection for him and for the first time in a long time felt that maybe my relationship status was not all doom and gloom.

Except for one thing of course.

Chapter 33

We had gathered the children together and were going to tell them our "news". I had been trying to avoid doing this and had already successfully evaded the conversation twice (with the help of Angelica throwing two well-timed hissy fits, I hasten to add) but it had become nearly impossible to hide now as I could no longer button my trousers. A few people at work had commented that love must agree with me whilst looking pointedly at my stomach – translated, that meant that they thought I was a fat cow who had lost all self-control and interest in my appearance just because I'd bagged myself a man. If only they knew what my reasons were for looking like a porker! They'd know soon enough though, along with everybody else.

We had lined the children up two weeks ago and had been about to explain the reason why we were gathered together when all hell broke loose in what will forever more be referred to as the "Phonegate" scandal.

We had just finished eating a Chinese and Owen and I were clearing away the plates when bloodcurdling screams of both temper and fright emanated from the living room. Upon investigation we found Angelica staring at Carly with her teeth bared and Carly looking like she might jump out of her skin at any given second.

I immediately went to Carly and stood in front of her lest Angelica produce a weapon, so great was her apparent unhappiness.

"And the problem is …?" I enquired.

"I'll tell you what the problem is," Angelica snarled. "The problem is –"

"That you can't speak in a civilised tone of voice quite obviously," Owen said reproachfully. "Wind your neck in, Angelica, and stop behaving like a fishmonger's wife. Whatever it is can't be that big of a deal."

"She was looking at my text messages," Angelica cried whilst dramatically pointing at Carly whose eyebrows were now reaching her hairline.

"Did you have Angelica's phone, Carly?" I asked in a stern voice.

"It beeped, Mummy, and I just wanted to see what the noise was and I accidentally pressed something and then she went mad and started shouting at me," Carly said before starting to wail.

"I don't think she meant it," I said to Angelica (I foolishly thought that this would be the situation resolved but Miss Teenage Attitude of the Year thought differently).

"Well, you would say that, wouldn't you?" Angelica spat with barely concealed contempt. "It would be awful if Mummy's perfect little girl was anything other than a friggin' angel, now wouldn't it?"

"She's six years of age, Angelica, and as they don't teach text jargon at school I very much doubt that she saw anything that would be of any interest to her on your precious phone. As for her being perfect, can I just say that no child is perfect but she certainly does not need to be demonised in this way by you of all people."

"And what is that supposed to mean?" she roared at me.

"Oh for God's sake, you figure it out," I said, tiring of squaring up to the ball of insolence in front of me who wanted to throttle somebody if the look in her eye was anything to go on.

"Oh yeah, that's right, Frankie –"

(I hated the way she said my name. She drew out every syllable as if it was a bad word so that it sounded like "Frrrrraaaankkyyy".)

"Turn it all round as if it's my fault! That brat should never be near my stuff."

I felt and must have looked as if I had just been

slapped as Owen quickly intervened with a loud bark that made everyone jump.

"Go and get into the car now, Angelica," he said in a voice that was not to be argued with. "But before you go I'll have that." Owen gestured towards the mobile phone that was in the tight grasp of Angelica's hand.

She looked stricken for a moment before fixing both Carly and I with the most satanic look I had ever witnessed. It bore so much menace that I gave Carly a squeeze of reassurance before looking away myself.

"Out now," Owen instructed before my front door was nearly forcibly removed from its hinges.

"I take it now is not the best time to discuss expanding the family then?" I asked unnecessarily.

"Hummph," Owen snorted in annoyance. "I'd like to reduce part of it, I think. I wonder how much I'd get for her on eBay?"

"I thought she was priceless?" I asked.

"Oh yeah, she's that all right," he said with a furrowed brow. "I need to go. I have to have a long hard talk with my daughter about how cold and draughty a park bench would be to sleep on."

We had engineered the same situation a week later and this time I decided that I would cook, hoping that perhaps producing a home-cooked meal and eating it together might create the illusion of a "happy family" so to speak. Needless to say it was an unmitigated disaster from beginning to end with Phonegate being replaced with, and I quote: "I'm not hungry, Daddy. I knew she was cooking so I went to McDonald's before I came to get something decent to eat."

I grinned and bore the insults whilst wondering what the annoying little trollop actually ate in McDonalds seeing as she didn't eat "the carcasses of dead animals". A McVegemite Sandwich perhaps or a McNutcutlet burger or a McBeansprout stir-fry perhaps (you could have a lot of fun with this particular game if you had the time and imagination to focus for long enough)?

Owen was again going home to talk about the disadvantages of sleeping on the streets and we were left with no option but to reschedule the conversation that had to happen sooner or later yet again.

And now, here we were – all together again. There were no phones in sight. No food was being consumed or made in any manner or form and I was firmly hoping that the person who came up with the quirky little phrase "third time lucky" was smiling on us.

I started to focus on the here and now again.

Ben and Carly were looking expectant if slightly wary (a side effect of being in the company of a psychopathic teenager) whilst Angelica was staring at me in her usual belligerent fashion. (No change there then.)

I had made Owen promise that he would tell them as I hadn't got the nerve. In truth I was petrified as to what Angelica's reaction was going to be.

"She always said she wanted a little brother or sister," he told me.

Yeah, with the same mother and father as she has, I thought with my stomach knotting.

"Do we have to tell them all together?" I wheedled for about the fortieth time. "Should we not tell them separately and avoid any fireworks?"

"There won't be fireworks," he said. "Look, I've made Angelica promise that she'll start behaving herself from now on and she says that if I'm happy that she'll be nice to you. She's a good kid really."

(Yeah, when she's sleeping.)

He then started looking all misty-eyed and stupid and I wanted to hit him. God, but he was gullible. She had him well reeled in.

Now, Owen clasped his hands together and grinned at everyone. He was as nervous as hell. I knew it and his daughter knew it as I could see her eyes narrowing in suspicion.

"Can we get on with this, please?" she said in a bored tone. "Some of us have lives, y'know."

I could see Owen's eye starting to twitch and felt sorry for him.

"Frankie and I have some good news that we'd like to share with you."

"Depends on what your definition of good is," Angelica muttered just loud enough for me to hear.

"How would you feel about having an extra addition to the family?"

"What's a na – an – diton?" Carly asked, screwing up her nose.

"It means another person," Angelica said quick as a flash, fixing me with a particularly nasty look. "Personally I think there's too many people in it already but what does my opinion matter?"

"Angelica," Owen said in a warning tone.

She blinked slowly and deliberately and turned away.

"Owen," I said sharply in exasperation. At the rate he was going I'd be nine months pregnant and heading to the labour ward by the time he let our other children know what was happening.

"Look, kids, we have some really good news and we hope that you'll be as happy as we are about it. We're going to have a baby."

There was a stupefied silence and a variety of expressions greeted me. Ben was chewing his lip and looking thoughtful, Carly was smiling brightly and Angelica looked rather lost.

"When are we getting it, Mummy?" Carly asked with great interest. "Can we go and get it tomorrow?"

"No, darling, we can't. The baby won't be ready to be born for another six months."

"Where are we getting it from?"

Oh great, just the question I was looking forward to.

"We're going to get it from the hospital, darling."

"Why, Mummy?"

"Because that's where the stork leaves it."

"Are you sure, Mummy? Casey Murray's got a new baby sister and she said that her mummy got really really fat and that the baby came from her belly button. Maybe our baby will come out of the front of your tummy?"

"Ben," I said loudly in the hope of distracting Carly, "what do you think? Are you happy?"

Ben looked quite non-committal for just being told that his mother was going to produce a baby.

"S'all right," he said. "Will it be very noisy and cry all the time?"

"Well, all babies cry, pet, but hopefully this one will be just like you and be very good. You were sleeping through the night when you were six weeks old and a great little feeder."

I was grateful that my children seemed to be so accepting of the situation. I looked at Owen and saw that he was surveying Angelica with a wary expression. She was staring at the floor and saying nothing. In fact the silence was deafening.

"Angelica," he probed gently. "Are you all right, love? What do you think?"

She still didn't answer and I was about to make a sarcastic comment when I noticed fat tears plopping onto the knees of her jeans. She had her arms wrapped around her chest almost as if she was protecting herself and for the first time since I saw her in hospital, my heart went out to her.

I sat beside her and put my hand on her arm. She didn't shrink away which was miraculous in itself and let me know that she must be very confused indeed.

"Ben, can you take Carly into the kitchen, please? You can get biscuits from the cupboard and a glass of milk."

I frowned as Owen sat at Angelica's other side. She still hadn't moved and the tears were continuing to flow.

"I'm sorry, pet," said Owen. "All I've ever wanted is for you to be happy. Just because we're having a baby doesn't mean that I'm replacing you in any way. You'll always be my special girl." Owen wrapped his arms around her and she buried her head in his shoulder.

"I'm not crying because I don't think I'm special," she said. "I just wish that it was me."

"That you were pregnant?" I asked incredulously.

"No! That I was the baby."

She was staring at my stomach and watching as I rubbed my small bump in a circular motion with my hand. It was a habit I had got into but I stopped when I realised how insensitive I was being.

"It's just that I can see that you really want this baby," she said in a choking voice. "Both of you do. It must be nice to be wanted and needed."

I placed my arms around her and gave her an awkward hug. "Angelica, please believe me when I say that I have never wanted to be anything else but your friend. I don't want to take the place of your mother but I do want you to know that you are wanted and needed. Carly looks up to you – she's always excited when she knows that you're coming to visit. She thinks of you as a big sister." (Slight economy with the truth but you can only work with what you have at a moment's notice).

She shook her head and then covered her face as loud wracking sobs emanated from behind her fingers. I felt completely helpless as I looked at Owen whose eyes were filled with tears.

"Angelica, can we call a truce, please?" I asked. "Please give me a chance."

Angelica removed her fingers and looked at me. "Why do you want to do that?" she asked.

"Maybe it's because I want you and need you," I said defiantly. "Your daddy certainly does and his happiness is everything to me."

"Dad, can I go now?" she said, not looking at me. "I have a really sore head and I want to lie down. You can stay here for longer if you want but I really want to go home." She stood up abruptly.

I motioned at Owen, telling him that I thought he should leave with her.

He seemed to understand and, getting up, put his arm around her and steered her towards the door.

"I'll phone you later," he said, blowing me a kiss.

I willed Angelica to look around and give me at

least some hope that she was going to give me a chance. She didn't and as usual I was left with the feeling that I didn't measure up.

Ben and Carly came into the room when they heard the door closing and Carly gave me a sheepish look.

"Mummy," she said slowly, "Ben told me that he knows where babies come from and it's not from the stork."

Chapter 34

I phoned Owen after the children had gone to bed and he told me that Angelica was very upset and had cried herself to sleep. I felt wretched with guilt concerning my lack of understanding when it came to the girl. She made it very hard, I reasoned. Dealing with her was like trying to pull against a gale-force wind.

"Why is she so upset?" I asked, fully expecting to hear my name mentioned.

"I think it's just reopened old wounds concerning her mother and the fact that she was abandoned for want of a better word."

"And what about me?" I asked.

"What about you?" he said.

"Is she not feeling a bit put out that of all the women in all the world you had to choose to have a baby with the one that she likes the least."

"Actually, Frankie, I think you'd better sit down for this as the shock may kill you."

"Oh no. What have I done now?"

"Well, apparently you're not that bad. Angelica says that she wouldn't mind trying to get to know you a bit better but she's afraid of what her mother's family will say."

I was baffled by the control that absent parents who acted like they were childless or suffering from amnesia had over their children and how their families behaved like they were martyrs who should be enshrined. I thought of Nebby Peg and snorted in disgust.

"I take it that we're talking about good old loveable sweet Auntie Brenda upon whom the sun rises and sets," I said.

"The one and only," he responded. "She becomes more poisonous by the day."

"We should introduce her to Great-granny Peggy and they can create their own secret society in honour of their beloved family members who are useless parents."

"I think that might be dangerous," Owen said. "They might enjoy it all too much."

I sighed. "Look, I have an idea. Where will Angelica be in the morning?"

"She'll be like every other teenager who's on their summer holidays – she'll be in bed and unless you're armed and dangerous I wouldn't even contemplate wakening her."

"Perhaps I'll leave it until tomorrow afternoon then," I said thinking out loud. "I'd like her to be in a receptive mood."

"Frankie, what are you planning?"

"I don't know yet myself but I'd like to try something if that's all right with you."

"No harm in trying," he said, sounding decidedly unconvinced. (Oh ye of little faith.)

"I'll try and I'll do it for you," I said. I realised when I had the words spoken that I actually did mean them.

The phone rang again almost as soon as I put it down. Owen back again, I thought.

"What have you forgotten?" I asked in a sing-song tone.

"I haven't forgotten anything," Ruby said. "Although apparently you've forgotten how to answer the phone like a normal person."

"I'm sorry! Owen is literally just off the phone and I thought that he was ringing back to tell me something else."

"You sound a tad chirpier," she said. "I take it everything went all right tonight. Did Princess Angelica not show up or did somebody gag her?"

"Actually it has been a very surprising night. Angelica was very upset but things didn't kick off the way that I was expecting."

"I bet she was upset," Ruby growled. "It wouldn't

be nice for anybody to discover that they were no longer the Queen of feckin' Sheba."

I started to laugh but quickly curbed my giggling when I remembered the tears splattering all over Angelica's trousers earlier.

"She's not that bad," I said. "I know – I know," I added quickly as I heard Ruby start to splutter and cough on the other end of the phone. "She took the news really badly but she didn't have a hissy fit or anything – she just seemed really sad. She was sobbing and she actually said that she wished that she was the baby because she wanted to know what it was like to feel wanted and needed."

"Wow," Ruby said. "Wow," she repeated.

"Another word, please," I said.

"Shit."

"I've had an idea. I'm going to try and meet up with her tomorrow and maybe take her out for a while and do something that she likes. I'll take her down to Belfast and we can check out the shops and maybe I'll buy her something nice."

"Are you mad?" Ruby said. "What are you doing that for? I'm sure you've better things to be spending your money on rather than trying to humour that sour little tyrant. She's done nothing but make you miserable, Frankie, and I think you should seriously consider getting your head tested." She sounded quite cross. "Are you still having the headaches you talked about?"

"Sometimes, I suppose."

"Are you sleeping any better?"

"Erm, again, sometimes although not the way I used to. Was there something specific you wanted or have you just phoned to annoy me and do a health check?" I asked, hoping that she'd shut up and give my head a holiday.

"Actually I phoned to tell you about someone who I think might be able to help you."

"I don't need a psychiatrist thank you very much," I said swiftly.

"I wasn't talking about a psychiatrist, I was talking about an old faith healer that I heard about today. His name is Thaddeus McCrory and he lives in the mountains in Carrickbeag and apparently he's a legend."

"Ruby, what the hell are you prattling on about?" I said, feeling impatient. "I don't need a faith healer. I'm perfectly all right."

"I didn't say that you needed one," she said. "I just think it would be good if you went to see him. He's rough and ready but he comes highly recommended and his speciality apparently is pregnant women."

"Why? Has he some sort of a fixation or something?" I recoiled, imagining a dirty old man looking for an excuse to get a grope.

"Frankie," Ruby said reprovingly, "he's not like that. He apparently has a direct line to God. You're not sick but a blessing from him wouldn't do you any harm.

He's cured people of all sorts of complaints. Things that are far more serious than a bit of insomnia and a sore head. I've been worried about you. You've been through a really tough time these past few years and now that you do seem happy and are pregnant I just want everything to go well for you."

"This faith healer – has he made the blind see and the lame walk and does he have a beard and wear sand shoes and speak Hebrew?" (I'd never been big into cures and charms and the like.)

"Oh fine then," Ruby said. "Don't believe me. I hear that he has real heat in his hands and that they hold all his powers. His mother passed them on to him before she died."

"Well, he can keep his hot hands away from me," I said.

"Would it really do any harm?" Ruby asked. "With all the stress you've been under lately you and the baby could be doing with all the help you can get. Look, take his number and if you change your mind and stop being so stubborn then you can give it a whirl."

"Fine, you're worse than my mother when it comes to cajoling me into things."

I took the number and idly stuck it in my back pocket before going up the stairs. I could hear Ella and Hammy gently talking in their room and when I looked in on my two big babies I saw that they were both sleeping softly. I blew them kisses and undressed, admiring my changing shape in the wardrobe mirror as I did.

I got into bed and lifted the novel that I was currently reading but then put it down again, deciding that I had too many real life situations to solve never mind trying to unravel the plots and twists in someone else's imagination. The question was where should I start? What would I do tomorrow to try and convince Angelica that I was not the stepmother from hell?

Chapter 35

I felt inspired and brilliant. It was twelve o'clock and I'd been up since nine and was simply buzzing with ideas, much to Ella's amusement.

"Excuse me but have I missed something? Are you going to all this trouble for 'that spoilt brat who irritates me beyond belief' or is this another 'symptom'."

"Oh, for God's sake, not you too! I've already had the third degree from Ruby. There's no big mystery. I haven't suddenly gone mad or anything. I've just decided that as we're stuck with each other we might as well make the best of it. I've attempted to suggest things before but maybe I didn't try hard enough."

Ella gave me a reassuring squeeze as she bustled about doing her laundry. I noticed that she seemed illuminated. I thought in a strange and confusing way that my pregnancy had given her a focus and temporarily distracted her by bringing out her caring nursing side.

"Right, I'm going to make tracks," I said cheerfully as I grabbed my car keys. "Wish me luck and take good care of my babies."

"I will," Ella said.

Ben and Carly were running around the garden like two raving lunatics, being chased by Hammy who was waving a garden hose at them and threatening to switch it on.

I felt jittery and nervous as I put the key in the ignition. I was trying not to think about the possibility that Angelica might well slam the door in my face or that she might see me at the door and pretend not to be there. I really wanted to try and make this work for all our sakes. I couldn't bring a baby into a world that was so full of aggravation and I couldn't put up with much more of it myself either.

I reached Owen's cottage and saw that the curtains were all open and hoped that Angelica hadn't left the house already to do whatever it was teenagers did these days.

There was no answer to the first ring of the door bell but by the time the chime had stopped reverberating for the second time Angelica had opened it a crack and was peering out at me in wonderment.

"What do you want?" she asked rather accusingly. "Daddy's at work."

"I know he is," I said. "And if I wanted to see him that's where I'd be looking for him but, as you are the one I want, that's why I'm here."

"What do you want me for?" she asked defensively, opening the door slightly more so that I could see her hand on her hip in her usual stance. "I don't want to talk about last night."

"Angelica, please. I'm not here for a row. It's the last thing I want. I came here to see if we could do something together today."

"Like what?" she said with a sneer.

"Something you'd like to do," I said tentatively.

"I'd like to go back and eat my breakfast in peace," she said.

"No problem." I could feel beads of sweat beginning to form on my upper lip from the sheer pressure of the situation. "What time would you like me to pick you up?"

"Frankie, what is this?" she asked incredulously. "Since when did you become my new best friend? You don't like me, remember? And the feeling's pretty mutual."

"Do we have to be like this all the time?" I asked, hoping to appeal to her good side. That's if the stroppy little cow has one, I thought – sorry – I mean – if the poor confused, mixed-up, motherless teenager who has issues had one.

"What other way would you like me to be, Frankie?"

"Well, maybe we could make an effort to get on for your father's sake. He is our common bond in that we both love him and want to see him happy."

"You've only known him five minutes," she said. "How could you possibly love him as much as I do?"

"Oh for goodness sake, Angelica, I am not about to enter into a discussion about who loves your father more. This is not helping anyone. Can you not try to be agreeable for even five minutes or is that too much of a challenge?"

She nearly closed my fingers in the door only that I had the good sense to move them in time. I put one hand on my forehead and the other at the base of my back and walked around. This was not how this was supposed to happen. We should have been halfway to Belfast now talking about the latest trends in Top Shop and what good concerts were coming up in the Odyssey. The day wasn't supposed to end five minutes after I arrived with me being sent home almost minus a few of my digits.

I marched over to the front door and opened the letter box.

"Angelica, I'm leaving now. If you change your mind you know where I am. I've taken the whole day off and I'd like to spend it with you. Can you imagine what your father would say if he came home to learn that you and I were taking the time to get to know each other and weren't fighting? He'd be thrilled with both of us and you'd have had a nice day out too. I hear that there's a sale on in River Island."

There was no response so I got into the car and prepared for Ruby to say "I told you so". She'd probably been rehearsing her speech already.

I sat in the car and prayed that the door would open but of course it didn't and I'd already played my trump card. Angelica had a weakness for the clothes, shoes and jewellery in River Island but if that hadn't worked she obviously wasn't going to play ball with me in any shape or form.

Reluctantly I turned the key in the ignition and drove away. I might as well go to work. At least it would keep me occupied and save me from moping.

There was plenty to do in the college. The staff barbecue was coming up at the end of August and I still hadn't organised for the local papers to attend. Mr Reid maintained that if prospective students saw the staff enjoying themselves in their "civvies", they would probably be more inclined to enrol for the new term in September. Owen and I were going to keep well out of lens shot this time though; and the event was definitely not going to be videoed.

I arrived at the college and sighed deeply. I wanted a different story to tell Owen. I wanted to phone him later and tell him Angelica and I had a wonderful day shopping together and I wanted her to reiterate those sentiments whilst telling her father what a hip and cool stepmother she had. Perhaps I was just too ambitious; maybe deluding oneself was another symptom of pregnancy.

I answered my mobile and heard Ella's voice asking excitedly how I was getting on.

"I'm not," I said flatly. "I'm back at work which is where I should have been in the first place instead of coming up with half-baked mad ideas that were never going to work. Why didn't you talk me out of it before I went?"

"Trying to talk you out of anything is like trying to reason with a rabid dog," Ella answered at once. "I remember you saying something similar about Angelica at one stage. Perhaps the problem is that you two are just too alike."

"I am nothing like her," I answered sharply. "Are you really trying to insult me, Ella? I am not a stubborn, outspoken, mad teenager in case you haven't noticed."

"Well, you're not a teenager," she answered.

"How are my children?" I asked. I was tiring of this stupid conversation.

"They're wonderful. We're going to take them out soon. I promised Carly that I would buy her some new earrings and I never break my promises to my favourite niece."

I could hear Ben's voice in the background. "Carly can't be your favourite niece, Auntie Ella, cos she's your only niece. You can only pick a favourite out of a group."

"Shut up, Ben!" came Carly's voice. "My Auntie Ella is never wrong and she says that I'm her favourite so you keep quiet!"

I laughed at her indignant tone.

"I wish you'd convince your mother and your Uncle Hammy that Auntie Ella is never wrong, darling," said Ella. "Life would definitely be much simpler if they'd both listen to me."

"Oh ha ha," I said. "Right. I must go and face the music."

I was not looking forward to having to admit defeat on this one and I knew that Ruby would be merciless in her response.

I walked nonchalantly through the door and could hear an animated conversation taking place in reception and it was with shock and surprise that I realised that it was Ruby and Mandy who were chatting in such a friendly manner.

"Whaaaaaaaaaaaaat?" Ruby said a few moments later when we were walking down the corridor and I was looking pointedly at her with a smirk and raised eyebrows.

"'Right, Mandy, I'll see you later. Sure why don't you give us a shout when you're going for lunch'," I mimicked in Ruby's husky voice.

"She's not as bad as I thought she was," Ruby said. "In fact she's quite nice. She was saying that there's a quiz on in the Swiftstown Hotel on Friday night and that they're one player short. I quite like quizzes so I thought I might go and offer my services."

"Really?" I turned to look at her. "In the twelve years I've known you you've never revealed that you like quizzes. Is this a closet fetish or maybe it has something to do with some of the other players on the team. There wouldn't a certain man who'll be lending the team his expertise just in case there are any questions about photography would there?"

Ruby blushed from her hairline down to her neck and looked at the floor.

"I knew it," I said triumphantly. "Stop looking so fierce, Rubes. I think it's great. He seems like a nice fella even though I could cheerfully strangle him with his camera lead for all the trouble he's caused me but that all seems to be forgotten about now so if you and he get it on that'll be fine with me."

"What do you mean 'get it on'," she asked, looking quizzically at me. "It's a quiz night not a teenage disco, Frankie. Somehow I think the other participants might have something to say if we suddenly start snogging in the middle of the general-knowledge round."

"There's always afterwards," I said. "Make sure you sit beside him and tell him you're hungry. There's nothing like a nice meal and a bottle of wine to create the perfect atmosphere for a date."

"Yes, thank you, Cilla," she said. "Hey, what are you doing here anyway? I thought this was your day for trying to befriend stroppy teenagers – or, let me guess, the little brat wouldn't take you up on it. Well? What was her excuse? Washing her hair, was she? Ungrateful wee bitch. There's not too many would have even tried."

"Climb off your soap box, Ruby," I sighed. "It'll take more than one attempt to persuade her that I'm not The Wicked Witch of the West."

"I wouldn't hold my breath," she answered. "Why should you have to prove anything in the first place? She should know that you're not out to hurt her in any way."

"But that's the thing, Ruby – how does she know that? Her own mother, who carried her for nine months and gave birth to her, decided after seven years of being with her that there was another life somewhere more appealing and ran off and never came back. If your own flesh and blood can do that to you, what could someone else not do, especially if they have just stolen your father away from you and are now going to give him another child to distract his attention away from you even more?"

"I suppose when you put it like that it makes sense but she's still a stroppy cow with an attitude problem."

"Yes, well, she is a horrible teenager so some things just have to be expected. It could also come with the genes – her aunt's a force to be reckoned with and a terrible influence to boot. I wish I could freeze time and keep Ben and Carly the way they are forever."

"What are you doing here?" Owen asked as he entered the Admin Office where Ruby and I were talking.

"I decided to come to work after all," I said brightly, not wanting to admit defeat.

"She's back at work because she went to see Angelica and got the door shut in her face," Ruby said.

I shot her a look but she ignored me.

"If I was being offered a chauffeur-driven shopping trip to the city where I could buy all sorts of lovely clothes," she said, "I think I'd jump at the chance. In fact, you wouldn't like to take me instead, would you? I'm sure I'd appreciate it."

Owen looked at me apologetically. "I'm sorry, Frankie. I'll have a word."

"No," I said emphatically. "That will turn her against me even more. Least said is soonest mended. Just leave it with me and I'll try again in a few days. I can be very persistent, y'know."

I needed to put my thinking cap on and get into the head of a teenage girl. What would I like to do if I were one? Suddenly I had an idea and I could feel both Owen and Ruby staring at me as I started rifling through the Yellow Pages like a madwoman.

Chapter 36

I was so excited. Owen and I were sitting in the waiting room of the Radiology department in the South Swiftstown Hospital and I was waiting most impatiently to hear my name being called. Despite the fact that my bladder thought it was swimming in the Irish Sea, I couldn't wait to see the first images of my baby. As the next patient was called I shifted uncomfortably in my seat and Owen placed a reassuring hand on my knee.

"Are you all right?"

"I desperately need to pee but besides that I'm holding up." I had plenty of visual stimuli to occupy me as I was partaking in the age-old tradition of all expectant mothers: I was having a bump competition. Who had the biggest baby bump? Who didn't look pregnant from behind? Who did? Who was bigger than me and what would they be thinking about the state of my belly if they were having similar thoughts?

"I shouldn't mention waterfalls or alert you to the fact that there's a fountain in the next waiting room then, should I?" Owen said playfully and I swatted him with the back of my hand.

It was with relief I eventually heard my name being called.

"Mrs Colton, please."

"Call me Frankie," I said as I entered the room where the white-tunic-wearing radiographer was standing holding the door open. I was not "missus" anything any more.

"Right," she said with a raised eyebrow.

I could tell that she thought I was being pernickety because I was in a mood; little did the woman realise that the mere thought of being referred to as Missus (Mrs Tony Colton in particular – ugh!) made me want to hurl and that took very little these days.

I looked around the room and decided that it hadn't changed very much since I was here looking at Carly wriggling around in my womb.

I perched myself on top of the leather examination table and pulled up my top, preparing myself for the feeling of cold jelly on my tummy. I suddenly started to feel nervous. I could hear Ella's words about how stress isn't good for the baby ringing in my ears and I squeezed Owen's fingers tightly. He squeezed me back and rubbed the back of my hand and gave me a reassuring wink.

The radiographer uncoiled the ultrasound equipment and placed the probe on my tummy. I saw a blur of black and grey and scrutinised her face for any sign that she was about to tell me that my pregnancy was a figment of my imagination and that I was just a fat bitch.

She made a noise and pursed her lips and I felt frantic.

"What?" I said jumping.

"Mrs Colton, I must urge you to say still," she said, jumping with me.

"I'm jumping because I think there's something you're not telling me and I told you not to call me feckin' missus," I said with tears suddenly pricking my eyes. Goddamn it, why did I ever wish that I wasn't pregnant? I was a horrible person and I deserved everything I got. I turned and looked at Owen who patted me on the hand again but I could tell he was concerned as well.

"I'm going to have to change the machine," the radiographer said as she took the probe away and started to push buttons and wheel the equipment towards the door.

Oh feckity feck feck. She was trying to spare my feelings instead of telling me the truth. The equipment was fine: it was me and my baby who weren't.

As soon as the door closed I burst into floods of tears which hadn't ceased to flow by the time the radiographer made a reappearance five minutes later with a larger version of the scanning equipment.

"I'm a big girl. You can tell me, you know," I said sniffing.

"Tell you what, love?" she asked.

She was calling me "love". This was definitely not a good sign. She had looked at me like I had horns when I first entered the room and now she was calling me love. There was something wrong. I just knew it.

She grunted again as she slid the probe over my stomach.

"Aha," she said. "There you are. I thought I saw two heartbeats but I just wanted a more focussed image to pick it up."

"Pardon," I said, looking at Owen who was mirroring the shock that must be just as evident on my face.

"Twins," she said simply. "Do they run in any of your families?"

"Not mine and they don't in yours either, do they?" I asked Owen in a whisper.

"Well, actually, my father was an identical twin and I had a twin brother who died at birth."

"Thanks for telling me," I muttered as the radiographer started to press buttons and take measurements. Why on earth didn't he tell me this before?

(Quite important to warn your expectant girlfriend that it could be twins, do you not think?)

"There's an arm and a leg and the other one is tucked in behind. Look, you can just see a little hand waving."

I looked at the monitor and all my fears and anxieties melted away as I focused on the miracle that was evident in front of my eyes. My babies were waving their first hello to their bewildered mammy and daddy so we should at least be pleased that they were alive and well. Five minutes ago I had been scared out of my wits that I was going to receive bad news and now instead I had two reasons to be overjoyed.

Two reasons to be happy. Two reasons to get even fatter than I had anticipated. Two reasons to be twice as sick (it was all making sense now), two reasons to get nervous about giving birth (*twice!*) and two reasons why my mother wasn't just going to have one coronary. She was now going to have two.

"Frankie. I've been worried out of my mind," Mammy stated when I eventually switched my phone on three hours later.

In three hours Owen and I had stared incessantly at each other whilst taking it in turns to utter expressions of shock and surprise and talk about the lorry-load of nappies we would need.

"It can't be that bad," Owen said. "Two's not bad when you consider that some women give birth to quadruplets and quintuplets. Two's nothing really. It'll be wee buns. Easy peasy."

At that point I reminded him in no uncertain terms that it wouldn't be him pushing and straining and ripping and tearing in an effort to bring them into the world.

"Don't be so melodramatic, Frankie. Think about Ella. She would give her eye teeth to have the chance you're being given on a plate."

I was thinking that I should be counting my blessings when I realised that I would have to tell Ella that instead of bringing one baby into the world I would be bringing two while she had none. Oh great.

"Frankie, what's wrong with you," my mother demanded. "Why are you breathing like that? Do you need to put your head in a paper bag?"

"No, I do not," I said irritably.

"What's the matter," she said, her voice growing high-pitched. "There's something wrong. What is it? Is the baby all right or have they found something?"

"They've found something all right," I said.

"*What?*" she shrieked.

"They found another baby."

"Pardon?"

"That's just what I said," I laughed hysterically.

"Are you delirious? Do you have a temperature?

George, come here. There's something wrong with
Frankie. She's not making any sense."

"Is that a change from usual then?" I heard my
father mumble.

"Mother, do stop panicking. When I say that they
found another baby I mean that there's two. I'm
expecting twins."

"Oh dear God! George, get me a chair. I think I
feel faint."

Chapter 37

I was part relieved and part terrified by Ella's reaction to my news. Instead of being upset as I suspected she might have been, she hadn't stopped talking about what type of pregnancy I would have in front of me and her graphic details about the birth and how little time I would have between both babies being born had me wishing I could sew my legs together.

"Did they ask you about getting a special scan done?" she asked the next morning.

"They did mention something when we were leaving about a scan which would tell if the babies are identical or not," I said as I continued to sort out my ever-growing laundry pile.

"Yes, they'll be able to see if the babies are joined to one placenta which means they're identical or two which means that they're non-identical and two eggs have been fertilised instead of just one."

She looked animated as she was talking and had a faraway look on her face and I knew that she was imagining what her own reaction would be if she heard this news. I could just see her and Hammy being overjoyed, instead of worrying about the amount of nappies they'd have to deal with and how much space they were going to need.

"You can come with me to the scan if you like," I said impulsively. I wanted my sister to experience this with me and not because she was a midwife and a well of information (too much information sometimes). It was just that I wanted her to be part of it all. It might even give her the incentive she needed to extend her stay.

"I wouldn't want to impose," she answered quickly.

"Why would you think that?" I asked. "Owen won't mind and I could certainly do with a friendly face there who will explain everything to me in layman's terms instead of a pile of medical gobbledy-gook."

"In that case I would love to be your gobbledy-gook translator."

"It *will* be you some day," I said.

Quickly she stood up and started to tidy the kitchen sideboard. She always did that even when we were younger to ease her agitation and mask her feelings.

"We'll see," she said. "I got my period again this morning so it definitely won't be this month."

Her disappointment was evident and Hammy's

noticeable absence and her inability to meet my gaze meant that to make matters worse they'd been arguing about it again.

"Not this month but maybe next month," I said cheerfully.

She smiled weakly. "What I need, Frankie, is a miracle. Nothing short of a miracle will do. We've been doing everything right. I have an ovulation kit which I got from the hospital which is so sensitive that it can nearly warn me a week in advance of when I'm going to ovulate. We've been having sex at all the right times. I've been lying with my legs in the air in all sorts of flamin' mad positions in the hope that gravity will help his sperm find an egg but still it doesn't happen. Why me, Frankie? Why is this happening to me? I see all sorts of women coming into the maternity ward to have their babies and the sad thing about it is that at least one quarter of them don't want to be there because they have enough children or they're teenage mums or simply sometimes because they're too selfish and they don't want a child complicating their lives and ruining their houses and their weekends."

I was shocked by the sheer force of Ella's reaction.

"I'm sorry," she said grabbing my hand. "It's so insensitive of me to be ranting and raving like this to you, especially when you have enough problems of your own."

"Your problems are my problems," I said. "And we'll

find a solution somehow. You see those articles in the magazines all the time talking about miracle babies."

"Well, nothing short of one is going to do." Ella let go of my hand and began shuffling things around.

The back door closed and Hammy came in bearing flowers while Ella's tidying got even more intense and erratic. I saw this as my cue to leave them on their own as I prepared to make the journey that I'd been psyching myself up for all day.

Although the fuss about the baby or babies, should I say, temporarily put my plans on hold I hadn't forgotten about my idea where Angelica was concerned. I was hoping that now Owen had told her our "twin" news that she might be more receptive to spending some time with me.

I pulled the door gently without closing it fully and left Ella and Hammy talking quietly. Through a crack I could see Hammy massaging Ella's shoulders while she stared at the ceiling.

Ben and Carly were playing outside and both came running when I emerged from the house.

I ruffled my son's spiky hair and gave Carly a quick squeeze.

"Can we do something with you, Mum?" Carly asked in an earnest little voice.

"Well, as it happens I do need to take you two out for a while later. We need to go and buy new school uniforms."

The animation on the children's faces disappeared and was replaced by quite obvious disgust. Ben looked sullen whilst Carly was wrinkling her nose and looking pensive.

"That's not a proper treat," she said.

"It's not a treat at all," Ben said reproachfully. "I hate the thought of having to go back to school. I like being at home with you and Auntie Ella and Uncle Hammy."

"I know, son, but unfortunately it's only a few weeks until school starts again and I don't want to leave getting your uniform until the last minute in case they've run out of something."

Ben looked decidedly unimpressed by this suggestion and continued to look solemn.

"You should be excited, Ben," I said, changing tack. "You'll be able to make the under-twelve football team this year after your birthday."

I left my trump card until the end and was finally awarded a half-hearted grin in response. Ben had experienced a lot of changes this summer. He hadn't mentioned his father in a while but I knew that the thoughts were still simmering in the back of his head and that it would take very little to bring them bubbling to the surface yet again.

"I'll tell you what – why don't we go and see Granny Celia for a while first and then we'll go out and get ice cream or something before we go shopping for school. I'm going to leave you with granny while I go and do a message."

"Where are you going?" Ben asked in a suspicious voice. "Are you going to see Owen? Before Owen we used to go lots of places and do things with you but now you never have time anymore."

"That's not true," I cried, feeling stung by the accusation that I had been a less than attentive mother lately. "You know that I haven't been well and that things have been a bit hectic with having Auntie Ella over to stay and me being busy at work."

"And having to go and try and make friends with Angelica too," Carly said.

"Who told you that?" I asked.

"Angelica told me. She was laughing and saying that it was really funny."

"Did she now?" I said.

"She said that it was fun to watch you fall all over yourself and then she said something about freezing."

"Freezing?" I asked puzzled, feeling sure that Carly had picked up the wrong end of the stick somewhere.

Carly looked thoughtful. "Oh, I remember! Mum, what does it mean when someone says that hell will freeze over before something happens?"

I felt my stomach sink and did not like where this conversation was heading at all.

"It means that someone really doesn't want something to happen."

"Angelica said it. She said that hell would have to freeze over before you and her would be friends."

I was horrified that the tyrannical little shrew would fill Carly's head with such notions and was even more put out that neither my son nor daughter seemed the slightest bit annoyed about the statement. I tried, however, to cover up my feelings of hurt as I encouraged them to tell me more.

"When did she say all this, darling?" I asked gently.

"Yesterday."

I frowned and wondered where on earth they had seen each other yesterday.

"We forgot to tell you that she called over when you and Owen were at the hospital."

"Why would she do that?" I asked.

I noticed that Ben was giving Carly a look and saw her suddenly shrinking behind my legs.

"Carly," I said in a warning voice, "remember when we had that conversation about not having any secrets from one another and I told you that you could tell me anything?"

"Yes," she said in a small voice while Ben continued to stare at her with his eyebrows knotted.

"Well, tell me what she said."

Ben was shaking his head at Carly.

"What did she say?" I asked, directing my attention towards my son.

"She said that it was a private conversation just

between the kids," Ben said in a whiny voice which let me know that he knew I had him cornered.

"Listen to me," I said in my most menacing voice. "Whatever she has promised or threatened I'll double it."

(I couldn't believe that I had to bribe my own children to talk to me and was making a mental note to go round to Owen's and personally shave off all Angelica's hair and trample her make-up.)

I had in my pocket a voucher which I had been planning on giving the warped little minx. I had gone to the hair and beauty salon last week and bought it for her, thinking that we could go into town and pamper ourselves. The method in my madness with regards to the voucher was that I felt that she could get anything that she wanted and not feel that she needed my permission. I thought that I had covered every angle, but obviously not.

"Please, Mum, don't be cross," Ben said.

"I won't be cross if you're honest and promise to never hide anything from me again," I said.

"She says that you and her daddy aren't good for each other and that if you ever got married that we'd be really unhappy."

"And she said that we had to make a plan, just like The Famous Five always do," Carly said, swept away by the romance of it all and obviously picturing herself as an amateur sleuth.

"And what type of plan did you have to come up with?" I asked, barely managing to maintain an even tone.

"We had to try and think of something to break you up."

"And we're going to meet her again when you're at work next week," Carly said. "Oh-oh," she added, looking at Ben and shrugging her shoulders as she realised that she had well and truly given the game away.

"Don't you worry about meeting her," I said firmly. "I'll make other arrangements."

"What are you going to do, Mum?" said Carly.

"I'm going to take my special babies out for the day and spoil them rotten," I said firmly. "But first I need to go back into the house and see Auntie Ella."

I turned on my heel and walked back into the house where I could see my sister and brother-in-law still deep in conversation and oblivious of my presence.

"Sorry to interrupt," I said, knocking the door gently. "Here, sis," I said throwing the envelope at her. "Take that into town and treat yourself to a makeover. Why don't you book a nice restaurant for a meal, Hammy? Ella will be a new woman by the time she's finished with that."

"That's the best idea you've had all day," Hammy said with a smile.

I left again and was gratified that someone was pleased with the way their day was going because I was anything but.

Chapter 38

It was getting dark and we were driving home from the fun park in Belfast where the children had been on every amusement known to man when my phone rang again.

I knew I was being stubborn but I simply didn't feel like talking to Owen. I looked and saw that he had rang me four times. I shouldn't have been blaming him for his daughter's behaviour but I couldn't help it. I couldn't stand by and watch my child behave like that.

"Why did you throw your phone away, Mum?" Carly asked inquisitively as she watched me. "And why are you making those faces?"

"What faces? I wasn't aware that I was making any faces."

"You were going like this," she said as she sat

forward and bared her teeth and put on a scary face in the mirror.

(Oh dear, I must have been getting carried away again.)

I looked around at her and smiled and told her that I was playing.

Too late I heard the screech of brakes in front of me and felt myself spiralling into panic as I tried to frantically stop the car by jabbing my foot controls.

The car jolted violently as I hit the one in front. The children screamed in terror and I heard the sounds of metal crunching and glass breaking. I was aware of being thrown hard against the steering wheel and could feel my seatbelt cutting into my flesh as it was pulled under force.

My first worry was for my children who were crying in the back and trying to comfort each other.

"It's all right, Carly," Ben was saying as he put his arm around his little sister.

I heard her scream, "There's blood, Mum!" and she started to sob uncontrollably.

I manoeuvred myself awkwardly to look at where they were sitting and my breath caught in my throat as I winced from the pain in my abdomen.

"It's all right, darling," I said, determined to stay strong.

The door of the car in front opened and I saw a man run towards me.

He opened my door and on seeing the children moved to the back of the car to get them out. He spoke to them in a gentle tone as he helped them out. It was only when they were out of the car that I give vent to my pain and a loud moan escaped from my mouth.

The man came quickly to my aid. He was talking on the phone when he came to the door.

"Quick as you can, please. There's a woman and two children involved. Little boy, about ten I think, has a broken nose and a wee girl of around six who is in severe shock and holding her arm."

"Are you all right, love? Can you move?" he asked me.

"My back hurts and I have a terrible pain in my side and I'm —"

I was just about to tell him that I was pregnant when he started to point at my leg and talk louder into the phone.

"She says she's hurt her back and her side but she seems to have done something to the top of her leg as well as she seems to be losing a lot of blood."

I could feel my already white shocked skin further drain of blood as realisation dawned on me.

"Oh Jesus. My babies. Please help me. It's not my leg. I'm pregnant with twins. Please don't let me lose my babies!"

Chapter 39

I saw the doctor's face and didn't need to hear the words to know what he had to say wasn't good. Owen was by my side holding my hand and crying and Ben and Carly were in another part of the hospital with Mammy, Dad, Ella and Hammy who had all rushed there when they had received the news. The man who I had crashed into was very understanding and had phoned my parents before the ambulance left.

"Frances —"

"Frankie," I said matter of factly. If he was going to tell me that I had just lost my babies the least he could do was to call me by my proper name.

"Frankie," he started again. "The scan showed that the impact of the crash ruptured the placenta and as a consequence I'm afraid that you've lost your baby."

Owen and I looked at each other for a second before the two of us started to speak at once.

"There are two babies —"

"It's twins —"

The consultant flicked through his notes and disappeared again.

What was in actual fact a wait of around forty seconds felt like a whole day as our future and the lives of our babies hung in the balance.

"I'm sorry, Mrs —"

"I am not Mrs fecking anything! I am Frankie. Now are my babies alive or what?" I shouted with Owen continually patting my hand.

I shrugged him off. He was irritating me.

"We're going to have to do another scan. Your notes haven't come through from the other hospital yet and we didn't realise that you were pregnant with twins. The ambulance personnel didn't have it in their notes."

"For feck's sake," Owen breathed as a porter came in to wheel my bed back to the radiology unit for the second time.

"Shut up," I snapped. "Go and find Ella for me. I need her."

Owen looked confused but didn't argue as he rushed off in the direction of the Accident and Emergency department.

Ella appeared at my side just as I was being scanned again and the sight of her made me weep.

I could feel her tears on me as she held me whilst I was scanned again.

Anyone for Seconds?

I moaned as they continued to probe and look at my womb.

"Please hurry up and tell us," Owen said in the background.

"It appears that the placenta has indeed ruptured. However, as you have two placentas and one is intact and there is still evidence of a heartbeat it appears that you have lost one baby but that the other one is still alive. We'll have to keep you in for observation of course but it looks good so far."

"What's good about it?" I cried in anguish. "My baby is dead."

"At least we still have one of them," Owen said.

"Get him out of my sight," I whispered to Ella as I turned my head towards the wall.

"I didn't mean to upset her," I heard Owen say as he remonstrated with Ella who was asking him calmly to wait outside.

"Please, Owen. Let me handle this. She needs me right now."

I heard retreating footsteps and breathed a sigh of relief in knowing that he had gone away from me.

"It's all right, I'm here," Ella whispered before I was wheeled into my own private room just off the main ward.

"What about Ben and Carly?" I asked.

"They're fine. They're downstairs in casualty. It could have been a lot worse. Ben has a sore nose and Carly has a sprained wrist but apart from that they'll be fine with some TLC. They can stay with Mammy and Daddy tonight and so can Hammy. I'm going to stay with you."

"No."

"Save your energy, Frankie, and don't argue. I wouldn't want to be anywhere else – besides, us nurses get special treatment when we're getting put up by the NHS for the night. There's something you need to do first though."

"What?"

"You need to talk to Owen."

I stared mutinously ahead, unable to put my feelings into words and unsure whether even if I did anyone would understand.

"He's lost something as well, you know."

"He's lost a lot of things," I whispered after she had left.

Owen appeared with red-rimmed eyes and immediately reached for me. I shied away from him and he awkwardly moved back from me and sat at the edge of my bed.

"I didn't mean what I said. I know this is hard for you and I'm sorry that I wasn't with you. Where were you all day?"

"Spending time with my children."

"I tried to ring you."

"Well, maybe I wasn't in the mood to talk," I snapped.

"Have I done something to upset you?" he asked after a pause. "I know that you've had a horrendous time but have I unwittingly annoyed you in some way?"

I grunted and said nothing, wishing that he would just go away and leave me alone.

"Frankie, please talk to me," he implored as a nurse came in to change my drip.

"I'm really very tired and not in the mood to be interrogated," I said, loud enough for the nurse to hear.

"I think she's had enough for one day," she said quietly as I closed my eyes and feigned sleep.

"I'll be back tomorrow," he said.

I didn't answer him.

"Your hair's nice," I said to Ella as I sleepily noticed that she had come back into the room.

"Shhhh . . . go back to sleep," she whispered.

"Was I sleeping?" I asked in surprise.

"It's two o'clock in the morning," she answered, peering at her watch in the half light.

"So you never got to go out last night?" I said, now awake and wanting to talk.

"We were going to go to that new Italian restaurant in town but then I got an urgent phone call about my sister and because I love her dearly I decided that she was more important than my stomach."

"I'm sorry," I murmured.

"So you should be," she said. "You totally destroyed my evening. I did enjoy my pampering session though. You shouldn't have gone to all that trouble for me."

"I didn't," I said. "I wish I had done it for you though."

Ella looked at me questioningly.

"I got it for Angelica," I said. "I needn't have bothered though. The vicious little bitch simply doesn't deserve it. Not only does she not want me but she now wants to turn my children against me as well."

"Surely not," Ella said. "She was perfectly nice the other day when she came around to see them."

"You knew she was there and didn't tell me?"

"Why did I need to?" Ella asked, looking alarmed.

"The children told me that she came by to talk to them about the best way they could all put their heads together to break Owen and me up."

"The sneaky madam! She came in and told me that she wanted to take them outside to plan a surprise."

"No planning required any more," I said coldly. "She's got what she wants. She can have Owen back all to herself because I am fed up with the whole thing."

"What do you mean?" Ella asked, straightening herself and sitting forward in the uncomfortable-looking armchair she was slouching in.

"I mean that it's over. Finished. Single parenthood is beckoning again."

"You don't mean that," Ella said worriedly.

"I bloody do."

"Mammy is going to have a blue fit. She'll be joining you in the bed. I think you're being very rash and to be honest I think you're being unfair to Owen."

"Why?" I demanded.

"Have you actually told him any of this or given him the opportunity to speak to Angelica about it?" she asked. "I thought not," she added, looking at my face. "Give him the chance to explain. You can't expect parents to accept all responsibility for the actions of their children. It's not all his fault that she is as she is. Sweet suffering Jesus, if Mammy and Daddy had to bear the brunt of all our actions they'd be six foot under by now with all the worry and stress of it all."

"That's not the point, Ella," I said. "I'm weary of the whole situation. Everyone has their breaking point. If Owen had dealt with Angelica properly in the first place none of this would have happened. I understand that he's in a difficult situation and that he's trying to compensate for the fact that her mother left but he doesn't seem aware that his daughter puts me in a difficult place every time she opens her mouth. She really is vile. I just had to get away from her yesterday and look how it ended up."

"It was an accident, Frankie," Ella said gently. "It wasn't anybody's fault."

"Yes, it was," I said. "It was hers. I was furious with Angelica but looked behind me to reassure Carly in the car that everything was hunky-dory when it happened. So it's her fault and Owen's for not dealing with it. And you can't convince me otherwise. It's over."

"Oh well, if you just want to throw in the towel and let her win," Ella said with an eyebrow raised.

She knew that she had hit my Achilles' Heel. I was always a very poor loser and hated to be beaten at anything. There used to be fights that would have made Jerry Springer nervous over the Snakes and Ladders board when we were younger.

"It's not about winning or losing," I said. "It's about having the will to keep struggling and fighting. Angelica told my children that hell would have to freeze over before she would be my friend. What sort of an environment is that to bring Ben and Carly into or any more children for that matter?"

I was overwhelmed with sadness when I thought about my poor surviving baby. I wondered if it was missing its little brother or sister. I knew I was. I had only just started getting used to the idea but I would have loved them both and been the best mother possible. The thought of my baby made me all the more determined to do what I felt was necessary.

Anyone for Seconds?

"I'm going to tell him tomorrow," I said. "I'll tell him that I can't do this anymore and that for the sake of all my children including the unborn I cannot possibly live with Angelica."

"If that's how you feel," Ella sighed.

"It is," I said resolutely.

Chapter 40

Three days had passed when I woke one morning to the sound of voices outside the door of my private room. I blinked and groggily lifted my hand to shield my eyes from the sun which was shining through a crack in the curtains. I tried to turn on my side and gasped in pain.

The voices outside became more audible and I thought I recognised one of them and strained to hear what they were saying.

"Please let me see her just for two minutes. It's really important."

"This is not a drop-in centre. This is a hospital where we have strict rules about visiting. They are there for a reason, mostly because our patients are not fit for the excitement and fatigue that visits create."

"I promise that I won't cause her any stress. Please, just for two minutes."

I heard a series of tuts and mutterings before the voices faded away. Whoever it was had obviously got their marching orders.

I heard the door open but didn't turn around as I knew that I was due more medication.

"Frankie."

My eyes sprang open as I realised that Maura Byrne was in the room with me.

"I thought you weren't allowed in to see me right now," I said in surprise.

"You heard the Nazi dressed as the Ward Sister tell me off then," she grinned.

"What are you doing here?" I asked, eager to get rid of her. I liked Maura but she was standing in the enemy camp so not exactly a welcome sight.

"I heard what happened," she said tentatively. "I'm really sorry, Frankie. It must be awful for you. It's awful for everyone. From a purely selfish point of view I was looking forward to having twin nephews or nieces or one of each. I love children. I have no interest in having any of my own but I'm a world-class auntie."

I looked at Maura and saw that she had tears in her eyes.

I wished that people would warn me when they were planning to drop in and say such things. Things that were actually very nice and endearing and in danger of weakening my resolve.

"What's happened between you and Owen?" she asked, breaking the spell.

"So that's why you're here." I curled my lip. "Sent you to fight his battles for him, has he?"

"He doesn't know I'm here, Frankie, and I'm sure he would fight every inch just to keep you as he loves you so much. The trouble is that I don't think he knows what he's fighting about."

I sighed and focused on the cracked tiled ceiling above my head with its surgical-looking lights.

"Frankie, I'm not here to give you a hard time. I don't want to hurt you any more than you're already hurting. I want to help you and I just wanted to let you know that my brother thinks the world of you. You're really good for him. I didn't realise what had happened when he went to Dublin that time and if it's any consolation he got a right mouthful and a thick ear when I next saw him."

"If I was so good for him he wouldn't have done that to me and he wouldn't be letting his spoilt brat of a daughter treat me the way she does."

"I knew it," Maura said in a tight voice. "Where there's trouble you'll always find her."

"That's not a very nice way to speak about your niece," I commented. "I thought you were Super Aunt."

"Even my superhuman powers can't stretch that far. We all know what she's like. Well, most of us do, my blind, deaf and completely besotted mother being the exception to that rule. She was, however, very upset when she heard what happened."

I made no comment and instead examined my nails. It was nothing I hadn't heard before and no doubt excuses would be made.

Poor Owen's wicked wife ran off and left poor ickle Angelica and him all on their ownsome.

Well, I was starting to have some sympathy with the woman. If I gave birth to the female version of *Damien* I think I'd run for the hills and not look back either. I wondered had Angelica always displayed demonic tendencies or had I sent her to hell altogether (no pun intended of course).

"It's her, isn't it?" Maura said.

"Look, to put it mildly I don't have the energy for this whole thing any more. I love Owen but life is just too short to keep fighting a losing battle. Us staying together would make too many people miserable and I think too much of my children to put them through any more heartache."

"And what about Owen's heart?" she asked. "That's his baby that you're carrying. He's already lost so much – does he have to lose his chance to bring up a child in a stable relationship as well?"

"But it wouldn't be a stable relationship. It would be so unstable that it would be horizontal. It's not my fault, Maura. I wish with all my heart that things were different but they're not. I have to concentrate on my surviving unborn child. I don't have time to worry about Owen and I have even less time to concentrate on humouring Angelica when she is intent on rebuffing me every time I try to get close to her. I've tried talking to her, I've suggested trips out, I've told her that I'll leave her anywhere she wants to go with her friends and every time I've opened my mouth I've got my suggestion thrown back in my face. I'm tired, Maura. I just don't have the energy anymore."

"I'll talk to her," Maura said, standing up.

"You do that, Maura. But don't do it on my account because my mind is made up."

"Please," Maura said with a beseeching look. "He really loves you and he wants this baby so much. He's good to your children and they seem to love him. You know that they wanted to go with him the night of the accident except your mother wouldn't let them. Your little girl was swinging from his neck and she called him Daddy when he was looking at her wrist."

My chest swelled with emotion until I thought it was liable to explode. I couldn't speak.

"I'm going to leave you now but please think about what I've said. Life might be easier but would you be happy? Would your children be happy and would that precious little baby be happy knowing that its father can never be a proper part of his or her life even though it's his deepest desire?"

Maura left and gently closed the door. I'd like to go

back to blaming my hormones for the unrest that was present in my mind but I knew that simply wasn't true and felt my steely mindset start to crack.

My door opened again and I saw the consultant come in followed by a lady wheeling a scanning machine. I wrapped my hands protectively around my stomach when I saw it.

The doctor saw my face and tried to reassure me.

"We just need to make sure that everything is as it should be and that the baby is all right," he said.

I wearily lifted the surgical gown I had on and said a silent prayer. I was almost afraid to look at the screen.

"There's the heart beating steadily and there's a leg and the head and the spine and, look, there's a little hand."

I looked at the screen and watched as my baby greeted me and let me know that he or she was alive and well against all the odds. My tiny miracle. A tiny miracle that had done nothing wrong and deserved a normal proper family, a little voice chided me. I shrugged it off as I fixed myself.

I was tired and wanted to close my eyes.

Chapter 41

Twelve weeks had passed since my ordeal and in that time I had grieved, moped, devoured my mother whole several times over and fallen out with anyone who dared to tell me that I was "lucky" to still have one baby. I didn't consider myself lucky at all. I had lost my baby, a part of me, and the fact that its twin remained was wonderful but irrelevant to the sense of loss I felt when I remembered the gush of blood and the doctor's words.

I had come home from hospital a week after the accident and had tried my best to settle back into life. Ben and Carly were aware that something horrible had happened and were being extra loving towards me. Ben drew me all sorts of pictures and I had so many homemade Get Well cards from Carly that I could no longer see my mantelpiece.

"Everything will be all right, Mum," Carly said stroking my hair. "Granny says that God will take care of everything."

I tried to hide my disgust. I had usually managed to get to Mass every Sunday but my belief in God had waned since I had lost my baby and my man in one fell swoop. Obviously it was not God's fault that Owen was a twerp and that his daughter was unbearable and it also wasn't his fault that I hadn't been paying attention to the road but I needed someone to blame and the Almighty seemed the obvious place to start.

Ella had been dividing her time between Edinburgh and Swiftstown in order to help my recovery. (I bet she was regretting that decision.) She had settled into my home and was a great help with the children as well as being a live-in counsellor/agony aunt/punching-bag for me to vent my anger on. Having something to do had obviously helped her too as she had put on a stone and gone up a dress size and was more like I remembered before.

Gradually, though, I started to feel more positive and decided to look on the bright side. Things could have been a lot worse and I reasoned that I had to keep up my strength for the sake of my other precious bundle who was now kicking the life out of me and giving Ronan O'Gara a run for his money.

Life had continued as normal in other ways and I had been glad of the temporary distraction when

Carly had progressed into her second year in primary school. Ben had also left the house on the first day of September, happy in the knowledge that he had a great year's football ahead of him. The weeks following had been a series of days that merged into each other where I concentrated on taking the children to and from school and helping them with their homework when they returned. I didn't go out, except to do the occasional spot of grocery shopping and my social life had become non-existent and would have disappeared altogether if it hadn't been for Ruby and Ella bringing me the latest released DVDs and encouraging me to go walking.

I had decided to take some time off work but had been gratified to find out that both Owen and I still had our jobs after a review had been conducted and it was deemed that the newspaper had exploited a situation for their own benefit. A full apology had been issued on the front page of one of the August editions after the new editor was threatened with court action (by Ruby). And as it came just in time to attract the attention of more prospective students, it had been cited as a productive PR exercise (although Mr Reid stressed in a strangled and high-pitched tone of voice that this did not mean that he wanted any of his staff to think that this was an invitation to start making home movies of any description.)

Halloween had come and gone and I had tried to

distract myself as best I could by making outfits for Ben and Carly and engaging in all the excitement of going trick or treating with them. I hadn't joined in all the fun although I would have scared the shit out of everyone with my very lifelike impression of a zombie and that was without the help of a wig or theatrical face paint.

Owen and I had gone our separate ways but help had come from a very unexpected source mid-November. When Maura had come to see me in the hospital all those weeks before, her words had initially fallen on deaf ears as had her mother's. Esme had tried to tell me that Angelica was a good girl (helllloooo?) who simply needed love and affection to bring out the best in her to which I had responded by telling her that that person providing it wouldn't be me (was she mad?). I had neither the inclination nor the patience for it anymore and I heartily regretted ever setting eyes on Owen who had visited me every day and beseeched me to rethink my decision but to no avail. I told him that I loved him, wished him luck (he'd bloody need it) and promised that he could have as much contact as he liked with the baby but asked him not to come near me again. I had surprised myself at how calm I was about the whole situation but as my emotions were numb I was incapable of feeling anything.

I had expected Maura to try and reason with me and

I had braced myself knowing that Esme might call but what I hadn't prepared myself for was the possibility that Angelica might appear.

I was feeling tired and sore and depressed when the doorbell rang one evening. I asked Ella to answer it and told her to tell whoever it was that I was in bed. I closed my eyes and heard the low hum of the television whilst listening to voices in the hall.

"Who was it?" I asked when I heard the door opening.

"It's me, Frankie," I heard.

I wondered for a split second if the medication I had been prescribed produced hallucinogenic symptoms as I could have sworn that the voice belonged to Angelica.

Either that or I was seriously overtired.

"Frankie? I know it's late but can we talk? Just for a wee minute?"

There it was again. I screwed up my face and opened one eye to convince myself that I was imagining things but instead came face to face with my worst nightmare.

"How did you get in here?" I demanded, looking at Angelica and wanting to run away. I was in no fit state to be attacked verbally or otherwise and for a moment I wondered if she had bludgeoned Ella at the door in order to gain access to my home.

"I let her in," Ella said as she opened the door a

crack. "Angelica wants to talk to you and I think you should give her five minutes and listen to what she has to say."

My sister was a traitor. How could she do this to me?

"Please, Frankie. It's been really hard for me to work up the courage to come here so please don't send me away."

I wanted to slap her. Did she just say that things were hard for her? Hard? Would she like to walk in my shoes for a day? I looked at her and decided that her horns seemed to have receded slightly. She looked nervous and vulnerable and unsure of herself.

"Five minutes," I agreed. "Starting now."

"Frankie, my dad's miserable without you. He's not sleeping, he's losing weight and he's really sad. I haven't seen him behave like this since my mum left and it's scaring me. Please talk to him. He really loves you and he wants you and the baby more than anything else in the world."

I was speechless. Was this a joke?

"Frankie, I know that it's all my fault. I shouldn't have made things so difficult for you. I guess I just didn't want to share my dad but Auntie Maura said something that made a lot of sense to me."

"What did she say?" I asked. This, I was dying to hear. What on earth had Maura said to produce such a dramatic change? Had she crushed mood-altering drugs into Angelica's food? Was she bribing her? Was she threatening her with violence if she didn't make amends?

"She told me that there would come a day when I would go to college or that I would start work or go out for the night and that I'd meet somebody. Somebody special who I'd want to spend the rest of my life with. I'd want to bring him home and introduce him to Daddy and when I got his approval I might decide to marry him or go away with him. The point is that if I ever did leave and set up home with somebody else that Daddy would be on his own and he'd be lonely. Auntie Maura says that it'll take me so long to find a man who'll be willing to put up with me that Daddy will be shrivelled and grey and too old to be dating so he'll die alone and sad and it would all be my fault."

I tried to stifle the first smile that I had threatened to crack that evening but couldn't help myself.

Angelica gave me a small smile in return and shrugged her shoulders.

"Frankie, I know I'm a nightmare. It's not Daddy's fault that Mammy left and I know that it's not mine but for so long it's just been me and him and it's hard to change."

"I know," I agreed. "Change is difficult for everyone to cope with but it can be done if it's approached in the right manner."

"And would you be willing to approach it again?" Angelica asked.

"I don't know what you're suggesting, Angelica, but I can assure you that I'm in no mood for riddles."

"It's not a riddle, Frankie. It's perfectly simple. Please come back and make my dad smile again and I promise that I'll adapt and cause no more problems."

She looked like Angelica. She was wearing the clothes that Angelica favoured and she sounded like Angelica but this girl had to be a stunt double of some description or else the demon teenager had been cloned (God help us all!).

"I suppose what I'm trying to say is that I'm sorry for being such a foul-mouthed vindictive little bitch."

I couldn't have put it better myself but I still wasn't sure what I was meant to do. Angelica had been one of the main factors which caused our relationship to break down but, even if I was to take everything at face value and there was no ulterior motive, how could I be sure that Owen would want me back?

"Did your dad send you here?" I asked finally.

"No and you can never tell him that I came to see you. If you do get back together with him I want him to think that it's been your decision and that you haven't been pressurised in any way."

I had a little laugh. "Angelica, if I was susceptible to buckling under pressure my mother would have me living with her, wrapped in about two tons of cotton wool. Don't worry – if I was ever to make the decision to get back with your father it would be strictly because I want to."

"And do you want to?" Angelica asked, looking at me anxiously.

"I want a lot of things. I'd love to be able to rewind time and have you behave like this when I was pregnant with both my babies. Then I mightn't have gone to Belfast and had that accident. I had to get away, you see, or I might have been up on a murder charge by now. I'd just found out that you had gone sneaking behind my back and had spoken to Ben and Carly about the best way to split your father and me up. I guess that was the straw that finally broke the camel's back for me. I tried so hard to become your friend, Angelica, and let you know that I wasn't the enemy or that I wasn't going to steal your father but you just wouldn't give me a chance and involving my children in your games and trying to turn them against me was the last straw. I just couldn't take any more. So you got what you wanted and your father and I lost our baby."

"Frankie, that's not fair!" Ella cried, coming into the room having managed to unglue her ear from the door.

"It's okay," Angelica said contritely. "I deserve it. I don't care what you think of me but I want to do this for my dad. You might not have been my first choice for a stepmother but you're definitely my dad's first choice. He's always talking about you."

Well, at least she was being honest.

"I'm well aware that I was never your first choice, Angelica," I said. "But I doubt if any other woman would have fared any better under the circumstances."

"As I said, I didn't want to share my dad but I realise now that you never wanted to take him away from me and even if you had he wouldn't have gone."

"No, he wouldn't," I said sternly. "He loves you very much, Angelica, and I'm sure that you don't expect him to live like a hermit to prove it to you either."

Ella and Angelica were both staring at me with new hope.

"That doesn't mean that I'm going to run straight back into your father's arms this minute. And have you given any thought to the fact that he mightn't want me to either?" I felt incredibly sad at the thought. "A lot has happened over the past few months. We're both still grieving and that's probably not the best frame of mind in which to go making life-changing decisions."

"But you'll think about it?" she asked softly.

"I might."

"How's the baby?" she asked as she watched me gently rub my side.

"It seems to be fine," I said, rubbing more vigorously as I felt a sharp kick.

"What's it doing now?"

"It's moving around," I said.

We looked at each other for a moment before I took her hand and gently placed it on my stomach. She gave a little start and began to smile as she felt her half-sibling squirm.

"Active little thing," she commented.

"Thank God," I said.

"Will you at least think about what I've said?" she asked again.

"I'll think about it, Angelica, but I can't say any more. I do, however, really appreciate everything that you've said and I'm glad that you came to see me."

At that moment Carly came bustling into the room and looked positively panic-stricken when she took in the scene.

"Mum's sick," she said in a warning tone as she came and put a protective arm around me.

"It's all right, pet," I reassured her. "Angelica just came to see how I was."

"Did you?" she asked, adding resentfully, "I don't want to meet with you to talk about Mum anymore."

Angelica flushed a deep red and looked at the floor. "I know it was a terrible thing to do and I promise that it won't happen again." She looked thoroughly ashamed of herself.

Carly looked at her warily for a few moments and then said, "Can Angelica come up to my room and see my new doll?"

Angelica smiled at her and shook her head to indicate that it mightn't be a good idea.

"All right," I said. "Angelica and you can go to your room while Auntie Ella and I have a little chat."

"Well?" Ella said after the girls had gone upstairs.. She was nearly beside herself with excitement.

"Well nothing. She apologised and I accepted and that's it."

"What do you mean 'that's it'?"

"I don't know what you all want me to do, Ella. My head's all over the place and I don't know what to think. This is so unexpected. I never in a million years thought she would ever come looking for me to ask me to take her father back. I'm only used to the Angelica who hates my guts and makes voodoo dolls in my image."

"Is Owen going to be coming here again?" Ben asked excitedly two minutes later as he entered the room followed by Angelica and Carly.

"I don't know, darling."

"We miss him, Mum," Carly and Ben said in unison and, as I looked at their faces and remembered how Angelica had felt the baby move, I knew that the decision was being taken out of my hands.

Chapter 42

Owen was surprisingly receptive to my suggestion that we should perhaps try and be friends and see where it led when I approached him several weeks after Angelica's visit. I wouldn't have blamed him if he had told me to piss off and shut the door in my face. He was, like myself, however, displaying some symptoms of being very wary and kept looking at me like I might chew the head off him at any second.

I had gone to visit him at home when I knew Angelica would be at the youth club. Ruby had tipped me off that he was taking some time off work and also told me to behave myself and not be rude. (As if?) As soon as I entered his house I felt as if I had "come home". As we were now into the month of December and the weather had got colder there was the delicious welcoming smell of a turf fire. Music was playing softly in the background and there was a pot of homemade soup bubbling merrily on the stove. If I didn't know any better I'd say that he had been forewarned.

"You haven't been talking to Ruby lately, Owen, have you?" I asked.

He sucked in his cheeks and tried to maintain a straight face but as he was a very bad liar he didn't succeed in fooling me.

"She just can't help herself," I said.

"She cares," Owen said. I knew that he wanted to add "more than you" to the sentence but didn't.

"I don't know why I acted so badly. I was very emotional and angry after what happened but I shouldn't have taken it out on you or anyone else for that matter," I blurted out. "I guess I've been carrying around a lot of emotional baggage from the past that I need to let go off. You're nothing like Tony and you did everything right in proving it and I know that I've treated you badly. I didn't mean to though. I do love you, Owen."

Owen opened his mouth to say something but I silenced him with my hand.

"Let me finish. I've had a lot of time to think lately and done a lot of soul-searching. It's not easy to admit that you've behaved like a prat so don't put me off my stride. When you left me and went to Dublin and didn't contact me it was like Tony happening all over again and I suppose I never got over that. I built it into a massive deal in my mind and anything that happened after that just added fuel to the flames and helped to convince my irrational mind that I was going to be hurt again. Angelica has really annoyed me but you aren't responsible for her actions. We're all shaped by our past experiences, after all, so I'm not one to talk."

Owen looked at me for a moment and then folded his arms and settled himself back in his chair. "I know that you were carrying the baby and that you were the one that went through the physical pain of losing it but it was my baby too and not only had I to contend with my own loss I also had to deal with losing you as well. Women just can't help running away from me. You acted like it was my fault, Frankie, and that wasn't fair. I wouldn't have wished that on you for anything."

His eyes had filled with tears and so had mine.

"I'm sorry, Owen. I'm so sorry," I whispered.

"Do you mean it, Frankie?" he asked, suddenly grabbing my hand and kneeling down beside me. "Are you willing to try again? I need to know that you're serious about this because if you're not I'd rather that we just went our separate ways. There's only so much I can take."

I looked at him and noted that his eyes were sunken through lack of sleep and that his skin was so pale that he would have nicely blended in with his buttermilk-coloured walls. He had indeed lost weight and was looking shabby, not at all resembling the sharp-talking dapper hunk with glasses that I had first fallen for. He was a broken man and I had reduced him to this. Did he deserve this? Did he deserve all the anxiety and the stress that being with me was bound to create?

He seemed to read my mind as he leant forward and planted a soft and gentle kiss on my forehead.

"I love you, Frankie. I always will."

"I love you too, Owen," I said in a choked voice before flinging my arms around him and hugging him tightly.

Eventually he extricated himself from my vice-like grip and helped me up from where I was sitting. He took both my hands in his and surveyed me for a moment.

"Come with me," he said as he led me upstairs.

(I was not in the mood but if that's what it took to seal the deal I supposed that I could lie there and think of Ireland.)

We went into the bedroom and I mentally chastised myself for not wearing my best underwear. Elasticated maternity pants were sure to be the ultimate passion killer. Owen, however, didn't seem to be interested in going anywhere near the bed so perhaps I was safe after all. He was noisily rummaging through his top drawer and cursing loudly and wondering where he had put "it".

"Aha!" he proclaimed triumphantly as he apparently found what he was looking for and put it in his pocket. He looked around the room and started to talk to himself again.

"I wonder where the best place to do this is?" he said aloud.

(Steady on. This is no time for exploring new positions.)

"I know. We'll go out into the garden, Frankie," he said. "You've always loved it there."

(Just because I liked the rose bushes did not mean that I was willing to start acting like a depraved eejit. I was up for most things but this did not appear on the list.)

"Owen, it's freezing," I said tentatively. "We'll get our death out there."

"I'll be very quick," was his response.

(I suppose he hadn't seen me in a while.)

"Fine." This was obviously a no-win situation.

I followed him down the stairs and sighed as we walked into the garden.

"Are you ready?" Owen asked.

(Jesus, whatever happened to spontaneity? I wasn't used to being warned in advance.)

Owen knelt down in front of me and took my hands in his. "I've been waiting for this moment for most of my life, Frankie. I wanted to save this for someone very special. I never gave this to Jane as I never got the chance – besides, I don't think she would have appreciated it like I know you will."

He unzipped his coat, put his hand in his pocket and retrieved a little box and then he turned it around, opened it and revealed the most exquisite ring I had ever seen. Nestled in the middle of a cluster of tiny diamonds was a large emerald stone which sparkled and shone in the light emanating from the kitchen window.

I put my hand to my throat and continued to stare at it.

"It was my grandmother's engagement ring," Owen explained. "I had it valued a few years ago and it's worth a small fortune as it's a real antique. It's very precious to me, not because of its potential value but because of its sentimentality. I loved my granny very much and in order to keep her memory and her spirit alive the person who wears this ring must mean just as much to me."

I held my breath as he removed the ring from the box and held it in front of me.

"Frankie, will you do me the honour of becoming my wife?"

I opened my mouth, decided I didn't know what to say and closed it again. This was all just too much to take in.

"Frankie?" Poor Owen looked like he might pass out with the stress of the situation so it was only right that I put him out of his misery.

"Owen, I love you very much but I'm not sure that I deserve this or the sentiments that are behind it. I've treated you really badly and I think that if your grandmother was here that she'd probably like to kick my ass from one end of the garden to the other for being such a fool."

"My grandmother would have loved you," Owen said. "You share a lot of the same qualities."

"Was she half mad, neurotic and stubborn as well?"

"No. She was kind and warm and loving but she could be fiery too and we all used to run for cover when she was in a bad mood. What do you say? Will you have me?"

"Of course I'll have you," I said.

I slipped the ring on to my finger and it fitted perfectly. It felt like it had been made for me.

"I had it made into your size. A bit presumptuous, I know, but I really hoped that you would say yes. Ella gave me your old wedding band so I used that to get the measurement for your ring finger."

I held my hand in front of me, looked at Owen and decided that I had made the right decision. I was also most relieved that I didn't find myself having to strip in the garden and also made a mental note to kill Ella. Again. Since when did my sister get so sneaky?

Chapter 43

When I arrived home my family appeared to be camped out and lying in wait for me. (Oh great, I was being ambushed.) The news that I had gone to see Owen had obviously spread like bushfire. I could see the top of Ben and Carly's heads as they peered around the side of the curtains and Mammy and Daddy's car had magically appeared in the driveway.

"Hello, Frankie," Ella said jovially as I entered the living room where they were all gathered drinking tea. There was almost a party atmosphere.

"Hello, Ella." I was wiggling my eyebrows at her and beckoning her to come into the hall with me.

"What's wrong?" she asked.

"Why would anything be wrong?"

"No reason. How did things go with Owen?"

"All right. We've just decided to be friends. I don't think we'll be taking it any further."

The look of pure shock and confusion on Ella's face was reward enough for my little white lie. I could nearly see the cogs in her mind whirring as she processed the information whilst being privy to what Owen had been planning.

"Why?" she asked weakly.

"He got my ring size wrong and I just couldn't bear to be with someone who's attention to detail was so bad."

There was a stunned silence before I proffered my hand and flashed my ring finger. I was so going to enjoy doing that over the next few days. My ring was absolutely breathtaking as was my man.

Ella squealed and started to dance a jig which alerted everyone else to the fact that something major had happened.

Mammy nearly suffered a fit when she came into the hall and saw Ella dancing me around at the foot of the stairs.

"Ella, put your sister down this minute. I do not want any more trips to hospital until that baby is ready to come into the world."

"If we can't celebrate the day she gets engaged, Mother, then we're a sad and sorry lot."

"I beg your pardon?"

Carly bounded from the living room keen to

know what was going on and be involved in all the excitement. "Why are you both shouting?"

"Your mummy and Owen are going to get married, sweetheart," Ella said as she finally allowed me to sit down on the bottom step and lifted Carly up.

Both my children began to scream, Mammy cried and Daddy stood at the living room door and looked bemused but happy.

"You're not planning on getting married before the baby comes, are you?" Mammy asked tentatively.

"Of course I am, Mammy. I'll go to the camping shop and get a tent for a wedding dress and have St John's Ambulance on standby in case there are any other catastrophes. What do you think? I may be slightly unbalanced at the minute but I'm not totally mad altogether."

"Oh good."

"Aren't you happy?" I demanded.

"If you're happy then that's all that matters."

"I know *I'm* happy. I asked you if *you* were happy, Mother." I was starting to feel decidedly peeved. The woman was impossible to please.

When we first started to go out but I hadn't got round to introducing him (was scared he'd run away) she gave out because she wasn't being included. When the fecker did run away she did nothing but worry about how her reputation had been sullied in the local papers and ate the jaws off him when he came back. Then she was happy that we appeared to be sorting ourselves out but now that we were taking the ultimate step towards matrimony she couldn't seem to work up enough excitement to so much as break a sweat.

"Of course I'm happy, love. I just want everything to work out for you. I don't want you to have to cope with anything else. You had enough to deal with after that other shyster took himself off."

"Tony did me a favour, Mammy. I hope he's taken root where he is because the last thing I ever want is to have to lay eyes on him again."

"Why would you?" Ella asked. "Isn't he playing happy families and old Nebby Peg grieving because he's emigrated?"

"But that's just it, Ella. When one thing starts going well in my life something else falls spectacularly apart."

"God! Stop being so pessimistic. Should we not be cracking open a bottle instead of meeting trouble halfway and pre-empting disasters that might never happen?"

"You can have bubbly if you want. I think that Bubs (my affectionate name for my bump) and I will stick to the safe option." I opened a carton of pure orange juice and began to drink thirstily.

"Auntie Ruby!" I heard the children squeal excitedly.

I'd known that it wouldn't be too long before she put in an appearance. I'd shared a rushed phone conversation with her when I left Owen's house and had nearly been left deaf in one ear with the amount of screaming she was doing.

"Oh my God! I am so excited! I'm not talking about it now though. I want all the details face to face later!"

I went into my hallway and discovered to my surprise that Ruby was not alone. She was accompanied by an elderly man with silver hair and a weather-beaten, kind face. He was wearing trousers and a colourful waistcoat and had a very endearing smile.

"Come into the living room," I beckoned, leading the way, then stepping aside to usher him in.

"Don't kill me," Ruby whispered pulling me back out to the hall.

In the living room the elderly man was introducing himself at length to my mother who was hanging on his every word.

"Why would I kill you?" I asked Ruby in alarm. Mammy was now gesticulating wildly to get Daddy's attention.

Instead of answering, Ruby drew me into the living room.

"You're not into all that black magic, are you?" I heard Mammy ask. "Because I think I would draw the line at that. A wee prayer probably wouldn't do any harm though. Frankie doesn't always get to Mass, you see, so somebody needs to look after her soul."

"Frankie," said Ruby, "let me introduce you to Thaddeus McCrory."

Who?

"Thaddeus is the faith healer I was telling you about."

(I *so* was going to kill her even though he didn't look as creepy as an old man with hot hands should.)

I gave her my foulest look and then politely shook hands with my uninvited guest who seemed suddenly not to be the slightest bit interested in me.

Ella had just come into the room and almost as soon as she entered Thaddeus rubbed his hands together and held them out to her.

"Sit down, my dear," he said gently.

Ella did as she was told and shot me a quizzical look which made me want to laugh.

"Will you allow me to bless you?" he asked, looking intently at Ella as if he could see inside her.

Ella gazed back at him, then nodded in response and didn't take her eyes off him until he moved to the back of her head. The room was silent as we watched him gently massage her head whilst whispering words with his eyes closed. He stopped after about five minutes and Ella looked like she was in some sort of trance.

"I'm sorry. I don't normally do that but something instinctively told me that you needed my help. How do you feel?"

"I feel fine. Wonderful actually," Ella said. "What did you do to me?"

Anyone for Seconds?

"I gave you a blessing. I know that there is something missing in your life and that you have a very strong faith. I sensed it as soon as I came into the house even though you weren't in the room."

Everyone was silent. Even the children seemed transfixed by the stranger in our midst.

"And you and your wee baby will be just fine," he said to me as he began to massage my head (and mess up my flippin' hair).

Whether it was the power of suggestion or what, I must say I felt wonderful after he had finished, deeply relaxed and content.

Soon after Ruby announced that she and Thaddeus had to leave and gave me an apologetic glance and a tight squeeze of congratulations as we stood in the hall.

"Sorry, pet. I really wanted to do that for you and I knew that you wouldn't go to him so the mountain simply came to Mohammad."

"I'm glad you did. Look."

We both looked towards Ella who seemed to be basking in some sort of glow and had a dreamy faraway expression on her face.

"If he has helped my sister, he was worth it," I said as Ruby left. I just wished I knew how he was going to help her to achieve her ultimate goal.

Chapter 44

Sometimes I seriously believed that by opening my big mouth I automatically jinxed myself. I had been fretting to Ella about Tony making a reappearance, and although that didn't seem to be on the cards anytime soon I ran into Nebby Peg for the first time in months (as I hadn't seen in her in a while I had hoped that the old bat had been forcibly put in an old people's home).

I was in Tesco's doing my Christmas shopping when I spotted her. I attempted to do a three-hundred-and-sixty-degree turn with a trolley which had a wonky wheel but instead of speeding away in the opposite direction I only succeeded in drawing more attention to myself.

"Frankie, how lovely to see you," she said.

(I know that it was the season of goodwill but I

didn't think that Nebby Peg knew anything about that.)

I smiled, not trusting myself to speak in case I burst into tears. If she made any horrible comments about Ben and Carly or the loss of my baby I didn't think I'd be able to take it.

"I heard what happened."

I made no response and instead eyed the long French baguette that I had just placed in the trolley with my other groceries. It would be a great waste of lovely bread but I wondered if I could use it as a weapon if she turned nasty.

"I was sorry to hear about the accident. I hope the children are all right and that things go okay with you." She looked pointedly at my bump as she said this.

I resisted the urge to ask if she'd had a personality transplant since we last spoke, which had been the fateful day of the foot-splattering incident in Newcastle.

"Thank you," I croaked. It was all I could manage under the circumstances. I was in shock.

"Must be going. Say hello to the children for me." She walked away with a nod.

What? No unforgivable comments? No put-downs? No questioning of my abilities as a mother? No sarcasm or remarks about my love life? God, life was going to get really boring now.

I paid for my purchases and unloaded my groceries into the car and headed straight to my mother's for a postmortem of events. I was glad to escape from the madness of the supermarket and its pre-Christmas panic as I had a sore head and my ankles were doing a wonderful impression of looking like inflated balloons.

Mammy opened the door and I nearly knocked her down in my enthusiasm to get into the house. I noted that Ella was there too and was glad that they would both be able to submit reasons as to why I hadn't been annihilated on sight.

"Oh my God, you will never guess what just happened!" I said.

"What?"

"I just met Peggy Colton and she was actually civil to me. There were no barbed comments and she didn't make a show of me in public. She actually wished me well in a roundabout way. Now what do you think of that? First Angelica and now her. Have I changed or has everybody else just cottoned on to themselves and realised that they were behaving badly?"

I was hoping for tea, a slice of cake and a discussion but instead Mammy didn't appear to have heard me and Ella was fidgeting and picking her nails.

"Is something wrong?" I finally asked.

"Nothing for you to worry about," Mammy said quickly. (Translated this meant that ordinarily I would be worrying but as I was pregnant and not allowed to worry then I wasn't going to be told.)

"Mammy, credit me with some cop-on, please. If

there is something wrong with either one of you then I'd rather hear it now than later."

"There's nothing wrong exactly," Ella said, looking nervous.

(Exactly. Another word I disliked. That meant that there was something wrong but by putting the stupid and wholly ineffective word "exactly" at the end of the sentence the speaker hoped that you wouldn't feckin' notice.)

I began to tap my foot impatiently and waited for someone to speak.

"I was going to talk to you later, Frankie, but I suppose I might as well tell you now. I'm going to go back to Scotland."

I was aware that my face had probably just fallen flat and that my bottom lip was threatening to start wobbling but I had good reason. I had got so used to Ella being around that the thought of losing her was like someone removing my right arm.

"I'm sure you've missed Hammy terribly, Ella. You've been wonderful and had the patience of a saint. I know I've been a pain."

"Don't be silly, Frankie. I love being with you and the children. It's just that I love being with Hammy as well and I really miss him, especially as it's coming up to Christmas. There's also the little thing of us trying for a baby. I think it would be easier to try and conceive if we were in the same country at least."

I smiled and had to agree. Even the Angel Gabriel would have trouble with that scenario.

"I'm sure Hammy's been asking you to come home?"

"No. He knows that you've needed me here and I would have stayed longer but I know that things are going to be okay for you now that Owen and you are together again so I'm happy to leave."

I knew in my heart of hearts that she was right and that it would be selfish of me to expect her to stay away from her home and job and husband for any longer. I hated the thought of it though. I was missing her already and she hadn't even left yet.

"When were you thinking of going?"

"Today is Thursday so I thought that if I rang work and told them that I would be coming home on Saturday evening they could maybe slot me in for a shift on Monday."

"So soon?" I gasped.

"I'm going to make it easy for everyone including me," Ella said. "Quick and painless. It'll be hard for me to leave you all but I'm only a fifty-minute flight away so I'll be back soon."

"It won't be the same without you," I said.

Mammy had yet to speak. She was sitting quietly at the table looking at us both.

"I think it's a very sensible idea, Ella," she said finally. "You should both go back to your respective lives which have been much improved by you being together."

(Very philosophical, Mammy.)

"I think that this trip has been very worthwhile for both my girls and that you've both benefited from it so I'm happy to let you go, Ella, even though I hate losing you again."

Her eyes filled with tears but I knew that she was right in everything she said. Ella had been like my guardian angel sent to protect me and get me through one of the worst times in my life. By the same token it also seemed to have been good for her as she was much more relaxed and had got a break from dealing with the misery of her infertility alone.

"Okay," I said finally. "I'd love to barricade the door to stop you but I can't and I wouldn't. You have been such a rock to me, Ella. I only hope that I can repay the favour some day."

"I'll be back as soon as the baby's born, darling. And that won't be long now."

"No," I looked at my bump which had really taken shape and was like having a football up my top. I had ten weeks to go which was bringing me up to the middle of February.

"I guess we'd better go home so that I can help you pack."

"The packing will do itself tomorrow," Ella said. "I'm more interested in talking about Nebby Peg and getting to the bottom of why she's being so nice to you."

"God alone knows," I said, no longer caring.

"Maybe she feels guilty?" Mammy interjected.

I refuted that suggestion instantly. The woman wasn't capable of such an emotion.

"Maybe she's decided that she's too old and tired to continue to fight a losing battle," Ella said.

I thoughtfully sipped the tea which Mammy had set in front of me but came to the conclusion that the old battleaxe (Peggy, not my mother) got too much pleasure out of being spiteful to simply give it up. No. There had to be another reason and I was dying to find out what it was.

Chapter 45

When Owen heard the news that Ella was going back to Scotland he took that opportunity to introduce a proposition which would give me plenty to think about and provide a welcome distraction to the fact that I was losing my sister.

We were sitting in Owen's house drinking tea and eating hot toast and butter in front of his fire when he hit me with his brainwave. I was sighing with contentment but feeling disgruntled at the same time, because I had to go and collect the children from my mother's and then go home, when he began to speak.

"Are you cosy where you are?"

"Are you joking?" I answered, feeling my eyes getting drowsy as a result of the heat from the fire.

"Wouldn't it be lovely if you didn't have to leave?" he responded.

"I'll say," I was already imagining how nice it would be to be lying there in my baggy pyjamas and slipper socks instead of having to go home where Ella would be starting to pack.

"Well, do you not think that we should do something about it then?" he asked with raised eyebrows.

"I can't stay, Owen. I'd love to but Ella will need my help with packing. Besides, I want to spend time with her before she goes. And anyway Mammy wouldn't be able to keep the children. She's being very good as it is, taking them when she can."

"No – no – no," Owen said smiling. "I wasn't suggesting that you stay tonight."

I frowned, rubbed my eyes and wished that he would get to whatever convoluted point he was trying to make.

"What I am suggesting is that you make life easier for yourself, Frankie. Easier for you and nicer for me. What I am proposing is that we stop this toing and froing between two houses. All this running about isn't good for your blood pressure or your ankles."

I surveyed my swollen feet and tended to agree with him.

"I think that you and Ben and Carly should move in here with Angelica and me," he said with a smile and a flourish.

I was shocked. Although we were getting married sometime in the near future and had talked before about the possibility of living together at some point I had always decided against it purely because I felt Angelica would hate it and make life unbearable for us. At least with the current arrangement I could escape if things got heated. (Which they hadn't been in a while but two hormonal women under the same roof was a recipe for trouble.)

"Erm . . . well . . . Owen," was all I could manage in the form of a response. I wasn't sure how I felt.

Obviously I was pleased that he wanted to have me with him and that he was concerned for my welfare but I just didn't know if I was ready to leave my independence totally behind me. I loved Owen's home but I was also sentimentally attached to my own house. It represented my first tentative steps towards putting my life back together after Tony had left me. Our marital home had been too big and expensive to keep and was full of unwanted reminders of the past so I had to move out in order to provide myself and the children with a totally fresh start. My house in the middle of a small cul-de-sac in Swiftstown was not the height of grandeur. It was a small modest abode. But I had decorated it to my tastes, taken out my own mortgage and stood on my own two feet and stuck my middle finger up at anyone who had ever doubted my abilities to carry on after the loss of the useless man in my life.

Owen seemed to sense my train of thought.

"You don't have to sell your house or totally give it up for that matter. You could rent it out if you wanted," he suggested thoughtfully. "I'd just like to have you here with me so I can look after you properly and I know that you love this house."

I looked around me and had to agree that I felt totally comfortable in my surroundings and did truly love Owen's home which was also very spacious although I momentarily wondered where we would all sleep.

Owen seemed to again pre-empt my thoughts and took me by the hand and led me up the stairs.

Obviously I had been up his stairs before (well . . . I was heavily pregnant after all . . . ahem!) but I had never surveyed it as ever being a potential home for me or my children before.

"There's plenty of space for everyone and room to extend were we ever to decide that we needed more room." He said this with a wink and gestured at my swollen belly. (I sincerely hoped that he wasn't suggesting that the reason for any home improvement was because he wanted his own five-a-side football team as at this moment in time my leaky nipples, swollen ankles and large girth were dictating that this was never going to happen. Dream on, mate!)

Owen's bedroom was large but decorated in the fashion of a single man – which Owen had obviously been when he first moved in. The furniture was dark mahogany and the sheets which adorned the black leather sleigh bed were black and grey although he'd had the presence of mind to scatter some black and silver satin cushions for decoration. There were black and white photographs of John Wayne and Charlie Chaplin on the walls, along with a multicoloured tapestry which had been bought on a trip to Mexico when Owen was in university. His en-suite bathroom was decorated simply in black and white and I smiled when I saw his razor and deodorant sitting beside the sink. I also noticed that his towels were blue and cream and frowned. I would co-ordinate the towels to match the tiles and make the place my own with the addition of the vast array of body lotions and deodorants which I had in my possession. I stopped and smiled and realised that I must have already made my mind up. Normally it took me a while to make decisions as I liked to weigh up all pros and cons before committing myself but this one was obviously pretty easy and also the right one or I guessed I wouldn't feel so good about it.

I had a quick look in Angelica's room which was tastefully decorated but as usual looked like the scene of a particularly violent robbery.

"I keep asking her to tidy up but she maintains that she prefers it to feel lived-in."

"Lived-in?" I repeated. "Is that a code word for bomb site then?"

I was starting to waver and swallowed hard as I

tried to figure how the neat and tidy (compulsive, obsessive) side of my personality would cope with this, especially as it wasn't my home.

Owen led me into the three other bedrooms which I now looked at with new eyes as I could already picture them housing my children's things.

"So what do you think?" Owen asked finally, once we had retreated back downstairs and I was putting my coat and scarf on.

"I think it's a nice idea," I ventured.

"Nice," Owen repeated, looking like he had just tasted something sour in his mouth. "I was hoping for a more enthusiastic word like wonderful or brilliant or fantastic." "Well, it is all those things, Owen, but have you consulted Angelica about any of this?"

"Well, no, not exactly, but . . ."

"Come back to me when you've talked to her and make sure you tell her that it was your idea and that I'm not moving in on top of you just to spite her or destroy her reputation in any way."

"Okay, okay. I'll speak to her but I promise it won't be a problem."

He kissed me on the forehead and the nose and then finally on the lips and I felt so secure in his arms that I wished I didn't have to leave at all and was suddenly filled with the hope that Angelica wouldn't mind us infiltrating her space as more than anything else I wanted to be with Owen.

Chapter 46

I found myself back at the airport two days later and had a lump in my throat the size of a rugby ball as I watched Ella check in. Ben, Carly and Owen had all come for the spin and were there for moral support should my hormones run amok and turn me into a snivelling heartbroken wreck (again).

Owen had called in the previous day and found me in floods of tears at the kitchen table.

"It's all right, love. I know I'm not Ella but I promise that I'll take equally good care of you."

"It's not that," I whinged, producing a jar of beetroot. "I'm sad that Ella is leaving but I hurt my hand trying to open this and I really really want some with my lunch."

"So the cause of your distress is all down to a pickled vegetable then?" he said trying not to laugh, which had served to only enrage me further.

"Don't laugh at me," I said. "I'm delicate."

"Your stomach's obviously not delicate," he commented as he watched me delve into the jar with a fork and sigh with contentment as I began to eat.

"Are you sure you don't want ice cream with that?"

"I'm not that bad. Well, not yet anyway."

"I suppose I'd better make a move," Ella said, once she had handed over her luggage.

"But it's early yet. You've still got loads of time," I said.

"I know I have but I hate goodbyes so I'd rather just say 'see you later' and go and get a cup of coffee and read a magazine for an hour."

I knew how she felt. Goodbyes made me crazy.

"I think that's a very good idea," Owen said as he gave Ella a tight hug. "Thank you so much for everything."

"No need to thank me," Ella said. "I was just looking after my little sister which is not hard to do."

The children both launched themselves at their aunt when she held her arms out to them and she closed her eyes tightly as she enveloped them both in a bear hug.

"Look after your Mum until I come back, won't you, my darlings?"

The tears began to flow and my head started to ache and thump with all the stress and pressure.

"Look after yourself, pet, and remember I'm only a phone call away day or night if you ever need me."

"I think Hammy would have something to say if I interrupted your first night back for a chat at an ungodly hour of the morning. I'd say he'll have other things on his mind. I'm so glad that you're looking so much healthier now. Everything will be fine."

"One way or another I know it will," Ella answered. "And on that positive note I'm going to leave."

We hugged tightly and with a last lingering look I watched as she went towards the doors of the departure lounge.

Owen put a secure and comforting arm around me and held me close.

"You'll see her soon again, love. Absence makes the heart grow fonder and all that."

"I couldn't be any fonder of her than I am already," I said, loudly blowing my nose. "I love her so much. She's been so good to me."

I had developed hiccups by then so between hiccupping, sobbing and talking in a stilted voice to Owen I really must have been a sight for sore eyes but I didn't care about any of that. My beloved sister had just left and I didn't know how I was going to get used to life without her. I'd miss her smile and her kindness and her hugs and her wisdom and the way that Ben and Carly lit up when they saw her.

"Don't be upsetting yourself or anyone else," Owen nodded in the direction of the children who were looking at me sadly and trying to come to terms with their own loss.

I quickly pulled myself together. I wiped away the last of my tears, blew my nose, caught sight of myself in a mirrored shop window and nearly had a heart attack.

"Sweet Jesus, why did nobody tell me that I looked like a sick beached whale?" I uttered as I took in my puffy swollen eyes, red nose and my free-flowing maternity top that had a stain on the front of it and hair that would have made Worzel Gummidge jealous.

"You don't look that bad, love."

I gave Owen my best withering look and reminded myself not to listen to him in future when asking his opinion on my appearance before I left the house.

"You're in the middle of Belfast, pet. Who on earth are you likely to meet that knows you? You'll never see any of these people ever again and when we get home I'm going to run you a bath and let you watch soppy DVDs in bed all afternoon.

I had agreed that we would stay with Owen for the weekend as a trial run for "the real thing". Owen had discussed his "idea" with Angelica who so far was agreeable but I wanted to make the transition as slowly as possible so that it wouldn't be too big a shock to her system.

I thought longingly of *Love Actually* and *Steel*

Magnolias and looked at my husband-to-be and knew that I was well and truly blessed and had to admit that what he said was logical. Nobody knew me and so what if they thought I looked like a messy blimp? Their opinion didn't matter.

"Granny Peggy, Granny Peggy!" I heard Carly call.

This had to be some sort of very sick joke. Owen must have put her up to it just to scare me. Well, I didn't think that it was very amusing and I was about to tell him so when I ran straight into my wizened nemesis.

Nebby Peg looked at me appraisingly and I could tell that she thought that I was obviously letting myself go.

I look murderously at Owen as of course the entire situation was his fault. Wouldn't know anybody, eh? Wouldn't care what they thought, eh? How feckin' deluded was he?

"Frankie," she said simply in an annoying condescending voice.

"Peggy," I answered, still wondering what the hell she was doing there. Surely to God the pensioners' club weren't that hard up for places to go and things to see that they had to resort to taking their patrons to the airport for the day?

"We've just left Auntie Ella. She's going on one of those," Carly said, pointing to a plane by way of explanation and thus breaking the silence.

"I'm here to meet someone myself," Peggy said.

I snorted in response. Whoever it was, God help them. If Peggy was there to welcome people to the country the economy would suffer greatly from the dramatic decrease in tourism.

"And there he is now."

I turned, unable to help my curiosity, wondering who Peggy could possibly be meeting and it was with shock, horror and complete and utter disbelief that I came face to face with her visitor, his stunning companion and their new baby.

Chapter 47

Owen looked at my pale face, Peggy's gleeful expression (things couldn't have worked out any better for the old hag) and the resemblance between Ben and the newly arrived traveller and very quickly came to the correct conclusion.

I was rooted to the spot and felt as though my limbs had all been put into a clamp as I couldn't seem to move them. I had also lost the power of speech and was feeling decidedly ill (not pregnancy-related for once).

Tony looked at me and his face registered surprise and shock in equal proportions. He then looked at the children and I saw his expression soften as he surveyed them both.

"Grandma, how are you?" he greeted his grandmother enthusiastically, giving her a tight hug and for the first time since he left I witnessed her looking genuinely and sincerely pleased. "I knew that you said that you'd be here but I didn't expect all this."

I wondered what he meant but quickly worked it out when he looked at the children again. Surely he didn't think that me and *my* (I'd like to stress that word with extra emphasis under the circumstances) children were here to welcome him and his floozy? His floozy who looked effortlessly glamorous with her glossy mane of dark hair, brown eyes and perfect figure ten seconds after giving birth. (Bitch, bitch, bitch!)

Carly left my side and moved closer to Tony. "Are you my daddy?" she asked quietly. "Granny Peggy showed us photographs of you one day."

Tony had the good grace to look ashamed of himself before hunkering down in front of her. "Yes, pet, I'm back."

"Glory be and Alleluia!" I announced in disgust. "Let's bring out the red carpet and sing a song now that you've remembered your children."

I could feel Ben digging his fingers into my arm. Although Carly seemed interested in the fact that her father was standing in front of her, Ben didn't seem to want to move from my side.

"Hello Ben," Tony said as Carly continued to look shyly at him.

Ben mumbled and walked away kicking an empty coke can in front of him before a litter attendant lifted it with a frown and put it in the bin.

"I think it's time we went on our way," Owen said when he had eventually recovered from his own shock.

"So soon," Tony said, looking puzzled. "But we haven't even been properly introduced."

"I'm Owen." They shook hands firmly. "I'm Frankie's fiancé."

I saw the look of momentary disbelief and was mildly placated.

"Tony. I'm Frankie's —"

"Bastard of an ex, useless father and all-round tosspot!" I finished, shaking with rage. How dare he stand there exchanging pleasantries with people and assuming that all had been forgiven and forgotten after leaving me high and dry with two children.

"God, Frankie. Do we have to continue like this? Surely I've given you enough time to get used to the situation now," Tony said in a bored voice.

"Oh I'm sorry," I said slowly, every syllable dripping with sarcasm. "I suppose you think that I should be grateful to you for giving me space while you just left with her," (suitably filthy look directed at stick insect) "giving no explanation to your children and making them feel completely unimportant. Ben has been so confused about everything and it's no wonder, he thinks he's been replaced." At that point I looked at the baby boy who was nestled in his mother's arms, blowing bubbles and looking disarmingly cute. "I don't know what you were expecting, Tony, but if it was a welcoming committee and being told that what you did was all right then you're crazier than I thought."

"But I thought you and the children –"

"You know what thought did, don't you?" I spat. "Please don't tell me that you seriously thought that we were here for you. This is a very unhappy coincidence as far as I'm concerned. I was here to drop my sister off and for no other reason."

He looked crestfallen (good – multiply that by a thousand and you'll feel like I felt when you left, you prick!)

"Some things obviously don't change, as you can see," Peggy interjected with a sneer. "Lovely to meet you again, my dear," she crooned as she hugged the stick insect and inspected the baby who I had to admit was making me ache for my own little bundle. But weren't Ben and Carly once like that or had Tony simply blocked them from his mind altogether?

I turned on my heel and started to stomp off, eager to follow Owen who had wisely decided to take Ben and Carly outside and away from the unfolding scene.

"Bet you're glad you're not still with her when you look at her now," Peggy said loudly enough for me to hear.

"I know – rough and shaggy definitely aren't the trends for autumn," the coat-hanger said whilst laughing in a nasal way and shaking her mane of dark hair.

"Neither are marriage-wrecking, poaching yourself a sperm-donor or being a slut when you first met my husband!" I roared back.

"Frankie, we need to talk!" Tony called out. "I need to make arrangements to see the children."

"I'd find myself a good solicitor then if I was you," I retorted before making my way to the nearest exit.

I stood against a wall outside and gulped deep breaths of air. I put my hands protectively around my bump and vowed that I was not going to allow myself to get any more worked up about this than I was already. Why was I surprised? I had predicted that something like this was going to happen. I just hadn't expected it so soon. No wonder Nebby Peg had been acting weird. Everything had started to make sense.

My phone rang as we sat into the car and I answered my mother wearily.

"Don't sound so glum," she said. "Ella will be back before you even have time to miss her properly."

I had forgotten all about Ella. "I know she will," I agreed in a monotone.

"How are the children?"

"They're fine," I lied as I watched their faces flicker between puzzlement and annoyance in the back of the car.

"Are you sure you're all right?" she asked again.

I shot out of the car and held the phone until my knuckles turned white.

"No, I'm not all right. Tony's here."

"Tony's there," she repeated slowly as if I had lost my mind and was having hallucinations.

"Yes, Mother," I snapped. "Tony just arrived in the country with his home-wrecking, glamorous friend and the children, who are totally confused now, and I had to run into him with me looking like a sack of shit!"

"Language, Frances. I don't think —"

I hung up. I wasn't in the mood for being lectured or fighting or anything else. I was tired. Tired of everything going wrong.

I looked into the backseat of the car where my children were sitting looking pensive and wondered what I was going to do. Just what the hell was going to happen now?

Chapter 48

Ella was horrified when she heard what had taken place after her departure.

"God, I'm sorry, Frankie," she said softly.

"Why are you sorry?" I asked.

"Well, you wouldn't have been there only for me."

"That is technically true," I pondered. "You and your lousy bloomin' timing."

"My timing might have been bad for you, hon, but someone was certainly glad to see me. Stop that, Hammy!"

She giggled and I smiled as I imagined what they must be getting up to. They had been separated for the best part of three months, give or take a few weekend trips back to Edinburgh, so they had a lot of making up to do. I sincerely hoped that Thaddeus's spell or potion or whatever was lingering and doing its job and that a pregnancy would be the result of their amorous delight in being reunited.

After I got off the phone from Ella I redialled and turned to Ruby for her ever-wise words of wisdom and found her similarly loved up with Mandy's older brother, Luke.

"He's what? The big shit! I've a good mind to go and take him out right now so that he won't cause you any more bother."

"*Take. Him. Out.* And how exactly would you do that, Ruby?"

"Hmm, my bare hands would be weapons enough, I'd say. The cheek of him! And he actually thought that you were there to greet him and the skinny tart? How stupid is he?"

"Very stupid, I think you'll find," I sighed. "Although not stupid enough not to know his rights. I can see trouble ahead. I told him to get a solicitor when we were parting company in the airport and I bet you any money that that's what he'll do. He'll get a solicitor, fill them full of shit about what a family man he is now that he has a baby with Twiggy and I'll be left without a leg to stand on."

"Hold on a minute," Ruby said, sounding angry. "He was the one who chose to leave and emigrate to another bloody continent. I hardly think that that qualifies him for the Father of the Year Award."

"He'll make out like he had no choice and blame

me," I said, starting to panic. I couldn't bear the thought of being dragged through court and being made a mockery of. I had watched enough of *Ally McBeal* to know that court was not a pleasant place.

"Frankie, go and have a drink and chill out and stop working yourself into a lather, please," Ruby instructed.

"I'm about to produce a child and probably have an ex-husband who is spying on me at this very moment in the hope of exposing me as a crap mother so I don't think that now is a very good time to be getting sloshed, to be honest."

I could hear whispering on the other end of the phone and realised that Ruby was entertaining so I decided to stop barraging her with my problems and left her to enjoy her evening.

Ruby's relationship with Luke was blooming and still at the honeymoon stage where they spent every waking moment together.

No one had been more surprised than Ruby (who suffers from self-esteem issues and is blind to her own loveliness) when Luke asked her out after the pub quiz, which was their unofficial first date. Apparently the rest of the participants were unimpressed with their behaviour, however, and Ruby was banned from partaking in such an event in the future as Luke was incapable of concentrating due to the effects of her specially purchased Wonderbra and flirtatious antics. They had been together for over three months and the "famine" as Ruby liked to refer to her uneventful love life had come to an end.

Everyone seemed to be in the throes of passion at the moment with the grave exception of *moi* who would rather sleep the clock round than engage in any type of activity. Owen was suitably understanding and gave me cuddles and foot massages every night and was happy to do so. My ankles were massive as was my ever-expanding bump and I found that once the theme tunes for the soap operas had trilled from the television that was the signal for my bedtime where I attempted to get comfortable (gravitational impossibility).

Angelica had also been attentive and was actually very sweet when she put her mind to it. She constantly asked me how I was feeling and was interested in every development in my pregnancy. She still had her off days, mind you, although the difference was that I knew that the cause was plain old teenage hormones and mood swings as opposed to gunning for me. If I had been told of this dramatic change in behaviour in the bad old days when she was a walking nightmare I think I would have fainted with shock.

I probably also wouldn't have believed that my problems with Angelica would have been replaced by worse problems with my stupid ex-husband who I thought had ridden into the American sunset never to be seen again (obviously wishful thinking on my part).

I got up from my position on the sofa, looked out

over the garden and started to wring my fingers and could nearly hear my heart thudding as I thought about what the next few months might hold in store. What lies would my children be told about me? Would I be painted as being hard to live with (which I obviously am not), would they be told that I chased him away (in Nebby Peg fashion) or would I murder the philandering little pillock before he had the chance to open his mouth?

"You look worried, pet," Owen said as he came into the living room with a glass of wine in his hand. "A penny for them."

"I'm having so many thoughts that I don't think a penny would cover them all," I said. "Try a twenty-pound note and then we might be in business."

"I don't know what you're so worried about," he said eventually. "No judge in the land would grant him any type of significant access after the way he's behaved."

"Judge!" I shrieked, unable to contain my horror. "So you *do* think that it'll end up in court then?"

"No. Frankie, hold on a minute and stop being so melodramatic."

"I am not being melodramatic – I am being realistic," I answered in an indignant tone. "I just love the way that everyone tries to pretend that everything is going to be all right when it's painfully obvious to me that a crock-load of shite is about to hit the fan and splatter everywhere. I just can't believe that this is happening now when I should be so happy. I've got you, I'm pregnant and so looking forward to having the baby, Ben and Carly seem pleased with the situation or at least they were until Arsehole Features appeared again and Angelica has finally accepted that I'm not out to destroy her life. What happened? Did some cosmic force in the sky decide that I was having it too easy and decide to get their ginormous wooden spoon out and stir it all up a bit. You know, just for once, just for change, I'd love things to be normal and quiet for a while. I get so sick of always looking over my shoulder."

"Well, there's always the alternative then," Owen said quite calmly.

"The alternative?" I repeated. "I didn't know that there was one."

"There's always one."

"Do you want me to guess?" I said with growing impatience.

"Well," he said slowly, "if you don't want to constantly be looking over your shoulder and you want to avoid a court summons and put yourself out of your own misery then you can always tackle the problem head on."

"What?" (I was contemplating shaking the information out of him at this stage. I hate big build-ups. Just get to the bloody point, please.)

"Go and see him yourself before he has the chance to go talking to solicitors and seeking legal advice. Be the bigger person."

"I am five foot nothing and therefore not a big person, Owen, and if you think that I'm going to go running to him and offering my children on a plate then you have another thing coming. Please credit me with some self respect."

"This has got nothing to do with self-respect, honey. It's got to do with sorting things out before you stress yourself into an early labour. You're both adults and Ben and Carly are your very precious children and therefore your common bond. Surely for their sake you can come to some arrangement that will suit everybody. You don't have to hand them to him on a plate but you do need to realise that, no matter what, he's still their father and has rights."

I opened my mouth to retaliate (the reference to absentee parents having rights always made me want to spit nails) but I quickly closed it again as I realised that Owen had a point.

"So you think I should suggest a meeting with him then?"

"Why not?"

"But I have no way of getting in touch with him except through Nebby Peg and I'd rather put a bullet through my foot than go anywhere near her. She'd see it as me giving in and have a right old field day."

"But that's my point," Owen answered in an aggravated tone. He got up and started pacing the room and chewing his lip. "Let me put it very simply, Frankie, by using my own personal circumstances with Angelica to illustrate. If Jane was to appear back from whatever end of the world she's been hiding out in all these years and she expressed an interest in seeing Angelica, then I would try my best to facilitate it. Angelica is old enough to make up her own mind but I'd encourage her to give her mother a chance nonetheless because when all is said and done the woman gave birth to her and part of her is in every breath that Angelica takes. I don't know why she suddenly ran off and left the way she did. Maybe she was sick. Maybe she felt trapped. Maybe she was a selfish bitch who cared more about herself than about her baby. But whatever her reasons for leaving, if something ever brought her back then I'd like Angelica to go and talk to her and fill in the missing pieces of the jigsaw."

I looked at Owen and saw the pleading look in his eyes and felt guilty about being such a wuss. I had to concede that he was probably right. (I hated when that happened.)

I yawned loudly and decided that as I had a lot to think about I would go to bed and do just that.

"Please, Frankie," Owen said after I had kissed him goodnight, "I'm not telling you what to do. I'm just telling you what I'd do if I were to take a leap of faith."

Anyone for Seconds?

I nodded and found that my future husband had just grown to the size of a giant in terms of what sacrifices he'd be willing to make for his only daughter. I supposed that he was right and that the children were the most important thing.

I was just going to have to find the least painful way to approach the matter without losing too much credibility in the process.

Chapter 49

Christmas had come and gone and had passed by most peacefully. (Who was I kidding? How many Christmas parties was I likely to be invited to?)

Owen and I had done things in style this year and cooked dinner at his house. (When I say Owen and I, I mean him.) I couldn't get out of the habit of calling it "his" house. He corrected me every time and encouraged me to think of it as my home.

He bought me lovely things for Christmas. I got an eternity ring, a collection of CDs, which Owen created especially for me with all my favourite songs (for the labour ward) and some new books. But the best gift and the one that I liked the most (after my very sparkly ring, of course) was a book detailing and showing pictures of how to enhance your home and make the most of its features. There was a particular section relevant to older houses with lots of character that I read every day while dreaming of what I would do if I wasn't heavily pregnant.

Owen had presented me with it on Christmas morning and told me that he wanted me to use it.

"I want you to put your own stamp on this place," he had said with an encouraging smile. "Maybe when you do that you'll start referring to it as 'your house'."

Santa came to the children and also to Angelica and I know that she appreciated the thought and effort that had been put into co-ordinating her clothes, jewellery, CDs and books.

"I did it all naturally," Owen joked as Angelica *oohed* and *aahed* in delight whilst looking at her new things.

"Sure you did, Dad," Angelica said before giving me a massive hug which made my day, my Christmas and my whole world.

I had spent most of Christmas evening lying talking and laughing with my sister, on the phone, who was also delighted with the presents I had bought her. She had also received an unexpected phone call from Thaddeus McCrory.

"Who?" I asked in confusion.

"The faith healer, Frankie."

"Oh, Mr Hot Hands himself," I joked.

"Frankie, all joking aside. That man is brilliant. He

has real power. I can even feel it when I talk to him over the phone and I'm hundreds of miles away. I've rung him a few times but he rang me earlier to wish me a Happy Christmas and to tell me that he had said a special prayer for me today."

New Year was also relatively quiet. I toasted in 2009 by sipping a solitary glass of red wine, eating a few Pringles and then downing half a bottle of Gaviscon to overcome the heartburn they caused. Owen and I watched television in front of the fire, looked towards the future with anticipation and talked companionably into the wee small hours when we fell asleep in each other's arms.

I prayed that the ease and comfort that I felt on the first day of the new year would prevail and seep into the days ahead but as usual things never went according to plan (for me. Ever).

A few weeks had passed since Owen and I had our "discussion" concerning Tony and I still hadn't managed to get my head in gear to do anything. Matters weren't helped by the fact that I had started to feel very unwell.

I woke up on a bright Tuesday morning in January to find that my face had swollen to twice its normal size and that my head was literally bouncing with pain.

Owen took one look at me and, before I had the chance to comb my hair or get properly dressed, he had me frogmarched down to the local health centre and was threatening the receptionist with unrepeatable things if I didn't get to see the midwife immediately if not sooner.

The midwife asked me to climb up on the examination table (abseiling equipment required at this stage) and felt my stomach. She then took my blood pressure and asked for a urine sample and when all three tasks had been completed she pursed up her lips and made lots of *oohing* and *aahing* noises. After the doctor had been consulted and a bed secured I found myself back in hospital again much to my utter disgust.

"Pre-eclampsia," the doctor said without further explanation when he had finished examining me. The staff had taken pity on me and given me the same private room on the ward as I'd had the last time.

I studied him hard until he eventually realised that I hadn't a notion what he was talking about.

"You have all the symptoms," he continued. "You're suffering from fluid retention which presents itself as swelling of the hands, face and ankles."

(And makes you look like a cross between the Michelin man and a blimp).

"You also have protein in your urine and your blood pressure is very high."

"Huh, I'd say that probably has more to do with

my stupid ex-husband than it has with my pregnancy," I muttered.

"Pardon?" he said, looking at me over the top of his rimless glasses.

"Nothing," I answered sweetly whilst wondering why all male gynaecologists had to look so stern. You'd think that they'd be happy to have the dream job. I'd say most fifteen-year-old boys would give up their eye-teeth just to be privy to some of the sights they saw.

"So when will I get to go home?" I asked, looking outside at the winter sunshine and wondering when I'd get to sit in Owen's conservatory again with a blow heater at my feet, gazing out towards the lake.

"You might be out in a few days or you might have to accept the very real possibility that you could be here for the duration of your pregnancy as this is an extremely dangerous condition which needs to be closely monitored."

I looked at Owen and felt sure that my pregnancy was making me hear voices in my head.

"What did he just say? It sounded like he was telling me that I might have to stay here until the baby's born but I know that can't be right."

Owen looked scared as he took my hand and began to rub it.

(Why me??????)

As it turned out my condition did improve. It improved right up until the morning that I was due to go feckin'-well home and then it decided to do a complete U-turn. I wasn't blaming my illness though. I was laying the blame far closer to home.

Angelica had come to see me the evening before and as we had been getting on so well I was pleased to see her and welcomed her with open arms. My open arms, however, got a frosty reception and she seemed to recoil at the gesture. I was perturbed to say the least.

"Are you all right, Angelica?" I asked in concern (technically as I was the one in the hospital bed she should have been asking me this question).

"I'm fine," she answered in the most unconvincing tone of voice I had ever heard.

"Yep and I've just seen a pig flying passed my window smoking a cigar," I retorted. "What is it? Are you having boy trouble or have you had a fight with one of your friends? You and your father haven't fallen out, have you?"

"Why does there have to be anything wrong?" she answered sullenly.

"Erm, because when people are happy they normally smile or at least attempt it."

I was getting peeved now. It was me who needed to be cheered up. I didn't think that I could cope with the strain of anyone else's misery.

"Have I done something to upset you?" I asked tentatively. I was nearly afraid to ask the question in case I got an answer that I didn't like. I had been trying my best to keep out of her way when we had been in the house together and had only interacted in conversation if she had started it and was a willing participant. We had been getting on quite well as it happened but as usual when things started to go well I should have smelt a large rat.

"Every situation doesn't have to be about you Frankie, does it?" she sneered with an ugly look of contempt on her face. She flicked her hair in irritation and began to pace around the room and my heart sank. I knew that she was about to let me have it between both eyes and I didn't think that I could handle it.

"Hold on, Angelica —"

"No. You hold on, Frankie. These last few weeks I have heard nothing but you moaning about all your different problems. Most of which have been self-inflicted if you ask me. The fact that your ex-husband is a scumbag is not anyone else's fault. You should have noticed the signs when you first started to go out with him and stayed well clear. Why did he run off and leave you? Did you ever ask yourself that? Maybe he was tired of listening to you as well."

I could feel my eyes starting to sting as the tears came. I was shocked at the forcefulness of her tone and couldn't believe that she was speaking to me in such a manner. Had she really only come here to abuse me?

"Angelica, what have I done to deserve this?" I asked, now openly crying and totally upset.

"Yeah, that's right, Frankie. You be the martyr and start feeling sorry for yourself again. It's not like anybody else has problems to deal with or feelings that can be hurt."

I looked at her in total confusion and began to wreck my brain thinking of what I could have possibly said or done to make her behave in such a vicious fashion towards me when I was so vulnerable. I should have known better than to think it would last, I decided bitterly, looking at her and wondering how she could be so cold and heartless.

Owen entered my room at that point and I quickly turned my head so that he wouldn't see that I had been crying.

"Hello, darling. Have you come to visit the patient then? Isn't she looking much better?" he said without looking at me.

Angelica grunted in response and started to flick the zip on her jacket up and down in rapid succession until I could no longer bear the raspy sound.

"Angelica," I said loudly, "please don't do that! You're driving me mad."

"Welcome to my world," she said harshly before walking out of the room, leaving Owen staring after her.

He turned to me. "What the hell −" he began before I put up my hand to get him to stop.

I wasn't going to have anyone else having a go at

me. My head was pounding and I was sure that my blood pressure was about to explode out through my ear in a re-enaction of that scene from *The Exorcist* where there's vomit everywhere.

"I am not having this," Owen uttered before kissing me and telling me that he'd see me later.

I tried to stop him but it was too late and what little energy I possessed had been spent in trying to defend myself against Angelica.

I couldn't understand what had happened and no matter how often I ran over the events of the previous weeks in my head I still couldn't come up with an explanation for her outrageous behaviour.

We had been getting on so well lately. She had even started to confide in me about things that I knew she would never discuss with Owen. If Owen had known that we had spent one particular evening talking about what "getting to second base with a boy" involved, I think he would have had a heart attack and kicked the two of us out. That had been an enjoyable time.

We had both curled up at opposite ends of the couch and giggled our way through a tube of Pringles and a large bar of chocolate until I could no longer keep my eyes open. She had kissed me on the cheek and said goodnight and I had hardly seen her after that except for a few fleeting moments here and there. Nothing bad had happened. There had been no "words". We hadn't been angry with each other and I hadn't chastised her or annoyed her in any way. In fact I had bought her some new clothes the previous week when I updated Ben and Carly's wardrobe and, come to think of it, I'd been a tad put out that Angelica's reaction had been so blasé. I'd thought that she would be pleased but she had hardly noticed.

Was she distracted and annoyed and had I failed to pick up on it because of my own problems? I thought back and tried to remember if I had seen her eating a decent meal lately and was frustrated when I couldn't remember.

I prayed that she wouldn't stop seeing me as her friend. I didn't want to be Frankie the punchbag anymore. I cared about her and I wanted the feeling to be mutual.

Chapter 50

As it turned out I had been right in my diagnosis and by the time the nurse came to take my blood pressure the following morning it was sky high and its owner was like a wound-up spring.

"You need to learn to relax, Mrs Colton," the doctor said in a patronising tone of voice. "Breathe deeply and be calm. All this hyperactive behaviour is not good for your baby."

I peered over the bedclothes at him and wished that I had a 44-calibre machine gun. The pompous, arrogant little tube was talking about me like I was a child with ADHD instead of a heavily pregnant woman who had every right to feel overwrought and anxious.

"You won't be going home today, Mrs Colton."

(Was he still talking?)

"We'll have to keep you in for observation."

(Observe me quietly then, please.)

"Check her blood pressure every half hour, nurse, and let me know if there is any change in her condition."

I looked after the doctor in disgust and only sheer will-power kept me from sticking my middle finger up behind his back as he left the room.

The nurse obviously sensed that I was annoyed with him and jerked her head towards the door as she spoke.

"He hasn't got a clue, y'know. They're all great at the textbook stuff but when it comes to recognising real feelings and hurt they're a bit slow on the uptake. Don't pay any attention. It'll all blow over. I have a daughter the same age myself and she can be a right little madam, I can tell you."

I looked at the nurse in surprise and wondered how she could possibly know what had happened. Then I remembered that she had been on duty when Angelica had come to see me the day before.

I thought back and my eyes started to sting. I shrugged my shoulders in an effort to remain aloof to my feelings of hurt but it didn't work.

"There, there," the nurse said kindly, while gently patting my hand. "Don't be upsetting yourself. The little one knows when you're feeling down."

I sank back on to my pillow and felt totally drained and must have slept for hours as by the time I woke up Owen was sitting at my bedside watching me sleep with a most perturbed look on his face.

"How are you feeling, love?" he asked in concern as he saw my eyes flickering awake.

"All right, I suppose," I answered groggily, rubbing my eyes and feeling my forehead. I squinted at Owen and recognised all the signs of aggravation and stress in his face. I hadn't seen that look since the day he left the front of my house in a rip-roaring temper with Angelica in tow.

"A twenty-pound note for them," I jested, hoping to lighten the mood. It didn't work as all I got in response was a grunt and a crease-lined forehead that even the miracle that is Botox couldn't cure.

"I just don't know what to do or what I've done for that matter. Her whole attitude is terrible. She left the house in a complete temper this morning and nearly took the front door with her. She seemed to be spoiling for a fight from the minute she got up and she wouldn't talk to me when I asked her what she thought she was playing at when she gave you such a hard time yesterday."

"Owen," I said reproachfully whilst exhaling deeply. The last thing I wanted was for him to have a go at her and make her feel that he was taking my side.

"What did you want me to do, Frankie? You're sick and lying in hospital and feeling and looking like absolute shite –"

"Oh charming!"

"Well, you're not at the peak of health, darling, so you can't expect to look your usual gorgeous self."

(Nice comeback.)

"Therefore I am not letting her get away with speaking to you in that way. I was so ashamed of her. You're so vulnerable at the minute and instead of supporting you she just heaps on the pressure!"

I stroked Owen's hand and shifted my position in the bed. Thank goodness I had a room to myself. I don't know how I would have coped with all the drama had there been an audience watching.

"Hormones?" I suggested.

"You women and your flamin' hormones," he said testily. "No, I don't think that's it. There's more to it than her simply being in a bad mood. Something must have happened."

"Like what?"

"Well, if I knew that I wouldn't be sitting here giving myself an ulcer thinking about it, would I?"

I closed my mouth and shut my eyes. I was so tired. Before I had the chance to doze, however, two whirlwinds came into my room and planted themselves at either side of the bed.

"Hello, darlings," I said as I drew my children close to me. I always gained great comfort from their affections which I knew were born of wholly unconditional love which I didn't have to fight tooth and nail for.

"Mum-mmy," Carly said in a slow drawl which I

knew meant that she wanted something, "did you remember about my play?"

Play? Play? I thought quickly as a pair of seven-year-old eyes scrutinised me closely for signs of recognition. My mind was blank. I was usually a dab hand at remembering things like that but obviously it had slipped my mind.

"Of course I remember, darling," I lied unconvincingly, hoping that Owen would quickly interrupt with a short but subtle synopsis of what she was talking about.

He didn't. He seemed to be as oblivious as I was.

It didn't matter; however, as Granny Celia came quickly to the rescue.

"Of course she remembers, darling," my mother said. "She remembers that you said you were playing a sunflower in the school production called *Mary Mary* and that all the funds made are going towards getting an outside play area for the nursery school."

"Oh, *that* play," I said. I had a hazy recollection of Carly saying something about needing green leggings a brown top and a home-made yellow flower hat. I was normally quite good at all that *Blue Peter* type of artsy-crafty stuff but at that moment could cheerfully have done without it.

"When is it on?" I asked.

"It's on Wednesday at one o'clock," Carly said, looking at me pleadingly. "Will you be able to go?"

As it was Monday and I had just been told that the likelihood of me seeing the light of day was remote for the foreseeable future I didn't like her chances. Poor Carly would be like an orphan, I thought morosely. The only child there without a parent. The psychological wounds would be dreadful.

"Leave her alone, Carly," my mother chided. "She mightn't be out of hospital on Wednesday and if she is she'll have to rest at home. You want your baby brother or sister to be born healthy and well, don't you?"

Carly looked thoughtful before springing off the bed and looking excited.

"We could ask Granny Peggy to go, couldn't we, Mum? Granny Peggy and Granny Celia could sit together and watch me."

The look on my mother's face at that point in time was truly priceless. She seemed to be having difficulty breathing if her snorts were anything to go by and if she was trying to hide her abhorrence of the suggestion she wasn't doing a very good job.

"Erm, I'm sure Granda George would like to sit beside Granny, darling," she said in a tight, indignant voice.

"Granda said he couldn't go, Granny. He said that he was going to be spending the week planning what he was going to plant in his garden in the spring and when he looked at all the pictures he would think of me in my sunflower costume."

Daddy hated plays. He hated crowds in general. They made him itch around the collar and he would end up opening the top button of his shirt and then Mammy would fall out with him for looking shabby. Oh joy! I was so glad that resting was the only order of the day for me.

"He will be coming with *me*," Mammy said sharply.

There was no way that she would be sitting anywhere near Peggy Colton. Not without a wooden cross and a clove of garlic anyway.

"We could always ask Daddy to come and watch," Ben said thoughtfully.

He had been sitting quietly chewing his lip throughout the conversation and I wished wholeheartedly that he had stayed silent.

Carly looked delighted with the suggestion and looked towards me for approval which was definitely not forthcoming.

"It's a possibility," Owen said, also speaking for the first time.

I looked at him with a mixture of horror and disbelief. What was he trying to do – make my blood pressure dance?

"Granny, could you take Ben and Carly outside, please?" I said. "Owen and I need to have a little chat."

"You're not surely suggesting that –" Mammy began before she noticed that I was pointing towards the door and grinding my teeth in an agitated fashion.

"I'm going now," she said in a wounded tone. "Far be it for me to have an opinion. Come along, children. Kiss your mother goodbye and tell her that you'll see her later."

Carly threw her arms round me and gave me a tight squeeze. I stroked her blonde curls and nuzzled into her neck which smelt of ice cream and flowers. Ben leaned towards me and put his head on my shoulder. He didn't give hugs these days. It was no longer the cool thing to do apparently.

"Daddy's never seen where Carly and I go to school," he said before leaving me and walking towards the door.

The statement hung in the air as I looked towards Owen who was staring at me pointedly.

"What?" I said in irritation. This was a closed subject as far as I was concerned.

"Were you listening?" Owen said.

"No," I snapped. "Deafness is another symptom of pre-eclampsia."

"Selective hearing, you mean," Owen said quietly.

"What is your problem?" I asked, throwing my legs out of bed and getting up to pace the floor as I frequently did when I was worried.

"Frankie, he's not going to go away. He's still here and he's not invisible and the sooner you realise that fact the better."

"We were invisible to him for long enough, Owen.

What am I supposed to do? He decides to come here for a visit, for a holiday, for six months, I don't know, and all of a sudden I'm meant to be the accommodating ex-wifey who has conveniently forgotten what an insensitive, heartless asshole he is. Have you any idea what it's like to think that life is ticking over just fine, that your marriage is stable, your children are happy and that life is good only for it all to be taken from you. That bastard came home one day and announced that he was leaving. He told me in the same flippant tone of voice that he used to tell me that we were out of milk or the electricity bill needed to be paid."

Owen squeezed my hand and I knew that he felt my pain.

"I do know what it's like, love," he said gently. "I know all too well."

(Memory loss and complete insensitivity must also be symptoms.)

I knew that Owen was empathising with me but still felt miserable as unwanted memories flooded my mind. I had thought that Tony and I were the real thing. We had survived Nebby Peg and her meddling and a great family tragedy as well as the usual stresses and strains that most couples are faced with, so I thought that we had passed all the tests. How wrong I had been.

I would never forget that day. It had started normally enough. Tony had gone to work and I had dropped Ben off at school and taken Carly, who was an active two-year-old, to the shops with me to buy things for dinner. I had bought steaks with all the trimmings and was going to surprise Tony with a beautiful meal that evening. I felt sorry for him because he had been doing a lot of overtime and I thought he needed a break and a treat. In hindsight I realised that he had been doing overtime for Stella and not for his boss. No wonder he looked permanently exhausted. Leading a double life would have been pretty strenuous.

I had cooked the steaks, roasted vegetables, had a shower and changed my clothes and Mammy had taken the children for me but the evening hadn't gone according to plan. Instead of a romantic meal for two where I would tentatively bring up the subject of us having another baby, I was faced with Tony who looked shocked at first to find that we were alone but then obviously saw the empty childless house as the prime opportunity to break the news to me.

I will never forget the feeling of the blood draining from my face as he told me that he didn't love me anymore and that he couldn't cope with the pretence any longer. Apparently it wasn't fair to me. Apparently I was supposed to be grateful to him for setting me free. I didn't want to be set free. I wanted to keep the vows I had taken on my wedding day, I wanted my children to have a father and I wanted to run away and hide and pretend that his words were the product of a bad dream where I would wake up panting and thanking God that it wasn't real. But it was real. It was all too real. After Tony had finished trampling my heart into a thousand pieces and added insult to injury by telling me that he had fallen in love with somebody else, he had gone into the garden and made a hushed phone call before going quietly upstairs to pack his things.

"I'll get the rest of my stuff later," he had said as I looked at my dinner napkins and wine goblets in disbelief and tried to make sense of why my whole world had just been turned upside down in a matter of minutes.

"So that's it," I said. "We don't talk about it. You don't give me the chance to say anything. You just come home from working late, announce you don't love me and then walk out of my life forever." I began to cry as the enormity of what was happening hit me like a ton of bricks. "You must have had this well planned," I said through my tears. "Did you and she sit and talk about when and how you were going to break it to me. How long has it being going on?"

He didn't answer me.

"How long?" I screamed as a dinner plate smashed against the wall, swiftly followed by every other piece of crockery sitting on the table. The dinner service had been a wedding present. It was ironic, therefore, that it was ending up in the same broken state as the event it was given to mark.

"Nearly two years," he answered nervously, not taking his eyes from the steak knives which were within my reach.

"Our daughter is two," I said limply. All the fight had just gone out of me. What was the point in arguing? The decision had been made and nothing I could say or do would reverse it. I sat and thought about how happy I had been after Carly was born. I had always wanted a little girl to dress in pink and I couldn't wait until her tiny blonde tufts of hair grew longer so that I could create pigtails with ribbons. Carly had been around eight weeks old when Tony had announced that he had been given a promotion and that although it would mean more money, it would also mean an increased workload and late nights.

Tony seemed to sense my train of thought and where it was leading me. "I met Stella after I got the promotion. She joined the sales team and I was asked to take her under my wing and show her the ropes."

"Someone needs to define the meaning of wings and ropes to you," I said bitterly. "I don't think wings are a reference to jumping into bed with your apprentice and I don't think that bondage was what they had in mind when they mentioned ropes."

"It wasn't like that," he said in a defensive tone of voice. "It wasn't a purely sexual attraction."

"I do not want to hear details!" I shouted covering my ears. "Do you really think I need to know how your sordid little affair was conducted while I was sitting at home with our baby daughter and our son foolishly thinking that you loved us and that you always would? What about our children? Did you spare them a thought while you were cheating on them and me with someone else?"

"I didn't mean for any of this to happen. I never meant to hurt you or Ben or Carly. I always thought that we would be together too but obviously things change and sometimes you can't control them."

"You could try," I said feeling my anger build inside me. "So what has she got that I haven't?" I shouted. "Is she younger? Is she richer? Is she prettier? Was I not enough for you? Were our children not enough for you?"

"It just happened."

He seemed unable to offer any other explanation and I felt drained. I wanted to lie down in a dark room and never wake up again. What had I done to deserve betrayal by someone who I trusted implicitly? I must have been very stupid not to have recognised the signs earlier. The late nights, the business calls which Tony couldn't take in front of me, the changes in us. I put his lack of interest in me down to the fact that he was tired. I didn't think he was tired of me.

Chapter 51

I lay awake and counted the tiles on the clinical-looking ceiling above me. Owen and I had talked for what seemed like hours. The sister of the maternity ward, who was normally quite liberal about my visitors as I was in a room of my own and therefore not annoying any other patients, ended up by coming in, looking at her watch in a suggestive manner and asking Owen if he had no home to go to.

Now, hours later, our chat was still continuing in my head and causing turmoil. I felt as if I had an angel sitting on one shoulder and a horny devil on the other one who were both giving me conflicting advice.

I understood the point that Owen had been trying to make; I just didn't know if his suggested course of action was appropriate or wise or if I had the stomach for it.

He thought that I was being stubborn and pig-headed and that my actions would come back to bite me some day and I, on the other hand, had accused him of being soft in the feckin' head.

"Do you want to have two teenagers who are hell-bent on going to find their father because you've had a disagreement or they don't like the rules in our house?" Owen had asked.

"They wouldn't do that," I said. (Mind you, I had difficulty picturing my flaxen-haired daughter as anything else but a bouncing, happy little girl.)

"Angelica was a cute seven-year-old at one stage," Owen said sadly. "She used to sing and dance and play and be full of energy and joy but losing her mother soon put paid to that. She still had her happy moments but ultimately she was very sad. I don't want the same thing to happen to Carly or Ben for that matter. They're both at crucial ages where they could be badly affected by the decisions you make now. I had no choice but to accept what happened as I had no way to contact Jane but you have a choice, Frankie. You can do the right thing now and save yourself and the children a lot of heartache in the future."

"You seem to forget that my actions as they stand now could be saving them from a lot of hurt as well, Owen. What if, hypothetically, I was to give him access to the children and they started to get close to him and then he and the stick insect decide that they want to go back to America? What's he going to do? Come to an arrangement with Aer Lingus that they'll meet halfway across the Atlantic Ocean every other Sunday?"

"It's a risk you'll have to take, Frankie. If it were to happen nobody could accuse you of not giving him a chance."

"And why should he get a chance?" I asked defensively. "He doesn't deserve one. He never gave either me or his children a second thought when he left. Why am I suddenly being expected to make all these grand gestures? What has he done to prove himself worthy since he's been here? Nothing, that's what."

"But he doesn't have to, Frankie. You can do it and show that you're a woman of courage and conviction and that you have a conscience even if he doesn't. Look, don't make any decisions about it now. Just think about what I've said. Weigh up all the pros and cons and think about what the children would want. You heard them tonight. They're curious as much as anything and why shouldn't they be?"

"Okay, okay," I held up my hands in defeat. "I'll think about it and let you know but whatever decision I come to is final. No more pressure. Agreed?"

Owen didn't answer me and he wasn't getting off that lightly.

"Agreed?" I said in a firmer tone.

"All right," he sighed.

"Why does this matter so much to you anyway?" I asked.

"It matters because I love Ben and Carly like they were my own children and it matters because I love you more than I have ever loved anybody in my whole life including Jane. I don't want to see you getting hurt in years to come and being filled with regret because you had the chance to do the right thing and didn't take it."

I smiled at him and leaned my head on his shoulder and wondered what I had done to deserve such a wonderfully selfless man.

Now, lying awake after Owen had left, my thoughts found their way back to the painful path that they had travelled earlier where I was transported to the bad old days when it was a monumental task just to get up and get dressed in the morning. Sometimes I didn't get dressed. Sometimes I would slob about in my dirty dressing gown and eat cornflakes dry from the box and contemplate the sad state of affairs which was my life. I found out at that time who my real friends were and smiled fondly as I recalled how sensitive and caring Ruby had been. She had gone out of her way to think of distractions and treats which she hoped would take my mind off the sadness and depression that had threatened to engulf me. They didn't always work, however.

We would go to the cinema where we would watch a film and she would laugh and I would look at all the couples and want to burst into noisy tears and tell the world how piggin' lonely and ugly and worthless and stupid I felt. We would go out for food and similarly loved-up couples would arrive and ruin my appetite and my night. I couldn't bear to see other people happy when I felt so miserable.

After Tony told me that he was leaving and walked out the door that terrible night, I had crawled into bed and lay there looking into nothingness whilst trying to block out what had been said. I had thought that if I concentrated hard enough my memory might erase it and then the acute pain in my heart would leave.

The children missed Tony terribly at first. Ben was mystified as to where his daddy was hiding and had convinced himself that we were in the middle of a very real game of hide and seek where Daddy would jump out and surprise him. Of course it didn't happen and gradually he had stopped asking. Carly was young but my heart ached every time she pointed to the door and said "Daddy" in her lispy baby voice.

I knew that our relationship was over but I had always thought that, no matter what, Tony would stand by his children. That had been the biggest shock of all. He had lost his own parents at a young age and had felt a void and to my horror and amazement he seemed prepared to put his children through a similar experience.

"You're going fecking where?" I had asked though clenched teeth, barely able to contain my anger when he had told me that he was going to be moving to America.

"Frankie, calm down. It'll be for the best. It'll give you a chance to find your feet on your own. It wouldn't be fair to be living under your nose with Stella."

"Oh I get it now," I had said snapping my fingers. "I'm sorry for being so dim. I'm supposed to be grateful to you for your thoughtfulness. I'm supposed to smile and say thanks for not rubbing my nose in it and give you my blessing so that you can start a new life in America with your tart and forget that your children or I ever existed."

"Don't be so fecking stupid —" he began but he didn't get the chance to utter another word as I roughly shoved him towards the door.

"Get out, Tony!" I shouted not caring if the neighbours heard me or not. "I'm glad that your dear sweet mammy is not here to see you behaving like this towards her grandchildren."

I had cried and cried after that. The weeks had merged into months and birthdays and Christmases and anniversaries had passed and gradually with the help of my parents and Ella and Ruby I had started to feel slightly more human again.

Anyone for Seconds?

Men had come and gone. Most had run a mile when they heard that I was the mother of two children, scared that I was ensnaring them to be part of a ready-made family. It hadn't mattered though as I wasn't ready for a relationship. I was too scared. The wounds were still open and sore and I was not prepared to be hurt again. I didn't think I'd ever trust a man again until I met Owen and he changed the way I thought about things. He made me realise that men could be hurt too and that women could be just as evil. Our mutual experiences of betrayal and desertion had brought us together and I was glad they had.

Still sleepless, I lay and thought about what Owen had been through and how he would handle it if he were faced with the decision of whether or not to encourage Angelica to meet her wayward mother if she ever came back. He was confident he could handle that but I wasn't so sure he could.

I was still staring at the ceiling when I made my mind up. The only question now was how many people it would affect and who would get hurt the most.

Chapter 52

Another few days had passed and I had been sent home from hospital only to be admitted again with my blood pressure soaring once more. Carly had taken part in her play and had been pronounced the best sunflower ever to grace the boards at the local community centre. My father had abandoned his plans for his flower garden and potting shed to go and proudly watch her and Mammy had made her outfit and beamed the whole way through the performance. Granny Peggy was also there and so was Tony much to the annoyance of my mother. I don't know what she was more upset about: the fact that I hadn't forewarned her or the fact that Tony had shaken her hand and told her that she was looking well for her age.

She had stormed into the hospital and had nearly required sedation to lower her tone.

"The cheek of him, Frankie! How dare he take the opportunity to manhandle me in public when I wasn't expecting it and couldn't —"

"Belt him with your handbag!" I finished laughing.

"Well, I'm glad you find it so amusing, young lady, because I found it thoroughly stressful," Mammy sniffed.

"Well, you can stop being stressed. You have to be happy because your two daughters are going to be together again in less than twenty-four hours."

Ella had decided that there was far too much excitement going on in Swiftstown and was most put out that she was missing all the action. She had decided to take a week off work and fly over to see us all.

I could see Mammy's brain going into overdrive as she absorbed this news.

"But why is she coming home, Frankie? Oh God, please tell me that she and Hammy haven't split up!"

I tried to tell her that this definitely wasn't the case but she was on a roll and therefore not interested and not listening.

"She better not come home looking anorexic again. It's a disgrace, that's what it is. Starving children all over the world and your sister looking like she's been transported straight from Ethiopia and dipped in white paint!"

Mammy was a tonic even if she didn't realise it. She was really comical when she was in one of her "moods" and I couldn't contain my mirth. I laughed until my sides threatened to split (not a good thing when you're fit to burst as it is).

"She wasn't anorexic when she left Mammy," I said when I could speak. "You know that she was nearly back to her old self and she told me that she would never allow herself to get into that position again – so stop worrying."

My better humour was helping me to view my "situation" in a less tragic light. If I came up with the right plan I could come out a winner. The children didn't have to lose either. They'd get to see their "father" (term applied very loosely as he was still viewed as the devil incarnate) and to make up their own minds. The worst scenario would be that they would meet him, learn a few facts and feel disillusioned and let down. But, happily, all wouldn't be lost as they would still have Owen. I was also hoping that the new baby would provide a timely distraction.

Tony going to see Carly perform in her play had been purely providential. Tony and Owen had met each other in the street one day (I couldn't help it but every time I thought of the two of them meeting I imagined them in cowboy hats squaring up to each other at high noon) and Owen had taken the opportunity to tell Tony that his daughter might be glad to see him if he chose to watch her perform. Tony, allegedly, had been most grateful for the information and shook Owen's hand in response. It was a tiny step in the right direction but there were still things I had to do.

"Mammy, could you do me a favour and get me a contact number for Peggy Colton?"

Mammy looked all around the room as if a voice had just spoken to her from on high.

"Mother!" I waved from my propped up position in the bed and she studied me, blinking very fast and with a furrowed brow.

"Now, Frankie, I know you're not well but that's no reason to lose all sense and start being foolish. What on earth do you want bloody Peggy Colton's number for?"

"I'm going to ring her and ask her to get Tony to meet with me. I think we should come to some arrangement about the children."

I jumped ten feet in the air as my mother let a roar out of her and feet came running in all directions.

"There is something wrong with her," she said, pointing at me as if I had suddenly developed smallpox or rabies or suggested that my estranged husband see his children.

"What seems to be the problem?" one nurse asked kindly.

I mouthed at her and shook my head whilst rolling my eyes and trying to look in the direction of Mammy but succeeded only in making the young student more concerned. I think she was worried that I was having some sort of seizure.

"I'm fine," I said emphatically. "I'm feeling better than I have in a long time. There isn't a thing wrong with me. You can tell the doctor that I'm fighting fit and ready to go home any time."

Mammy was standing with her back towards me and even though I couldn't see I knew that she had her disapproving look painted all over her face.

"I'm sorry to bother you, nurse," she said. "I didn't mean to cause a scene I'm just trying to reason with my daughter because she's making a huge mistake but she won't listen."

The nurse looked perplexed as Mammy began to tap her foot on the tiled floor in irritation.

"I'm a grown woman and if I make mistakes then I can be held accountable for them," I told the nurse. "I am simply having a disagreement with my mother. If you have any cures for a condition known as Acute Drama Queen please let me know as she needs a large dose of the antidote."

Mammy rounded on me with her cheeks flaming mad and then grabbed her handbag and stormed out. I sighed. I hadn't wanted to fall out with her. She just made it so difficult. She gave a whole new meaning to the saying "mother knows best", and that was on a quiet day.

Owen was delighted when I told him I'd had a

change of heart. He was less than thrilled, however, to learn that he would have to go and pay Peggy a visit. We decided that Sunday would be a good day for Owen to talk to Tony about seeing the children, as I had learned, on good authority aka Ruby and her superior snooping skills, that Tony liked to visit Peggy on a Sunday and bring his son with him. Aww sweet, I thought, whilst making gagging motions and wondering where the Stick went if she wasn't with Tony. Perhaps she had learnt the hard way that Peggy couldn't be taken at face value.

Chapter 53

It was Wednesday when I had decided that I would take a leap of faith and let Owen do the needful with Tony. But by the time Sunday came and I was back home again, Owen and Ella, who had arrived home, had to convince me I was doing the right thing as I was sure it would be an unmitigated disaster of the highest order.

"This is the bloody craziest idea I've ever had," I said. "No, actually, wipe that comment. This is the second maddest idea as the first one was when I married that arsewipe in the first place."

"Frankie, will you please calm down and stop working yourself up?" said Ella. "Owen's only going to Nebby Peg's to see if Tony's there which he mightn't be but if he is you should count it as a bonus because then you'll get a response quicker."

"A bonus," I said in a derisory tone. "Stop talking about him like he's a lotto ball. And stop thinking he's something special because he's flamin' well not!"

I looked on as Owen and Ella exchanged a look. They might as well have had a full-scale conversation about my state of mind as their eyebrows bobbed up and down and they made faces and nodded in my direction.

"Feck off," I declared crossly before marching out of the living room and into the kitchen in a fit of pique. It was okay for them; they didn't have all the worries and fears that I did. They weren't the ones risking their children's happiness, and for what? It wasn't like I would be given any thanks for stepping out on a limb. Nebby Peg and Tony would just look on it as their rights being facilitated and still see me as the unsophisticated blimp with a bad attitude.

Ella came into the kitchen, looking sheepish. She was also continuing to put on weight and seemed to be in a more cheerful disposition these days, much to my delight. Right now though, I wished she'd go away and leave me alone.

"Are you all right?"

"Never been better," I snapped as I stared out the window and watched as Ben and Carly, wrapped in their winter scarves and gloves, kicked a ball around the back garden, completely oblivious to the monumental changes that were afoot which would ultimately change their lives and shape their future.

411

"Frankie, you are doing the right thing. You're being very brave and I'm proud of you."

I continued to look out the window and saw Ben turn round, register that I was watching him and happily kick his ball with a flourish and wait for my reaction. I immediately clapped and blew him a kiss and he blew one back and grinned at me. He looked so like Tony when he smiled. He had a cheeky but very endearing grin which I knew would always get him out of plenty of tight corners and probably into the arms of plenty of lovely ladies in the future. I grimaced as I thought of my little boy entering the dangerous world of coupling and suddenly I felt like I'd been hit with a brick.

"That could be me someday, couldn't it?" I said to Ella.

"You someday what?"

"I could be like Nebby Peg."

Ella took a deep breath and moved her mouth around as she searched for an answer. "I know that you are awkward and grumpy and that you are very strong-willed, Frankie, but there's no need to be as self-deprecating as all that. You'll never be like Nebby Peg. You're far too nice."

"I didn't mean it like that," I answered impatiently. "And I'm only grumpy because I'm tired and people won't leave me alone and awkward because I can hardly walk anymore. What I meant was that God forbid Ben might one day make a mistake with a girl and have a child. I sincerely hope not, and I'll be having strong words with him when the time is right and telling him to take the necessary precautions and to ignore any rogue genes of the Colton variety, but if he did I wouldn't like to see him miss out on anything."

A look of understanding passed over Ella's features and she squeezed my arm and looked out at my son who was now in his element and putting on a football show extraordinaire for both his mother and his aunt.

"You'd die if you thought Ben had a child that he'd never see. Everyone makes mistakes, Frankie, but the children shouldn't have to suffer just because their father chose to mess up. He is part of them and they have the right to know him. You never know, Frankie, this might be a good thing for everyone. You can introduce Tony to the children slowly and let him visit them here and then, if he does get on well with them and they want to spend time together, it will give you and Owen more time on your own when the baby comes. On the other hand they could meet him, have their curiosity satisfied and decide that they don't want him to be part of their lives and if they do you can always say in years to come 'Well, kids, I did try, y'know'."

I smiled and gave Ella a hug. "When did you get so smart and practical?"

"Excuse me but I always was like this. Besides, I've

had plenty of time and practice at rationalizing things lately."

I nodded in understanding and not for the first time mentally kicked my own arse for being insensitive. Ella would handle this situation so much better if it was she who was in the middle of it. Not that I was wishing her to end up a single mother and Hammy an absentee father, mind you; that was stretching my imagination too far. They were the perfect couple destined to grow old together and always be happy.

Ella not having children was too hard for us to contemplate so we chose not to think about it. She was made to bear her own children and would love every second of it, unlike me who looked upon my pregnancy as purgatory on earth. Her arms were made for nestling and protecting a baby within them, her smile was made for directing towards her young and her whole attitude was fitting to make her the best mother in the world.

She seemed to read my mind.

"If I can't have a baby myself Frankie, I'll find another avenue for all the love I'd have given my own child. Our lives are mapped out for us already and if it's not meant to be then there's a reason for it and somewhere along the line that reason will become clear."

"So you reckon that when I met Tony and went

through all the aggravation of fending off Nebby Peg before we got married, then got married only for him to make a laughing stock of me, that that was already written in the stars? Some feckin' angel somewhere had a very warped sense of humour the day he decided to guide me in that direction."

"All your experiences have made you who you are today, Frankie, and without being the person you are you might never have found Owen and be as happy as you are together. Sometimes having too much of a good thing makes you complacent and complacency means that you don't appreciate fully how lucky you are. Maybe that's something Tony has recognised. Perhaps seeing the kids again caused stirrings of emotion that he had tried to put to the back of his mind."

I looked at Ella and nodded towards the door, indicating that I was ready to face the world again and together we went back to Owen who no longer looked perturbed at my reaction; instead he looked positively pissed off and as if going to visit Tony was the furthest thing from his mind.

The source of his annoyance had just slammed the door and was walking nose in air towards the driveway with a gait which spelt out in capital letters that she was fed up with the world and determined to show it.

"Oh lovely," I said watching Angelica's retreating back in dismay. "Can anything else happen today?"

It could and it did as five minutes later my mother came panting into the house followed by my father who apologised before she opened her mouth.

"Don't do it, Frankie!"

"I am doing it, Mother," I said resolutely. "We are doing it," I said as I put my arm around Owen and said a silent prayer that everything would work out all right. Let's hope my masochistic "angel" gave me a happy ending to this particular chapter.

Chapter 54

After Owen left to embark on his mission and I had checked on the children and then lain my weary body down on top of our bed (I was now becoming accustomed to viewing Owen's bed as my own), my thoughts drifted back to the scene which had greeted Ella and me earlier. What the hell had happened to Angelica and why did she seem to have in her possession a personality which could change entirely from one day to the next? She had seemed so content before whatever was annoying her took its toll and created a monster that Frankenstein himself would have been thrilled with. I sat up in bed and looked towards the door.

My inner voice was already screaming at me to leave well enough alone and not to cause any more contention than there already was but I'd had plenty of practice ignoring it in the past and wasn't about to change now.

I stood and looked at Angelica's bedroom door like the handle might bite me if I touched it. In some ways I wished it would as I was apprehensive about what I might find. Some things were better left unknown but at the same time I couldn't stand by and let this teenage girl who I had come to care for put herself firmly on the road to self-destruction. There had to be a reason for her bizarre behaviour and although she probably wasn't stupid enough to leave potentially dodgy articles, which could lead to the grown-ups in her life getting some answers, in her room I might just find a clue somewhere.

I entered Angelica's boudoir and immediately wrinkled my nose at the smell of stale clothes and shook my head in frustration at the untidy state of the room which looked as if a mortar bomb had exploded in the middle of it. Finding anything in the midst of all this chaos would make finding a needle in a haystack look like a piece of cake, I thought grimly, but with determination I decided to give it a go anyway.

An hour later I was no further forward and had begun to wonder what I expected to find. There was no evidence to suggest that a boy or indeed a girl (I am officially a woman of the world) was involved. There were no love notes or hearts bearing her name along with the name of the person who was starring with her in a tale of unrequited love. There were no condoms, no phone numbers or pamphlets suggesting that there was any need for a trip to an STD clinic and no discarded pregnancy tests. I found no brightly coloured pills, no syringes or crack bongs (okay, I do admit that my imagination had gone spasmodically into overdrive at that stage) and I saw nothing suggesting that she was involved in anything illegal. In fact, if truth be known, all I found was a perfectly innocent if infuriatingly messy teenage girl's room.

In exasperation I took a last glance around to make sure that everything was exactly as I had found it. I was dying to fold her clothes and put them in her drawers, put her shoes in pairs and set them neatly against the wall, lift the outdated magazines for recycling and put her crumbling and broken eye-shadow and blusher compacts into her stained and dusty make-up bag but I couldn't. How Angelica managed to locate anything was beyond me but I felt sure that as a sniffer dog could detect the scent of its prey Angelica would know instinctively in the manner of all teenagers who put their privacy on a par with breathing that an intruder had invaded her territory.

I closed the door and went to phone Ruby who would provide no answers but who would cheer me up and probably make me laugh.

She answered on the first ring and sounded breathy and excited.

"What were you doing?" I asked suspiciously.

"Just talking about you, hon. Weren't your ears red?"

"No," I answered. "So what have I done now?"

"Not a thing. I just saw Angelica looking very pensive and deep in conversation over dinner."

"Dinner?" I said in surprise. "I offered her lunch earlier on and she turned her nose up at it and looked at me as if I was trying to feed her dog food. Little Miss Attitude is back."

"In fairness, Frankie, I don't think she was having such a great time where she was. She looked positively miserable actually."

"She was probably moaning to her friends about how horrible her life is and how her stepmother is the root of all evil," I said grimly.

"Oh, she wasn't with any friends," Ruby countered quickly. "She was with that aunt of hers – the one that looks like a bulldog with a hangover – and some other woman."

"Oh, she never said. Normally she tells Owen when she's going to meet the lovely Brenda. She stormed out of here about two hours ago and looked like she had the worries of the world on her shoulders."

"Oh well, don't worry about her, Frankie. I think you have enough on your plate at the moment. How did Owen get on today?"

"I don't know yet. He hasn't come back yet but I suppose no news is good news."

"And how are you feeling. How's the bump?"

"Oh fine," I said, moving my hand over my swollen belly in a soothing circular motion and feeling my baby move around in response to my touch.

"Well, you just concentrate on looking after yourself and it and don't worry about Angelica. She'll be fine."

I curled my lip and shook my head. Ruby meant well but she had no comprehension of how soul-destroying living with a disgruntled teenager could be and I very much doubted that Angelica would be fine any time in the near future if her behaviour of the last few weeks was anything to go by.

"I'd better go," Ruby said eventually with a despairing sigh, obviously taking my silence as her cue to leave.

"I'm sorry, Rubes," I said in response. "I don't mean to take my problems out on you. I'll have a longer chat with you later when Owen comes home and I know more about what agreement he's come to with Tony."

Owen arrived home approximately fifteen minutes later looking for all the world like a puffed-out peacock who'd had a good day being noticed. He was extremely pleased with himself and his abilities as a mediator and as such couldn't wait to tell me that

Tony had responded favourably to his suggestion that we try to come to an agreement for the sake of the children who *were* at the end of the day the glue that linked us all together.

"He was really emotional, Frankie."

"He should try being eight months pregnant then if he likes emotion so much."

"No, seriously."

"I am being serious."

"Well, okay then. He was delighted that you're willing to give him a chance. Look . . ." Owen paused for a moment and spread his hands out in front of him in a thoughtful fashion as if to collect his thoughts before he put them into words. "Frankie, the guy knows that he messed up and messed up big-time at that. He knows that he put you through hell and that he was unfair to the children and a crap father but he wants to try and make amends now. Better late than never," he added quickly, looking at my face and sensing my incredulity and anger.

"Too little too late," I responded with a quick but very insincere smile.

"Frankie, I thought you'd got over this," he said in a voice that only served to fuel my anger.

"You make it sound so easy, Owen. I wish I felt as confident as you do about it all but then it's not your children who may end up getting hurt yet again!"

"They are my children, Frankie," he retorted

immediately, "and if that does happen then I'll simply be here to pick up the pieces. We owe it to *our* children to see that they grow up feeling that their parents did right by them. I'm sure it's not a nice feeling to wonder where your father disappeared to or why he left in the first place but it would probably be worse to learn that the same man wanted to make the effort but wasn't allowed to."

Owen didn't say anything more. He just kissed me on the cheek before leaving the room. Leaving me alone with all my thoughts. My fears. My feelings of inadequacy.

Chapter 55

I woke after tossing and turning fitfully and once my eyes had become accustomed to the dim light I registered that it was actually ten past one in the morning and that I had been asleep for around six hours.

I got up slowly and sat on the edge of the bed. I was worried. Where on earth was Owen? Why had he not come to bed? I had got used to his strong arms encircling me and protecting me every night and I missed them. I shook my head as I recalled my reaction to his news earlier. Why did I have to keep overreacting like I had a screw loose every time Tony seeing the children was mentioned? I had done the right thing. I just needed to trust Tony now and hope that he would do the right thing also.

I thought of the Serenity Prayer that hung pride of

place in a decorative frame in my mother's living room:

> *God, Grant me the serenity to accept the things I cannot change*
> *Courage to change the things I can*
> *And wisdom to know the difference.*

I recited the little prayer inwardly and realised that I could apply this to a lot of areas in my life. New Year's Day had long since gone but it wasn't too late to try and implement a few better-late-than-never New Year's resolutions.

The landing light was on when I entered the corridor outside our bedroom and I could hear muffled voices downstairs. I wrapped my dressing gown around me tightly and went to investigate, suddenly realising that I was hungry and that a glass of milk and a digestive biscuit would be very welcome. I looked in on Ben and Carly, switched off Ben's PlayStation which was still humming and turned out Carly's light as she had fallen asleep looking at her picture books. Owen must have put them to bed. I felt instantly guilty. Here was this wonderful man who had my children's best interests at heart, who loved them so much that he didn't want them to get hurt and who made sure they went to bed at the appropriate time so that I could get my rest, even though I had shouted at him and made him feel bad (yet again).

I tiptoed down the stairs and heard Owen and

Angelica talking quietly. Suddenly, however, their voices became raised and I frowned.

"Angelica, don't lie to me," I heard Owen say. I knew he was upset by his tone and was picturing him taking his glasses off and rubbing his eyes in weariness like he always did when something was annoying him. "Where were you until this time? It's twenty past one in the bloody morning. You didn't even phone to say that you were going to be late and your attitude when you left the house earlier was less than desirable. Why do you always have to be so difficult?"

There was no response (surprisingly, as the stroppy little mare usually had an answer for everything).

"Well?" I heard Owen repeat, his voice firmer than before.

"I was out," Angelica snapped in a defensive tone.

"Don't you speak to me like that," Owen retorted angrily. "I'm not the one who has proven myself to be wholly irresponsible. I've been worried sick about you – you could have been lying in a ditch somewhere. Anything could have happened to you."

"Well, it's a pity it didn't then," Angelica said with a strange quiver in her voice. "There'd be a lot less trouble for you and everyone else if I wasn't around and at least if I died you wouldn't have to feel guilty about not wanting me around anymore. Because I know that is how you feel, Dad. You'd be happier if it was just you and Frankie and *her* children."

I winced at her tone and was aggrieved that she actually thought that this could be true. I also noticed that she had put a lot of emphasis on the word "her" when she was referring to my children, making it very clear that there were two camps within the house. Them and us. I sighed and stroked my bump which was having its usual lively spell when I was supposed to be resting. I prayed again that the impending birth of the baby who would be a half brother or sister to all the children involved would act like a glue which would cement us all together and provide a common bond which would bring us closer.

"What friends?" Owen asked abruptly.

"What do you mean?"

"I mean who were you with? Whose parents allowed them out so late? I want to know so that I can speak to them and tell them that even if they're okay with their children running around in the middle of the night I most certainly am not."

I smiled and remembered similar conversations taking place in our house when Ella and I had ripped the arse out of our parents' good nature and stayed out beyond our curfew. I also remembered how annoying it was to be referred to as a child when you were fifteen going on sixteen and made a mental note to talk to Owen about it.

"I am not a fecking child!" Angelica screamed.

"You are *my* child," Owen roared back, "and as

long as you live under my roof you'll abide by my rules and do as I say."

"That can soon be rectified," Angelica answered, her voice hostile and cool.

"Oh really? And where exactly are you planning on going?"

"You'd be surprised at the options that are open to me at the minute," she answered loudly before opening the door, fixing me with an accusatory stare (obviously because I'd been caught earwigging again) and stomping up the stairs at high speed.

I tentatively went into the room and sadly watched as Owen held his head in his hands.

"Owen," I said quietly, "I'm sorry about earlier. I didn't mean to upset you. I came down to look for you and couldn't help hearing what just happened."

Owen said nothing. He simply sat back in his chair, entwined his fingers and looked at the ceiling. He looked resigned.

"Who the hell was she with until this time and more to the point what was she doing?" he asked worriedly. "I hope she hasn't got herself into any trouble."

I opened my mouth to tell him that I had made a full forensic examination (*CSI* style) of her room but promptly closed it again as I realised that this news might not be received well. After all, what right did I have to do that? It wasn't my place.

"Look, I'm sure she was just doing what all teenage girls like to do – she was catching up with her friends, talking about boys and music and when the next disco will be." I hoped I was sounding more reassuring than I felt.

"How do you know that?" he snapped.

"Well, having been a teenage girl once myself I'd like to think that things haven't changed that much in the last fifteen-odd years."

"Well, she can forget about going to any discos any time soon," Owen said. "She's grounded until she proves that she can be trusted again."

This was not what I wanted to hear. Not because I didn't think Angelica shouldn't be punished but from a purely selfish point of view I knew I was liable to bear the brunt of her bad feeling as Owen would be at work and I had the misfortune to be on maternity leave now and therefore at home all the time (oh goody goody gumdrops).

"Owen, don't you think you're being a little harsh?" I reasoned. "She didn't kill anyone and you have no evidence to suggest that she was up to anything worse than a bit of gossip and having a laugh."

As I said the words something came into my mind about Angelica "having a laugh" or maybe it was that she wasn't "having a good time". I racked my brain. Where had I heard that? Suddenly I remembered my conversation with Ruby. I was about to tell Owen that perhaps Angelica wasn't to blame at all and perhaps he should talk to Brenda but something stopped me. Angelica hadn't actually corrected him when he had assumed that she was with friends so maybe for some reason she hadn't wanted him to know where she was or who she was with.

I decided that as she was grounded that I would have plenty of time to talk to her about it. And that as I had refrained from telling her father what I knew maybe she wouldn't view me as the enemy when I asked her why she had been with Brenda and why Ruby had thought that she looked so sad.

Chapter 56

Ruby was a welcome sight for sore eyes as she waved and approached the table I was holding for us at one of the local coffee houses. It was lunchtime and extremely busy and I had nearly kissed the young waiter who finally told me that there was a table free in the vicinity.

She kissed me on the cheek and plonked herself down in front of me. She looked radiant. She'd had her hair cut in a softer style, her face which was normally devoid of make-up had been given a light dusting of bronzing powder and her eyes looked bigger with the addition of some mascara and well-positioned eyeliner. Her lips were glossy with lip balm and at that moment upturned in a huge grin.

"Well, doesn't being in love just suit you down to the ground?" I commented laughingly.

"I am not in love," she said in the most unconvincing tone of voice I had ever heard.

"Aye right," I murmured. "I like your makeover. Your hair really suits you."

"Yes, it's a bit less wild than it used to be. Mandy goes to this hairdresser who specialises in shorter cuts and she made me an appointment last week."

I couldn't help laughing again when I thought how much things had changed. Mandy used to hide if she saw Ruby coming and Ruby used to think that Mandy was the most annoying person on earth. Oh, how the love of a good man changed your perspective and helped you to accept things and overcome fears that you wouldn't normally want to tackle! My situation with Angelica was another prime example and precisely what I was here to discuss. I reckoned that if I was going to talk to Angelica about where she had been the previous day I might as well be in possession of all the relevant facts as I had no doubt that she would probably try to deny it or at best contradict me.

"So what's this all about?" Ruby asked quizzically after we had scanned the menu and ordered coffee and sandwiches.

"Well, I think that something must be going on with Angelica," I said.

"So what else is new?" Ruby muttered. "Is there ever a time when she's not up to something?"

I voiced my concerns to Ruby who looked puzzled, concerned and annoyed all at once.

"I don't understand why she would feel that she had to lie about it," Ruby said as she took a bite of her prawn sandwich. "Doesn't she see Brenda all the time or had things cooled off between them?"

"I don't think she had been seeing her as often," I answered thoughtfully. "I had put that down as one of the reasons why she and I had been getting on better and why the house had been quieter and less charged with a bad atmosphere."

"Hmmm, it definitely sounds as if that woman is a bad influence on her. Although, as I told you yesterday they weren't on their own, there was another woman with them."

I tried to think who this might have been but simply didn't know. Perhaps it was a friend of Brenda's (did the bad-tempered freak actually have any friends who were willing to admit to the fact in public?) or another family member. I was puzzled. Owen had always said that nobody else had ever taken an interest in Angelica except for Brenda and anyway there were no other aunts, only uncles who were younger and probably didn't understand. I didn't think that Brenda would bring just anyone into the company of Angelica. After all, from what I had gathered she went to extreme lengths to cover up the fact that her sister had done anything wrong and was very preoccupied with protecting the family name.

"What did she look like?"

"Her usual charming sourpuss self. That woman has a beak on her that could curdle milk."

"Not Brenda," I chided. "The other one."

"I didn't get that good a look at her," Ruby said, "but from what I could see she had blonde hair, was quite thin and had a funny-looking tattoo on her neck."

"Was she a punk rocker?" I asked, bemused.

"Who knows?" Ruby sighed.

I decided that that was enough talk about Angelica. I wanted to hear all the juicy gossip about Ruby's new and improved love life and wanted to put my complicated family issues behind me for a while.

"So tell me about the delectable Luke," I asked while eyeing a particularly large piece of chocolate fudge cake in the desert trolley and ordering us two more coffees.

I arrived back to the house just in time to catch Angelica in the act of packing her things but thankfully she wasn't alone. Ella had obviously dropped by to say hello (or if she told the truth she was escaping as she was staying with Mammy this time) and was sitting talking to her in a very mild-mannered and calm fashion.

As usual I reacted in completely the wrong way. It was a good job Ella was there or else Owen would probably have had every reason to blame me for his daughter's sudden departure.

"What the hell are you doing?" I demanded as I witnessed all Angelica's worldly goods being shoved untidily and messily into a few bulging holdalls.

"Frankie, can I have a word?" Ella quickly intervened and took me to one side, sensing that I was about to have the mother and father of all fits.

"Jesus, Ella, Owen's going to go mad," I said. "They had an argument last night but it wasn't that serious. She's been grounded for coming home late but it's not the end of the world."

"There's a lot more to this than you realise," Ella said. "I let myself in earlier and we've been having quite a good chat."

Ella wasn't usually prone to exaggeration but she had to be adding on a few details to the "real" version of this story. "Good chats" did not happen with Angelica at the best of times and were not likely to occur at the minute as she would rather shout and strop than talk civilly to anyone.

"Are you quite finished talking about me behind my back now?" Angelica appeared at the door looking more hostile than ever and, more worryingly, with her coat on.

I took a deep breath and tried to follow Ella's example by being calm. "Angelica, please stop overreacting. I'll speak to your father about you being grounded. He doesn't want to spoil your fun. He's just worried about you. Fathers and their daughters, y'see — they're very protective." I accompanied this last statement with what I hoped was a companionable shoulder-rub.

Angelica acted as if I had just burnt her with a hot poker and roared at me. "Stop trying to be all matey all of a sudden! You don't want me either so I'll go where I am wanted for a change!"

"And where is that exactly?" I asked sarcastically, aware that Ella was vigorously shaking her head at me in an attempt to get me to keep quiet.

"As if I'd tell you that. I hope you'll be very happy together, Frankie. Thanks for stealing my dad and my house!"

She tried to shrug past me but as I was standing sideways and my bump was huge she wasn't going to get very far. She shrank back and looked at me and for a terrible moment I thought she was going to hit me but instead she sighed and retreated back into the house.

I saw this as a window of opportunity and asked Ella to leave.

"Are you sure?" Ella asked.

"Look, I'm fine. Thank you for whatever you did to keep her here until I got home but I'll handle it now."

"Please try and be understanding, Frankie. She's gone through things that we could only ever contemplate with horror."

"I'll do my best. I need to talk to her about some other things too and it looks like if I don't do it now I might never get another chance."

I felt strangely serene as I re-entered the sitting room where Angelica was sitting, looking pensive and fidgety. I knelt down at her knee and hoped that I wouldn't get her knee cap shoved in my mouth once I started to speak.

"Angelica, please don't push me away," I appealed. "I don't want to do this. I want to help you. I don't know where you keep getting this idea that you're not wanted because you are. The house wouldn't be the same without you and your daddy would be heartbroken were you to leave. He's fought so hard to make you happy all these years. Please don't throw it back in his face over a silly argument."

She said nothing. I wondered if she had heard anything I said or was just trying to pretend that I wasn't there.

"When you left yesterday I didn't realise that you were meeting Brenda, Angelica."

If I had thought that she wasn't listening I was now proven wrong as she visibly blanched in front of my face.

"How did you know that?" she asked in a quiet voice.

"I didn't see you myself but Ruby did and she said that you didn't look very happy. Has something happened? Please talk to me, Angelica. I'm not your mammy but I'd like to think that you could still look to me for advice if something's bothering you."

She sneered at me and roughly shoved me out of the way as she got up and made to leave the room.

"Why do you have to keep running away, Angelica? Why can we not sit and talk about whatever it is that's annoying you?"

"You can sit wherever the hell you like but I'm going to take action."

"Meaning?" I asked.

"Meaning that I'm fed up and I'm going. Nobody understands. Nobody will even notice."

"Try me?"

"No."

"Yes."

"No."

I shifted position and almost immediately realised that something wasn't quite right and I wasn't simply referring to the fact that my stepdaughter and I were in the middle of yet another stupid pointless argument.

"Angelica, you can't leave. I need you."

"What the hell do you need me for?"

"I need you because my waters have just broken and this baby isn't supposed to be here for another three weeks," I gasped before moaning out loud as a sharp pain tore through my abdomen.

Chapter 57

"Shit," I breathed as I attempted to manoeuvre myself into a more comfortable position on the floor.

Angelica was looking at me with scared, wild eyes which was exactly what I didn't want to see. I needed to be with someone who would be in control and steer me safely in the direction of the hospital.

"Do something," I squealed in a high-pitched, frantic voice.

"Like what?" she asked in an equally panicked tone.

I looked at her and watched as she seemed to be steeling herself. She had taken her coat off and was now rolling her sleeves up. I watched her in fascination and wondered was she about to go and start boiling kettles and throwing towels on the floor like they did in all the best films.

"Ella's a midwife, isn't she?" she said suddenly.

"Good thinking, Batwoman. Can you ring her?"

Angelica pulled her mobile out of her coat pocket and started to dial.

I noted the time as another contraction took hold of me. I wanted pain relief. All the pain relief I could get my hands on. I was not going to give birth on the sitting-room floor which I had been planning to partially carpet as part of my official "putting my stamp on the place" ceremony. It would need to be feckin' carpeted now, I thought, as I surveyed the puddle which was seeping into the floorboards.

I jumped as I heard a loud piercing sound.

"What the hell is that?" I muttered.

"It's Ella's mobile," Angelica said apologetically. "She must have left it here."

I took deep breaths. Not because I was a great advocate of breathing exercises but because I needed to do something to calm myself down.

"Try phoning your father, Angelica. Try his office first and if you don't get him there then try his mobile although it's doubtful that you'll get him on that. His signal is terrible at work."

I howled as another pain gripped me. They were seven minutes apart and coming at me in waves.

This was not how I had envisaged the birth of my baby. I hadn't made a birthing plan exactly but I had had an idea of how things were going to go. Obviously I hadn't anticipated the event happening three weeks before it should have. I certainly hadn't expected to be on my own in the house with Angelica and seemingly cut off from anyone with any experience or other useful attributes (like a driver's licence for instance). I had hoped that Owen would be there when it happened. I pictured him running around in a frenzy, collecting my case, packing away the CDs which he had so lovingly prepared for me and all whilst uttering words of reassurance and love. We would arrive at the hospital, quickly, where I would be put straight into a wheelchair, taken to the wonderful local Midwifery Led Maternity unit where I would be offered the chance to have a water birth and refuse, naturally, as I hated water. Instead I would opt for a comfortable bed, copious amounts of gas and air, Pethidine, Morphine, an epidural, an anaesthetic and any other pain relief available.

My thoughts were shattered by a bloodcurdling scream which did not emanate from my person. Angelica was standing looking at the phone and shouting in frustration.

"Daddy, where the hell are you? Why can you not answer the phone?"

"Did you try both numbers?" I asked.

She nodded miserably. "Will I phone your mother? Ella might be there."

"Oh God no!" I yelled without even considering it as a feasible option. Mammy would be on the floor beside me which would not be at all helpful under the circumstances.

"Ruby?" she suggested.

"Yes. Ring Ruby and tell her . . ." I trailed off as I felt another contraction begin. I had watched a television programme once where someone had said that you should visualise your pain like a ball of fire which you should try to extinguish by hanging your head and imagining that you had a bucket of water beneath you.

"What a load of bollocks!" I exhaled sharply feeling no better for all my efforts.

"What's a load of bollocks?" Angelica enquired.

"Never mind," I answered. "Did you get Ruby?"

"I'm still trying. She's engaged but at least she's there."

I moaned. Ruby being engaged was as bad as her not being there. She could talk for Ireland and knowing my luck probably would at that very moment.

"Leave messages with both your dad and Ruby and phone an ambulance, Angelica," I instructed. The contractions were now five minutes apart and getting more severe, and my pain threshold was shite.

Angelica quickly did as she was told and then dialled 999. I heard her giving my name and details and was surprised that she was so well aware of my due date. Perhaps she did occasionally listen and take interest in things, even if she didn't make it obvious.

"Frankie, how far apart are your contractions?"

"About five minutes but they really hurt," I said. "I'm scared," I added and could feel my bottom lip beginning to wobble.

Angelica was listening intently to what was being said and nodding her head. "I understand," she said. She wrote something down on a piece of paper and thanked someone called Paula.

"Will they be here soon?" I asked.

Angelica pretended not to hear me.

"Angelica?"

"That girl was really nice, Frankie. Seems to know what she's talking about. She said that if you got any worse that I could phone her back and that she could talk us through what to do."

"Why would we need to do that?" I asked.

"She said that the ambulance would get here as quickly as possible but that it will still be ten to fifteen minutes probably."

(Please tell me that wasn't her way of telling me that this Paula person thought I would have already given birth before the feckin' ambulance arrived.)

"Don't you need to take those off?" Angelica said, nodding in the direction of my stretched-to-capacity, elasticated maternity trousers.

I shook my head quickly, closed my eyes and tried to think happy thoughts: like what I was going to do to Ella for being stupid enough to leave her phone behind, Owen for not being at his desk and Ruby for being a motor mouth.

Angelica was pacing around and wringing her hands. I patted the floor beside me.

"Come and sit beside me. It's lonely down here on my own," I said with a half-hearted smile.

She gingerly eased herself on to the floor (whilst managing to avoid all wet patches) and looked expectantly at me.

"You might have to deliver this baby – your wee brother or sister," I added with a quivering voice.

"Well, if that's what has to be done, I'll do it," she said resolutely.

"You'll not leave me?" I asked. (I had to be sure. I wasn't convinced I was going to be able to get through this experience as it was, never mind lean over, cut the cord and comfort the baby who no doubt would be outraged and scarred for life at the indignation of being born on a cold wooden floor.)

"I'm not that bad, Frankie," Angelica said as I grasped her hand and used it to help me get over the next contraction. "It probably wouldn't have worked out anyway. Who was I kidding? It's easy to say that you want someone when they're all grown up and don't need a lot from you. She left all the hard work for my dad to do."

I was confused by Angelica's rabbiting. Was she talking to me or herself?

"Who did?"

"Look, Frankie. I'm not proud of this but when you went into hospital for the first time with high blood pressure my Aunt Brenda came to see me and told me that she had a surprise for me."

I nodded at her in encouragement.

"I went to her house and, when I arrived there, there was someone else there – someone I hadn't seen in a long time."

I breathed hard as a particularly brutal contraction took its toll on my body.

The door opened and I had never been so glad to see either Owen or Ruby in my entire life. I cried with relief and sobbed in Owen's arms as he tenderly hugged me and told me that everything would be all right.

"We got here as quick as we could," Owen said. "Ruby got the message Angelica had left and came to find me as soon as she could."

"You shouldn't leave people messages like that when they are holding hot cups of coffee, honey," Ruby said kindly to Angelica whilst pointing at a rather unsightly stain on her otherwise pristine white shirt.

"Sorry," Angelica said smiling. "Oh look, there's the ambulance now!"

I sighed with relief but didn't stay content for long as yet another contraction rose to a crescendo and then subsided.

"They're getting really close now," Angelica said, looking worriedly at me. "You had the last one only about two minutes ago."

Ten minutes later and I was still in the same position, although with the added comfort of a tank of gas and air which I was sucking on as if my life depended on it. I had also just had a shot of Pethidine but alas my epidural was just going to be a longed-for figment of my imagination as I was destined to have my baby in front of Owen's old-fashioned stone fireplace.

The ambulance crew had come into the house and examined me and then much to my dismay announced that it was too dangerous to move me in case I gave birth to our baby in transit. (No − I didn't fancy making the headlines in the local paper for having the baby halfway down the M1.)

Owen was with me and so was Angelica. They were both holding my hands and I knew that they would be there until they heard our baby cry. The three of us were in for the long haul together.

Chapter 58

As it turned out I could have had five or six round trips to the hospital in the time that it took my cervix to dilate. I was still puffing and panting two hours later and happily attached to a new canister of gas and air which was making me feel deliciously floaty even though my nether regions were in bits. (Never mind the joy of having a baby. The gas and air alone makes it all worthwhile.) I had been moved into one of the downstairs bedrooms and thankfully was no longer having to face the indignity of delivering the child on the floor.

"Not long now," Ella pronounced as she examined me again. She had been my rock, my saviour, the best sister in the world ever and I rejoiced that she had taken the wise decision all those years ago to study midwifery as her chosen career path. She had arrived about ten minutes after the ambulance crew when she had discovered that she must have left her mobile phone behind her. Thankfully she was alone.

The children were with Mammy, having been informed that I was feeling tired and needed a break.

When I had given birth to Ben the experience had been rather traumatic but lovely all the same as the pain was soon forgotten when I had been handed my baby boy. Tony had been with me and cried all the way through it like a big girl's blouse (although what the hell he thought he had to cry about had been beyond me). My labour with Carly had been very quick with no complications and I had been delighted with my beautiful daughter. But there was one thing missing on both those occasions which was very obviously present this time. The togetherness I was experiencing with Owen and the love that we had for each other was better than any pain relief and carrying me closer to the time when our baby would actually come into the world.

Given the current circumstances I probably could have been forgiven for being annoyed and out of sorts and also could have been excused for shouting and roaring at the man responsible for all the suffering. (I love the way women in labour always blame the man as if they themselves were drugged or sleeping when conception took place.) I, however, couldn't have loved Owen any more at that particular point in time if I'd tried. He held my hand, gave me sips of water and murmured words of encouragement in my ear and told me at twenty-second intervals that he loved me.

Angelica came in and out to check on my progress and seemed genuinely concerned for my welfare. I would have imagined that I would have been slightly uncomfortable in baring all to my teenage stepdaughter but she had been remarkable and had gone up one hundredfold in my estimation in terms of her level-headedness and maturity.

"I want to push," I gasped as an overwhelming urge took over me. Animal-like noises were coming involuntarily from my throat and Owen was going to need to undergo bone surgery to replace what I had just broken by crushing his poor hand.

The paramedic had taken over Ella's position at the foot of the bed and my sister was now where I needed and wanted her most – at my side. Angelica had also joined them, her eyes wide with horrified fascination (best form of birth control ever for a teenager methinks) as she watched me struggle.

Ten minutes later the room was awash with emotion as our baby son entered the world. I cried with relief, happiness and sadness as I was aware that I should have been preparing myself to give birth for a second time.

"He's beautiful," Owen breathed, his voice thick with emotion.

"I've delivered hundreds of babies but no experience will ever surpass this," Ella said, wiping her tears away.

Angelica had yet to speak. She seemed mesmerised and unsure of what to say or do.

"What do you think of your little brother?" I asked, expecting that she would probably correct me and refer to him as her half-brother.

"I think he's perfect. He's the most beautiful thing I've ever seen," she said quietly.

Owen smiled and kissed me for the hundredth time. "You are amazing. Have I told you lately how much I love you?"

"You're slipping up. Not in the last minute."

Ruby had also reappeared from where she had been hiding in the kitchen and was positively giddy with relief (or was it caffeine from all the coffee she had consumed?) when she saw that finally it was over. Ruby did not possess a strong stomach and therefore had chosen to keep out of the way. Even now she was studiously averting her gaze in case she saw anything that would give her nightmares.

"Oh my God," she whispered as she looked at our son and marvelled at how gorgeous he was.

Ella was hopping from foot to foot, holding her mobile and looking at me expectantly.

"Okay, you can tell them now," I said. I knew that she was dying to impart the good news to our parents who would be amazed (Daddy), shocked (Mammy) and horrified (Mammy again) to discover I had just given birth in the house but happy and relieved (both) to know that we were all well.

My new son and I were being moved to the hospital where we would be given a proper check to ensure that everything was as it should be and I couldn't have been happier given the fact that I was being put in an ambulance with my undercarriage badly in need of a few stitches.

Life didn't get much better than this. Did it?

Chapter 59

I was more tired than I had ever been in my life and so happy I could have shouted my love for my family from the rooftops.

The baby (no name had been decided yet so that would be how he would be referred to until inspiration came) was sleeping peacefully in a crib beside my hospital bed. We were both fighting fit and doing well by all accounts and allowed to go home the following day. Owen had stayed as long as he could with me but as soon as he had heard that we would be returning to the cottage he announced that he had to go and do a tidy-up that "Kim and Aggie" would be proud of.

Mammy and Daddy had also called in, bearing bags of gorgeous new baby clothes and smiles that threatened to split their faces open.

"He looks just like your father," Mammy had pronounced when she first saw our little bundle.

"Well, he doesn't have much hair and I suppose he is a bit on the podgy side round the middle," I laughed as Daddy made faces at me and allowed his new grandson to tightly grasp his forefinger.

I thought that he bore a lot of resemblance to Owen actually. Babies, of course, changed appearances at a rate of knots but for the moment I was happy to say that he looked like his doting father.

I had been disappointed that Ben and Carly hadn't come to the hospital with them and assumed that they must have been with Owen until Mammy told me in a stilted hushed tone that they were actually with Tony.

I was upset for a nanosecond until I remembered that I had promised myself and everyone else that I would stop being a neurotic lunatic and deal sensibly with the situation.

"He offered," Daddy said by way of explanation. "He rang the cottage looking for you and Owen told him the good news and gave him our number. He phoned and said that he'd only be too happy to take the children for a few hours while we came to see you."

"You're not angry, are you?" Mammy asked, regarding me anxiously. "We didn't want to upset you and thought that maybe now would be a good time because you're –"

"Slightly preoccupied," I finished. I felt like a queen who had been unceremoniously usurped from power by her most loyal subjects. My children were with their father after weeks of soul-searching and negotiations and nobody felt that they could include me in the final decision. I concluded that it was my own fault for being totally irrational and paranoid. It was for the best. I would have to keep repeating that to myself.

"And everyone thought that from a purely practical point of view that it was quite sensible," Daddy finished, looking somewhat scared.

I looked at my parent's troubled faces and shook my head. "It's fine. I hadn't expected it to start so soon but it had to happen sometime so why not now? Did he pick them up?"

"Yes," Mammy answered stiffly.

"Did you speak to him?"

"I spoke to him," my father answered gruffly. "I told him to have them safely back to us by seven o'clock this evening. He's taking them out for tea and going to have a chat with them and, don't worry, there'll be no funny business."

"Funny business, Daddy?"

"He's not taking them to Neb– . . . God, you even have me doing it now! To Peggy's. And he's not going to be introducing them to anyone else either. It's just going to be them and him. Quality time and a bite to eat. I suppose it'll do for a start."

"It will," I said. "You will ring me and let me know that they're home safe, won't you?"

"Of course we will, love. You can speak to them yourself later and they can tell you how they feel."

"I hope he doesn't say anything," I worried out loud.

"Say anything about what, love?"

"Me?"

"Do you think the man actually has a death wish that he wants granted?" Mammy answered.

"But he will probably try to blame the whole sorry situation on me and they might want to believe him and then where will we all be?" I asked, panic rising in my voice (and all thoughts of not hyperventilating going swiftly out the window).

"Frankie," Mammy said gently, "sometimes you just have to have faith in the Man Above and also have faith in your children. Ben is ten now and he knows who's looked after him all these years and who has been noticeably absent and Carly doesn't know him at all and she's very protective and loving towards you. They won't be easily fooled. Besides I don't think that his prime reason for wanting to see them is to bad-mouth you. He's probably just realised what he nearly lost or might still have lost."

I looked at my mother in admiration. Sometimes she really surprised me with the amount of sense she spoke.

I looked at my new son, said a quick prayer to the Almighty asking that he take care of all my children and protect them from virtual strangers who might or might not want to take their mother's name in vain. Then I closed my eyes and fell into another exhausted, hazy sleep.

Chapter 60

The wheels crunching on the gravel outside the cottage signified the end of our journey home and opened a new chapter for us as this was when our baby son would be properly introduced to his new surroundings. Technically he had already seen most of them as a result of his untimely entrance into the world but I wasn't worried about technicalities – I was just glad to be home.

A solitary blue balloon decorated the front door and a banner was visible through the sitting-room window. In we went, Owen carrying his son nestled in his little car seat, dressed in a tiny blue snowsuit and mitts.

Mammy, Daddy, Ella and Hammy (who had come over to meet the newest member of the family), Ben and Carly, Angelica, Ruby and Luke were all there to greet us with beaming smiles and *oohs* and *aahs* as they surveyed the baby.

"I could eat him," declared Ruby.

"Putting you in the notion, Rubes?" Luke asked swiftly, only to be put on the receiving end of a particularly menacing stare.

"I'll just enjoy this one, thank you," Ruby said with a shudder.

"I'll soon have him indoctrinated into my way of thinking," Hammy said gleefully whilst rubbing his hands together before producing the tiniest Caledonian Thistle football strip I had ever seen.

Everyone laughed including Ben who was clearly delighted at the prospect of having yet another ally when it came to his madness for "the beautiful game".

Carly came right up close to my armchair to study her tiny brother who was now snuggled in my arms. Her mouth was in a perfect O.

"Would you have preferred a girl?" I asked.

"I've got Angelica," she answered, "so I guess another boy is all right. I'm just glad that I'm not the baby anymore."

I glanced around at the others. They were all noisily chatting to each other. "How did you get on with meeting your daddy yesterday?" I said quietly. I couldn't restrain myself from asking. I was dying to know.

"It was okay, Mum. He took us to McDonald's and said he was sorry."

"Sorry for what?" I was shocked.

"Sorry for leaving. He said that he never meant to make us feel as if he didn't love us because he does."

"He also said that you had done a very good job with us because we have nice manners!" Ben had come bouncing up and overheard us. "And that he knows it must have been hard for you on your own."

I wondered if Tony was being patronising but decided to take it as a compliment. At least he hadn't said anything bad about me (or had he?)

"Is that all he said about me then?"

"He said that we had to be good for you because you were going to be busy with the baby and that you were a good mum."

I smiled in spite of myself. Forgive and forget – wasn't that what people advocated should be done in these situations? (Well, forgive anyway.) We had all moved on after all.

I told the children that they could go and play and looked towards Angelica who seemed to be standing quietly in the background and not offering much conversation. I mouthed a greeting at her and asked if she was all right but wasn't sure if she was ignoring me or if she simply hadn't seen me. I sincerely hoped that it was the latter.

I hadn't seen her since I had left the house two days previously in an ambulance and was looking forward to speaking to her.

Owen had disappeared but was soon back, having turned down our bed and prepared a bath for me to submerge myself in.

I kissed him on the cheek and left my son in his capable hands – though I didn't think that he was going to get much of a chance to handle him if my mother had anything to do with it. She would be rivalled soon enough, however, as Esme was on her way up from Dublin (we were honoured) and Maura was also going to be putting in an appearance.

On the way to the bathroom I met Angelica in the corridor. "Hi, honey," I said gently. "I didn't get the chance to thank you properly for all your help the other day. You were marvellous. Exactly what I needed."

She looked at me and shrugged. "I did the best I could, Frankie. There was no one else around so it was up to me to help. I'm sorry I was a pain. It's probably my fault that you had the baby early in the first place."

"I think my waters would have broken anyway, Angelica, so don't be worrying. I'm just glad that you didn't leave." I shivered. That just didn't bear thinking about. I wanted her to confirm that she wasn't leaving now but was scared to ask in case she told me something I didn't want to hear. At least she was still here now and that was all that mattered.

My bath was lovely and I felt refreshed and ready for anything (good job as a disruptive night lay ahead consisting of four hourly feeds and broken sleep). I put on a pair of my comfiest tracksuit bottoms and a baggy top, sprayed myself with deodorant, fixed my hair and then prepared to meet with my son's admirers.

Esme had arrived and was cradling the baby tenderly and making cooing noises as Maura looked on.

I looked at Owen and he agreed with a nod that the time was right to finally announce the name of our precious boy.

"He's wonderful," Esme said, turning her eyes towards me. "So beautiful and so like his father and grand-father."

"So I'm told, Esme," I answered, "which is why we could think of no more fitting tribute than to name him Jack Owen Byrne after the great men who went before him."

Maura let out a small gasp and Esme began to cry quietly while clutching her grandson tightly.

"Thank you, Frankie. Thank you so much. He would have been thrilled."

Things were getting far too sentimental and I was threatening to cry yet again when there was a knock on the door. I hoped that whoever it was wouldn't stay too long but was dismayed and horrified in equal proportions when I opened the door to discover that the caller was none other than Brenda and she was not alone.

Chapter 61

I stood and looked and was speechless for a few moments. The last person on earth I wanted to see today was Brenda and I didn't appreciate her bringing her cronies with her either.

"Who is it?" Owen shouted from the kitchen.

"Wait here," I commanded as I partially closed the front door and went to where Owen was sitting.

"It's Brenda," I hissed, "and she's not on her own."

"I'll soon sort that," Owen said.

Angelica came into the room.

"Your aunt's outside," I said. "Do you want to go and see her for a few minutes? Maybe she'll leave if she speaks to you. I'm sorry, Angelica, but I don't want her in this house and especially not today."

"Is she on her own?" Angelica asked, her face devoid of all colour.

"She seems to have a friend with her," I said. "You'd probably know who it is better than me."

Owen made his way to the door and I followed just in case he needed somebody to smack Brenda one if she was going to be difficult. Angelica hung back and appeared unwilling to come with us.

Suddenly, as Owen reached the door, he seemed to lose the use of his legs and sat down heavily on a nearby chair. While I was getting over the shock of that, I heard Angelica begin to sob and when I swung around I found her clinging to Ella who had joined her in the hall.

At this point Brenda breezed into the house like it was her God-given right while her companion chose to remain outside, looking decidedly uncomfortable.

As Owen was still sitting there looking ghastly for some unknown reason, it fell to me to halt Brenda's progress.

"This isn't a great time, Brenda," I said. "We have a new baby and a houseful of guests as you can see. Was there something in particular you wanted?"

I was surprising myself by being so controlled. Brenda scared the shit out of me and I was normally a jittery nervous wreck when I had the misfortune to be in her company but today I had decided I was putting up with no nonsense. Besides, Owen and Angelica looked as if they had lost the run of themselves entirely and I wasn't going to have the day

I brought my new son home tarnished with that particular memory.

"We wanted to speak to Angelica," she said airily.

"Well, clearly Angelica doesn't really want to talk to you," I said as I looked towards Ella who was still holding Angelica tightly.

"We don't recognise you as being of any importance in Angelica's life so butt out!" Brenda countered angrily. "This has nothing to do with you."

"Apart from the fact that you're standing in my house," I replied through gritted teeth.

"But it has everything to do with *me*," a voice said quietly.

I looked towards Owen who had stood up at least but seemed to be transfixed by Brenda's crony outside the door.

"Why don't you come in?" he said to the blonde-haired woman who looked like there were a million other places she would like to be at that moment in time.

"I'd rather not," she said. "I can see you're busy. Congratulations on your new baby."

Owen didn't reply. Instead he went over to where Angelica was still clinging to Ella and clutched her elbow.

"I'll take over from here," he whispered to Ella.

Just then Maura emerged from the living room and gasped when she saw the state of her niece.

Owen gently manoeuvred Angelica until he was able to half-carry, half-help her walk through to the kitchen where he sat her down and began stroking her hair. She was still crying as if her heart would break and vigorously shaking her head. Myself and Maura stood there rather helplessly but then, hearing voices, I realised that Brenda had barged into the living room so I headed back there. Now it was Esme who was standing at the front door, looking at the stranger outside as if she had seen a ghost.

In the living room my parents, Ruby, Luke and Hammy were sitting silently as if they had just stumbled into the middle of an extremely private argument (which of course they feckin' had, thanks to bloody Brenda and her capacity for gross insensitivity).

Brenda seemed totally oblivious to the distress she was causing and continued to stand haughtily in the middle of our sitting room whilst giving everyone the evil eye and daring any of us to challenge her. Perhaps what she hadn't banked on was coming face to face with a post-pregnant hormonal woman who disliked having her territory invaded so rudely.

"Go and join your friend outside please, Brenda," I barked, jerking my head in the direction of the front street.

"I'm here to see my niece and I'll be here until I do," she snapped.

I grabbed her by both shoulders and steered her towards the kitchen where Angelica could still be heard sobbing in distress.

"Can you see enough now?" I roared. "See what you've done to your niece who you pretend to care about so much? Angelica, sweetie, do you want to see your Auntie Brenda right now or shall we agree to phone her later?"

"I don't want to talk to anyone," Angelica said, her breath catching in her throat.

"I think Angelica has made her feelings pretty clear, Brenda. Don't make me physically throw you out."

"You?" she was laughing at me.

"Yeah me," I answered before getting her arm in a death grip and frogmarching her to the door and out, past an incredulous Esme. "Now stay out! Are you so stupid that you can't see the damage you're doing and have always done? That poor child has only ever wanted a mother. She never asked for all this pointless game-playing which serves no purpose but to give you kicks, seeing as you can't seem to get them anywhere else."

"Why, Jane?" said Esme to the woman outside. "Why did you do it? Have you any idea of the trouble and heartache you've caused?"

I had already guessed that Brenda's companion must be her sister but to hear her name out loud made it real. I would have thought that I'd be more shocked but so much had happened over the previous few days that I was now somewhat unshockable.

Anyone for Seconds?

I took a moment to look at the woman. The woman who, since I had ever known Owen, had been portrayed in the guise of a pantomime villain who everyone loved to hate. No horns were visible about her person. She didn't look bad or as if she had been spawned from the devil. In truth, she looked fragile and scared, a bit like Angelica had looked when she had been lying in her hospital bed all those months ago. She was dressed demurely in a pair of slate-grey trousers, flat heels and a simple white shirt. Her blonde hair was tucked behind her ears and she was wearing plain diamante studded earrings. My eyes wandered to her neck where a birth mark was visible. It looked strangely like a tattoo and it was with a jolt that I realised that this must have been the woman who Angelica had been dining with the previous week. I felt wretched as I thought of how distraught Angelica must have been. I could see the resemblance between Jane and her daughter and wondered for the millionth time since I had met Owen and first encountered the situation how anyone could abandon their child in a such a crude and detrimental way.

Jane made no answer or no apology. She sighed and turned away from us both. Brenda stepped in and began to chide her in a stage whisper. "Pull yourself together. You can't let them win. You have every right to be here. Walk in there and claim what you rightfully own."

I heard Esme's sharp intake of breath and was in danger of collapsing with shock myself. In fairness, however, Jane didn't seem too sold on the idea of doing anything either.

"Win? Claim what you rightly own, Brenda?" I said incredulously. "This is obviously all just a game to you where 'winning' is the ultimate prize but let me tell you that what you should be concentrating on are Angelica's thoughts and feelings. Has anyone thought to ask her what she thinks about any of this? She's not a trophy – she's a living breathing human child who's been badly hurt."

I heard my baby son calling for me and realised that it was feeding time. I excused myself and gave Esme a reassuring squeeze before I made my way back inside where I saw that Mammy was in control of the situation and already giving Jack his bottle.

Owen appeared from the kitchen. He looked stressed and miserable and I felt terribly sorry for him.

"If you're going outside I'd get rid of the Chief of Police out there before I spoke to Jane."

"You know?" he said, stopping in his tracks.

"I was outside with your mother and the pieces of the jigsaw all started to fit together. How long has Angelica known that she has been here?"

"Quite a while it seems," Owen said ruefully. "I think she first made contact with her when –"

"I first went into hospital and she suddenly started

seeing me as the enemy again," I finished. I was sad for Angelica but glad to know that I wasn't the sole cause of her unhappiness.

"Is Mother all right?" Owen enquired.

"She's fine. Shocked, I think, but fine all the same. How is Angelica now?"

"She's as well as can be expected when her long-lost mother and Trojan aunt appear out of the blue shouting the odds on the day that her new brother gets brought home from hospital. She feels terribly guilty, you know. She knows that she's been horrible to you."

"I'm so sorry, Frankie," Angelica said as she appeared, sniffing into a tissue. "I've just been so confused about everything. Brenda phoned me one day to say that Mu – I mean Jane was coming home – and asked if I wanted to see her. I decided that I would like to meet her as curiosity got the better of me and I wanted to know why she'd left and why she'd come back now after all this time."

Angelica paused as Owen and I held our breaths.

"And?" Owen prompted.

"She hasn't really said much to me. Brenda did all the talking."

"Well, isn't that a shock?" I said. "How do you feel about it, honey? Do you want to see her?"

"I really don't know. I'm a bit numb really." She looked at her hands which were shaking and I put my arm around her and let her rest her head on my shoulder.

"Thanks, Frankie."

"For what?"

"For being here," Angelica said before going back into the kitchen.

"They've gone," Esme said as she came back in the house. "Jane persuaded Brenda that it wasn't a good time and asked her to leave."

"Owen, I think that Angelica should talk to her mother," I said. "Will she ever have another chance? Who knows what will happen if she leaves again? She may never come back and would that really do anyone any good?"

"I'd have been quite happy for her not to appear today, that's for sure," Owen said.

"Well, sometimes things don't work out quite the way we'd like but fate has its own way of sorting things. I'd probably have preferred it if Ben and Carly had never seen their father again but they have and they haven't changed. It's early days but sometimes you just have to have faith in your children and in the Man Above."

I caught my mother's eye through the door which was partially ajar and smiled. She could be a wise old bird sometimes.

Chapter 62

Owen and I were sitting in companionable silence and watching our son as he lay looking at his feet in wonder. He was now three months old and still looked like his father (if tiny spectacles were available they would have been identical).

It was a Sunday night and Owen was rubbing my feet whilst humming in tune with the stereo which was playing softly in the background. The cottage was quiet but all that would change soon. I was sure of it.

Just as I had predicted our peace and tranquillity was shattered some thirty minutes later as the rest of our little family returned from their respective outings. If anyone had told me that we would have found ourselves in this situation less than eighteen months after meeting, I think I would have needed open-heart surgery to recover. But no matter how ludicrous or complicated our circumstances seemed to outsiders it was what we had to do for the best to make sure that our children were happy.

"How was Daddy today then?" I asked. "Still got the cold?"

"No, he seems better now," Carly answered solemnly. "Baby Lawrence is better as well. Poor Stella still has it though and she looked really ill."

(So there was a God. Yeah, yeah, I know I wasn't supposed to think like that but I couldn't help it. I was only human after all.)

"Really ill?" I said with what I was sure was a gleam in my eye.

"That's awful," agreed Angelica. "Bet her hair was all lank and greasy and her face was covered in spots, wasn't it?"

"No," Carly answered innocently. "But her nose was all red and it was peeling and she kept having to put Vaseline on it."

"Poor Rudolph the Supermodel," Angelica whispered and we both laughed conspiratorially.

"And what about Great-granny Peggy? Did you go and visit her in the home?"

"We were going to go but Tony said we better wait as she hasn't been in great form lately. He says she's very cross."

"I'll bet she is," I murmured before Angelica and I shared another knowing look.

Anyone for Seconds?

It seemed that Stella and Great-granny Peggy hadn't been getting along too well. According to the children Nebby Peg had been very critical of poor Stella's childcare techniques and seemed to think that she and Tony weren't that well suited! (Sound familiar?) Tony hadn't reacted very well and as a result it had been decided that perhaps it would be better for everyone if Granny Peggy went to live in pensioners' accommodation where there would be people to keep an eye on her. The fact that they couldn't find any closer than fifty miles away in Belfast only served to infuriate dear old Nebby Peg further with the result that no one had seen her in a few weeks (were hiding out until the tablets started to work). I'll bet the old bat was sorry she hadn't stuck with me. No matter how bad things had ever got I don't think I could have done that. But it was no longer my concern and I no longer cared.

I turned my attention back to Angelica.

"And how did you get on?"

"Jane's fine. She's flying back to Antigua soon though so I'll probably not see her for a while."

"And how do you feel about that?"

"Whatever. She wanted me to go out to her during the summer holidays but I'm not sure I want to."

Owen's eyes shot up into his hairline. "It's up to you, honey. If you want to go I'm sure we could manage to fund it for a few weeks. It might be nice for you to see where your mum has been all this time."

"She's shown me plenty of photos. I think I'd rather stay here. I'd miss my wee man too much." Angelica blew softly on Jack's face and was rewarded with a bubbly gurgle in response. She was a very attentive big sister who truly loved her little brother. She was extremely protective of him (Rambo wouldn't have a look-in) and was afraid of missing any stages in his development.

It turned out that when Jane left she had literally gone to the other side of the world to escape. She hadn't had any plan to go anywhere in particular but had opened an atlas and decided to go to the first place her finger fell on. Owen hadn't been the least bit surprised to hear that this had been Jane's decision-making process.

"She always was a free spirit," he had said. "I knew that she wouldn't have had it well planned. She hardly took any of her things with her. They were left all over the house as reminders for me to trip over."

It transpired that Antigua had been where Jane's fingertip had pointed towards so that was where she had gone and set up her own beach bar to woo the tourists. She said that she thought about Angelica every day but that she simply hadn't been able to stay in Ireland. She had been suffering from depression (possible post-natal which had been left untreated) and felt that it would have done more harm if she had been around as she would have ended up hating her only child which could have been more destructive than living with her absence. I didn't know what the answer was. I only knew that in one way I was glad that she had left as I was madly in love with her ex-husband and good friends with her daughter.

Angelica and Jane had been getting on a lot better since Auntie Brenda had been sent on an extended holiday to help run Jane's business. Apparently there had been problems with the staff and I had no doubt they had all been left with skid marks in their pants as a result of meeting Brenda for the first time and realising that there was no escape.

Ben came and sat beside me. "Can you come and watch me play tomorrow night, Mum? We're playing Dunmore in the under twelves league semi-final."

"Of course we'll be there," Owen said and was greeted with a huge grin. Owen tried to attend all Ben's matches and was usually hoarse upon his return so great were his attempts at being louder than the cheerleaders present.

"I asked Tony if he'd go and watch me but he says he's busy. How come he's always doing something else when I want him to come and see me play, Mum?"

I looked at my son's earnest face and my heart went out to him.

"I'm sure Tony would like to see you play but maybe you just didn't give him enough notice," Owen said (intervening as usual at the right time with the most diplomatic advice). "Why don't you give him your match schedule the next time you see him and then he'll be able to plan ahead."

"I could do that or I could send it to Uncle Hammy," Ben said with a grin.

I had spoken to Ella the previous week and she had started the conversation by saying that she would like to come and visit but our chat intrigued me as she told me very casually that she was bringing a few extra guests that she would like us to meet.

"Who?" I asked.

"Never you mind."

"Excuse me. Are you planning to sleep in the garden?"

"No, I'm sleeping in the lovely room that you will have prepared for me and I'm sure that Ben and Carly can bunk in together.

"But –"

"But nothing, Sis. Stop being so nosy. All will be revealed in due course. Just trust me."

I resigned myself to the fact that she wasn't going to tell me anything more and that if I pushed her she would simply fill me full of outrageous lies.

After she had finished speaking to me she had her usual chat with Angelica and I was delighted that the two of them were continuing to get on so well.

Mammy was beside herself with curiosity and kept

constantly asking me in the manner of a Nazi interrogator whether or not I knew anything. Daddy didn't seem to mind. He was too preoccupied with planting his garden to speculate and had an avid helper in Carly who was convinced that as she had been a sunflower in the school play that she had green fingers also.

I had only two weeks to wait and I was counting down the days.

Chapter 63

Two weeks had all but passed and were practically uneventful if you discounted the fact that Ruby had rung me breathlessly the previous weekend to ask if I would be her bridesmaid. I had subsequently been left partially deaf in one ear as she had shrieked her delight at finally being convinced that her spinster shelf no longer wanted her on display.

"I've done it, Frankie. I've actually fecking done it. What will my mother do now that she no longer has to say endless prayers to St Jude –" (the patron saint of hopeless cases for those of you not in the know) "in the hope that her daughter might some day be taken pity on."

"Ruby, you seem to be totally unaware of how attractive you really are. I've always told you that it would only be a matter of time. And, yes, I would love to be your bridesmaid. Any excuse for a drunken hen party and dressing up in a posh frock for the day."

Upon enquiry I ascertained that Mandy was to be the other bridesmaid and nearly needed to be resuscitated for the shock.

"We're good friends now," Ruby said somewhat sheepishly.

I couldn't see her but knew that she was making faces and cringing on the other end of the phone line.

"And if I had told you that this would happen when you were making voodoo dolls in her exact replica and threatening her every time she opened her mouth you would have –"

"Had a fit, I know, but I love her brother and love makes you so much more tolerable of people who you used to think were really irritating but are in fact quite nice really when you take the time to get to know them."

Mandy no longer worked for Redmond College but was now instead devoting all her energies into writing the gossip column of the newspaper where Luke was currently photographer and I knew without reading it that she would be very good at her job indeed.

Ben had played well in his league semi-final game and actually scored one of the best points of the match (I'm not biased honestly) but was to come home dejected after losing to a stronger team. He did, however, have a victory in another sense as shock, horror, his father, the no-longer cold-ridden Stella and their lovely little baby came to watch and cheer him on. Owen, Carly and I were also in attendance whilst Angelica looked after Jack. Stella and I had regarded each other somewhat frostily at the beginning (this being the first time that we were actually to come in contact with each other since she referred to me as "shaggy" at the airport all those months ago). We managed to thaw out towards the end of the match, however, and had quite an interesting conversation about which formula milk was best. Tony and I also managed to have a chat about the children and I felt quite grown up (at thirty-three years of age) when I managed not to stick my tongue out as he walked away. I think Owen might have had something to do with his being there but when I asked he admitted to nothing (without looking me in the eye).

Angelica had continued to see Jane until she went back to Antigua and after the initial period of noisy tears, had not reacted with the pent-up emotions that I thought she would on seeing her mother again. I hadn't given it much thought but would have presumed that all the years of hankering and yearning for this woman would have resulted in them having a closer relationship. It seemed, on the contrary, however, that

Angelica wanted me to remain her confidante when it came to matters of the heart, doing her laundry and being her closest ally when it came to scrounging the very last penny of pocket money from her father. It turned out that maybe I had done something right and that all my perseverance and patience (I am practically a saint when it comes to this virtue) had paid off.

Ella was due home in two days' time and my mother and I were having an ongoing competition to see who could guess who her travelling companions were going to be.

"Does Hammy have any nieces and nephews?"

"They're too young to be hauled over to Ireland, are they not?" I countered.

"Maybe she's bringing over some of her nursing companions?"

"Oh please, Mother, her workmates would so not want to come to Swiftstown on holiday."

"And what may I ask is wrong with Swiftstown?" my father asked, speaking for the first time as he washed his hands after another busy day working with the earth.

"Absolutely nothing, Father," I answered. "It's a wonderful place."

"Leave Ella alone. Stop ruining the surprise for me," Daddy said. "If she had wanted you to know she

481

would have told you over the phone. You women are all the same. Never content unless you're gossiping and putting the world to rights."

Mammy and I stared after him in affection and decided to take his well-meaning advice.

Ella arrived at the airport positively glowing. I had been reminded, as I walked through the austere reception area, of the frail figure who had greeted me some time before and had shivered at the memory. Hammy followed her carrying two suitcases and was subsequently tailed by two young people, who looked like they were in their mid-teens. The boy was tall and gangly with jet-black hair and was wearing faded jeans and a Liverpool football top (he'd fit in immediately). The girl who was wearing leggings and a long top with boots wasn't quite as tall but had the same dark colouring as her companion and was very pretty with large eyes which were rimmed with kohl eyeliner.

"Say hello to James and his sister Annabelle," Ella said by way of introduction as the boy and girl surveyed us shyly before following Hammy into the airport shop to buy drinks.

Mammy and I looked at her expectantly.

"I got the idea from being with Angelica," Ella explained. "When most people are looking for a child they always want a cute cuddly baby to begin with. Not everyone is so excited by the older children out there who need help. I got pretty close to Angelica the last time I was here and felt that I really made progress with her. She still talks to me on the phone."

"I know that," I remarked.

"Hammy and I decided that we didn't want to go for IVF and adoption is so time-consuming and difficult that we might well be too old by the time a child becomes available. So we decided that the next best thing would be to become foster parents."

"Oh wow," was all I could muster as a response while Mammy held Ella tightly with tears coursing down her cheeks and told her how proud she and Daddy were of her.

There was a party atmosphere in the cottage that night as everyone sat around the large oak table, which took pride of place in the kitchen, and got acquainted. James and Annabelle were lovely although I didn't doubt that they had been hard work and were still troublesome at times from what Ella had told me of their turbulent backgrounds. I looked over at Angelica and she smiled back (between making cow-eyes at James who was quite handsome in his own angular, scruffy, teenage boy way).

Ben and Carly were also quite taken by our guests and of course delighted to see their aunt and uncle again. Ella was totally smitten with her youngest nephew and wouldn't allow anyone else to hold him or go near him while she was in the vicinity.

The door bell rang whilst I eventually extricated Jack from Ella's arms to put him to bed.

It was with surprise when I opened the door that I realised that the visitor in our midst was none other than Thaddeus McCrory.

"Gosh, Thaddeus, I don't know what you're doing here," I laughed as I led him inside. "I thought your specialty was pregnant women and I can assure that it's taken me too long to get my waistline back to risk losing it again so soon."

Owen nuzzled my ear with his arms wrapped around me. "Now, darling. Never say never. We're aiming for our very own five-a-side football team so that Ben can get practising properly before Liverpool sign him."

"That is indeed my speciality, my dear," the old man answered, "but it's not you I've come to see."

There was a pregnant pause (pardon the pun) before he approached Ella and gently led her to a nearby chair where he began to whisper and gently massage her head.

As realisation dawned, my mother and I clung to each other and then immersed Hammy in the biggest bear hug that he had ever been party to.

When Ella was finished she too was enveloped.

"I guess it's true what they say," Ella said quietly, her hands reverently cupping the small mound now visible beneath her top. "Once you stop worrying about it, it can happen naturally and it did."

Anyone for Seconds?

I looked around the room at my wonderful husband-to-be, my children and back to my baby son, who was quietly sleeping in my arms. I grinned broadly at my stepdaughter, looked fondly at my parents and at my sister who was glowing with happiness and realised that everything I had wanted for so long, hadn't always appreciated and had nearly lost was centred there.

"And you know what else they say?" I said through my tears, whilst handing Jack to Owen. "They say that the best things come to those who wait."

And with that I lifted the teapot from the stove, raised it in the air and asked cheerfully, "Anyone for seconds?"

The End